CRAZY FOR CORNELIA

CRAZY FOR CORNELIA

CHRIS GILSON

WARNER BOOKS

A Time Warner Company

This book is a work of fiction. Names, characters, places, and incidents are the product of the author's imagination or are used fictitiously. Any resemblance to actual events, locales, or persons, living or dead, is coincidental.

Warner Books, Inc., 1271 Avenue of the Americas, New York, NY 10020

Visit our Web site at www.twbookmark.com

 A Time Warner Company

Printed in the United States of America
First Printing: March 2000
10 9 8 7 6 5 4 3 2 1

Library of Congress Cataloging-in-Publication Data
Gilson, Chris.
    Crazy for Cornelia / Chris Gilson.
       p.   cm.
    ISBN 0-446-52536-7
    I. Title.
PS3557.I4743C73   2000
813'.54—dc21

                                                    99-30155
                                                      CIP

To Carolyn

Part One

Dress Grays

Chapter One

Kevin Sebastian Doyle searched for something to admire in 840 Fifth Avenue, but could only see a musty stack of limestone and money.

At the corner of Fifth Avenue and 65th Street, he stood across the street from the apartment building in the cold, exhaling vapor through his nostrils as he squinted to confirm the number on the gray awning: 840. The building had no invented name like the Beresford or the Dakota. Kevin figured it didn't need one. In this building, the names lived inside—families like Vanderbilt, Lord, and Morgan.

The face of 840 Fifth surprised him. Its location oozed wealth the way the cheap old building he grew up in leaked asbestos. But he'd expected a shimmering tower to fortress these fifteen-room apartments overlooking Central Park. Instead, under the gloomy December sky, 840 Fifth Avenue squatted on the corner of 65th and Fifth like a sullen dowager with dirty skirts.

Kevin's father, a career doorman at another prewar building on Fifth Avenue, had told him that Old Money let the outside of their buildings grow seedy to hide their grand lives from the grumbling peasants. An "eccentricity," he called it.

Kevin's father knew little secrets about Old Money. Over the years, he also tried to identify with it in awkward ways. One day he brought home a moldy 1930s edition of *The Emily Post Guide to Etiquette* and asked his family to study it. Kevin had opened the Emily Post book and, deadpan, read a line out loud, "Even a tiny home with only one or two servants . . ."

His mom had snorted and rolled her eyes at his father's sad efforts to know his employers, and Kevin felt reality rip through his chest thinking about her.

She had died suddenly just eighteen days ago.

For years he had struggled to make a living as an artist. Now he longed to work on the piece he had dedicated to his mom. Instead, since she was the only family member who had encouraged him, slipping him what little spare cash his conscience let him take, he would be going to work as a doorman.

He gripped the heavy stack of blue-plastic-wrapped uniforms over his shoulder, slippery as a stack of weasels, and crossed the street. The two uniformed doormen standing just inside the black wrought iron and glass double doors of 840 Fifth came to attention as they saw him approach.

One of the doormen poked his head out of the heavy door and blocked the entry.

"Can I help you?"

The large-framed black man with cropped gray hair was in his fifties. His watery eyes appraised Kevin, who probably looked suspicious in his black leather jacket, torn jeans, and scruffed-up Doc Martens.

"I'm Kevin Doyle. Starting the job today." He spoke more slowly than usual, working hard to take the punch out of his voice.

"Take the side alley and come around back to the service door. I'll go meet you."

Inside the building's staff room, the doorman broke into a friendlier grin and offered his white-gloved hand for Kevin to shake, a big man's easy grip.

"Andrew Stiles, fifteen years at this building. I know your dad and your Uncle Eddie. Eddie got you the job, I guess." The older man's lined face softened as he looked closely at Kevin and picked up on his rawness. "Sorry to hear about your mom."

"Thanks." The cork he'd stuffed into his feelings was working loose, but he shoved it back.

He watched Andrew take his doorman cap off and absently wipe his forehead. Under the hat, Andrew Stiles wore a little black skullcap that said, "I love Jesus," with a red heart for the "love" part.

Kevin decided that Andrew wasn't a religious nut, because his eyes seemed gentle, not zealous. But they weren't dulled, either, more like his edge had been sanded off from years of "Very good, sirs." Andrew put his cap back on like a man with a sense of place. The whole building could collapse around him, but Andrew Stiles would dust off his epaulets and man the door.

"You'll find a locker over there with your name on it," Andrew told him. "Suit up and come out to the lobby when you're ready."

So Kevin stood in the empty staff room, painted the same garish yellow as the light in a subway station. Burnt coffee burbled from a stained Mr. Coffee machine, and an ancient floor heater hissed in the corner. Under the secret treasures of this building, Kevin marveled, the staff room could be a museum exhibit of the other New York City, the one where he grew up. He looked at the cracked Formica table and could see his mother in a housedress laying out dinner for his family.

He found the hulking metal time clock bulging out of the wall. On the steel time card organizer beside it, he located the tip of a card sticking up with his name on it. He clocked in at 11:56.

The heavy *ker-chunk* of the hammer jolted him violently like an electrical shock. By reflex, he hit the time clock back, a good slam that stung his hand. Kevin squeezed his eyes shut. Eighteen days after his mother died, he still couldn't let his anger go. His shoulder ached from carrying the plastic-bagged uniforms twenty blocks. To make it through this day, he would need to bite the bullet until his teeth turned to chalk.

One of the banged-up lockers had his name written on a strip of masking tape across the door: "Doyle, Kevin."

He removed the blue bag from one of the winter uniforms and stripped down to his shorts. He unfolded a shirt and slipped his arm through one heavily starched sleeve that felt like sandpaper. Next came the gray wool pants. He knotted the plain black tie, slipped on the scratchy dress-gray jacket. Then he tugged on his snug white gloves, one finger at a time. Finally, he took the officer-style cap with the black patent leather brim and wiped a fingerprint off the shiny surface.

Kevin studied himself in the cheap plastic mirror on the wall next to the lockers. His tight frame filled out the uniform when he pulled his shoulders back, although he wouldn't pop any buttons puffing his chest out. He worked out at home with a cheap set of dumbbells, since he couldn't afford to join a gym.

Kevin put his hat on, angled it to the left, slightly low. Lines had started to creep into his forehead over the last two weeks. Getting middle-aged at twenty-five.

Then he took the chrome whistle on a black lanyard that he would use for calling cabs and slipped it around his neck. He forced a big smile and talked to the mirror, pointing his white-gloved finger.

"Doyle comma Kevin," he snarled. "Don't fuck with my whistle." But under the buzzing fluorescent overhead lights that washed the room with a factory-floor tint, he looked more like a Salvation Army officer with a bad attitude than a guardian.

He definitely needed to push Mr. Leave Me Alone way back on the shelf and practice Mr. Friendly and Helpful.

He crinkled his eyes, improbably blue. Kevin's mother was Black Irish, with Moorish blood that left Kevin with choirboy eyes and jet-black hair. She raised Kevin and his sisters in a walkup on Tenth Avenue, whacking and cajoling them to avoid temptation and soldier on without complaint. She had also chosen to nurture Kevin's artist's eye. She called it the "spark of the divine."

"Who are you?"

Kevin turned to the fleshy man who had appeared beside him, also in doorman's uniform. He had a broad face with drooping jowls and wide, cunning eyes. His body stood almost double-wide—a human wheelbarrow.

"Kevin Doyle." He put out his hand, a little wary.

"I am Vladimir Kosov," the man took it in both of his. "I go off duty now. I was captain of twelve doormen at the Hotel Leningradska in Moscow. We will talk, you and I." He pointed to the door with his forefinger. "Now, Andrew wastes."

"He what?"

"Andrew wastes for you in the lobby."

"Oh. Thanks."

Kevin closed his locker and watched Vladimir drop heavily onto the bench, grunting like a football player under his gear.

He walked down the hall to the end where the cheesy linoleum floor stopped at a door marked "Lobby."

Showtime.

He expected to see crystal chandeliers and velvet furniture, maybe authentic Old Masters mounted on silk wallpaper. But the lobby loomed dark and austere. The gray fabric that covered the walls looked just like his flannel doorman suit. Muted, recessed lights kept the lobby just bright enough to walk through without bumping into furniture. He could barely make out the fragile, maroon-silk upholstered chairs and a small couch perched around a table that appeared to be teak, polished to shine in the dark. They don't want us to read on the job, Kevin decided.

He found Andrew guarding the door with his hands folded behind his back, standing next to a small shelf jutting out from the wall beside the door. The doorman's shelf, which Andrew kept neat and burnished, had a manila file and folded-up newspaper stacked neatly on top.

"So," Kevin struggled to think of something positive to say, "I guess this is the place to be, 840 Fifth."

"Best building in Manhattan. Small enough you get to know all the owners real quick. A nice class of people."

"Nice class of people" jammed sideways in Kevin's head. The cocoon of wealth made people negligent, even criminal, because they stopped thinking about anyone else.

"Where does your dad work again?" Andrew asked him.

"2000 Fifth, with Uncle Eddie. He got my dad his job fifteen years ago."

Andrew pursed his lips. "So I guess you're following in your dad's footsteps. And your Uncle Eddie's."

"Yeah. The Doyles, we own the door."

"So let's start at the beginning." Andrew shifted to what Kevin guessed was his training voice. "This building's a co-op. You know what cooperative ownership is?"

"I know cooperation's the opposite of what they have in mind. The owners can break the Fair Housing laws, only let in who they want as neighbors."

"Well," Andrew had to agree, "this building got famous by who they wouldn't let in." He stopped to open the door for an older man blessed with a strong chin stuck up at an angle, pink skin, and swept-back silver hair. "Good afternoon, Mr. Blanchard."

"What's the Yale-Harvard score?" the man barked to nobody in particular.

"Yale, fourteen–seven, first half, Mr. Blanchard," Andrew told him. "This is Kevin Doyle, new man on the door."

The man stopped in front of Kevin, tipping slightly to the left. "What was the matter with the old one?"

"I hear he retired, Mr. Blanchard." Kevin braced himself against the whiskey fumes.

"Well, there's always room," Mr. Blanchard said, nodding at him.

"Excuse me?"

"Always room at the bottom, son. Remember that."

Was he supposed to answer? His mother had taught him to be patient with old people because they could be fragile and confused. But Blanchard spun on his heel with surprising agility and wandered off toward the brass elevator doors at the other end of the lobby.

"Hey, Andrew," Kevin said. "Wasn't that game yesterday? Harvard won."

"Yeah, but Mr. Blanchard went to Yale, and he can use a little cheerin' up. His son, Bill, he's gettin' a divorce and he just told the old man he's going to tell the world he's homosexual."

"Blanchard told you that?"

"Hell no. The owners don't tell us shit. Maids, butlers, that's who we hear all the information from." Andrew chortled. "They're happy to tell you anything makes their bosses look like fools."

Andrew removed the fat manila file from the doorman shelf and handed it to Kevin.

"So here's all the building rules. No smoking. No drinking. No fraternizing with the owners."

"Uh-huh," Kevin said, flipping through the stack of papers. One fell open to reveal twenty-five neat rows of blocks with handprinted names and apartment numbers. Small head shots of people cut out of newspapers and magazines were pasted in the boxes.

"That's a visual aid for you." Andrew tapped his finger on his collage. "Job one for a doorman is security. That's what we do, keep the building secure. Anybody you don't know shows up, you got to find out politely who they are. That's why you got to know your owners. We got one hundred and twelve people living in forty apartments. This here gives you all their names and apartment numbers so you can memorize 'em. I put in their kids, dogs, servants, everybody they allow in the apartment. Some photos, too, whatever I could find. Hang on, here comes 11B."

Andrew nodded toward the street. Kevin saw a very old man with a skeletal face and wisps of white hair fluttering in the wind. He held his thin, gnarled hands in front of him like a dinosaur's claws, helped along by a young, heart-faced blonde wearing a shiny black fur coat.

"Got 'em. Count Dracula and Courtney Love," Kevin whispered to Andrew as he swung open the door.

Andrew ignored him. "Good afternoon, Mr. Geddy, Mrs. Geddy. This is Kevin Doyle, new man on the job."

Kevin practiced touching the brim of his hat like Andrew, working to keep his smile hoisted up even though his real emotions were scraping bottom and his jaw ached.

Mr. Geddy nodded his skull and exposed his gums in greeting. The woman flickered an interested glance at her new doorman before she turned her eyes back to her husband. Kevin watched her walk hubby to the elevator, expensive haircut bouncing on her fur collar. He wondered what she allowed her husband to do with his claws for the privilege of living in 11B.

"So what'd you do before this?" Andrew asked him.

"Three years, I worked Bellevue, nights," Kevin said, leaving out his art for the time being. "I was a physical aide, no medical training or anything. Mostly I kept the patients company. Or restrained them."

Andrew seemed interested. "Mental patients?"

"Most of them. Some of them were faking it to stay out of jail. 'Had a delusional belief I was Jesse James, made me rob the convenience store,' that kind of stuff. Thirty-days observation in Bellevue buys them a 'get out of jail free' defense."

"Why'd you leave?"

"I snuck a patient out to see her kids one weekend. The tough part of security at Bellevue was sneaking back in. She got caught, I lost my job. It was just a night job to get by. I was studying—"

They both heard a high-pitched scream from outside.

"Incoming," Andrew said.

They opened both doors for a triple-wide wicker stroller pushed by a stressed-out nanny in a white uniform. Two of the three bundles inside, a baby boy and girl, were asleep, their blond heads slack. The third screamed in a wavy, high-pitched yowl. The parents walked behind them, a fine-featured couple in their thirties, their faces screwed up painfully at the sound.

Kevin bent down and put his face in front of the shrieking baby.

"Hey, gorgeous," he said, wiggling his ears. Gotcha. The little girl stopped bawling in mid-cry, her mouth hanging open in the goofy, wondrous way of all kids, even rich ones.

Kevin used his taxi whistle to chirp for her. She smiled like a burst of sun.

"Mr. and Mrs. Eames, this is Kevin Doyle," Andrew said.

The father smiled at Kevin and pressed a five-dollar bill into his hand.

He waved it away. "That's okay," Kevin told him brusquely. These people probably saw doormen as mutants bred to push doors and perform courtesies, if you kept feeding them treats of currency.

While the Eames family arranged itself in the elevator, Kevin peered at the photos in Andrew's file, memorizing the children's names. Even in the semidarkness, Kevin felt a shadow falling over his shoulders and the little hairs stirred on the back of his neck.

"Hey, Dumbo . . . *ping!*"

The familiar voice growled behind him as he felt a sharp burning in both ears. He turned around to see his Uncle Eddie's round, ruddy face with its heavily ridged forehead set in permanent irritation. His hair was buzz cut with open spaces, like a lawn that needed reseeding. Eddie kept his fingers poised to snap against Kevin's ears again. He wore civilian clothes today, not his doorman uniform. His thick, pub-brawler arms stuck out of rolled-up jacket sleeves with a N.Y. Knicks logo on his pocket.

Kevin knew from experience it would take a moment to hear past the painful ringing. And he'd have to swallow his bile at Eddie. His uncle was the closest thing west of India to a sacred cow, at least to the Doyles. He was the only family member who could provide union jobs, which had kept the other men in the family from decking him for fifteen years.

"You still got big ears, kid." Eddie turned to Andrew. "When he was little, he had ears like Dumbo. I used to sneak up and ping him. We had ourselves a little fun."

"Turned my life around, Uncle Eddie."

"Tell you what, just call me Eddie. We don't want to give hiring relatives a bad name. Did I just see you turn down a tip?"

"I guess."

Eddie shook his head sadly at Andrew. "He's a mutt, but he's my late sister's kid. Kevin, tips are life's blood. Tips are mother's milk. You're a doorman now. You see a resident standing in front of you, that's not a person, okay? That's a bag of groceries."

Eddie handed Kevin a plastic card. "Your union card. Welcome to Local 32A. International Brotherhood of Portal Operators. I'm your delegate now. Your employer is the building manager of this property. But you got a grievance, you come to me."

Eddie handed Kevin a second card.

"This is your Platinum Health Plan card from the union. It gives you the same health care as anybody living in this building. Maybe even better. Choose your own doctor, best hospitals, get your meds, you don't pay squat."

Eddie handed him a piece of paper and a pen. "Sign there, says you got your health plan. I got you a sweet deal, kid. Nobody gets a doorman job two weeks before Christmas."

"Yeah," Andrew agreed. "Just standing there, you get maybe two thousand for Christmas. If you always grab their bags before they ask, always know the right time, weather, you get maybe four, five thousand bucks."

"You owe me, kid," Eddie said. "I'll be around. Take care, Andrew."

Eddie lumbered out the front door, a potbellied fireplug in a team jacket, disappearing just as a gray limousine pulled directly in front of the awning.

"Heads up." Andrew nudged Kevin. "Here comes Chester Lord. He's chairman of the co-op board for the building, makes the rules around here."

Kevin watched a clean-featured man in his early fifties climb out of the back seat of a limo that looked smaller than life, like it was built in the Black Forest by elves. Chester Lord glided into the building. His medium frame, in a striped tie and blue blazer, could have lost ten pounds. Though his sandy hair had thinned a lot, he combed it straight back with no effort to hide the bald spots. A WASP thing, Kevin realized. They never combed their last few strands of hair all the way over their heads or wore hairpieces. A guy like Chester Lord let his dome get shiny and didn't care what anybody thought.

"Good afternoon, Mr. Lord," Andrew said.

"Hello, Andrew." The crisp voice was soft, hard to hear. He arched one eyebrow at Kevin. "Are you the new doorman?"

"Kevin Doyle."

The man squeezed his hand and let it go. In the awkward pause, Kevin sensed a shyness.

"Well, good luck to you."

"Thanks."

Andrew waited until Chester Lord was whooshed up in the elevator. "Something you got to know about the Lords."

He took the folded copy of the day's *New York Daily Globe* off the shelf and handed it to him. Kevin peered at the newspaper, opened to the fifth page, barely able to decipher the print in the lobby's gloom. He held it close to the weak light to get a better look.

There was a column titled *Debwatch*. The script typeface looked like a wedding invitation. It was written by somebody named Philip Grace. Under a bold black headline, "Corny's Social Swim," Kevin studied a grainy picture taken at night. A girl of maybe twenty in a soaking-wet dress stood in the fountain in front of the Plaza Hotel. The column called her a "wilding deb" and "party girl." The girl seemed wired enough. Still, her eyes didn't look to Kevin like she was having any party.

She looked pretty, like his younger sister, Marne, but with finer features. Deb features. Delicate even in the muddy pixels of the newspaper photo. His sister Marne was the anti-deb. A firefighter, she'd had to fight the guys in her Brooklyn squadron for acceptance. She became one of the guys when another firefighter tried to stick his hand down her shirt, and instead of getting huffy like they would have expected and filing a sexual harassment claim, she broke his fingers.

But this girl in the photograph never had to fight for anything in her life. She just slid down a lucky birth canal and popped out an heiress. He tried to wrap his mind around what it would be like to go through life without a financial worry.

"The girl who'll always have everything." Kevin shook his head. "Look what she does with it."

"Maybe." Andrew's forehead twitched. "Son, it's going to be hard on you here if you don't cut the residents a little slack. They got problems, too."

"Sure." Problems like having the chauffeur blow-dry you after a cold swim in front of the Plaza Hotel.

"Anyhow, this young woman is Chester Lord's daughter. Chester, he's a pleasant man, usually. But young Cornelia has got some impulse-control issues. You know what I'm saying?"

"No problem."

"The other thing," Andrew went on, pointing to Philip Grace's byline. "This here's a sneaky reporter. He'll try to get you to tell him when Cornelia might be on her way in or out. He makes a living taking nasty photos. Sticks to this building like a roach on cheesecake, figures Cornelia's always good for some kind of show. He'll offer you money. You take it and anybody finds out, it'll get you fired like you been vaporized. Get me in trouble, too, not training you right."

Kevin stared at the girl in the picture. In his neighborhood, nobody would even notice that kind of behavior. Unless maybe she puked on your new shoes. But the tawdry photo of the debutante both irritated and fascinated him.

His dad would call it another eccentricity, winding up drunk in a public fountain and not even enjoying it. Maybe it was a bored-party-girl thing. Or maybe she was just crazy as a bedbug, and everybody covered up for her.

Either way, he wondered what his mother would think of him now, having to tip his hat to a girl like that, staggering by him giggling, smelling of stale champagne.

Tomorrow, no matter how long he worked, he would need to check on the neon saint he'd dedicated to his mother.

Chapter Two

*I*n Penthouse A, Chester Lord IV leaned over and lightly kissed his sleeping daughter's forehead.

It felt warm and moist, covered with wisps of her straw-blond hair. He tried to imagine Cornelia's face lighting up the way it had before her childhood slipped away. Before this odd young woman who drank too much and danced in public fountains moved in.

Chester sat by her bed and wished he could invite her to dinner, just the two of them in the apartment, to talk things out. Instead, he would have to explain to her why she would be grounded until he talked to her psychiatrist and Tucker Fisk, to come up with some sort of a plan.

He sighed heavily. He had allowed so many opportunities to reach his daughter get away. Perhaps irretrievably. Lately, that thought felt like an anvil in his stomach. She never actually rebuffed him, only seemed to live her life dancing to music he couldn't hear. To put it mildly. He had clung to the notion that they would one day share a cleansing effort to talk out their differences. Now all they shared was grief frozen in time. He worried whether Cornelia had finally lost any desire to cut through the silence that had hardened between them over the past ten years.

Chester fought to ignore the color scheme of his daughter's bedroom. One side of the room was all red, the other side all black. It bore little resemblance to the sweet sanctuary that once housed precious antiques, a collection of crystal, and her own gleeful artwork and school projects. In one mad week, she stripped the room of all personal things, as if to deny him any clue to her personality, and installed stark utilitarian furnishings. All that she kept from her childhood was her giant fish tank full of colorful creatures, which, to her credit, she tended carefully.

Now she slept doped up on medications that the unctuous psychiatrist Dr. Bushberg had prescribed. The sight of her blond head on the pillow pained him. Her mother's Devonshire-cream skin and delicate features still made her look so innocent and vulnerable. Chester squeezed her hand and left the room, forcing himself to keep the slump out of his walk.

Other duties called.

"Just don't come to the board meeting," he muttered to Cornelia.

He crossed the long, dark second story, passing the gym. When Elizabeth was alive, that room had hammered with the clang of free weights and the hiss of the hydraulic workout machine. Chester used the machine only as a coat rack.

He passed sconces that once hung in Napoleon's castle at Waterloo, and glanced in the gilt-etched mirror between them. Though he was hardly trim, Chester looked presentable. Wall-to-wall anxiety kept a sparkle in his eyes. And he had not yet suffered the Dorian Gray effect that strikes WASPs suddenly in middle age, collapsing a youthful face overnight into cracks and folds.

Chester had inherited the seat on the 840 Fifth Avenue co-op board from his father, and felt crushed by his duties as its chairman. He had no question that the owners at large needed him to stand up to the reactionary owners who dominated the board. He secretly thought of them as the Amazing Stone Heads of Fifth Avenue—blockheads stuck in the ground like the relics on Easter Island. Nursing prejudices formed as spoiled children in Herbert Hoover's time, they still tried to snub every applicant whose surname ended in a vowel, inviting lawsuits. Chester knew that these geriatric brats would all cling to their seats until death removed them.

At least Chester had prevented 840 Fifth from becoming a total viper pit, tangled with bickering and litigation. He tried to keep the truly disagreeable applicants away from the board, not even allowing them to go through screening. Then he dealt with the most irate and arrogant rejectees. When they bellowed and stamped their tasseled feet, threatening to sue over some real or imagined slight, Chester's pacific nature became an asset and not the liability it tended to be in his business.

If he couldn't understand the dizzying world of high tech that was changing his company, or even handle his own daughter's behavior, by God, he could still choose his neighbors.

He stepped heavily down the broad sweep of staircase. His ancestral co-op's elliptical, marble-tiled foyer stood two stories high, with a wraparound balcony. An oversized crystal chandelier dangled from the vaulted ceiling. It had flickered inside the Palace of Versailles on the day an angry mob beheaded its former occupant.

Crossing the foyer, Chester Lord IV avoided the paintings of the three Chester Lords who had come before him.

Chester had already indulged a secret fantasy after his father died. Although he couldn't bring himself to break tradition by removing the faces of the Lord men from the great foyer, he did take the life-sized paintings of all three ancestors and order them reproduced as shrunken eight-by-ten prints. It usually amused him to pass the tiny heads, which he'd cut down to size as surely as a Borneo headhunter. But today they managed to burrow annoyingly into his thoughts.

In their line of one-child families that produced only sons, the Lords' starter fortune came from Chester Lord I, who founded the Lord & Company investment bank in 1900. That mother lode made it difficult for his son to fail. Yet Chester II seemed bent on losing the money anyway, growing too fond of wintering in Palm Beach to shuttle back and forth to Wall Street and then cashing out all of Lord & Company's stock market holdings. When the stock market crashed in 1929, Chester II barely got his hair mussed.

Lucky Granddad.

When Chester's father, Chester Lord III, took over after World War II, he invested in the black arts of Madison Avenue—advertising and network television—pumping Lord & Company into an even richer and fatter enterprise.

The tips of Chester's ears burned whenever he thought about his father. Today had brought back his eleventh birthday party at the Westchester Country Club. When Chester missed a putt, his dad hectored him to keep shooting until all his friends and relatives drifted off. At twilight, forty-seven putts later, he finally sank the ball.

Chester glumly forced himself to study business at Yale, aching to change his major to social anthropology. He envied those students with their beards, tangled hair, and sloppy jeans, who seemed to bear the real problems of the world. During his college years, Chester would gaze out the window of Finance 101 and fantasize. He had read *Coming of Age in Samoa* by Margaret Mead. How he yearned to run off to study those gentle islanders who only made love, not war.

But, of course, Chester had to join Lord & Company.

None of the cunning, pin-striped men who reported to his father took young Chester seriously. Sometimes he imagined that they snickered as they passed him. He knew that the top managers met after work at watering holes like "21" and never invited Chester to join them. They dismissed him until his father got a snootful and said at the firm's Christmas party, "A Lord will always run Lord & Company, even if he runs it into the ground."

How prophetic. In the 1970s, Chester tugged at the short leash his father allowed him by investing in John Delorean's new automobile. In the 1980s, he sought safe harbor in the savings and loan industry. But he was soon fleeced by its slickest operators, who bankrupted their S&Ls while buying yachts with twenty-four-karat-gold faucets for themselves. He constantly stood trembling before his father's desk, explaining why money practically bled out of his business ventures.

The berating only stopped when his apoplectic, workaholic father finally blew an artery and was wheeled out of his office on a gurney. Chester fearfully took over the presidency. He floundered while the crafty managers around him circled and snapped. He knew they were lining up outside buyers to force him out.

Desperate to find a loyal right hand, he hired his old Yale roommate's son as his protégé—a fierce blond Young Turk named Tucker Fisk, a football star at Yale with a Wharton MBA who had already cut a blazing swath through Wall Street.

Tucker proved to be more protector than protégé. As much as Chester shrank from confrontation, Tucker roared with the joy of it. On the day they called Bloody Tuesday, Tucker lined up and summarily fired the executives who wanted Chester out. Then he terrified the loyal ones by demanding letters of resignation to keep in his desk in case they should even think about disobeying him. On Bloody Tuesday, the halls of Lord & Company rang with trembling voices swearing lifelong allegiance to Chester Lord. But Tucker fired most of them anyway. He replaced them with his own people, young zealots with laptops who looked sixteen years old to Chester and leapt at Tucker's orders.

Then Tucker forged a bold and profitable alliance between Lord & Company and Koi Industries of Hong Kong. Chester recoiled from the Kois, father and son. They were no better than modern-day pirates. The Kois would somehow get ahold of plans for competitive products, probably by industrial spying, and quickly build cheaper knockoffs. The Koi sedan they called the Panda looked like a toy Honda. The Koi computer blatantly violated Compaq and Intel patents. Still, Tucker's partnership with the Kois coined money for Lord & Company. Secure in his role as president and chief executive officer, Chester practically sweated gratitude. He couldn't even complain when Tucker pressed him to move the firm from its fine old quarters on Wall Street to the garish Koi Tower on Madison Avenue.

Chester stopped to stare at his dad's shrunken image. He wondered what the old man would think of the brassy new Koi Tower.

By the time his right loafer left the staircase and landed on the marble floor, Chester passed the only life-sized paintings, of Elizabeth and Cornelia. His daughter's smirk mocked him.

How could he meet people today, after Cornelia's latest humiliating appearance in the tabloids? His upper body slumped again. Then he rasped to himself, *Good God, pull yourself together.* Whatever happened to the code of his class, "Never complain, never explain," immortalized by one of the Fords when police stopped him for drunken driving.

Chester squared his shoulders. Duty compelled him to greet his guests with head held high, despite the damnable article about Cornelia. He crossed the black and white tiles of the smart foyer and headed for the living room. The family co-op consisted of twelve rooms, fashionably crammed with the plunder of centuries. A sweeping hundred-foot penthouse terrace, relandscaped each season, dwarfed the tallest trees of Central Park and the spired gothic skyscrapers of the West Side.

By all rights, Chester should feel like Captain Zeus on the bridge of a mighty Olympian ship. His view of Central Park and the West Side was unbroken to the Hudson River and the Palisade cliffs of New Jersey. Instead, he longed to hide anywhere, even in one of his bathrooms.

He felt his heart skipping wildly. But it was only anxiety, not a deadly heart attack. He felt like a man held together by Brooks Brothers and Scotch tape. Perhaps he'd be better off with a massive coronary like Dad. At least it would all be over soon, and he'd have quiet and tranquility, a nice long nap. He took a deep breath, wiped his palms on his pants.

So what if he didn't show up for the board meeting? They would reject all the applicants anyway. If tomorrow he pulled the covers over his head and stayed home from Lord & Company, Tucker Fisk would run the business without him. What difference did Chester make to anyone? With all his means, his influence, he couldn't even help his own daughter.

When Chester passed the bathroom and saw his slumping frame in the mirror, he seized up in fright. He quickly pulled himself up straight and pressed on.

Promptly at 3:00 P.M., late enough to justify cocktails but early enough so they wouldn't doze off, the members of the 840 Fifth Avenue co-op board gathered in the Lords' sitting room. They consisted of four WASP males and a German Jewish widow—375 years of experience snipping coupon bonds with Tiffany scissors.

The board members perched on fussy eighteenth-century chairs designed for people who wore powdered wigs and complained of gout. Chester nodded to his Scottish butler, O'Connell, a sturdy, inscrutable presence. O'Connell still wore a plaid kilt and long socks under his jacket and tie, and still rolled his r's in a thick Highlander burr after thirty years in New York. His large red hands busied themselves with ice cubes and ashtrays.

Chester sat at his living room desk.

"All right"—he glanced around the room—"let's get to new business. As you know, the Biddle apartment has been put up for sale by Eloise Biddle's estate. We have twelve applicants who meet the financial criteria. We'll vote today on which of them, if any, we should invite up for an interview."

Nobody objected. Thaddeus "Tad" Eames, a white-haired clubman who had never worked, licked his lips.

Chester read the first name on the list.

"Is he anyone?" asked Lily Stern, widow of the man who had inherited one of the world's largest private banks. She scowled so easily, her face might have been made of aged parchment.

"He was vice president, Lily." Chester sighed as he added, "Of the United States."

Lily's face hardened. "No."

"Well, we have to at least consider them, Lily," Chester said.

"What for?" barked Tom van Adder, retired custodian of his family's philanthropic trust. "He's a Democrat, isn't he? Besides, there was a ridiculous picture of his wife in the newspaper—"

He froze in mid-sentence and looked at Chester, his voice dribbling off. The board members smirked guiltily, each reminded of today's picture of Cornelia in the *Globe*. Chester caught them in their dirty little moment: how they delighted in the misfortunes of others. What was the word for it? *Schadenfreude.* Such a remarkably German concept. Chester swallowed the acid swelling in his chest, the reflux of anger and shame, and pretended that the whole business wafted right by him.

"I think we should invite him up," Tad snarled. "Ask him what he thought he was doing taxing capital gains. We can send their rejection letter afterward."

"Oh, for heaven's sakes, Tad," Chester said. "If we're going to reject them, let's just do it. On approval of their application, yea or nay?"

"Nay."

"Nay."

"Nay."

"Nay."

"Nay."

Chester began to argue, then thought better of it. He said nothing, and his silence made the room so packed with treasures feel barren and empty. The board members glanced at each other, obviously feeling cheated by his refusal to fight back.

"Let's move on," Chester said. "We have a fellow who won the Nobel prize. Now he's secretary general of the United Nations. His wife is a surgeon."

"Good Lord, no," Tom van Adder sputtered. "He hails from one of the *debtor* nations."

"Tom's right," Chip Lindsay said, bristling. "Those foreign U.N. people have diplomatic immunity. They can get away with anything." He shuddered. "The next thing you know, the city will come after us to pay his parking tickets."

Chip had been ambassador to Bermuda during the Eisenhower administration and thought he knew politics. Like Chester understood nuclear physics. Now, on top of it, Chip had memory lapses and had even worn pajamas once to a co-op board meeting. He noticed for the first time Chip's unusually large teeth when he pulled his lips back over his gums.

"I say nay." Chip bobbed his head.

"Nay."

"Nay."

"Nay."

"Nay."

"Agreed." Chester nodded. "We'll just send them a letter."

In the periphery of his vision, Chester saw Cornelia, who had shuffled into the living room wearing an oversized black terry cloth bathrobe that dragged on the floor.

Corny, why now?

His daughter's blond hair hung in a tangle, half covering her eyes. She stood in the center of the room behind the Stone Heads, quietly observing them. He saw a hint of determination in her gray pupils, lit up with points of violet as though a furnace burned deep inside.

The fire brought Chester back to the years when Cornelia was young, purposeful.

Chester shut his eyes briefly. He saw his wife, Elizabeth, and their daughter sitting scrunched together in their favorite place. It was a little wicker love seat in the sunroom. Elizabeth would read to Corny from dog-eared books about the dead inventor Nikola Tesla. *Tesla Towers! Free electricity for everyone on earth!* For a woman of her background, Elizabeth's interest in the electrical wizard Tesla seemed as odd as Jackie Kennedy strapping a utility belt onto one of her Halston dresses and asking for a schematic of the White House. But Elizabeth had ferreted out the family's ancient role in Tesla's broken career, and the injustice of it inflamed her.

Chester loved Elizabeth. He had swallowed his puzzlement and indulged her interest in Tesla, who had died penniless in 1943. But he had sulked about her passing the wild Tesla business onto Cornelia. His daughter had picked up the crazy inventor's flame. Insisted that he listen to her little discoveries of Tesla's inventions. She seemed as determined as his wife to romanticize the man, and Chester could only retreat into glum silences. Now he guiltily recalled mornings when Elizabeth and Corny would chat about Tesla at the breakfast table. He had fought back with foolish acts of feigned indifference. He was supposed to drop Corny off at the Gramercy School on the way to his office on Wall Street. Instead, he sat reading the *Wall Street Journal* ostentatiously past 8:30 until Elizabeth scolded him and Corny finally cried that she would be late for class.

Childish of him in retrospect, but typical of their silent power struggles at chez Lord.

Still, the Tesla business was a thin shadow across so many cherished times. Elizabeth had loved Cornelia with an almost wanton streak. Thanks to her, Corny earned straight A's at school, threw herself into modern dance, and giggled with glee at every new challenge. Elizabeth had such strength. She had protected both of them. And he adored her.

Exactly ten years ago, Elizabeth died in a helicopter accident by the East River. He had taken Cornelia ahead to the cottage in Southampton, where Elizabeth had planned to join them. They arrived to a halting phone message from O'Connell, and he called his office to hear his father's gruff voice clinically explain the horror. The commuter helicopter had lost electrical power. It had swirled in the sky like an angry brick before crashing and bursting into a fireball. There were no survivors.

Chester had become a basket case, distant and troubled. He took to locking himself in his study and drinking martinis with no vermouth. He couldn't talk to his daughter, not that he didn't try. But he bore a mighty responsibility to Lord & Company, and perhaps he had found that easier to cope with.

He felt the weight of grief and remorse in his chest now, swelling like a hard medicine ball.

"Hello, Cornelia," Chester finally greeted her. "We're having a co-op meeting now."

"Chester," she said in her reasonable voice. "I have to go out, but somebody put a lock on my clothes closet."

She had stopped calling him Dad a couple of years ago, and he didn't dare ask her to call him that again.

"We'll discuss it right after the meeting." He tried not to dwell on what she must see as his betrayal of her. Actually, the idea of grounding her had been Tucker's. He hadn't resisted, not after the scene she'd created the night before.

Cornelia beseeched Chester with her intelligent eyes. The look shot an arrow of shame and doubt through his stomach. His daughter stood just like Elizabeth, he thought, casually in control of her trim body. Her straw-blond hair sparkled, and he caught glints of the sun on her fine cheekbones. Her alert eyes fought against her medication. Her lips, full and pale, formed a brave line of resistance that broke his heart.

His daughter's eyes held his for another second, then turned to the board members, who squirmed and shifted in their chairs.

"The issue on the table," she announced, her voice raised like a clear chime despite her medication, "is should a girl be denied clothes? Yea or nay?"

The board members coughed and looked away. Chester concentrated on his desktop, raising his voice only slightly. "Cornelia, please."

This would be not only a contest of wills between them, he knew, but another frustrating pas de deux, the two of them speaking but hardly on the same channel. He wished the board would disappear, beamed back to their own musty apartments. Yet, even if they disappeared and Chester and his daughter were left alone in the room to speak freely, somehow his plans for them always wound up in chaos. The simple act of talking to her had become as fraught with peril as setting himself on fire.

"The next name," he said, because he could think of nothing else to say, "is Chad Benson, chairman of Sweethold Financial."

While Chester spoke, his daughter floated in her bathrobe past the board members to the antique mahogany liquor cabinet. She opened it and began fishing around inside, pulling out a deck of playing cards. Shuffling them as she walked back to face the board, Cornelia stopped directly in front of Tad Eames.

"All right," Cornelia said. "I need clothes, so the game is strip poker. Jacks or better to open. Mr. Eames, are you in for that blazer?"

"No, no," Tad Eames stammered.

"Was that a nay on Benson, Tad?" Chester felt stubbornly committed now. Besides, he realized with only a twinge of guilt, he secretly disliked Chad Benson, a loudmouthed Wall Street slice-and-dicer. Maybe he could ram a nay through in the confusion, and some good could come of this.

The board members studied their shoelaces.

"Ah, no, Chester . . ." Tad began.

"Thank you. We have a nay from Tad. Have any others decided on this applicant?"

"Mr. Van Adder," Cornelia said, turning to the man, who now tensed in his chair like a schoolboy. "How about you? Can you afford to lose those slacks?"

"No," said Tom van Adder, his eyes following the trim golden leg that flashed very briefly under Cornelia's robe.

"No you haven't or no you don't like them, Tom?" Chester snapped. "If we can't agree, then we'll just send them a rejection letter. Now if you'll excuse us for a moment. Cornelia, in my study."

He touched Cornelia's drooping sleeve and they started out of the room.

Lily Stern called after them, "We all hope you're better soon, Cornelia."

Chester ground his teeth. The smug old battle-ax. However misguided her passions, Cornelia had more goodness in her than the entire board with their self-congratulatory charity balls, where the charity was lucky to squeeze out a few crumbs after they'd paid for the catering and entertainment.

They hadn't reached the den when his daughter shook off his hand, folded her arms, and glared at him.

"Locking my closet? Stop her before she dresses again?"

"We need to talk, Cornelia, but not now . . ." Chester fumbled. "If you'll just go to your room and read or something, Tucker will be over this evening and we can all talk this out."

"Did you and Tucker Fisk decide to lock up my clothes?"

"I'm . . . just concerned about you."

"Well, I hope you and Tucker have a good man-to-man talk, because I'll be going out."

"Where?"

"To South America."

"For God's sake, why?" Chester yelped, trying to divine a purpose behind this shocking news.

"Research," she said. "Some historians believe that Nikola Tesla went to South America to build a third tower, or at least left plans for other people to build one. Anyway, I'm going to find out."

Chester felt his mouth open and close as he tried to respond. "Cornelia, I don't resent your mother for having told you these old stories about our family." He had slowly drifted toward this view, now blaming Great-Granddad, the pinched old Puritan, for starting this Tesla mess. "But it's so . . . *late* to try to deal with it. There are other things you should be pursuing."

She cocked her head. "Like?"

"Well, ah . . ." They could discuss the distance between them. Even if it meant admitting how he had failed her. But he felt too weary to open that can now, for what might spring out.

She didn't speak, worrying a thread that stuck out of the terry cloth of her bathrobe with her fingers. Her eyes seemed to scold him.

He tried again. "Have you spoken to anyone else about South America? Dr. Bushberg? Tucker?"

She seemed to consider this. "Nobody you know, Chester."

"Cornelia, whenever you start in with this Tesla business—"

"I didn't start it," she snapped back.

She sounded so matter-of-fact about an idea so, well, crazy. South America? She could be kidnapped. He saw a vision of his daughter surrounded in a dark jungle by dope smugglers or rebel insurgents, sinister men grinning, gold teeth flashing. She could even be murdered. He swallowed, felt his throat very dry. He must find a way to protect her at any cost.

"Well, you're a grown woman," he said slowly.

"And it's my money," she added.

"Yes, it is," he said agreeably. "I'm not necessarily opposed to this trip on principle. A change of scenery might be good. It's just so sudden, you really have to give me a little warning about a decision like that. That's not unfair, is it?"

She chewed her lip. "No, I guess not."

"Then, please. Let me get through with the board. We'll have dinner together."

His daughter brightened a little. "When?"

"Uh, soon." He lowered his eyes.

At 4:00 P.M., Chester briskly ushered the board members out of his sitting room.

Instantly, he retired to his mahogany-walled study. The old, familiar scent of leather and crackling logs in the fireplace soothed him slightly. Chester liked to sit among the first-edition books, dusted of their cobwebs, which he no longer read, and photographs of the sloop he kept in Southampton but no longer sailed. The thought that he could still share traditions he loved with his daughter seemed flimsy now. He settled into his most comfortable leather chair and rubbed his eyes, trying to force his mind to focus.

For the first time, he had let the board have their way and reject all twelve applicants. He wondered who would sue. Oh, to hell with them. By the next meeting, the city's elite Realtors would submit at least one hundred new names.

Without being asked, O'Connell's craggy, vaguely disapproving face had appeared. He carried a silver tray that contained a sterling shaker tinkling with ice, a huge martini glass, and a plate piled with small crescents of lemon peel. O'Connell poured the drink, but allowed Chester to pick up one of the lemon peels, twist it, and plop it into the glass.

Chester nodded his thanks and let O'Connell disappear before drinking half the stiff martini in one gulp.

Cornelia presented such a hornet's nest, he could barely begin to think about what to do for her without feeling stung from all directions. Clearly she needed more professional help than she was now receiving, and immediately. The South American business numbed him with a radiating panic.

Chester had to consider the practical. Thankfully, Cornelia's share of the family's money was substantially tied up in trust. She received only the whopping interest she earned on her interest, which she'd spent over the past years on God knows what. She would be twenty-one on February 14, Valentine's Day, and he couldn't, wouldn't, snoop into her personal finances. A line had to be drawn. Fortunately, the trust was set up so she could not invade the principal. Nor did she show any interest in the block of voting stock in Lord & Company that she'd already inherited. It lay gathering dust in a vault on Wall Street.

Chester let his lids droop and saw Cornelia as a child, smiling at him as she dragged out her school science projects to show him. Cornelia had always run full tilt into life, bright and determined. But her mother's death had changed her, crushed her in peculiar ways. He held the icy glass and thought of the time she took his hand and urged him to share her newest interest. She led him to the utility room in their apartment, which he barely knew existed. There she focused his attention on the 252 different circuits that controlled their chandeliers and wall sconces and such. God, how she had grown into a cruel parody of that curious little girl, with her crazy Tesla obsession.

Crazy.

Twice now, that word had slipped in so easily. He had always managed to block it before.

Cornelia had progressed so rapidly, in her willful way, from grief to obsession. All of his good intentions, the parade of therapists, the efforts to reach her, had come to nothing.

She had been so young and fragile when Elizabeth died. Clearly, he should have put aside his business worries and protected her fragility. But he had felt torn. His own father, who had made little effort to hide his petulant dislike for Elizabeth, had chosen this time to rachet up Chester's troubles at Lord & Company. God, what a year. The stock market had just collapsed like a palace built on toothpicks, although of course he was obliged to say with a straight face that the smoking rubble was a mere correction.

Chester, you need to focus, his father had thundered at him through the chaos of the crash. He was expected to work eighteen-hour days at the firm. Scuttling back and forth between home and office, feeling an awful fire in his chest no matter what action he took, he had left a critical business plan in his kitchen freezer, more than once forgot to have his driver take Cornelia to see family and friends who might have comforted her.

Goaded by his father, he reflected queasily, he had taken the easy way out. It was always simpler to tend to business issues, where things seemed to sort themselves out eventually, than to the murky, unchartered depths of emotions. And Cornelia had been so painfully needy. When he stayed late at the office, she would wake up at night, screaming for her mother. The Gramercy School called him about attention problems. Obviously it was his attention she ached to have. But in those early days after Elizabeth's death, Chester could barely manage to heft himself up and shave in the morning. What all the so-called experts told him about handling grief made no dent. His brief foray into Zen, a measure of his desperation, proved as paper-thin as a Japanese party lantern. So he abandoned Cornelia, for a time, to a string of nannies and au pairs.

With his feeble paternal tools, he had still tried in his own way to break through. For years, he'd invited Cornelia aboard the Lord & Company business jet to fly them both to Palm Beach for Christmas. He wanted to soothe her with the balm of the Florida sun, the lush bougainvillea, and the old banyan trees around the Mediterranean-style house where Elizabeth and Corny had once played. But Cornelia had trembled and refused to board the plane, causing him to cancel at the last minute. Finally, when she was thirteen, she let him take her hand and climb aboard. While the engines still screamed on takeoff, the pilots received word of a severe thunderstorm ahead, and Chester told them to turn back. So they shared a silent ride home from the airport, his daughter lost in a book, responding to his efforts at conversation about school and friends with polite nods.

The cracks had already formed in Cornelia's personality by then, small fissures that ran to her core. In the past few years, they'd split open with ferocity. His now remote daughter began to nurse an all-consuming passion she would no longer share with her father.

The damnable Tesla.

Cornelia had convinced herself that if Tesla had been allowed to build his free-energy tower, it would have changed the world. The poorest families on earth could have all the free energy they needed. Cars and planes could run on clean electricity. He shook his head and chuckled bitterly at that. Here, take your Exxon card back with a life-time refund. Tear up those utility bills. Shut down that leaky nuclear power plant next door. And whatever happened to air pollution?

What an innocent child Cornelia could be.

No doubt those flinty men who owned energy monopolies at the turn of the century saw a glimpse of that free-energy future, too. The first Chester Lord did, and helped them put a stop to it. Chester I had slyly pulled the plug on Tesla. The inventor died a lonely, discredited recluse who spent his final years in New York City haunting public parks, feeding crumbs to pigeons.

Chester drained his martini. The warmth of the gin was shrinking the anvil in his chest to something more manageable.

Cornelia studied Tesla's life and work so wholeheartedly that she neglected her studies at Gramercy School. A withdrawn teenager, she revealed little sexual interest in boys. Nor in girls either, fortunately. First the child psychologists called her a late bloomer. Then a very late bloomer. Eventually she began spending all her time in activities she would not share with him.

A year ago, their contact had withered even more. She had begun leaving the apartment with a shiny blue hard hat under her arm at 7:00 A.M., refusing to tell him where she was going. She wouldn't arrive home until after midnight. When he asked her where she'd been, she'd say, "a museum," and nothing more. He had feared briefly that she was having an affair with a construction worker. Then he wondered whether wearing a construction hard hat every day for nine months could be a strange, symbolic act of birth. Clearly a matter for a psychiatrist. He insisted that she see a heavy-duty therapist named Dr. Bushberg, recommended by his own doctor, for as many times a week as he deemed necessary to try to break her fever of unresolved grief. She went, but told Chester nothing, though he fished meekly for signs of change.

For the past year, consciously or not, he had steadily abdicated his responsibility for Cornelia to Dr. Bushberg and Tucker Fisk.

Tucker Fisk.

He had come to believe, or to hope so fervently it felt like a belief, that his protégé could save her the way he'd rescued Chester at Lord & Company. The boy seemed to care a great deal about his daughter, courting her in his managerial fashion. Tucker used the force of his personality to shield her from trouble. And she didn't make it easy.

The fountain fiasco was only the latest embarrassment. Two years before, Cornelia had left her own debutante party halfway through, simply vanishing into the night. There had been whispers and odd looks within their social set. Next came a wasted half term at Vassar before she dropped out. She was too busy studying Tesla.

He had tried to phone Dr. Bushberg, conveniently out of town for the weekend. He thought angrily of how he'd grill the psychiatrist to his shoes on Monday to get answers.

Chester drained the small martini pitcher. The instant that he did, O'Connell appeared with another. It also went down smoothly, a calm glow inside him. Like the fire in his hearth. Then the door chimes jingled and he heard O'Connell's footsteps marching across the marble foyer. This would be yet another indignity heaped on Corny, a bodyguard Tucker suggested they hire to watch over her.

He stood up with a mighty effort. He and Tucker would have to put their heads together tonight and come up with a workable plan. He readied himself to greet the woman O'Connell brought into the den.

"Pleased to meet you." The woman stuck out her hand. "Sergeant DiBlasi, New York City Police Department, off duty today. The commissioner's a friend of yours?"

"Yes, he is." Chester took the woman's hand. She gave it a brisk squeeze he could still feel after she withdrew it. He felt concern for his slender daughter in this physically powerful woman's care.

Sergeant DiBlasi had a square face with shiny skin. Her straight hair was cut at her shoulders, and she wore a black blazer over a sweater and skirt. Her curveless frame couldn't be described as girlish, nor did it appear to be a female weight lifter's.

"You don't look . . . ah . . ." Chester wanted to offer a small compliment, but these days he measured his words to female employees carefully.

She flashed a professional smile that she ended as quickly as her handshake.

"Not as butch as you thought?" She chuckled without mirth. "I'll meet your daughter anytime. No point trying to hide the fact I'm here to keep her in."

"No," Chester spoke coolly, unfairly resenting the woman. "No point in that."

Chapter Three

*K*evin remembered, a half-hour into his second shift, why Andrew told him they called the Russian doorman Vladimir "Vlad the Self-Impaler."

In the stuffy heat of the lobby, Vlad fell asleep easily. While Vlad talked, his eyes drooped. Then his jaw sagged onto his chest, and his head flopped over after it. Andrew had told Kevin that one night Vlad fell asleep and crashed over onto the lobby's umbrella stand. A jeweled Cartier umbrella, which some resident had carelessly stuck in with the tip up, punctured a nasty hole in Vlad's cheek. Kevin could still see his white scar.

At least Vlad didn't snore. The shift passed uneventfully, if the boredom that threatened to saw Kevin's brain in half didn't count as an event. Even staying vigilant and on top of details, Kevin found whole hours where nothing at all occurred, leaving his mind cut loose to drift. Only four residents trickled in after midnight, and Kevin would kick Vlad's shoe to wake him.

That left Kevin plenty of time to torture himself in the muted good taste of the dark lobby, thinking about how his mother must have felt with her head and arms and legs in a wild, rolling jumble down the hard cement staircase of his parents' tenement building.

Kathleen Feeney Doyle fell from the fourth-floor landing, flailing around in the dark because the staircase light, a pathetic 89-cent bulb, had gone out. It hadn't even burned out. The negligent prick of an absentee landlord, who lived somewhere in Westchester County, hadn't paid the building's electric bill on time. Two days later, Kevin saw men installing a thin, slick roll of imitation Astroturf over the cement stairs, to give the impression of a carpet. The dim bulbs lighting the staircase came back on, too. The landlord had raced to pay the building's Con Ed electric bill before the building inspector came to check.

Kevin replayed the scene over and over, a horrifying movie projected on the back of his eyelids. Once it started, he couldn't shut it off.

She had lost her footing carrying a twenty-pound turkey in a plastic bag. That was going to be their Thanksgiving dinner. She shouldn't have been carrying it: a couple of hours later, Kevin and his two sisters would be there to help. But his mother could be stubborn as an Irish donkey.

Kevin's father, Dennis, had heard the commotion from their apartment, ran down the stairs to find her, and yelled for a neighbor to call 911. His dad then called Marne and she called Kevin. He arrived in time to see his mother at St. Agnes Hospital hooked up to tubes, doctors and nurses desperately trying to save her life.

"I love you, Mom," Kevin shouted to her.

But even with all the beeping and shouting and crowding around, the doctors couldn't reverse the damage.

Kathleen Doyle had been only fifty-one years old when she died. Born on a slag farm in Bloody Forehead, she had sailed to the U.S. and met Dennis Doyle in Brooklyn, soon becoming mother to Kevin, Marne, and his older sister, Helen. She came with more than a bit of the mystical Irish Catholic about her.

Like other Irish country girls from the moonlike rock towns of County Sligo, she was told that mothers whose sons became priests were guaranteed a place in heaven. You couldn't *know* that for a fact, she'd said, but he could tell those rural priests had pretty well convinced her. But even his mother realized that Kevin Doyle, child of Tenth Avenue and 17th Street, wasn't exactly priest material.

He could forgive himself for not giving the priesthood a shot. It hurt him more to be standing in the lobby with a monkey suit on instead of working on his art for her after she'd stood up for him. As a kid, he was the only Doyle to sit quietly and observe things with what she called his "artist eye." She made it her business to expose him to the world of art, dragging out her old Time Life books on art appreciation, showing him the pictures inside when he was good, and using the heavy picture books to whack him when he wasn't. Seeing Kevin as an artist meant a lot to her. She sacrificed so he could go to art school, even if it was only a trade school, the New York Institute of Art and Technology, that advertised on subway posters. His payback would be to perfect the neon sculpture he made just for her.

He couldn't save his mother now, but maybe he could still do something that would have made her proud of him.

Brace this time, Kevin thought, sliding his time card into the slot to punch out.

Ker-chunk.

Another jolt screamed through Kevin's body. As if the time clock was made by the folks who brought you the electric chair. He clocked out at 8:07 A.M. Two shifts, back to back.

He wondered if the men who ran the building would invent a funny name for him like "Vlad the Self-Impaler." He would try to earn one closer to "The Artist" than, say, "The Asshole."

Kevin had drunk gallons of coffee but eaten nothing, so his stomach made sloshing noises when he walked and he felt jittery. But he had plenty to do before he could even sneak up on the concept of sleep. Most important, he had to check on Saint Sebastian. His sculpture might need dusting, and nobody else would do it.

Kevin changed into his civilian clothes, thinking about neon. He could never seem to finish the sculpture for his mother. "It's not right until it's right," Max, his instructor, said. A real artist couldn't think any other way.

Max had convinced him that Saint Sebastian needed a better halo. He'd work all night if he had to, get two hours sleep, and do the next doorman shift. Sleep deprivation from this job would degrade the hand-eye coordination he needed to make the circle geometrically perfect, with no bumps. But he'd just have to keep bending it until it was right.

Walking outside onto Fifth Avenue, his face was stung by the fierce wind whipping over the stone wall of Central Park. The trees were stripped bare and rickety under a thin winter sun. His crusty jeans, boots, and leather motorcycle jacket didn't keep him too warm in late December. But his only winter clothes had been stolen, along with just about everything else in his rat's nest apartment on Avenue B, in the cold heart of Alphabet City. He bent forward, rounded the corner into another tunnel of biting wind on 65th Street, and headed east.

A few yards down, he spotted a man leaning against a dented Toyota, acting impatient and fidgety. Somehow Kevin knew this was the tabloid reporter Andrew had warned him about. He sensed the guy watching him through mirrored sunglasses that were stark against his dark-chocolate skin. His head was shaved—it was a pretty good skull, with a couple of lizardy wrinkles on his neck. A once-expensive but faded scarf flapped in the breeze. Over the shoulder of the man's camel-hair coat, Kevin saw a beat-up brown-leather camera bag.

As Kevin was about to pass him, the black man took his sunglasses off and separated himself, smooth as an athlete, from his hood-ornament position on the Toyota. Curious, probing eyes were sunk back into their sockets. His wide smile made him look like a man on his way to a party.

"Young man"—he moved with agility toward Kevin—"I'm Philip Grace. Congratulations on your new job." He came alongside and touched Kevin's arm lightly under the elbow. "Let me walk with you. What's your name?"

Confidence, Kevin thought. Maybe fake, but that's what confidence usually was. The guy had a way about him. His features weren't handsome, but made him look both engaging and disciplined. He also wore a small gold ring in one ear.

"Name's Kevin Doyle." He put out his hand.

"Well, Kevin Doyle, I see you're in a hurry." Philip walked familiarly close. His attention flattered Kevin a little, like a coach warming up a draft pick. Kevin glanced at Grace's coat. The collar looked shiny, as though the nap had been brushed up too often. He made an effort to camouflage himself, to loiter around 840 Fifth.

"So I'll just get right down," Grace said. "I bet you found out you're going to be making about thirty-two grand your first year with overtime. Let me suggest a way you could establish an extra income stream."

"You make it sound tempting, selling you stuff," Kevin said. "But I guess tempting is your business."

Philip Grace gave him a mock-rueful smile. "I see you been talkin' to my friend Andrew. Good man of his generation. Keepin' his place, and all. Now you look to me like a young man with a plan. What's your real life? My bet is, you're a creative guy. Writer, somethin' like that."

"Something like that," Kevin allowed.

Philip waited. "So *are* you a writer? Keepin' a journal on those people in the building? Ways of the WASP?"

"I'm an artist."

"Well," Philip told him, "some would say that if you make your money workin' as a doorman, then you're a doorman 'stead of an artist. But I say, you gotta give a creative person time and inspiration. What kind of art?"

"I do neon sculpture."

"Pink flamingos 'n' shit?"

"My dad thought I ought to do beer signs." It felt easy talking to Philip, so long as he could sniff the way the reporter's questions were headed. "He worked as a brewer for Schaeffer a long time ago."

"I remember Schaeffer. New York beer," Philip Grace said.

"Nobody else does," Kevin told him. "But I got involved making this sculpture of Saint Sebastian instead. You know the martyr with the arrows in his chest?"

"Long way from Schaeffer to saints." Grace chewed that over. "Like Hallmark stuff? Little red St. Valentine neon guy, with pudgy cheeks?"

"Bigger," Kevin said. "Life-sized."

Grace looked lost. "You mean neon *art?* Is it good?"

"Well . . ." The cold numbing his face, Kevin knocked his hands together and took a breath. "I can tell you it's almost perfect technically, except the halo's a little off and I can't get the neon to shimmer the way I'd like. I got it in a gallery, but like the owner says, 'It's not creative unless it sells.' So I guess the jury's still out on how good it is."

"'Cause I was thinkin'," Grace went on, and Kevin had to give him credit for plugging away, "maybe we could swing by St. Patrick's, ask if they need it for the altar."

Kevin cackled loudly at the thought of his Sebastian in the Irish saint's cathedral on Fifth Avenue. Yeah, they'd love it at St. Pat's, the priests probably throwing holy water to chase it out.

The two of them had already walked two blocks crosstown, were coming to the light on Park Avenue.

"Whoa." Philip put his hand in front of Kevin, holding him back.

A bicycle messenger from hell shot in front of them unexpectedly, wearing a black helmet and gloves.

"Thanks," Kevin said.

The city had hung festive white holiday lights on the spare trees in the center of the avenue, but they wouldn't start glittering until after dark. On top of all the coffee, hunger made Kevin feel light-headed. Philip Grace bounced along with him, just as hungry for information.

"I read your story yesterday," Kevin said. "What's your column called?"

Philip slipped his hand into the pocket of his once elegant coat and handed Kevin a glossy business card, fancy white letters on a black background.

Philip Grace. Debwatch. The New York Daily Globe.

He saw an office number and a pager. No address.

"I thought it up myself," Grace said. "A debutante watch. 'Debutante,' you look up the word, that's a girl gets it all handed to her, parents throw this *comin' out* party when she's eighteen. She's introduced to society, meanin' the white power structure. The 'watch' part, that's my job. I keep my nose down, see what all those debs get up to, 'specially if they like to run around, get into trouble."

Kevin waited. "Why?"

Philip Grace gave him an All-Star glower. "Kevin Doyle, the debutante is the last gasp of the great let-'em-eat-cake, guzzle-champagne-on-the-backs-of-the-poor American class system. The Golden Goddess of Inequality is what she is. When one of 'em falls off the pedestal, it's got social significance."

Uh-huh, Kevin thought. Just like this reporter, he'd grown up on the street. Even his baby teeth had been kicked in. Kevin knew exactly what desperation looked and smelled like, and he couldn't let Grace think he was getting over on him.

He stopped walking, and Grace stopped in synch with him.

"So, Philip, you bump into a lot of other newspeople on your beat?"

"Not too many." Philip sounded a little guarded, not so cocky.

"Well," Kevin pressed, "all due respect, but I was wondering if maybe you started out chasing Madonna and Leo, some real celebrities, but you couldn't handle the competition."

Kevin might as well have thrown a pail of ice water on him, because Philip froze. But, to his credit, he recovered quickly.

"See, I figured you for a man liked to dig in, Kevin Doyle. Yeah, I had my special problems, gainin' access. Got me three TROs last year."

"What?"

"Temporary restraining orders," Grace said proudly. "The white celebrities start cringin' when a black man jumps in front of 'em."

"And the debutantes don't?"

Philip laughed. "Damn, you don't give a guy any room. Let's just say I learned you gotta create a niche for yourself. Too many reporters out there. So I stake out my segment, debs worth dishin', and do my homework. This Cornelia Lord, she's a disaster searchin' for a photographer."

Kevin thought about the spoiled rich girl's eyes in the photograph. She'd been searching for something, but definitely not a camera. "You're saying, she's asking for it?"

"Don't matter. The public's got a right to know. You seen Corny yet? Man, that's a one-woman show. How 'bout I buy you somethin' to eat, we can talk about her."

Kevin felt the emptiness of his stomach and his wallet. But the only thing worse than hunger he could think of, even worse than being a servant, was being for sale.

"No thanks." He put his hands in the cold, frayed pockets of his leather jacket and flashed Philip a grin so he'd know this wasn't personal. "Just so we're clear, I gotta issue you my personal TRO on any resident where I work, okay?"

Grace started to speak, then stuck his hand out so Kevin had to shake it again, one businesslike pump.

"Well, I'll see you 'round the building, Kevin Doyle." Grace smirked. "Both gotta fight for our art, right?"

He strolled off, whistling.

Kevin looked at Philip Grace's card and wondered if he'd just done something stupid, passing up a fistful of cash. Then he tore it up and scattered the pieces in the wind.

He walked to Third Avenue, listening to his stomach gurgling. He had one dollar and some change in his pocket. Coffee or a subway token, but not both. He stopped at a coffee shop no wider than a bowling lane; a dirty blue neon sign announced, "The Waldorf-Estonia Luncheonette." Thanks to his neon teacher, he recognized the stylish letters as an example of the 1930s German Bauhaus school of signage.

The coffee shop looked generically shabby. Booths were jammed close together around the same chipped Formica tables as his building's staff room. Somebody had just swabbed the floor. He gagged from the smell of ammonia.

Regular working people hunched over the counter, sipping coffee and scarfing down Danish. The booths belonged to plumbers and other trade aristocrats who made their own hours and took time to order eggs and pancakes. He took a booth toward the back, then once again checked his pockets for spare change.

Kevin's eyes went glassy as he read the menu, four pages long, single spaced. The smaller and seedier the luncheonette, the more items they had on the menu. Where did they keep all this stuff?

"You want to order?"

A young waitress with a whiny voice stood over him, a mustard stain on her white sleeve, rolled up to reveal bleached hair on her arms with tiny black roots like an ant farm. She held her pencil stub to her pad as if Kevin were putting her life on hold. He asked for a small pitcher of hot water with a teabag on the side.

When the waitress left his water and complimentary soda crackers, he looked around to see if anybody was watching. Then he took the clogged-up bottle of Heinz ketchup and tapped on the "57" etched in the glass; the ketchup spurted like lava into the cup of boiling water.

Kevin stirred his instant tomato soup. It scalded his tongue, then filled his throat and chest, and finally dulled the aching in his stomach.

He snuck three cups of his homemade soup and six packages of crackers, watching to make sure the waitress didn't catch him. But she was busy snapping orders in shorthand through a window in the kitchen.

Kevin checked the time on the watch his father had lent him, an old promotional one that said on the rotting band, *Schaeffer is the one beer to have when you're having more than one.* He would really need to buy a more dignified watch for the job. But he already owed Uncle Eddie $2,000 for getting him the job. "The vig," Eddie had called it. Kevin snorted. That was Eddie Feeney deluxe, trying to sound like a loan shark to scare him. At least he wouldn't have to pay Eddie until Christmas Day, after he got his tips.

His eyes closed. He thought about the fact that he couldn't totally explain to himself, let alone Philip Grace, about the neon saint.

Because that's what Mom wanted.

On his eleventh birthday, she balanced *Art of the Renaissance* on her lap and pointed to the color reproductions of paintings like *The Adoration of the Magi.* Kevin stared at the halos, which popped out at him like golden saucers.

"The saints," his mother breathed. "Look at the coolers."

The colors. His mother loved an artist whom he thought she called Jotto, like the New York lottery. She pointed out all the paintings Jotto created, the frescoes inside churches with names like *The Ascension* with Jesus Christ taking off like a 747.

Jotto, he discovered, was really a fourteenth-century Italian painter named Giotto. And Giotto painted stories that had a kind of moral, if not always physical, beauty. One of Giotto's paintings of Francis of Assisi made Kevin see why the saint was a big deal to the Irish, because Giotto zeroed in on the saint's character. Francis grew up a spoiled young rich man's son who got sick and learned to be humble, then gave all his possessions back to his father and spent his life in poverty. He made his whole life an offering.

But his mom's favorite saint was St. Sebastian. The young Roman had served as an officer in the Praetorian Guard, protecting the Emperor Diocletian. Then Sebastian, that arrogant Roman prick, somehow got what his mom called a "spark of the divine." He became a true believer, a persecuted Christian, along with the poor people and the lepers. Diocletian liked Sebastian, so he ordered him to renounce his faith. When Sebastian refused, Diocletian threw an imperial-sized fit and ordered Sebastian shot by archers in his command, dishonorably fragged by his own men.

In *Art of the Renaissance*, Kevin's mother reverently pointed out Giotto's little-known *Lost Saint Sebastian*, stolen and then recovered from a Swiss bank vault. She told him it was the first painting she had ever seen. She had found it in the National Museum in Dublin, a *culchie* country girl with skinned knees trembling in front of the triptych of Sebastian with his chest full of arrows. She said it changed her life.

Just thinking about it made Kevin's chest hurt. Those sharp arrows probably made a hell of a thump even going into a tree. He wondered how they must have felt tearing through muscle and pumping arteries.

Kevin was jolted out of his reverie by the waitress speedwalking past him.

"Can I have another hot water, please?"

She ignored him and went to another table to take an order.

Kevin closed his eyes again for just a second. He saw Saint Sebastian hanging. The archers started to bang their bows on the ground. His eyes opened and his waitress was banging silverware on the table in front of him. He smiled at her.

"You were snoring like a pig in a trough," she said, like she'd caught him walking out the door with the cash register. "You see a sign outside, Eat 'n' Sleep?"

"No," he said. "I was just drifting."

"No more crackers, you cheap shit," she yelled, making people turn and stare. "Go outside. The cold's free."

"The cold's free in here." Kevin sighed, and got up to pay at the counter. He couldn't work up much hostility for the waitress. The tips must suck at the Waldorf-Estonia Luncheonette, and at least one of the customers looked like he belonged back in the psych ward at Bellevue.

A middle-aged man with a red face, who had missed about half his thick whiskers shaving, sat at the counter wearing a seedy old business suit. Nobody sat near him, because every few seconds he would suddenly jerk back on his spinning seat and wave with both hands, like a spring-loaded toy.

Kevin had seen plenty of people do that at Bellevue, wrestling with invisible demons or maybe thinking they were doing a breaststroke across the East River. He looked away.

On his way out the door, he snuck a curious look back and stopped. A fly landed on the man's food. Kevin watched the man jerk his body back and do his breaststroke again to chase the fly away. But the fly zipped right back a few seconds later, insanely persistent like all insects, and landed on the man's greasy hash browns.

Kevin stared, wondering how he could turn his observation into art. Someday, after he fixed Sebastian's halo, maybe he could create a neon sculpture about somebody like that. Somebody who looks from a distance like he's acting crazy. Then, after you get closer, you see he has a good reason.

Chapter Four

*I*gnoring the screaming wind on Lexington Avenue, Kevin looked for a phone booth that wasn't being used or vandalized.

His mom could play the Irish martyr sometimes. She could have asked his dad to carry the turkey up the stairs for her. Or waited for Kevin. Why hadn't he gotten there early enough to help her?

He couldn't crawl any lower than being responsible, even in a small way, for his mother's death. Or maybe he could. No matter how rotten things got, they could always be downgraded an extra notch. He felt a vague panic that he could still fail at neon sculpture and die his own Art Death. Then, for the rest of his life, he'd be a doorman.

At the corner of Lexington and 52nd, he found a pay phone that worked and punched in the number of the Stinson Gallery in SoHo. This was the sixteenth call he'd made to the owner, Jessica Fernandez. He hoped that this time she'd be there, since she'd never call him back.

"Stinson. Jessica Fernandez speaking."

"Jessica? Kevin Doyle. How are you?"

"Kevin, darling." She sounded pleased. "Come right over. I have something I'd like to speak to you about."

"About Sebastian?"

"You must be psychic. I'm on another call, sweetie." Her laughter tinkled before she disconnected him.

Kevin felt the gnawing in his stomach smooth out slightly. Jessica's greedy-merchant giggle promised good news. And she had invited Kevin to the gallery, not her habit. She practically lit matches to keep her artists away.

Kevin walked eighty-two blocks against the freezing wind to West Broadway, the main street of SoHo. Here, dozens of galleries dangled Real Art before the leather-and-Lexus crowd. Every Saturday, middle-aged lawyers and dentists struggled to pull their jeans over growing paunches. Then they drove to West Broadway to buy the kind of art they couldn't find on Madison Avenue. This crowd liked the gritty, nothing-to-lose artists of Alphabet City. But their Lexuses could disappear from Alphabet City in a puff of exhaust fumes, or crackheads might cut their leather jackets off their backs. Instead, they visited the Stinson Gallery. At the Stinson, SoHo's premier gallery, Jessica Fernandez showed the work of Alphabet City artists where it was safe for the patrons to see it. He suspected that Jessica Fernandez didn't know much about art, but she sure knew how to hype artists.

Kevin entered the vast, well-lighted space, carved out of an old cast-iron building with black Grecian columns. Slabs of glass faced the street, allowing sunlight to pour in. A tiny plaque outside read "Stinson" in letters designed to be illegible, to make buyers believe the gallery was their secret.

Jessica Fernandez, thirty-ish, was perched with her legs crossed at a small white desk, holding a phone between two fingers with nails painted blue metalflake. She looked voluptuous with moussed jet-black hair worn in a wanton, pillow-ready style, wearing a sleek black dress and silver jewelry. Her eyebrows stood up in little peaks while her eyes lazily appraised Kevin, and her candy-red lips made an insinuating smirk. But he never heard her talk about anything but business.

"Evan, it's not selling," she kept saying into the phone.

Kevin knew she had another forlorn artist twisting on the other end. He felt sorry for Evan, whoever he was. But he also felt a terrible worm of delight wriggling in his chest.

Another artist taken out!

He hated letting that selfish thought creep in. Young artists in New York fought to survive. They exposed their work bravely, hoping no one would smell their fear. Most would be poisoned to death. Only a few would get lucky. Now poor Evan felt Jessica's fangs locking in through the phone. The good part, although Kevin hated to admit it, was that Jessica's getting her venom out on another artist meant she wouldn't be hungry for a while. He'd be spared his Art Death this time.

Kevin made a point of looking at other pieces in the gallery before homing in on his Saint Sebastian. It seemed more businesslike, less desperate.

He started through the sleek but soulless space. The relentless white of the drywall sometimes disturbed him, suggesting a clinic for sick art.

"Evan, nobody cares what some artist thinks," he heard Jessica tell the phone, exasperated.

He approached his neon saint. It stood up on its pedestal in a corner of the gallery, roughly where the kitchen door would be in a restaurant.

Kevin contemplated his Sebastian. Giotto might have painted the first three-dimensional saints, but Kevin Doyle had sculpted the first saint that lit up.

Emotions laid bare, rendered by simple lines was the phrase he'd read in his mom's art book, describing how Giotto made the divine look human. He identified easily with Giotto, who started out a peasant. He'd cut and stripped saplings for his frames, mixed his own paints from patches of colored earth he dug from the ground.

It had taken Kevin two years to achieve the level of technical perfection in front of him. Two years and $995 a month to the New York Institute of Art and Technology—barely made each month thanks to his lousy night jobs, and a little help from his mom. At NYIAT most students make neon advertising signs. But a lucky few got to work with Max Freuhling, who Kevin considered a real neon artist.

Max taught him the science of flameworking, how to cut and splice the opaque white-glass tubing that was only a quarter-inch in diameter. Then how to bend the fragile tube over a fire, careful as a diamond cutter. He showed Kevin how to pump the noble gases of krypton and argon through the tubing to achieve the bright neon colors. He gave him the ability to take meaningless tubing, shoot it full of gas, and plug the creation into a wall socket to buzz lightly and throw off a brazen light that wasn't beautiful or subtle, but packed a rude look-at-me power.

Kevin had to admit that he brought a certain grace to flame-working. He had carefully sculpted the glass tubing so his simple design could be instantly recognized, and not just from the arrows sticking out of Sebastian's chest like a porcupine. His sculpture laid bare the character and emotions of Saint Sebastian through simple lines and curves. It hummed loudly, almost proudly, from the electricity stirring the juice of the noble gases pumping harsh and violent color through his saint.

He designed the sculpture to be life-size, but a little smaller than his own body because ancient Romans had been smaller than Americans. He created it with tubular strokes and squiggles. Sebastian's profile was proud, an uptown saint. The suggestion of arch features and curly hair worked, too. He had given Sebastian the outline of a broad chest, and bent two tubes perfectly to portray sinewy arms on either side of it, tied behind his back.

For Sebastian's flesh, he used a pink tone, as close as he could find to real flesh color. For the arrow wounds, he added little red circles around the holes he'd created with thin wires in the blank space of his chest. That's where he mounted the slim, pure white arrows. It was hard work getting the arrows right, keeping the shafts pointed out naturally and kind of gracefully, with the hint of feathers at the end. He could have faked them, made it easy. But, in his art experience, the easy way was always the wrong way.

Except for the garish colors and the slight bend of the halo, the sculpture was as good as any neon sculpture he'd ever seen.

Still, the track lights several feet over Sebastian's head made the buzzing tubes look stark and kind of flat. Kevin had struggled to give Sebastian an inner glow. His instructor's own neon work shimmered more subtly, although he used the same tubes Kevin did. Like real art. Kevin could never get that look.

And the saint's halo still disappointed him. It wasn't gold like the shiny halos Giotto crafted painstakingly, buying scraps of leftover gold leaf from artisans known then as gold beaters. Neon gases didn't burn gold. So, instead, he used the next best thing—a small curve of light blue that looked like the sky around Sebastian's head.

In blazing pink and white with little drops of red, Kevin had out-lined both the pain and hope of the flesh-and-blood martyr. At least it felt that way to him.

In the two years it took him to get it right, he tried to ignore the other neon students who had laughed their asses off at his subject mat-ter, not to mention his attention to detail. But if he didn't make it per-fect, what was the point?

The only thing that could make Sebastian's colored gases look less like a beer sign was if they adjusted the spotlights on the ceiling mount over his head. He'd ask Jessica for a ladder to do it himself, to make zero trouble for her.

"I'm hanging up now," Jessica Fernandez said loudly into the tele-phone. He heard a short scream escape from the receiver before it clat-tered into its housing. Jessica smiled brightly.

"Jessica." He tried to sound helpful. "I was just thinking . . ."

Jessica's smile held. "Kevin, I have to ask you to move your piece."

"Move it where?" he asked her.

"Out of the gallery."

Kevin felt dizzy. "It hasn't even been here three weeks . . ."

Jessica waved her hand dismissively. "Darling, people don't really get it. I have a bigger piece coming in and need the floor space."

Kevin looked back at the sculpture, his pulse racing and stomach boiling. "I can fix the halo."

She frowned and waved her perfect metallic-blue nails dismis-sively.

"Sweetie, a glass saint? I gave you mercy space. I mean, there used to be a neon gallery down the street called Let There Be Neon, or something." She wrinkled her nose.

"Where is it now?" Kevin asked.

"My point exactly. Neon's just too accessible. It's . . . mall art."

Mall art.

So this was what Art Death felt like. Words like arrows slamming through his deep tissue, piercing his organs.

"Too accessible?" he repeated.

"Yes," she said.

Kevin walked over to the Hoover vacuum cleaner placed on a

white pedestal. He knelt down and read the card aloud, very deadpan. "Hoover, $38,000."

Jessica folded her arms. "Don't be linear, Kevin."

Kevin saw in her blank face that she'd moved on. He stood up. It had happened just like his mother's death. You showed up and got the news. End of story. No appeal. Now all he could do was take his Art Death like a man. Not like some mewling puke, like poor Evan on the phone.

"Okay. Listen, Jessica. I appreciate you giving it a shot. You did a nice thing for me."

Jessica's face came unclenched. She actually walked over to him and touched his arm. "You're promising, Kevin," she purred. "You have an eye. But this isn't your time."

Kevin took off his jacket and wrapped it gently around the face of the sculpture.

"Keep in touch," Jessica lied.

Kevin unplugged the saint. The humming stopped and the bright color fizzled out of the tubes. It stood bleached and frail now, a skeleton. He made sure his leather jacket fully protected Sebastian's face and shoulders.

He lifted the piece with great care and balanced it. Kevin's eyes burned, but he said nothing as he struggled to cradle the fragile sculpture, eighty pounds with transformer, clutching it to his chest. Keeping the slender arrows sticking out directly in front of him so he wouldn't crush them, Kevin fought the door, got outside, and started walking. Jaded New Yorkers, who wouldn't miss a step walking around the bodies of a drive-by massacre piled up on the sidewalk, turned to stare at him. He shivered without his leather jacket.

He walked uptown like he carried a six-foot egg, trying to roll on his heels so he wouldn't jolt the thin glass tubing, glancing down to scan for dog shit he might slip on. His hands and eyes stung in the gusting wind. But he soldiered on until he reached the filthy old cast-iron building on West 14th Street, six stories high, that had been a sweatshop a hundred years before. He rang the bell labeled "New York Institute of Art and Technology."

Inside the closet-sized lobby, he managed to maneuver the leather strap that opened the horizontal doors to the tired old industrial elevator by pulling with his teeth and the finger of one hand, trying not to squeeze Sebastian's arrows. He stumbled inside the elevator cage. With a groan of pneumatics, it lurched up to the trade school that occupied the sixth floor.

Kevin opened the balky elevator door. On this floor, walls had been knocked down to create one large studio. He felt grateful for the blast of warmth greeting him from the fires that students labored over, usually oppressive even on a cold day. At twenty workbenches, students bent neon tubes into signs for bars and tattoo parlors. For protection, they wore shiny silver Mylar protective suits, welding masks, and thick gloves while they hunched over the flames.

When he'd told his mother he wanted to study at the New York Institute of Art and Technology, he charged her up with his own thrill over "ribbon fires" and "noble gases." Then her eyes almost popped out when she read the trade school's tuition contract and saw the $995 payment he'd owe every month. She told him to never, ever tell anyone else. Then she co-signed.

"At least," she told him, "if you can't become a priest, you can make me a Saint Sebastian."

In the beginning, Max Freuhling shook with hilarity when Kevin asked him about creating a neon saint as good, in its way, as Giotto's oils. But Max was a practical man, and warmed to the task of giving Kevin private lessons strung out to cost as much as his student could earn at dead-end jobs. Kevin was so poor, he lived in an apartment on Avenue B full of cockroaches that snapped, crackled, and popped like Rice Krispies when he walked across the dark floor at night. The bathtub in the kitchen needed to be sandblasted before he could use it.

"Hey, Sebastian's back home," a student greeted him, and the entire studio body began to snicker, the floor echoing with hearty laughter.

"Where's Max?"

"In the john," a smirking girl making a sign that said, "$8 Haircuts," told him.

Still clutching his burden, afraid to set him down, Kevin backed into the men's room. Soot from the studio floor covered the old sink and toilets. Max was just leaving a stall, a paperback copy of *Lolita* in one hand. He zipped up his fly and stood in front of Kevin, a jagged face with cool green eyes widely spaced. Max's hair, still ice blond though he was almost sixty, stood straight up on his head in oily spikes, and he wore brown corduroy pants and a scratchy turtleneck.

Max's accent was heavily German, even though he had lived in the United States for more than forty years. Kevin once asked him if he went to Berlitz for German touch-ups, but Max never laughed at anything except Sebastian. Kevin put his saint down on the floor very carefully and unwrapped his jacket. The sculpture seemed to look gloomily at a point over Max's head.

"Jessica told me to take it out of the gallery," Kevin said. "I guess you never went by to see it."

Max's eyes flickered their scorn.

"How could I have made Sebastian better?" Kevin asked him.

"Look at your bends." Max shook his head sadly. "Disgraceful. If you cannot bend, how can you make a halo?"

"Max, I need your help now. My mother died." He felt the hollow place in his stomach grow, regretting that he'd used his mother's death for sympathy. "I need to make Saint Sebastian perfect so I can sell it."

"Are you current with the school payments?"

"Only one behind. I can make it up out of my first check," Kevin said. "I've got a new job."

"The school says no." He shrugged in a European way, suggesting that he was stifled by unbending authority.

"Max, I've been paying them for four years. They can cut me a little slack."

"Pfft. The money is not for the *school*," Max said with a sneer. "It is motivation for you. When you sacrifice, you concentrate. You want a cheap education? All through the city, there are incompetent glassmakers. Go watch them make a bad fire."

"Max, I really need an hour with you now. Just a little time on the halo."

Max turned away from Kevin and walked out of the men's room, letting the door swing back.

"Put a suit on," his mentor grumbled without turning back. "I'll give you twenty minutes."

Kevin first put Saint Sebastian in a safe place, the room where the students kept their large pieces. He left him between a green sign for Heineken whose red star was too big, making it look like an old sign for a Holiday Inn, and a respectable neon Fat Elvis in the Las Vegas lounge suit.

He quickly put on one of the Mylar suits, and carried a black Pyrex face mask under his arm.

"Look," Max told Kevin when he arrived at his instructor's worktable. "My new pieces. Look at the bends. Perfect bends."

Kevin studied them, but it wasn't for the bends. As always, each piece revealed a technical perfection he couldn't fault. Who could? They were critic-proof. A neon square. A neon circle. A neon cross.

What dazzled Kevin was the shimmer of that subtle, elusive Max-glow that Kevin couldn't bring to his own work. Compared to Max's little pieces, the colors of Kevin's saint still looked as crass as the logo for a massage parlor. He could shrug off the saint's harshness, like Jessica Fernandez did, as "irony." But that "irony" crap was for people who couldn't do any better. His mom's saint deserved more.

"I have to make it glow like your pieces," Kevin said before he strapped on his mask.

"To make neon glow, you must be scalded."

"Scolded?" Kevin said. "I get scolded all the time."

"*Scalded.* Your heart feels scalded now, from your *mutter* dying, does it?"

Mutter? His mother, Kevin realized. "Yeah, that's how it feels."

It was the first time Max had ever spoken to him in a personal way.

"Good," Max told him. "Today, maybe you become a better liar."

"What?"

"Art is a lie that makes us see the truth," Max intoned. "You were always a bad liar, so you make crooked halos."

Kevin felt outclassed in their exchange, as he always did. Max had gone to art school in Europe. He used words like "deconstruct."

Max motioned for Kevin to switch on the burner. Kevin tightened the mask over his face, pulled his silver hood up over his head, and zipped it around the mask. He picked up a length of glass tubing for a new, improved halo. Feet apart, he faced his fire ready to bombard the tube and bend it into shape.

Kevin's hands didn't work.

Normally, his hands took over from signals his brain fed them. Today, his fingers inside the gloves felt like fat, mushy sausages.

He tried to focus his mind to send the signals. Place the tube in the fire. Move into it, using the gravity of his body. But his body seemed to produce no gravity.

A critical light had expired somewhere in his brain. Kevin stepped back from the workstation.

"What is the matter?" Max frowned.

"I don't know," he mumbled through the mask.

Then Kevin turned away from Max and walked out of the studio with his space suit on. He reached the freight elevator door, and as he closed it, he saw that Max hadn't budged from his flameworking bench, his hands on his hips.

"That suit is school property," Max shouted in a surprisingly theatrical voice, full of fury.

"I'll be back," Kevin mumbled into his Pyrex face mask.

He knew it was a lie when he said it, but the fullness of that didn't hit him until he stumbled onto the street. His space suit caused passersby to give him plenty of room. He felt his confusion like cement, hardening in his chest and setting into his brain. He needed to sit down at the curb.

Inside the mask, Kevin began to cry because he just realized, in his heart, that he would never see his saint or his mom again.

Chapter Five

*I*nteresting bunch of species. Colorful."

Sergeant DiBlasi tossed out microcomments as she peered into the fish tank in Cornelia's room. But she never took her eyes off her, Cornelia noticed, and kept her feet fourteen inches apart at all times, ready in case Cornelia should attack.

"Big tank, too, considering," the sergeant said. "Like in a seafood restaurant."

"You have to give fish a lot of space. Usually people just crowd them together." Cornelia got up off the edge of her bed dressed in her robe, since her wardrobe closet still had a padlock on it. She stood at the tank with Sergeant DiBlasi and pointed out the different varieties of exotic fish.

"That's Alice, the blue one wiggling her tail. She's always poking around in the other fishes' business. The big red one I call the Red Queen. See how she holds court? Other fish come to her."

"Alice in Wonderland," Sergeant DiBlasi said, nodding. "You feel like Alice?"

"Sure," Cornelia said. "She couldn't leave either."

Sergeant DiBlasi glanced around Cornelia's room, probably seeking out telling details, though she would find none. The room was naked. Once she had personal things, the small pieces of crystal and other objects her mother had collected from Europe, Central America, Asia, all over the world.

Then, one year ago, when she began her project, the Electric Girl had rolled up her sleeves and redecorated for efficiency. That way, she could just grab her hard hat every day and go to work with an uncluttered mind.

She had stripped the walls and laid bare the tabletops to keep things simple and avoid distractions. She had given away her sound system, even very personal things like her yearbook from the Gramercy School. Then she redecorated in functional red and black like a car battery, for life simplification, but also to put off visitors. Cornelia left only one personal touch, a photograph of a woman with blond hair to her shoulders who pursed her lips in a little smile. The silver-framed photo sat on a metal table next to her bed.

"Your mother?"

"Yes."

"Divorced?"

"She died."

"Sorry for your loss," the sergeant told her, like a recording.

Cornelia knew exactly when people she had just met made up their minds about her. Something settled in their eyes as though they had processed whatever data they needed, and would now treat her like a person they had just filed into inventory. These days, people formed their opinions about her more quickly. She observed that Sergeant DiBlasi completed her mental file right after seeing her mother's picture. She imagined the short form of the file would be *Spoiled Nutcase* with a few minor notations.

It saddened her. At times like this, she would love to share her secrets with a strong person like Sergeant DiBlasi, who did important work and knew a lot about life.

"What do you do in the police department?" she asked her.

"Armed robbery interdiction. Professional crews that hold up stores."

"Don't they shoot at you?"

The sergeant gave her a hard look. "Only if you let 'em."

Yes. She admired Sergeant DiBlasi. Especially the way she spoke, in clipped sentences to avoid superfluous chatter. She smiled, seeing both sides of the Alps in the sergeant's face. She had a Germanic squareness to her features, but her coloring was olive, Italian, and her lips rather full. Her hair was clean and glossy, worn without any particular style.

"Grounded tonight." The sergeant smiled tightly. "See a problem with that, Ms. Lord?"

"No." That much was true. She would have no problem with Sergeant DiBlasi. "But please call me Cornelia."

She felt a passing wave of guilt for what she was about to do.

Chester and Tucker Fisk settled into old club chairs, each angled slightly toward the fire O'Connell had built in Chester's study.

Tucker sipped mineral water. Then he flipped open the disk drive of his custom laptop, made by their business partner, Koi Industries. He intended to put on a show for Chester. With visuals.

Chester watched Tucker's agility on the laptop, feeling a ping of jealousy tinged with fear. The same model always jammed or crashed when he fumbled with it. He felt a clammy discomfort with the way they relied on their computers, Tucker's generation of cyberfiends.

Tucker's laptop computer was an unfathomable mystery to Chester. Made of tungsten with an eerie, almost extraterrestrial haze, it was flatter than a comic book. When Tucker popped it open by punching his personal code into the secret clasp, the wafer-thin halves revealed a flat, heat-activated keyboard on one side, marked with letters and symbols so microscopic Chester would have to fish out his tortoiseshell half-glasses to read them. Even then, many of the coded commands made no sense. But Tucker played his machine like an accomplished musician, making incredibly sharp and detailed pictures spring up on the silvery screen.

Only Tucker knew about Chester's technophobia, that he would fire up a space shuttle sooner than he would switch on a computer. He kept it one of Lord & Company's darkest business secrets. Investment bankers were expected to be comfortable with technology. In reality, Chester imagined himself a dumb and frightened turtle, head pulled back in its shell, attempting to cross the superhighway of global data. Without Tucker, he would be a flattened turtle.

Chester marveled at how easily Tucker Fisk controlled things. He studied his twenty-eight-year-old protégé, whose veins coursed with the ancient blood of Anglo-Saxon warriors. He was dressed in an Armani Black Label suit. The fine fabric was a bit vain for Chester, who took a certain pride in buying his suits off the rack just as he had in college, even though he could afford suits of spun gold if he chose. Tucker's blond hair, darker than Cornelia's, was brushed back in waves from a face with a heavy, pleasing coat of flesh that revealed little in the way of bone structure.

More than anything else Chester envied about him, Tucker knew how to take risks without hurting himself. At Yale, he had made quarterback on pure fearlessness. He wore an oversized protective helmet pumped full of air so he could wait that extra second to snap the ball without getting hurt too badly when they knocked him down. Chester searched his poker-player eyes, sharp as industrial metals.

He thought of the way those eyes danced on the day Tucker plowed through Lord & Company for Chester like a delighted Grim Reaper, the smug executives who had sneered at Chester begging to do exactly as he and Tucker instructed them. What a triumph, walking through Lord & Company and for the first time actually feeling like the boss. Tucker had created that moment for him, this boy who could forge mega-deals and intimidate older executives. With the magical tungsten wafer on his lap, Tucker could handle any problem.

With the exception of Cornelia.

"Perhaps you could explain," Chester finally asked him, "how she wound up in the Plaza fountain."

"She has a wild streak, but I'm working on that," Tucker explained in his careful baritone with its faint edge of Young Man In A Hurry. "I arranged a special Saturday for us. No pressure on her. I invited my college roommate, Tony, and his wife along. Corny didn't drink, and I thought I saw her take her medication. Anyway, she seemed okay. We all drove out to the airport to go dogfighting."

"Dogfighting?" Chester felt strangled. "My God, what were you thinking of?"

"It's not as dangerous as it sounds. It's just for thrills. More like a roller-coaster ride."

Chester glowered at him in disbelief. "She . . . hates . . . flying."

Tucker's eyes didn't even flicker. "I know. But I figured this was a good way to cure her. Look the devil right in the eye. Watch this video we took. Corny started out a little nervous, but once we got into a turn fight, she had a great time. Here . . . My friend Tony has two old fighter planes he keeps out at Teterboro."

Tucker showed Chester a grainy video on his laptop screen. It was taken from a camera mounted in the cockpit of what looked like a restored World War II combat plane. Tucker sat in the pilot's seat with Cornelia behind him, both tightly strapped in and wearing tan aviator suits and goggles. Chester could see, through the glass canopy of the plane, a crisp blue sky with puffy clouds circling the aircraft.

"These are T-6 fighter trainers," Tucker said, "made in the 1940s. They're in perfect shape, rebuilt engines. The only difference is, Tony had laser machine guns built on to tell when you score a hit on the other plane."

Chester fumed. But most of his pique was turned inward. He was the one who had, almost by default, abdicated his responsibility for Cornelia to Tucker. What did he expect? The boy had led a charmed life. He had no reference point for understanding Cornelia's fragility.

"Tucker, sometimes I just don't know. You had no business putting Cornelia at risk."

Tucker shrugged. "She wasn't. We showed the girls how to work their parachutes, just in case. And we gave them radios so we could all talk while Tony and I fought."

Now the video showed the yellow plane with Tucker and Cornelia taking off, apparently from a camera mounted on the wing of the other plane.

"I taxied out and took off with Corny, and we flew in close formation until we got to the airspace they keep clear for Tony."

The video revealed the other aircraft off the wing. A voice called, *"Fight on,"* and the blue airplane peeled off left. Tucker jerked his joystick left and toward him.

"Tony's in the blue plane. Now I'm going to get on his tail before he can get on mine."

In the computer screen Tucker's yellow plane rolled over, and Chester started to feel queasy imagining Cornelia's reaction.

"We were pulling over five Gs. I heard Cornelia yelling 'Yeah, yeah' on the radio. This is us doing yo-yos. We're climbing to pick up speed. Now I do snap turns around Tony's plane to stay out of his line of fire. Watch this."

Chester's heart fell as he saw his daughter's head bouncing around the cockpit of the plane rolling up into the sky, then diving and picking up speed, then rolling over again.

"I'm about to get on him now," Tucker said. "He's trying to get behind me but . . . here we go, Corny loved this part . . . yes!"

Chester saw a cockpit view of the yellow plane zip by into the sky right behind the tail of the blue one. He heard a rat-tat-tat like a video game gun.

"Nice shooting you, Tony." That was Tucker's scratchy voice on the plane's radio.

Tucker shut the computer off.

"We flew to the airport and came back to the city. Corny said she was going home to change, and she met us later at the Plaza. She had a few drinks, then she sort of wandered off and went into the fountain. Think about it, Chester. Whenever Corny's out of my sight, she gets into trouble."

Chester clutched his glass. He pondered their shared legacy at their alma mater, the old Kingsley School in western Connecticut. He and Tucker had shared it a generation apart, but prep school didn't change much. One could come out prepared to coast through life the way Chester did. Or like Tucker Fisk, who told him he had been a hall monitor able to punish his peers, one could learn early how to wield power without feeling guilty.

He believed that Tucker's fearlessness could help Cornelia unravel her own loss. But at times, he wondered if perhaps Tucker's joyous assault on life was simply insensitivity. Maybe he and his computer shared the same soul, all intelligence with no heart.

But what choice did he have?

When he had finally admitted to himself that he could find no purchase at all on his daughter's behavior, it seemed like he was waking up in a nightmare, his dread of Lord & Company all over again. Could he blame himself for turning to Tucker to help put her right as decisively as he had Lord & Company?

Chester took a gulp of his martini, at sea once again.

He often suspected that Cornelia dated Tucker just to make

Chester happy, so he could feel more comfortable with whatever she did with her time. Nothing seemed to spark between his daughter and his protégé. At least not so far as she was concerned. She might be the only young woman in New York City who did not consider Tucker Fisk the catch of the decade. And her coolness to the boy caused him to wonder whether it was simply her impaired judgment, or whether she saw something in Tucker that Chester did not.

Or maybe she just felt jealous.

He held this thought, rolling around in it like an epiphany. She might harbor feelings of jealousy about the close relationship between Tucker and Chester. It wasn't the bond of father and son by any means, but it could possibly, he supposed, seem that way to her.

"Chester," Tucker interrupted his musings as he drained his martini.

O'Connell instantly appeared at the door. "Will that be all, sir?"

"Um, would you like a drink?" Chester asked Tucker.

"No thanks."

The corners of Chester's mouth drooped slightly.

"Actually, a martini sounds good," Tucker corrected himself.

"Right," Chester said. "O'Connell, please get us a pitcher. Then you can go home."

The men talked Ivy League football while O'Connell poured the drinks.

When they were certain the butler was gone, Chester leaned toward Tucker. "I've grounded Cornelia in her room with a bodyguard."

Tucker Fisk nodded his approval as he sat back in his chair.

Tucker felt a spurt of adrenaline under his solid crust of calm. He enjoyed a certain thrill in doing battle even sitting in a club chair. And, in a matter of seconds, he would mount the assault of his career.

Tucker watched Chester frown at him in the ponderous way of the semidrunk. He tried not to wince at the gin fumes his mentor blew his way. Unfortunately, that had been his idea. Chester once preferred vodka martinis to camouflage his drinking. But Tucker convinced him that he should switch to gin, so people who did business with Lord & Company would realize that Chester was just drunk and not stupid.

But tonight, Tucker was grateful to see Chester good and loaded.

Here goes, he thought, keeping his goal in sight and beginning his long run.

"We have another problem that involves Cornelia," Tucker said. "It's about her stock in the company. You and Cornelia own just enough of the Lord & Company voting stock to keep control."

"What's the problem in that?" Chester snapped. "I'm afraid you're way ahead of me."

What else is new, Tucker thought to himself as he punched some keys on his laptop. A column of names and numbers appeared on the screen and scrolled down malevolently.

"Look at this," Tucker said. He turned the screen toward Chester for a view of this march of money. "I just got ahold of it today through our people on Wall Street. Han Koi is buying voting stock in Lord & Company for a takeover play. These are all dummy corporations that Koi Industries is using to buy a little here, a little there, you'd barely notice. Look at this company name, Yellow Apparel of China, Inc. They've bought up 18 percent of the outstanding stock already. Obviously they're planning a hostile takeover."

Tucker waited. He could imagine exactly what Chester was thinking, watching the pieces bitten off his family business. The screen mocked Chester Lord and all the Lords before him. He would now be stewing mightily over the treachery of the two-faced Han Koi, who had broken bread at Chester's home.

Chester had never really trusted his partner-of-convenience, old Han Koi. They weren't exactly separated at birth. Han Koi and Chester were both rich, but that was the only glue. Koi was a player in the real world, a self-made merchant who built an electronics conglomerate from a repair shop in Hong Kong. The old man's face could look like a serpent's head, tongue darting out and disappearing. Just talking with him repelled Chester, who had fought Tucker bitterly over the co-venture with Koi Industries. Chester wasn't a racist. He was barely a snob. But he didn't understand what a player had to do to make wheelbarrows full of money in the bloody new world of business warfare. And now his mentor would be feeling slimed by the chain-smoking Han and his useless son, Han Koi, Jr.

"Naturally, Han Koi used a Sun Tzu kind of attack. Very diagonal," Tucker said to goad him gently.

"Turn that off," Chester told Tucker angrily. "What do we do now?"

"Defense, pure and simple." Tucker had rehearsed this part carefully. It was the first few yards that were most important for a player to get his footing and build momentum. "If they make a run on the company, we've got to block them."

"Exactly," Chester said, his knuckles white, squeezing his glass. "I never trusted Han Koi. Duplicitous as hell, what he's trying to do. But it won't come to anything. I hold twenty-six percent of the voting stock and Cornelia holds twenty-five percent. That's a fifty-one percent majority between us."

Tucker licked his lips but said nothing while Chester searched his face.

"Oh, no. Cornelia would never . . ." Chester began.

Tucker measured his next words. The Cornelia problem involved a swamp of emotions, both Chester's and Cornelia's. But he made it his business to know what Chester Lord thought before Chester did.

"Not deliberately," Tucker spoke carefully. "But do you know where she goes all day?"

"Well, no . . ."

"Neither do I," Tucker said, which was true. Nor did he care if it was Saks or Bendel's. "Do you know why she's suddenly going on this trip to South America?"

"Something to do with Nikola Tesla," Chester answered with his eyes on his martini glass.

"But why would that come up now, Chester? Has she ever just taken off for another continent before?"

"Uh . . ." Chester shifted in his chair, making the leather squeak.

"I'm pointing out that there's a lot about her that we don't know for sure."

Chester's Adam's apple bobbed.

"What we do know is that old Han Koi has taken the trouble to count Cornelia's voting stock, too. And we can expect him to play dirty."

"How could old Han . . ." Chester fumbled.

"Corny turns twenty-one on February 14. She'll be able to do anything she wants with her voting stock."

"She wouldn't pledge it to Han Koi," Chester scoffed.

"Of course not. But in her . . . condition, she could be manipulated."

He would let Chester use his imagination for a moment.

"What do you mean?" A waste of time. Chester needed scenarios, faces.

"Well . . ." Tucker leaned in toward Chester, resting his arms on his knees. He had never felt more sincere in laying out a possibility. "Let's use a worst-case scenario. Han might get with some fortune hunter who could win Corny's confidence."

Tucker watched Chester fidget. Soon, Tucker knew, Chester would realize that he'd have to make a decision. He also knew it would be the most passive, least active solution. Chester possessed plenty of buried anger, but no guts. That's why he could always be led to the right decision. With Cornelia involved, it would just be a tougher game.

"The way I see it, you have two choices," Tucker said confidently, as though they could whip through this together with the wind at their backs. "You could hope for the best. Trust Corny to do the right thing."

He watched Chester take a swallow from his martini glass. *Be afraid,* Tucker thought. *Be very afraid.*

"Option two," Tucker said evenly. "We can be practical. Cornelia and I start talking seriously about marriage."

Chester frowned deeply. His gaze slipped to the framed picture on his desk of himself and Elizabeth on their honeymoon. Tucker noted that he didn't recoil or spit out his drink.

"What does that have to do with Cornelia's voting stock?" Chester finally asked.

"You need to make sure you keep it in the family. You know I've been attracted to Cornelia for a long time. These"—he waved his hand in dismissal—"brownouts of hers are manageable. If the psychiatrist can't deal with them, I can."

Tucker tried to read Chester's thoughts, but couldn't see clearly. This was a rainy, muddy field today. He would just grip the ball and slog through the next few yards on instinct.

"I was hoping that by this spring"—Tucker ran fifty yards—"I would ask you for Cornelia's hand in marriage."

Chester jerked involuntarily, spilling his martini on his toe. He didn't even notice.

Tucker waited.

"I just can't see that," Chester finally stammered, the grooves in his forehead making defensive trenches.

"Only because of her behavior," Tucker weaved expertly. "We'll work through it. The important thing now is to set a date."

"What do you mean?" Chester remained too perplexed to put his glass down. He held it in midair.

"If Cornelia and I got married on her birthday, Valentine's Day, she and I would own her Lord & Company voting stock in common. I would need her consent to sell it." He paused. "And she would need mine."

Tucker let Chester get used to that idea for a few seconds.

"I believe that I can give Cornelia what she needs. Stability. Patience. And continuity for the future. She's an only child, Chester." Tucker leaned forward slightly to deliver his money line. "We have the next generation to consider."

Tucker expected Chester to mist over, thinking about bouncing grandchildren on his knee. Instead, his lips tangled up as though he had started to speak but changed his mind about what he was going to say.

Tucker waited. *Hel-lo.* "Chester, are you with me?"

"Oh, yes," Chester stammered. "I see the financial angle, certainly. Very smart. It's just . . . I would feel better if Cornelia had mentioned a deeper relationship with you, Tucker. I feel like you're my own son . . . in many ways. I'd just like to see Cornelia more *excited* about you."

Tucker worked to keep his eyes from narrowing. "Chester, let me ask you something, man to man."

"All right." Chester's voice sounded high and strangled.

"Does Cornelia always confide her feelings to you? Who her friends are, that type of thing?"

"Well . . ."

"You see, Cornelia is a very *private* person. She has trouble expressing her feelings. I believe she's very spiritual."

"Spiritual?"

"I think so. She deals more in *unspoken* communication. Mind-to-mind kinds of things."

Chester seemed to drift. Tucker hoped he hadn't sounded too New Age. He needed to keep Chester grounded. "She and I are closer than you might think, but her problem won't let her commit."

Tucker went for the close aggressively. That's how a player always scored, knowing that only one of them, he or Chester, would come out of this room the winner. He needed that knife-edged focus now to hack through Chester's endless waffling.

"Chester, just let me speak to her about my intentions. I have a plan and it's a good one."

"You do?" Now Tucker caught a small point of hope in Chester's foggy eyes.

"Definitely." He smiled with total confidence. "Have I ever let you down?"

While Sergeant DiBlasi kept her under watch, Cornelia thought again about her last date with Tucker. Definitely what bad sex must feel like.

Tucker Fisk had to be the most peculiar young mogul in all of Manhattan. So skilled at making people do what he wanted, but so dense with her. He had promised her an adventure with a hint of such surprise and fun. Then he had taken her to an airport and jerked that musty old World War II plane through the skies in an obtuse attempt to impress her. She was flung around inside the cockpit, banging her head on the glass, feeling nauseated from all the twists and turns, her chest crushed by the force of gravity as he flipped the plane around like a matchstick.

What was he thinking?

The only way she could make it through the wrenching hour without throwing up was to clench her teeth and fantasize about Tesla. In fact, it ended up one of her most creative fantasies. So satisfying, Tucker could have taken a few more turns. She had completely forgotten that he was sitting in front of her in the airplane and she no longer felt sick.

Time to pick it up again, she decided, to recharge her batteries while she waited for exactly the right moment. Cornelia closed her eyes and garnered her energy, dreaming up her robust Electric Girl.

The dense South American jungle, a spiky dark net, enveloped her.

Her legs propelled her through the snarl of trees with giant fronds. Electrolytes tickled her nose, cleaning the air after a rainstorm. A roaring sound grew louder.

Beyond the last tangle of vines, she caught the bright orange ball of the sun. She broke out of the jungle to stand on a patch of cliff over Iguazú Falls. The falls rolled before her like a silvery mirror cascading into foam and mist. Maybe Tesla had been here. Why not? It was a breathtaking enough spot for a genius.

The Electric Girl slipped off her backpack, rummaged through it for a tiny model of the Tesla Tower. Then she took a breath and threw the toggle switch that produced bright threads of blue light across its miniature mushroom top.

"I am impressed." The voice came from behind her moments later, precise English with a mild East European accent. She turned to see Tesla, slender and intense, wearing khaki shorts and a peach-colored polo shirt.

His eyes owned her now, dark and infinite, letting her in and stroking her soul. "I know all about what you did for me in New York City. How you preserve my inventions. I keep up. And you are very beautiful. Where I was born, you would be called a princessa.*"*

He let the word flow, "preenchaysa." She could only nod.

"Why would a princessa *want to visit a recluse?" He smiled.*

"Because you have the most wonderful corona," she said. The curved band surrounded his head with a subtle, translucent blue, more heavenly than the sun and sky.

He motioned her into his Tesla airship. A match of her replica from the museum, the steel-ribbed antique gyrocopter.

"My antigravity aircraft," he told her. "Like the one you flew. Just more bells and whistles."

He lifted his shoulders and the rickety airship left the ground, elevated straight up in the air, and lounged at a few hundred feet. Then he moved his hand to the left and the airship peeled off into the sky.

"You are appreciated here, very much," he told her fondly. "Watch this. We will play together now."

The maestro twisted his wrist, and soon they hovered over Iguazú Falls. His eyes twinkled at her. In photographs he looked like a scientist, in real life like an impish artist.

"I didn't think you'd be fun," she admitted.

"Ah, you thought an electrical engineer would have no sense of humor," he said with a chuckle.

She touched his hand, moved by his tenderness. Then things began going wrong. Her hand on his caused the airship to suddenly jerk out of its glide pattern. It tipped over, spinning wildly.

"What are you doing?" It was Tucker's voice she heard now.

She saw night, with red and blue waves painted across the black. Popping white flashes burst in her eyes.

Tucker stood in front of her.

A black man in a long coat pointed a camera at her, which made obscene whirring and clicking noises, exploding flashbulbs in her face.

Her head throbbed. Police lights. The Plaza Hotel. Her stomach turned over. She felt something unsavory coming up her throat. Sake martinis. An unspecified number of them.

She stood in a fountain. Very cold, very wet, obviously very drunk. Possibly she had blacked out for a while. "Tucker," she remembered saying, "I'd really like to go home."

Oh, God. How had she let the fountain thing happen? Drinking, feeling trapped. She just wanted to cool off a bit in the foamy spray from Iguazú Falls. Cornelia opened her eyes and saw Sergeant DiBlasi's face two feet away, staring at her.

"I guess I zoned out," she apologized to the police officer. "It's my medication."

Sergeant DiBlasi nodded, and Cornelia could feel her watching as she shuffled into her bathroom. The door closed. She hadn't redecorated in here. The floor was still a rosy marble. Plump, fluffy towels hung over an ornate Queen Anne tub. She noticed that the sergeant had already removed all sharp objects or anything that could be used to hang herself, such as the pantyhose she had left hanging on a towel rack.

"Ms. Lord," she heard the sergeant say through the door, "I want you to talk to me while you're in there. Okay?"

"That's fine, but would you mind feeding my fish?" she called to her. "I don't know how long I'll be."

She imagined Sergeant DiBlasi looking suspiciously at the bathroom door, then at the fish tank. She heard a chair squeak and guessed that the sergeant now hovered over the tank. The fish would come up to the glass wall nearest her. The Red Queen and Alice and the blue eel would all work their mouths, hungry and pleading.

"Where's the fish food?" Sergeant DiBlasi called out, irritated.

"In the cabinet under the tank. Don't just pour it in though, okay? Use the rod with the little basket at the end to kind of swirl it around inside."

She could hear Sergeant DiBlasi banging around inside the cabinet, making more noise than necessary to find the fish food and the utensil.

"The eel's kind of stubborn," Cornelia called. "You have to shove the food right in his face or he won't eat."

"I think I can handle it," the sergeant called right back gruffly.

Cornelia sat on the side of her bathtub, waiting. She could imagine Sergeant DiBlasi jamming the metal rod in the tank, shoving it at the eel to release the food in his face. Then his tiny jaws would open.

"*Eeeeeeeek.*" That would be Sergeant DiBlasi's voice. The whole tank would be glowing like blue neon now.

She waited until after she heard a distinct *thump*, then walked out of the bathroom.

She stepped around the sergeant, who was lying on her back on the thick Persian rug and not moving.

But Sergeant DiBlasi would be fine. The temporary shock from the pulsing six-hundred-volt force field of her *Electrophorus electricus*, the electric blue eel, had sent a jolt from her hair follicles to her toes. Enough to knock her out, but nothing that would leave any lasting damage.

"See?" she whispered to the sergeant's face, now locked in an expression of surprise. "We weren't grounded after all." And she slowly began pulling off the sergeant's clothes to borrow for the evening.

* * *

The fire in Chester's study had burned out. Stoking the fire was O'Connell's job, and he had gone home. It smoldered with a damp, smoky aroma, but neither Tucker nor Chester wanted to break off their serious tête-à-tête to throw another log on.

Chester felt cold inside his shirt, his back and armpits damp. He had never had to deal with more confounding issues. Both his family fortune and his daughter's life were at stake. And Tucker promised a neat all-in-one solution.

What kind of husband would Tucker make for Cornelia? A strong one, certainly. The young man might finally make Cornelia feel protected. She never talked to him about Tucker, but that proved nothing. She never talked to him about anything. So what would be so wrong with letting the boy take it up with her himself? Even though she lived in her own little world, she never failed to exert her free will. Usually to his torment. She could just say no to him, if that was her wish.

He watched the young man's fingers fly over his diabolical laptop. Tucker had used even this brief pause in their discussion to catch up on some business for Lord & Company. Tucker tending to business once again while Chester drank and dithered. He felt a rush of warmth as he looked at the sleek blond head. How he needed Tucker. They made such fine partners, his protégé so young and fearless, Chester an older and more cautious mentor.

"Tucker, I've thought it over."

The young man stopped working. His head darted up with an enthusiastic smile.

"Speak to Cornelia about marriage. If that's what she wants, a February wedding would be fine."

Tucker's grin spread across his face, his huge gleaming-white teeth expanding like a row of refrigerator doors. He stood up and took Chester's hand in both of his. Not a hug, thank God.

"I'll speak to her tonight," Tucker said.

"Good. I don't want to keep her in the dark—" Chester began.

At that moment, the lights in Chester's study went out.

The electrical power was down, Chester thought as he looked out his study's bay window. But lights still twinkled across Central Park.

"Do you have any matches?" Tucker asked him.

Chester got up, feeling his way around the cold, blackened room. "Ouch." He banged his knee while rummaging around his desk, but found a matchbook. He fumbled as he lit one, and the whole pack ignited, almost burning his fingers. The flame cast a yellow halo over the two men. Chester carried the fragile light to the mantel and lit a beeswax candle housed in heavy sterling. He clutched the candlestick like a torch and carried it to the telephone, then called downstairs.

"840 Fifth."

"Are the lights on in the building?" Chester asked.

"Yes, sir," the doorman on duty told him.

"Well, they've gone off up here. Send up an engineer, please."

"You were saying?" Tucker asked him as Chester put the candlestick back on the mantel and settled into his seat.

"Yes. You can speak to Cornelia about your feelings." Chester kept his voice low. As they sat close together, Chester imagined that the yellow halo made them look like two conspirators plotting in a dark room.

"Don't worry," Tucker told him matter-of-factly. "She'll be Mrs. Tucker Fisk on Valentine's Day."

Chester stiffened in the yellow glow.

"If it's what she wants," Tucker added quickly.

A sharp knock rattled the study door.

"Come in," Chester called out.

The door swung open, but it wasn't the building engineer. Sergeant DiBlasi's thick outline stood in the semidarkness. Even in the dim light behind her, Chester could see that her hair stood out, wild and frizzy.

"Sir, it appears Ms. Lord has left the building."

Chapter Six

$\mathcal{V}$ibrating from the excitement, Cornelia left 840 Fifth by the back service door. She timed her exit so she could slip out just behind the noon-to-eight doorman.

The Russian, Vladimir, could often be caught napping.

Once in the alley, she hid behind a Dumpster. She held herself as still and patient as an urban guerrilla. Then she darted out and sprang for the iron fence, crawled over it, hopped down silently, and hugged the building's walls to blend with the night.

She allowed herself a brief whoop of triumph as she bounced on her Keds to the corner of Park Avenue. Then she took in a huge breath and blew into the shrill doorman's whistle she'd borrowed from a locker in the staff room.

The whistle brought a yellow cab to the curb. She gave the driver the address through the Plexiglas shield and smiled at the recorded cartoon-character voice that told her to buckle her seat belt.

The driver flung the cab from left to right, speeding up and braking harshly. She gripped the door handle as she considered her father's stubborn resistance. If only Chester could listen to reason without skating off into panic. Her father had exhibited only one mode—a sad, ticking-toward-crisis angst, regular as a metronome—ever since her mother died. She wished she could speak to him with a pure heart, the way she used to talk to her mother, but Chester tended to back away from her honesty. His fear-filled parenting style had become smothering, but always with that Chesterly degree of separation. He would retreat into his study, ask O'Connell for a pitcher of martinis, and hire a psychiatrist to do his talking for him. But now even calling a psychiatrist wasn't enough for him. Now he'd felt the need to bring in a bodyguard. Chester couldn't even play the tyrant with his daughter except by proxy.

She ached to tell him all about the Tesla Museum, sometimes wanted to just blurt it out and let them pick up the pieces together. Two years ago, when she first saw an opportunity to sponsor the fledgling Tesla Museum, she had visited his office at Lord & Company to broach the issue in a businesslike fashion.

"Dad, I've been thinking about what to do with all my money," she began.

But then Tucker Fisk had burst into her father's office and yanked him out with a few whispered words. Something about the Asian markets crashing and burning. Her father jumped up as though strings jerked his limbs and joined a group of frantic executives outside his door.

She waited a full two hours, then left. From that day forward, the Electric Girl worked alone.

It hadn't been her father's fault that an economic typhoon had chosen that particular day to blow in from somewhere in Asia and devastate their meeting. Still, on that evening she stopped calling him Dad and began referring to him as Chester.

They seemed so star-crossed, she and her father. If she could only make him understand the severity of the Lord family's wrong against Tesla.

But her hope for that cleansing moment had slipped away inch by inch. She clung only to the knowledge that beneath his parental confusion, his heart ached to love her.

One day, she willed against all prevailing logic and evidence, Chester would be stunned by what she had built and dedicated to the inventor. But until that day, Nikola Tesla didn't seem to be a topic that he could discuss rationally.

* * *

In the lobby of 840 Fifth Avenue, Tucker Fisk took his usual course through doors held open by others.

He brushed by the two doormen on duty, noticing only that one was black and the other white, as generic in their uniforms as packets of salt and pepper. He stepped into a small gray Panda limousine double-parked in front of the building. The car door shut with a tinny rattle, like someone at the factory had left a Coke bottle inside.

"We're looking for Ms. Lord," he told Mike. A lumpen man with dull eyes, Mike, the Lords' driver, was little more than a human autopilot. But he was obedient and discreet. "We're going to find her and bring her home."

"You say so, Mr. Fisk."

As the car pulled away, Tucker tried to settle into the limousine's cramped interior. This was a custom stretch version of a Koi compact car. They bought it as a business courtesy to the Kois, though both he and Chester had instantly regretted the decision. Padding the interior with plush seats and burled walnut paneling hadn't made it luxurious. The little Panda still felt like the inside of a cigar tube. As Mike headed downtown, the frame of the brittle, overstretched sedan groaned around corners, as if it might suddenly break in half.

Tucker punched "C" into his laptop and found his "Cornelia Lord" file. Among other data, it contained a list of all the clubs where Cornelia crawled with old friends from the Gramercy School. He had instructed people to bribe a waiter here, a bartender there, to satisfy Tucker's need to know about her nightlife. He still couldn't pin down how she spent her days, but so what? All that would change soon.

Cornelia Lord would be his wife. And, as far as creating problems went, she would be a nonfactor. Scrolling down the list, he identified a few clubs where she might turn up.

He had a thought and looked up. "Hey, Mike, you don't know where she'd go, do you?"

"Nope," Mike said.

Tucker grunted absently.

"Maybe she doesn't want to be found, Mr. Fisk."

"That's not her decision," Tucker said.

He took out his cell phone, little bigger than a matchbook cover with an antenna, and called his secretary at home.

"Cancel your plans for the evening," he said. "I need you to start calling nightclubs."

Cornelia sent the cab away and walked the last two blocks to the museum.

With her hands in her pockets, she enjoyed the bite of the strong wind that raged across the Hudson River and threaded through the canyons of the West Side warehouses.

Her trip to South America had taken on a new urgency. Before, her intentions had been deliciously random. The remote chance of finding Tesla's plans for a new tower, the thrill of escape and adventure, all these possibilities had been like wild mushrooms to be gathered up at some future date.

Now, with Chester and Tucker confining her as though she were some medieval princess swooning with hysteria, she needed to organize quickly.

Her pulse fluttered as she approached the building.

The new museum, not yet open to the public, might seem uninviting and a bit scary from the outside. It stood in a bleak warehouse district on the far West Side, occupying a brick building that used to be a car dealership. The ghostly outline of a Cadillac crest still appeared in the soot over the front door.

Her New York Tesla Museum.

And once inside, she could touch the man's genius. The force of his ideas filled the vast space.

Soon, visitors would come to see that it was Nikola Tesla, not Thomas Edison, who invented today's electricity. Edison merely got all the credit. Here, under one vast roof, they had gathered the evidence of Tesla's astonishing gifts. In the early 1900s, he discovered radio and television waves, X rays and particle beams. He'd lit the world's darkness, handed us all the sparkle and energy we take for granted. Then he lived to see each of his inventions taken away from him by some of the greediest men on earth. One of the worst was her own forebear, Chester Lord I.

Giving Nikola Tesla back his reputation mattered deeply to her.

For nine months, she had worked day and night to create the New York Tesla Museum as one of its principal founders. And she did it in total stealth. Nobody knew she helped to build it. Not even Chester. When the time came, it would be a surprise that he would come to view with respect and admiration. Or so she hoped.

But, until that moment came, the Electric Girl worked alone.

She opened the door with her key, fumbled for the light switch. The overhead xenon spotlights blazed on, those intense beams used to light the stages of rock concerts, illuminating the exhibits in their shafts of cold blue light. The temperature in the museum had purposely been set bracingly cold to conserve energy. Con Ed, the electrical power company formally named Consolidated Edison, didn't give away warmth.

In the light of the crisp spotlights, she trembled not so much from the chill inside the cavernous space as from the presence of genius.

The museum was her cathedral.

In the center of the great cement floor stood the forty-foot-high replica of the Tesla Tower, his invention to broadcast free electricity through the airwaves. The tower resembled a giant steel-girded mushroom with a bulbous top. If she pushed a button, it would begin to dance with blue licks of electric current. Tesla built two towers, one on Long Island and one in Colorado. Like Tesla's actual towers, the museum's replica couldn't broadcast electricity. But that wasn't the point.

On her way to the curator's office, she stopped to linger by her favorite exhibit. It was a full-scale model of an airship that Tesla had invented almost one hundred years earlier. His design, U.S. Patent #1665114, resembled a quaint Victorian helicopter, a ribbed aluminum cage with two propellers and a tufted velvet seat for two. With the museum's curator, Dr. Eugene Powers, she had commissioned an engineer to build this replica with an electrical engine. When they had taken a test flight over Connecticut, wiggling in the crosswinds, she had whooped with excitement.

She touched the aluminum frame and, through its cold sting, felt the warmth of moments shared with her mother in that sunny glass room of their apartment. She never went in that sunroom anymore. She thought about her visit to the museum just the night before.

After the horrible plane ride with Tucker, she had come to the museum to energize herself. Oh, had she needed a Tesla fix then. She

had obligated herself to attend some dull party at the Plaza, a sort of
starchy rave for Young Republicans.

As she stood by her Tesla helicopter, she yearned with all her
being to share the museum with someone whose world was not de-
fined by printed invitations. But would that person ever arrive on the
scene?

Would the Electric Girl always have to work alone?

For luck, she had touched the aluminum frame. Then she had
shut off the spotlight and trudged out to the deserted street, dressed in
her black evening dress over her practical Keds, passing the shadowy
figures of prostitutes who were the only other women in the warehouse
district at night. She hailed a cab to the Plaza, more than unfashion-
ably late for the party where she would join Tucker. He'd probably
have a new anecdote about the afternoon dogfight. He would certainly
emerge as the hero.

The fountain in Grand Army Plaza across from the hotel still
sprinkled bravely in December. It looked positively refreshing compared to the prickly heat she would feel in the crowd. The moment she
joined the black-tie mob in the ballroom, conversation dribbled off, as
usual. Really, could anyone stare like the women whose eyes drilled out
from those frantically smiling photographs in *Town & Country*? She
smiled thinking of that timber wolf grin, baring all teeth and gums.
The full *Town & Country* jawbreaker.

Tucker stepped from a clutch of snarky socialites to greet her.

"Corny, where have you been?"

"A museum," she hedged, weary immediately, looking toward a
long and tiresome evening.

"Well," Tucker said with a smile, "how about a sake martini?"

And she froze on that moment, because that's when all the trouble started. The flashbulbs. The cold, wet dress . . .

Well. One couldn't dwell on past mistakes when there was work
to do.

She crossed the cement floor to the curator's office.

She thought about Dr. Powers. He looked a bit like a dignified
werewolf, with his bushy silver Brillo eyebrows and beard.

When she had first sought out Dr. Powers and told him what she
wanted, he had dismissed her as one of the marginal Tesla groupies

who loved to spin government conspiracy theories about what the FBI or CIA or even KGB had done with Tesla's work. But, slowly and methodically, she had convinced that naturally skeptical man. He had grilled her to her shoes with questions. When she emerged from their first meeting—scheduled for thirty minutes, but lasting three hours—she was so soaked in perspiration she might have been staggering out of a sauna.

Then, after months of gauging her resolve, checking her out, working with her on a test basis, Dr. Powers had gradually turned from wary werewolf to her best friend, in a sense, and confidant. Finally, he had agreed to give up his Edison Chair of Electricity professorship at M.I.T. and be the museum's curator for a dollar a year. Such were the passions Nikola Tesla could stir in scientists and debutantes, if not investment bankers.

Dr. Powers kept his small space orderly and functional, his furniture industrial. If he ever hung his degrees, they would probably cover the entire wall, but he left his office the same distressed red brick as the rest of the warehouse. His only decoration was a large poster of Coney Island at night, dated 1904. The amusement park lit up like a magical city made of light bulbs or fireflies.

She admired the world in the poster as she planned her next step.

A friend would be such a delicious luxury now, just someone to listen. Her friendships had lapsed over the years, to put it mildly. She could count only her oldest friends to be a comfort. But should she risk contact with anybody?

Finally she called her friend Tina French. Tina lived on Sutton Place. She had a sense of humor, if not responsibility, and was given to mood swings. When she felt terribly upset, Tina always shaved her head, which advertised her current feelings quite effectively.

Cornelia heard a series of high-pitched beeps as Tina's phone rang. Tina carried a pager around with her, even though she had never worked for a living. Her grandfather had invented the hot-dog spit that turns frankfurters at refreshment counters, so her whole family lived on fat royalty checks. But Tina's nightlife, connecting with the right people at the right time, was important enough to her to carry a pager.

Cornelia punched in the museum's number. Tina would be on

her side, whatever the issue. They had been close since second grade, had seen each other when she'd worked long, frustrating days and wanted to blow off steam partying. It was good that she and Tina could always pick up and reactivate their relationship like a solar clock. She didn't have to tell Tina what she was doing. Tina cared about Cornelia, and she never judged.

Cornelia now called Air Brasília. She wrote notes in her neat, squared-off writing, jotting down times and flight numbers for Rio, São Paulo, and the quaintly futuristic capital city of Brasília.

"Obrigado!" she thanked the airline agent, practicing her Portuguese.

Line one trilled. "Tina?"

"*Corneee,*" Tina screeched. "Where have you been hiding?"

They agreed to join up below 14th Street, at a nightclub called the Meat Chest.

"Byee," she heard, drawn out as though her friend had fallen down a deep hole as she hung up.

Cornelia clicked onto Dr. Powers's Mac and went right to the official New York Tesla Museum Web site. She wouldn't know a soul in South America, and the prospect of such a free-spirited adventure made her scalp tingle. Of course, the Tesla Society would have members in Brazil. She would ask Dr. Powers for help, and query the discussion groups that shared ideas in excited bursts of text over the Internet. She typed in her inquiry three times, in English, Portuguese, and Spanish:

Tesla researcher traveling to South America needs immediate guidance on possible Tesla visits to your area, including papers/plans/evidence of Tesla Tower.

She tapped "Send" and settled back in the curator's chair.

A few on the fringes would talk about flying saucers that appeared over Rio in the 1950s, supposedly from some secret city where scientists worked on his antigravity theories. Obsessed Tesla groupies thrived in the woolly world of the Internet. But although their messages might wobble at the edge of sanity, responsible members of the Tesla Society's South American chapters would help her.

She left Dr. Powers's office, making clickety-click sounds on the cement floor as she walked to one of the exhibits, striped with blue light from the xenons. This was a life-size mural of the young, kinetic Tesla at the turn of the century, toiling in his laboratory on 33 Fifth Avenue, wearing a black suit. His shoulders danced with bolts of blue flame, running electricity over his body as a parlor trick for friends, among them Mark Twain.

She walked to their replica of the Tesla aircraft. It always excited her, the memory of that blissful day.

She had researched Tesla's original plans. Then she and Dr. Powers contacted a helicopter designer in Connecticut. At first the no-nonsense aeronautics engineer laughed at their plans; because Tesla's original design was so boxy and top-heavy, it didn't look as though it could fly at all. But they'd all worked together to come up with the gyrocopter. It ran on an electric engine with four batteries. Sputtering into the wind, flying the noiseless airship over the field, Dr. Powers had let her take the controls. He taught her how to bank the airship, then keep it in a wobbly but level flight. It was the best time she'd had since her mother died.

There had been few moments like that since. With the Chester-Tucker-Bushberg alliance squeezing like a python around her, the times when she counted on her Tesla fantasies to shut out the world were becoming both longer and more frequent.

Lately, her desire to snap her mind back to the here and now had grown more sluggish, like an insect caught in sticky syrup. It would be a good idea, she decided, to practice telling people about her work. Tina might be a good start; she could be trusted, primarily because she wouldn't care. She checked her Timex with its glowing Indiglo dial.

Tina would, of course, be late to meet her. Forget Eastern Standard Time. Her friend's internal clock was set to the rhythms and the revolutions of the club scene.

The taxi deposited her just after eleven, and she moved stealthily through the shadows. The corrugated doors that shut off the entrances to various businesses were sprayed with angry graffiti. She felt light and free in the meatpacking district, a frenetic hot spot by night.

She passed the blackened window of Hog Tits, a women's biker bar. A chrome cavalry of hogs—custom Harleys—stood outside in a line.

She poked her head in the door. Women with short hair and tattoos played pool. Glancing at the floor, she wondered if the bar had become gentrified. Instead of sawdust to soak up . . . well, whatever, she saw the peach-colored pages of the *New York Observer* strewn around. One woman, squat as a fire hydrant, looked up to glare at her. Cornelia gave her a friendly wave and took off.

Her body revving against the cold that made her nose run, she walked swiftly to Ninth Avenue and into an unmarked club, the Meat Chest. She walked down a flight of cement stairs and slithered through a gaggle of downtown types clutching drinks, listening politely to the band. The helium-voiced singer screamed words she only viscerally understood.

"Corny, look at you," honked Tina French.

Tina's makeup was so white and powdery it nearly matched her hair. It looked as though she had dunked her face in flour.

She was a reedy young woman, her slender body wrapped in slinky black club couture. Cornelia was delighted to see that her scalp had not been shaved recently, so she couldn't have been too depressed lately. Her hair, almost white-blond, had grown out in a spiky mass. They embraced and Tina held her out by the arms to look at her, giggling.

"I'm on my way to Brazil," Cornelia told her, then glanced at the other Pack members. Tina had not come alone. Tina never went anywhere alone. Tonight she'd brought the two Roberts, both also old friends from Gramercy.

"Our carioca Corny," said Bob Baylor, Robert No. 1, a distant cousin to the Mayflower Madam. Robert was needling her slightly, for a change. And showing off, too, by using the Brazilian term for natives of Rio.

"Do you still need a plane to fly?" Robert No. 2, Robert Selden, asked her, as though she were crazy. Robert No. 2 had a nasty streak, and his friends required mental antibodies to tolerate his often sharp words. Robert refused to be called Bob, believing it trite because it could be spelled either backwards or forwards. Robert also had special status as the only member of the group who once earned a paycheck, as a writer on the Conan O'Brien show.

"We were just talking about people who tend to be extreme time-sucks." Robert smiled with signature malice. "So it was funny you'd show up."

"Like your time counts," Tina shot back.

They all stopped to watch a very tall woman with an urchin's face and arms like sticks pass right through their group and wink at Tina.

"She's a model from Iceland, I think," Tina whispered to Cornelia. "Bob's been hitting on her all week. But it's a rather dry hole so to speak."

"Is she bisexual?" Bob asked.

"Sure," Tina said. "If you buy her something she'll have sex with you."

Tina French and the rest of the Pack, including Cornelia when she decided to join them, carried a certain élan in the Manhattan club scene, vanishing remnants of the dying breed of Old-Money WASP trust-fund delinquents. Money in Manhattan now was either made five minutes ago, or came from feeder cultures like Teheran or Los Angeles.

"What have you been doing?" Cornelia asked Tina.

"Well, *La Dolce Vita*'s playing at Angelika this week," Tina told her after a blank moment. "You have to see it. It's so explanatory."

It would definitely explain that outfit, Cornelia thought. She had seen the film in college, a bleak treatise of 1950s vintage on Italian aristocrats numbed by their money and the absence of value in their lives. Her friends dressed in a style that could be called retro-Euro to match the film, the two Roberts slouching in skinny continental suits circa 1960 and stringy ties.

Clothing meant nothing to her, but it mattered deeply to the pack. By next week, the boys could be wearing school ties and blazers and Tina would be wearing Donna Karan couture and slicked-back brown hair again. The point was, as soon as some arriviste figured out what to wear to mimic them, fast as lightning her friends changed to some new look. This left wannabes wearing costumes that fit in two days before, but now made as much fashion sense as showing up in a clown suit.

They all ordered martinis except for Cornelia, who asked for water.

"What's going on with Tucker? Are you engaged yet?" Bob Baylor wanted to know.

"He wishes," Tina said in a teenage voice, as though they were still in algebra class at Gramercy.

"We saw your picture in the *Globe*," Tina said, sounding a little jealous. "What is it about the fountain in front of the Plaza? I threw up in there once."

"Convenience," Bob said. "You're right there."

"Can we go somewhere and talk for a second?" Cornelia asked Tina.

They wound up standing in a lightly traveled corner of one of the club's seven rooms, all connected like a kind of funhouse.

"Did you ever wonder what I've been busy doing the past year?" Cornelia asked her friend.

Tina opened her mouth, about to say "Sure," but decided to retreat from that falsity. "I thought you were just shopping. And you said Chester made you see a psychiatrist."

"Tina, I helped build a whole museum devoted to Nikola Tesla. On the West Side. I'd like to take you someday."

Tina almost spit out her drink. "Did you give those people all your money?"

"Of course. I wish I had more to give," Cornelia said.

"What does your psychiatrist say about it?"

"Nothing."

"Well, you have to give them time." Tina felt on firmer ground discussing psychiatrists.

"No, I mean he really says nothing," Cornelia explained. "We have silent sessions. The first time I saw him, I told him everything. That was a year ago. I had nothing more to tell, so I just sit there twice a week."

"What do you do?" Tina asked.

"In the beginning, I'd wait for him to say something. He'd wait for me. It was a standoff. Then he started doing other things at his desk, but he'd be sneaky about it. Trying to look like he was writing something about me, when I could see he was paying his bills."

"You've been doing that for a year?"

"I just do it for Chester. I sit on Dr. Bushberg's couch and read for an hour, and he just fusses at his desk and talks on the phone. He doesn't even bother to pretend anymore."

"Chester doesn't pry into what you do? I mean, with your money?"

"No," Cornelia said, feeling sad about that. "He's too much of a gentleman. He wouldn't invade my privacy. And I think he's worried about what he'd find out. I've been trying to talk to him for years, but Chester loves the concept of status quo."

The two Roberts interrupted them, still looking fresh and untested despite the martinis and the wild strands of damp blond hair that slithered over their eyes. Being in their early twenties made all of them impervious. Or at least that's what they believed. Cornelia knew that no one, at any age, was safe from harm.

"What are you talking about?" Bob Baylor asked Cornelia.

"Nikola Tesla."

They stared at her in a dull, dumbfounded way.

"The tennis player?" Bob asked.

"Let's go to Lizards & Ladies," Tina said, to change the subject.

Cornelia protested, but they needled and dragged her along and there was little point in resisting.

To carry through their commitment to the *La Dolce Vita* revival, they had found a chromy 1960 Thunderbird convertible and a 1959 Triumph sports car, both sparkling white.

The Pack piled in and put the convertible tops down to head over to 14th Street. Beeping their horns, the cars split up like two mice to scamper around a tractor-trailer, then screeched to a halt in front of the bar. A tangle of yellow taxis, stretch limousines, and Town Cars had already stacked up in the dark alleyway. A nondescript storefront flashed a neon sign, "Lizards & Ladies."

Inside, the tiny club was packed wall to wall with delicious young model-and-actor flesh. Curiosities from the 1970s dangled from the ceiling in wicked parody: a Barbie doll wearing black bondage gear hung upside down with her legs forced around G.I. Joe's neck, novelty rubber chickens hung from meathooks like bats.

Behind the bar, a mountain of bras had been slung in a pile

against the mirror, women's panties and men's boxer shorts peeking out. They got there because women danced on the bar, if they were drunk or exhibitionistic enough, and shed their bras. Sometimes that was just a starting point. Ever since Mayor Guiliani shut down the topless bars in Manhattan and made the city a little *too* wholesome and corn-fed, it became a thing that club types did for fun.

The Pack's entrance sparked an instant buzz. The crowd made way, as much as they could in the crunch, so Cornelia's gaggle of friends could shove through. They ordered drinks from the rangy, gorgeous bartender, Girl-Tex. Guy-Tex, the other bartender, was much stockier, had eyebrows like caterpillars and a shaved head. Both women came from Texas.

"Hey, Corny," she said, "long time. We gonna dance tonight?"

"I sure hope not," she told her. "Water, please."

"You know we got a tradition here, honey," Girl-Tex shouted over the din, mock-staring Cornelia down. "If you don't drink, the bartender does."

"Amen," she told Girl-Tex.

Girl-Tex filled one glass with water and a shot of straight Baja tequila for herself. She tossed it back. Cornelia took a long swallow of water.

She felt hemmed in by the crowd. A stale, oppressive cloud formed by cigarette and cigar smoke settled above the bar like an inversion factor. She could feel it pressing trapped air on top of her, hot like a jungle. She drank the water and it cleared her nostrils.

She inched away from the two Roberts, tugging Tina with her. The boys had locked on to Girl-Tex, out-quipping each other to keep her attention as she built their martinis. Robert Selden stuffed something else in his mouth, probably a fistful of pills he used for mood management that terrified Corny when he took them with liquor. Robert batted away at least one family-and-friends intervention a week.

Tina looked more alert now. She blossomed after midnight when the crowd gave off a surging, oscillating kind of energy.

"You never really answered me about Tucker," Tina said.

Cornelia thought this over, wishing she could explain to Tina about the coronas. How seeing a sky-blue corona around somebody meant you couldn't go wrong. And a blackish, ugly corona meant you should run. And how Tucker Fisk exhibited no corona at all.

"Tucker can keep you off balance," she allowed. "On the surface, he's the perfect gentleman. Almost too perfect."

Tucker's ambition always thundered like hoofbeats under his skin. That was easy to spot. If only she could see his corona, so she could know whether or not to trust him.

"He seems to want to be with you," Tina said, her eyes wandering.

"I think I'm just arm candy. But I'm not sure. He's so close to my father, I can't really confide in him."

"No sex?" Tina asked, wide-eyed.

"Hardly. I'd rather like to know who I'm having sex with."

She had analyzed Tucker's parents, usually a good clue to character, but found no easy answers. His father, who had been nicknamed Sloopy in college, was a hearty but unsubstantial man. He had been Chester's roommate at Yale. Tucker's mother worked as a Wall Street lawyer. She was overly worked-out and always looked so bristling with anger and ambition that she might burst an artery just exchanging social chatter. She had obviously been the one who pushed Tucker. And she had succeeded, because Tucker did get things done. Enough to save her father at Lord & Company.

"Well, whatever else you say about him, Tucker's gorgeous," Tina told her in a dreamy voice, looking across the room.

"He knows it. I just wish I could decide what he wants from me."

"Well, why don't you ask him?" Tina said. "He's right there."

Cornelia turned and saw Tucker's head bobbing slowly over all the rest like a golden boat on the waves. Escape was impossible; she was trapped in the jaws of the crowd.

"Hi," Tucker said, with a drive-by casualness. "Sake martini?"

She took the glass gingerly, but didn't drink. She noticed that he did not say, "Your father is very worried about you."

"I came to apologize about taking you dogfighting," he lobbed out of nowhere. "I thought it would help you get rid of some bad memories, but I guess I really miscalculated."

She jerked her glass to her lips and half drained it. His eyes held hers. Their surfaces were like polished stones, impossible to penetrate. But his tone of voice, almost boyish, was a first.

After a moment she said, "I guess you did."

"And maybe I have a little trouble showing emotion, too," Tucker said. He frowned very seriously now. His voice croaked slightly, like a tree frog lived inside his huge frame.

"Tucker, what are you telling me?"

He thought for a moment. "Maybe I'm a little in awe of you. You're much freer than I am. I think I take myself too seriously sometimes."

By the time Tucker brought her a second martini, Cornelia began to understand how Tucker got along with people that he couldn't fire. He put them in a kind of trance. Like a spider she once read about that anesthetizes its prey. In Tucker's case, it seemed to be a sweet narcosis of flattery. He also had that boyish quality, such an earnest and apparently real interest in her that he had not revealed so plainly to her before this evening.

"I'm interested in the things you like to do, where you go every day," she heard him say over the noisy crowd.

"Tucker," she had to practically shout in his ear, "you're the most information-crazed individual I've ever known. If you really wanted to know, you could have asked me."

"I'm asking now."

"I'm sorry," she told him in the rather stiff, formal way that suggested she might have had too much to drink. "But I really don't think I want to get into that at the moment."

Tucker ordered her a third martini. After that she caught only loose fragments of Tucker's conversation more than the actual points he made, although his body language told her that he was working very hard to make points.

She spoke haltingly, struggling to connect things. After three drinks, her allergy to alcohol was seeping in. Her brain was becoming a fuzzball. Each thought drifted through wisps of cotton candy in fragments, at one-quarter time.

"Don't you think Chester cares about you?" he yelled.

"Yes, but my father seems to think I'm a train wreck."

She noted that he didn't say, "Oh, no." But he did say, "Is that what *you* think?"

"I do sometimes," she told him, the alcohol roaring through her brain now, loosening things a notch.

"What I'm saying, Corny"—Tucker made a face as sincere as one without a corona around it could look—"is if you feel that way, I'd like you to be my train wreck."

She closed her eyes and tried to gain a strategic perspective on this conversation that had suddenly become so full. A poor idea. The room swirled.

When she opened them, Girl-Tex, a blurry form in a white T-shirt and blue jeans, appeared, standing up on the bar. Guy-Tex jumped up after her.

"C'mon, Corny," Girl-Tex yelled for her. Cornelia headed gratefully for the bar. Girl-Tex held out her hand, got a strong grip on her forearm, and pulled her up.

The jukebox blasted "Radar Love." Girl-Tex started to dance a fierce two-step, her blue and yellow cowboy boots banging clunk-clunk-clunk on the bar. Guy-Tex started clunk-clunk-clunking with her own cowboy boots. Cornelia began to tap along, feeling the drums.

Below her, she could hear the two Roberts. They chanted, "Cor-ny! Cor-ny!"

She felt just right, stomping on the bar, charged and juiced, even though the crowd had begun to blur. Girl-Tex had wonderful electricity. She could almost see blue sparks kicking up from the cowgirl's boot heels.

The jukebox changed to "I Walk the Line." More women jumped up onto the bar now. A redhead ripped off her top, exposing a lacy black Wonderbra.

The music went on. She saw Tucker push his way through the crowd. He hopped onto the bar in one smooth move like he never stopped playing on the football field at Yale.

"Hi," she said.

"Hi. I thought maybe you'd like to go now." He smiled.

"Not yet, thank you," she said.

But now she was the one to miscalculate. Just as he began to wrap his beautiful black and gray suit jacket around her, the room circled diagonally. She felt herself falling backward.

Then the Electric Girl passed out.

"Good evening, 840 Fifth." Kevin took the call on the black phone box that hung by the front door.

"This is Tucker Fisk. I need you right now at the rear service entrance."

"I'll meet you there," Kevin said and hung up.

Vladimir had managed to doze off for most of their shift, perched on the padded seat that pulled down like an ironing board from the wall. Vladimir's jowls quivered as he snored, and his gray cap slipped over his forehead. The lobby's stifling heat, set to quickly warm the owners coming in out of the cold, sucked up all of Kevin's oxygen.

He shook Vlad the Self-Impaler before he could fall and hurt himself. "I've got to go in the back. I got a call."

Kevin walked briskly to the back door. Could the caller be a hoax? Philip Grace pulling a fast one? He didn't think so. Tucker Fisk had a good-sized ego, expecting Kevin to know who he was. He only knew because he'd studied Andrew's chart.

Kevin opened the back door, a double-thick metal slab with three locks. He saw Chester Lord's funny-looking stretch limousine idling with its side door open. And Cornelia Lord's boyfriend standing by the open door in a dark suit, his jacket flapping in the cold wind. His white shirt cuffs almost shone in the dark.

"What took you so long?" Tucker greeted him, his breath streaming in front of him. "Give me a hand."

"With what?"

Tucker grabbed his arm and pointed him inside the limousine. Sprawled on the gray velvet of the small back seat, the party-girl Cornelia Lord wasn't moving. He put his face near hers and felt a small breath on his cheek. She was alive, anyway. But the smell of an unfamiliar alcohol, kind of sweet, oozed out of her pores like toxic gas. He wrinkled his nose in disgust. Her blond hair flopped over her forehead. Kevin noticed that. Even though she was drunk and passed out, her tiny, perfect features still made her look like a model, except with a rich person's extra-creamy skin and a very young face shaped almost like a heart. A dewy line had formed over her lips, and her fine cheekbones had a pink stripe from the cold. The Girl Who'll Always Have Everything.

"Hey," Kevin said, shaking her gently. "You're home now."

She opened her eyes and fixed them on Kevin's cap.

"Great corona," he thought she said.

Then her eyes fell shut and she began snoring lightly, her face looking haunted. Kevin's pulse fluttered.

"What are you doing in there?" Tucker said, annoyed. "Get her legs."

Kevin grabbed her slender ankles while Tucker took her arms. Carrying her toward the door, Kevin thought he heard a sound behind the garbage Dumpster.

A silent explosion rocked the night in front of him, a pop-pop-pop of white flashes. Kevin held tightly on to her ankles.

"Thanks, folks," he heard Philip Grace say. The tabloid terrorist whipped from behind the Dumpster on a beat-up old Vespa motor scooter. He wore his mirrored glasses in the night, and a long white scarf with fringe at the end flapped from his neck. Grace gunned the gas and made the scooter whine like a Mixmaster.

"You cocksucker," Tucker yelled at him. "If you print that, I'll fucking kill you."

"You're just sayin' that 'cause I'm black," Grace shouted, cackling. Then he laughed again, pulled a little wheelie, and blew past them, shooting foul-smelling exhaust in their faces.

Tucker cursed under his breath while he and Kevin brought the girl inside, limp as a cadaver. Kevin suggested they take the service elevator, so they wouldn't meet anybody, and Tucker grunted.

Carrying the girl, Kevin watched Tucker study the floor lights changing over the door as they rode, so he wouldn't have to speak to the doorman. Kevin pretended to look at the lights, too, but discreetly glanced at the girl's face. The blond hair hung back, exposing small ears that stuck out a little.

"You never saw us tonight," Tucker said when the elevator door opened. He took his softly breathing prize from Kevin and strode off with her bouncing in his arms, a doll stuffed with sawdust.

On his way down in the clunky service elevator, Kevin thought about the woman's eyes. They'd opened for only a second, but weren't dull and wasted party-girl eyes at all. They had latched instantly on to something she found just over, or kind of around, his head.

Kevin felt his heart whomping, like he'd been through an ordeal. He didn't know exactly what to make of Cornelia Lord here in the flesh. If he looked at her without knowing anything about her life, he'd be pretty knocked out. When she opened her eyes, she looked as though she had what his mother called "a spark of the divine" inside her, a soft glow. But this was a girl who only lit up in real life by getting loaded, then passing out so people like Kevin and even her asshole boyfriend had to clean up after her. He couldn't deny that she was practically a Giotto to look at. But she had the character of a virus.

He just wondered, walking back to the lobby, what she meant by "corona."

To him, a corona was the electrical arc he made working on his neon. But Cornelia Lord didn't look like anybody who'd know what an electrical arc was.

Part Two

Electric Girl Blue

Chapter Seven

$\mathcal{E}$veryone knows the story of the Russian prince," Vlad the Self-Impaler began in his big, round storytelling voice.

Kevin stifled his yawn inside a tight smile.

At 8:00 A.M., Kevin had begun the second half of his double-header shift with Vlad.

Kevin pulled the worst shifts because he was new. Vlad got them because the building manager hated him. Vlad proudly displayed his laziness like a badge. Management couldn't fire him because of the union, but they didn't have to give him the choice shifts.

But as much as he hated carrying out bags and sorting mail, the Russian loved to talk. He worked to make each trivial event of his life into an epic told with pauses, arched eyelids, and dramatic gestures. Vlad never gave up his die-hard communism. He thought that any-body who ran any kind of business in New York, even a hot dog vendor, was a fang-toothed capitalist.

If the dry cleaner lost a button off Vlad's uniform, the Self-Impaler would spin a morality tale about his confrontation. But Vlad couldn't tell a story in real time. With all his dramatic flourishes, they always ran into overtime, longer than the event itself.

Kevin imagined that Russians valued storytelling because for so many years they lacked traditional American pastimes, like cable TV or showers. He managed to get through Vlad's stories because he liked to watch the Russian contort his rubbery face into different villains, the evil newsstand owners or reckless shoe repairman, who he claimed had shrunk his black brogues one size smaller.

His story of the Russian prince should be good for half a shift.

A cab pulled up outside discharging a tall, worried-looking man with a gangly body and long legs who seemed to half-fall out of it. When he reached the door, Kevin opened it to see that the man had shaved badly and dressed too fast in a tweed suit and tan raincoat. Kevin suspected he still had pajamas on under the suit.

"Good morning," Kevin asked without enthusiasm. "Can I help you?"

Vlad squinted at the man and interrupted. "Ah! Dr. Bushberg. Go up, please, they are expecting you."

"Thanks," the man mumbled and stepped quickly toward the elevator.

"That is Dr. Bushberg," Vlad stage-whispered, "headhunter to Cornelia Lord."

"If he doesn't carry a spear, he's a headshrinker," Kevin corrected him.

"Yes. Mr. Lord left word permitting Dr. Bushberg to visit. He pretends the doctor comes to treat Miss Lord for the flu. But the young Russian prince. The prince was a peasant boy, handsome and cunning. He worked like me at the Leningradska Hotel." Vlad's eyes misted. "It was better for workers there. For each doorman's shift we had eight men, only four KGB."

"Sure," Kevin told him. "Eight guys doing one job, plenty of nap time."

Vlad nodded in agreement. "A guest asked us to do something, we would tell them, 'This is impossible,' and they went away. We had no capitalist anxieties then." He pointed upstairs. "No need for head-shrinkers."

"Except to give lobotomies to the dissidents." Kevin liked to pull Vlad's chain.

Vladimir wagged his head. "CNN propaganda. The Americans have always sneered at us. 'Russians can't build computers any smaller than a barn.' But workers had dignity. It was the bankers and the Mafia who ruined our country."

"Well, I see why you came to New York City, to get away from people like that," Kevin said.

Vlad nodded. "So the young Russian prince came to New York City. He found work as doorman in a building on Gramercy Park, where all the residents have keys to the park. Very cozy. He was not afraid to use his charms on a young girl who lived in the building, a rich businessman's daughter. At night they met in the park. Soon, a romance." Vlad made a knocking motion with his hand. "The prince went to her father's door. He stood proud and declared his love for the daughter."

"And?" Kevin asked. He could feel his timing a little off, because he wasn't concentrating on the Russian prince. Instead, he thought about this Dr. Bushberg who'd gone upstairs, comparing this Park Avenue specimen to the psychiatrists he'd seen working at Bellevue.

"But the father"—Vlad made a show of rage—"the father slammed the door in the young man's face, told him he would have him fired. Or killed. He was a rich man in the fur business. He shouted he would never have a doorman for a son-in-law."

"So which was it, fired or killed?" Kevin asked.

Vlad snorted. "The prince would not bow and scrape to the rich father. He brought the girl to the top of the Empire State Building, got down on his knees and asked her to be his wife."

"He saw that movie." Kevin couldn't remember the name, a tear-jerker.

"What movie? He told the girl, 'Say yes or I jump now and kill myself.'"

Kevin raised his eyebrows. "He would've gone through with that?"

"Oh yes. It is very poetic, a martyr for love."

Poetic? Must be a Russian thing. He tried to imagine falling for somebody, then telling her you're a suicidal maniac. Where he grew up, that wouldn't make you any kind of a catch.

"I'd take the elevator down, either way," Kevin said.

"Ah, but she said yes. They eloped to Atlantic City, New Jersey." Vlad had a silvery thrill in his voice, like he believed his own story. "To keep his daughter near, the father forgave them. He gave the prince a job in the fur business and for a wedding present bought them an apartment in the same building. This story is true. My cousin who worked on Gramercy Park knew the Russian prince."

"The girl must have been something," Kevin allowed, "for a guy to go work in the fur business."

He let Vlad leave on his break and found himself wondering what a girl like Cornelia Lord had to tell her psychiatrist. Maybe she had herself talked into believing she had real psychiatric problems, like the patients he'd worked with at Bellevue. Sometimes they mistook their wives for fire hydrants, or told Kevin they heard the Captain and Tennille singing through their fillings. It was pretty sad.

But if Cornelia Lord really did have problems, he was pretty sure the psychiatrist who went upstairs wouldn't help much.

Dr. Bushberg came out of Cornelia's bedroom, frowning, and closed the door.

When O'Connell escorted him into Chester's den, Bushberg folded himself into the chair and pulled out a meerschaum pipe. They sat in silence while Bushberg fiddled with his pipe paraphernalia.

If the doctor had to spend this much time collecting his thoughts so profoundly, Chester worried, Cornelia's case must be severe. Or he could just be procrastinating, the same way Chester always had. He felt the now-familiar shame creeping up. This would probably be the moment where the psychiatrist would tell him it was all his fault, that he hadn't been there for her.

"Let's get to the point," Chester rasped. "What's Cornelia's problem?"

"Well," Bushberg hemmed, "I wouldn't like to rush into a diagnosis . . ."

"Rush? You've been seeing her for a year. What do you talk about?"

"I can't discuss what she tells me." He gave Chester a too-easy smile. "Professional ethics."

"I've paid you to treat her and I want an evaluation of her condition."

Bushberg reluctantly pulled out and flipped through an old notebook. "Cornelia is obsessed with an inventor named Nikola Tesla who's been dead for over fifty years," Bushberg said. "Something about an injustice to the man going back to the turn of the century."

"I know about Tesla." Chester waved his palm helplessly. "What does that have to do with going out dancing in bars, ending up drunk in fountains?"

Bushberg consulted his notes. "She may believe that her body contains more electrical impulses than the average person. Possibly she's self-medicating to calm herself down."

"Does she?" Chester asked seriously.

"Does she what?"

"Have more electricity?"

"No, we all have roughly the same amount," Bushberg said. "But she could be interpreting her anxiety as extra energy."

This was going nowhere, Chester thought. "When you started her therapy, I thought the medication you gave her was supposed to control her moods."

"It might," Bushberg said, "if she took her medication. But she doesn't. That's also fairly common."

Chester had a bad feeling. "When you talk about my daughter, it's as though you're speaking of someone you knew briefly, a long time ago."

Bushberg sucked so hard on his pipe, his cheekbones threatened to collapse. Then he banged it loudly on the ashtray.

"Professional detachment." Bushberg spoke each word carefully. "She can't become too dependent on me."

"I don't see that as a danger." Chester shifted uncomfortably. "I've tried to talk to her myself . . ."

He paused and Bushberg leaned forward, sounding pleased at this change of topic. Chester didn't like the look of Bushberg, but reassured himself that the man practiced on Park Avenue and billed Chester $6,000 each month for his daughter's sessions. He must know something. Perhaps all psychiatrists, Chester theorized, developed slippery personalities to slide in and out of their patients' lives without picking up any of their demons, like burrs that stuck to your pants along a country trail. Perhaps he should try confiding in the man himself. He certainly paid him enough.

"I've tried to talk with her several times," Chester said, "and it's as though we just miss."

"Oh, no. That wouldn't be wise, trying to talk to her yourself." Bushberg shook his head very somberly now, Sphinx-like. "I've given her an injection of antidepressants and tranquilizers. She should be under control for twenty-four hours and, if necessary, I'll come back tomorrow and give her another shot."

"And if that doesn't work?" Chester felt the back of his neck heating up.

"I wouldn't rule out the possibility of short-term residential therapy. I can recommend a private facility where she would get one-on-one attention."

"A *mental* hospital?" A snake pit.

"A very pleasant facility," Bushberg said. "Almost a resort really. I'm thinking of the Sanctuary up in Westchester."

"A resort?" Chester snapped. "A resort gives seaweed wraps and massages. A resort lets its guests leave. That's out of the question. And Cornelia doesn't belong in a mental hospital. Why can't we, well, give her bed rest and you can cure her here at home?"

"Oh, no, no." Bushberg shook his head vigorously. "That wouldn't be at all practical."

"Why not?"

Bushberg answered in a crushing wave of jargon that Chester went down trying to understand.

". . . Bipolar One Disorder . . . Episodic Alcohol Dependence . . ."

It all sounded like such gobbledygook. People of Bushberg's ilk only plowed into this level of jargon to fool lay people. Why did he suspect the psychiatrist wanted to wash his hands of Cornelia? Because he had tried but couldn't help her. Her condition had even worsened. He felt his anger build. Bushberg was probably struggling to avoid a malpractice suit, all this weaseling. Then he felt a sudden panic. Maybe Bushberg thought Cornelia could harm herself, but the groveling fool couldn't admit it to him.

"Are you telling me that Cornelia is at risk of hurting herself?" he asked coldly. "Yes or no?"

"Perhaps. I wouldn't rule that out," Bushberg said, unable to stop equivocating. "It needn't be deliberate. She could hurt herself purely by accident."

Chester felt the weight of decision closing tightly in his chest. He felt frightened for Cornelia.

"Why this sudden escalation?" Chester demanded. "You didn't think she was a danger to herself a week ago."

Bushberg seemed to jerk at that, gripping the arms of his chair. "It's very difficult for a family member to accept how suddenly the onset of a deeper problem can occur. Do you want me to phone the Sanctuary? There's a waiting list, but we can overcome that."

"No. You may not."

Bushberg's mouth remained open for a second. "Well, how do you want to proceed then?"

"Cornelia stays here." Chester tapped his desktop firmly with his forefinger. Genetic code was taking over for him, as it had for the Lord men all the way back to when Chester I could make even the mighty pucker by tapping the blotter of his desk in just this way.

"She needs to be heavily medicated then," Bushberg squirmed. "And she has to be closely supervised."

"Then we'll hire nurses for her around the clock." Chester stood up and O'Connell's craggy face arrived at the doorway.

Bushberg swallowed as he rose. "Of course, we'll handle it as you like, but I want to go on record that this wouldn't be my preferred treatment."

"Your preference is duly noted," Chester dipped his words in frost. "Cornelia stays here until further notice."

Chester waited for Bushberg to be gone. Then he spent ten minutes on the phone with his own doctor, whom he had known since they were classmates at prep school. "Tom, this Bushberg, are you sure he knows what he's doing?"

"He's a top man. Former head of the New York Psychiatric Association." His friend's deep baritone was a soothing balm. "Though I understand that he's gone through a wrung-out divorce with some financial pressure."

Chester frowned. "Would that affect his judgment of Cornelia's condition?"

"Only if he's suddenly doubling up on her sessions."

"All right." Chester hung up.

He would have to trust Bushberg against his better instincts. What did he know about psychiatrists?

He only knew that he would not make hasty decisions about his daughter, no matter what any of them said.

From the lobby, Kevin heard the bing of the elevator and saw Cornelia Lord's psychiatrist eject himself, a projectile of tics and hasty movements. He held the front door open for him, tipping his cap forward so he could eyeball the doctor without being noticed.

At Bellevue, Kevin had liked working with the shrinks. They didn't seem especially crazy, as a group, the way people joked about them. They worked hard. Some of them, especially the women, had as much guts as his sister Marne.

One doctor from Pakistan, so tiny her arms were like chicken bones, had actually walked into a utility closet to seek out a pumped-up, 250-pound male patient bellowing threats in the dark. Calmly, she talked him back onto the ward.

It made him wonder how, with indigent patients at Bellevue getting great shrinks like that, a rich girl like Cornelia wound up with this jittery piece of work named Bushberg. He stank of deceit, reminding him of losers from his neighborhood who committed to the shylocks for loans they couldn't pay back, then hopped around like fleas trying to avoid them.

Kevin drifted back to listening to Vlad.

"It is very important when you go to a steak house," Vlad explained one of his revenge schemes, "that you always say you are sending the steak back to the kitchen because it is too well done. Then they have to throw it away."

Kevin said, "Come on, you're just wasting food."

Vlad shrugged. "Capitalist food."

Chapter Eight

At eight in the evening, Cornelia called upon all of her energy just to rise out of her chair and climb into bed. She felt as though each of her limbs weighed three hundred pounds, and no possible effort seemed worth the trouble.

The previous evening was simply a black hole punched in her brain. Now her tongue felt as large and prickly dry as a cactus plant, her eyes were shrouded in mist, and she could barely find her limbs. All thanks to Dr. Bushberg's psychotropic drugs. It was her father's genteel way of keeping her manacled at home. Dr. Bushberg's medical headlock saddened more than angered her. Classic Chester, trying to keep an unsteady lid on the surface, while his own fear and panic kicked up underneath.

After Bushberg gave her the shot with the hint of a smile and left, her father had pulled a chair close to her bed.

"Dr. Bushberg told me something that disturbed me today," he began, sounding contrite.

She'd raised her head, struggling to keep her eyelids open to listen, but then the full weight of the drugs slammed against her as if she'd just walked into the side of a bus, and she had fallen asleep.

Why did they always just miss? It wasn't merely that Chester's judgment seemed to fail him, because her own sense of timing had not been infallible. Going out to meet Tina had not been a sound move, she admitted to herself. She felt needy and drank way too much when Tucker showed up and that undid her plans. Temporarily.

The Electric Girl must work faster.

On the other hand, she could not forget the surprising interlude with Tucker. Although she could only play back their words in fragments, and remember the two of them huddled together at the bar of Lizards & Ladies as the murkiest of images, she knew that Tucker had begun to open a curtain on himself.

Thinking clearly was difficult. She could review only one item at a time. Since what she needed to focus on was escape, she painstakingly checked items off her mental list.

Flight? Done. Air Brasília, tomorrow evening.

Money? Done. She would use only cash and her American Express Platinum card. The bills went to her own accountant, not her father's.

Research? Done. The museum had all the sources she needed. Now she only had to download replies to her e-mail inquiries.

Everything seemed in order. Still, little things could trip her up. Big things, too.

Like the nurse Dr. Bushberg had hired for her named Lucy Banks, R.N. That brown mountain of a woman in a pristine white outfit filled the butterfly chair so that none of the fabric could be seen slung over the metal frame. It was close to her bed on the red side of the room where the soft goods were, rather than the black side of the room where she kept hard goods like her metal dresser. Nurse Lucy seemed in a drowsy stupor. Her fleshy arms and legs that jiggled when she walked had settled down. Her eyes had grown deeply entranced by a Jackie Collins paperback with an iridescent cover. In about twenty minutes, Nurse Lucy would get up and give the Electric Girl another injection that would keep her pinned down to her bed. Oh, yes, that formerly tame weasel Dr. Bushberg had finally revealed his meanness. Fortunately, the Electric Girl kept some options open.

"Lucy," she said, working to lift her tongue and open her lips.

Her words echoed in her head as though she were trying to yell up from a deep well. Nurse Lucy looked up from her book, slowly. As a rule, Lucy didn't move very fast.

"What's that, honey?" Nurse Lucy said. Cornelia thought she had lovely eyes, like portholes looking onto a calm sea.

"It's really hard for me to get up. Could you please go into my closet and get me my heavy white bathrobe? I'm kind of chilly."

She had made a point of asking Lucy to do a lot of things over the course of the afternoon and early evening. One of them, going to the kitchen for her, had given the stealthy Electric Girl the opportunity to disable a closet door handle.

"Sure, baby," Lucy said, but didn't move before she finished the sentence she was reading.

Then Cornelia saw Nurse Lucy jettison herself out of her chair with startling vigor for such a big woman. Uh-oh. She hadn't suspected that Lucy's time in the chair was a recharging of her booster-rocket. Now the woman blazed across the room at the very moment she needed her to be deliberate and plodding.

But it was now or never.

She waited for the nurse to go a little farther into the depths of her closet. She had purposely hung the white robe as far back as possible, a fifteen-foot trek from the closet door.

As soon as Nurse Lucy had disappeared from her sight, Cornelia summoned all the energy inside her. She raised herself stiffly from the bed. Even her nightgown seemed to weigh a hundred pounds. When she hit the floor, she felt as though she were seeping through the carpet toward the earth's core. She lumbered in long strides for the closet, a race through water, her body more like a barge than a sleek submarine.

She put her arms straight out in front of her like Frankenstein to achieve forward momentum, huffing so hard she was sure Nurse Lucy could hear her.

Inside the closet, she saw Nurse Lucy's head turning, sensing her, then turned her bulk around to head back toward the closet door.

But the Electric Girl thumped ahead, holding her course. She reached the door first by one hundredth of a second. She felt for the doorknob and pulled. It shut almost all the way.

Almost.

She felt a devastating jerk that nearly yanked her onto the floor, and saw, through the crack of the door, Nurse Lucy's grim face. They each pulled like titans to gain an inch of space between the door and its frame. The door wobbled between them.

She willed her body to create more electricity, to ignite the reserve of adrenaline that she might still squeeze past the drugs. The door was only inches away from closing, but the torque from the Nurse-Lucy-pull was fantastic, as powerful as the yank from a big-wheeled tractor. She felt herself losing ground.

Then for an instant, Nurse Lucy faltered.

The Electric Girl whooped, grunted hard, and threw herself backward, pulling the door shut. Nurse Lucy yanked her fingers back so they wouldn't get caught.

A click.

The door locked. Nurse Lucy pounded hard on the inside of the door and called out, but nobody would hear her or investigate until early the following morning. The Electric Girl had already said her dull good night to Chester. O'Connell had gone home. She shuffled over to close and lock the door to her bedroom for good measure.

The Thorazine Shuffle.

She had researched the *Physicians' Desk Reference* carefully a year before when Bushberg began prescribing medicine. She knew that Thorazine, used to calm agitated mental patients, was the main ingredient in the cocktail Bushberg gave her. She slowly spun around as best she could, in a victory dance.

She had left a box lunch she'd assembled from the kitchen, a turkey sandwich, a bunch of grapes, and a bottle of Pellegrino inside the closet so Nurse Lucy wouldn't starve. Although that would probably take quite a bit longer than one night, given the woman's carbohydrate reserves. She wished she could toss the Jackie Collins book into the closet, but that would tempt fate.

She felt around her red bedspread to pull out a duffel bag, efficiently prepacked for a trip to the jungle. It weighed a lot with her hiking boots inside. She dug out her travel outfit, soft black workout clothes, and slowly slipped them on. Then she took a black jacket with thick lining from under the chaise longue and managed to pull the sleeves on with great effort. She didn't bother with her hair or makeup. This was no beauty contest. She pulled a black watch cap over her hair.

She unlocked the bedroom door, looked both ways, and slunk

slowly down the upstairs corridor. Chester would probably be in his study. She tiptoed down the staircase and shuffled ahead.

When she approached the door of her father's sanctum, she carefully lowered herself down on the floor, stretched out, and used her compact mirror at floor level to get a worm's-eye view. She saw Chester at his desk staring into space, a half-full brandy snifter in front of him.

Her poor dad. Cornelia felt a cold ping at the base of her spine. She worried about him. His energy had fallen so drastically over the past six months that she feared for his health. It would help him so much to give her his attention now, since they were as far apart as hostile countries.

She resolved that, as soon as she returned from South America, and she hoped it would be with a discovery that would impress him, she would make it her business to reach him. Her father understood duty, had told her time and again how important it was. He just couldn't comprehend hers.

Stomach pressed to the carpet, she crawled past the den door with her duffel bag held carefully on her upraised palms in front of her. She inched ahead as though she were pushing a peanut forward with her nose. It took her a full two minutes to clear Chester's door.

Ten feet past the study, she dragged herself to a standing position, pressed through the dark to find the utility room off the kitchen, and disabled the apartment's alarm system.

Then she opened the door out to the cramped service foyer and rang for the service elevator.

Her next maneuver, leaving the building, would depend on who she found on duty downstairs.

Chester Lord thought he heard a sound at the door of his den. He looked out in the hallway, but saw nothing. He sipped a long draught of brandy, feeling his nervous system race, and went back to staring out the window at the distant lights of the West Side skyscrapers twinkling over the dark forest of Central Park at night.

He had to stop fuming over Bushberg and set his mind to Tucker's plan. In truth, the Kois' hostile takeover play of Lord & Company frightened him to his shoes.

"A big, fat target," he muttered, that was all that being rich made a person today. In his snifter of 1890 Courvoisier, he saw a long line of scoundrels trying to slice off an unearned piece of the Lord pie. Now it was the Kois. Contemplating their villainy made him see the fine points of Tucker's solution.

Should he trust Tucker? Actions spoke louder than words, that tired but annoyingly apt cliché. Tucker had saved him at Lord & Company. Didn't he deserve the benefit of the doubt with Cornelia? He sipped thoughtfully, trying to recall how badly Tucker had ever really let him down. Tucker had been the one to urge the partnership with the Kois five years before. But now that Han Koi revealed his serpent's head, Tucker had stepped forward like a man, assumed responsibility. Tucker *did* have character. Chester's inability to glimpse it much of the time was just a generational thing, he concluded, like his inability to become computer-literate. He couldn't expect a boy Tucker's age to show his feelings exactly the same way as, well, Elizabeth had.

His tangled thoughts settled a bit. He inched like a worm toward that zone of solace, letting Tucker have his way. The boy would come through as he had in the past. And if Cornelia decided to marry him, perhaps she could feel protected enough to find her way back to, well, normalcy.

He ached to talk to Elizabeth. She had soothed him when he revealed the slender threads that held his confidence together. Their time together seemed only an instant now. Elizabeth's love used to evaporate so many of his doubts, when he had let her. He couldn't help that he was at heart a reticent man who kept his distance from other people, including his wife. And, in her way, she mirrored his own reserve. Elizabeth's emotions flowed freely with Cornelia, but could squeeze slightly shut with Chester. Perhaps that was what his father had meant when he told Chester, "Cousins can marry cousins, but Presbyterians should never marry Presbyterians." The important thing was that Elizabeth gave Cornelia her goodness and intelligence.

He took to his feet a bit unsteadily. His doubts and anxieties only poisoned what Tucker was trying to accomplish. If he were honest with himself, Tucker performed better at everything than Chester.

There was no doubt that, of the two of them, Tucker was the better equipped to save his daughter.

*   *   *

At his post by the door, Kevin watched a video monitor of the service elevator. He could see who it was, and felt a pinprick of curiosity.

"Hey Vlad, I'm taking a break," he told the Russian, whose eyelids were already at half-mast.

This morning, he had seen the picture of the back of his head on page three of the *Daily Globe*. It showed Kevin and Tucker Fisk carrying Cornelia Lord, passed out. "Don't Drop Deb," Philip Grace's headline read.

His copy of the paper was now carefully folded in his locker. Such total bullshit, and why he was excited about it, he didn't exactly know. Except that he enjoyed seeing Tucker's tortured face in the photograph, raging at the camera.

He didn't go to the staff room but stopped at the service elevator.

The door opened and Cornelia Lord stood inside. She wore all-black clothes and clutched a duffel bag, a knit cap on her head like an armed robber.

"Don't shoot," Kevin smiled, lifting his palms up.

She opened her mouth to speak, then held her lips open. Her eyes seemed to be fighting a dense fog. Still, a glimmer remained of the searching eyes. She trembled slightly.

"Hey, you okay?" he asked her.

Her face resembled cold white china. She barely moved for a second, didn't even twitch, then her head cocked slightly to the side like a puppy and her mouth curved around a word.

"Hello," she said. He could see it was an agonizing labor.

Kevin felt a twinge of sadness for Cornelia Lord. Her tongue seemed to be glued to the bottom of her mouth. As he looked her in the eye he saw, deep in the soupy gray, a dim sparkle. Then tiny pinpricks of violet light gathered and began breaking through the gray. She looked—he couldn't think of another way to describe it—happy to see him. She moved forward in inches and stuck her head out of the elevator, looking both ways to make sure nobody else was around. Color seemed to pump through her body as she stepped from the elevator into the dimly lit shadows of the service hall.

"Look, can I help you with your bag?" he asked her. She stood still. "Get you a cab?"

Then she put her hand lightly on his arm. She wanted Kevin to follow her. He fell into step beside her, but quickly got ahead.

He recognized her movement. The Thorazine Shuffle was what they called it on the psych ward of Bellevue. He'd seen it about a thousand times, patients slogging around on meds like creatures from *The Night of the Living Dead*. And there were other side effects. He remembered one patient complaining that her throat felt so dry, she worried that a brush fire would start inside it.

He slowed down to stay beside Cornelia Lord while she shuffled into the staff room. She really put her heart into it, he had to give her credit.

Kevin closed the door behind them.

"Thank you," she said with difficulty. "I really need your help."

She pronounced it *rilly*, maybe an upper-class thing. But his heart beat at the part about needing his help.

"I need you to lie for me," she told him, her tongue rolling around every word. "If my father comes looking for me, you have to tell him you haven't seen me."

"Are you trying to kill yourself?"

Her eyes flared. "No, of course not."

"Because I have to tell you," Kevin said, "that's a distinct possibility if you plan on drinking tonight. You're on meds now, right? You could get a bad reaction."

He'd caught her by surprise and she recoiled slightly. She slowly lifted her hand and almost—but not quite—touched his cheek. It was his turn to move back a little.

"I promise I won't drink. But I have to do something important. Just help me get out of here. Please."

Kevin thought about it. All he really knew about this girl was that Lord comma Cornelia would probably be trouble comma massive for anybody she touched. Look at what she did to her boyfriend, Tucker Fisk, that slick mogul, practically foaming at the mouth like a junkyard dog on page three of the *Globe*.

But Cornelia Lord had heart. She had to, sneaking out of whatever custodial care they had kept her under in Penthouse A, loaded up with Thorazine by her slimy psychiatrist.

He thought about the building rules he was supposed to follow.

What did they call it? Not "fraternizing" with the residents, namely Chester Lord's daughter. He had no doubt at all he could lose his job if he helped her.

"Let me go out to the alley first," he told her. "Or you'll have company. Follow me, stay in the dark when you get outside, wait for a cab, and get ready to run. Can you run?"

"Of course," it took her five seconds to say.

He went ahead and opened the service door against the cold. He knew that Vlad never watched the monitor inside to see the security vidcam mounted by the door over their heads. She followed him in what seemed like dog years. They got out the door. He walked up the short alley where he'd lifted her out of the limousine the night before, and onto the street.

He peered out into the dark and spotted two other photographers besides Philip Grace tonight. Philip's competition had caught up with him. They probably saw that Grace's *Debwatch* column won about fifty percent more space in the *Globe* today than usual, all because of Cornelia Lord. When he saw Philip's face, it wore a kind of gas-pain look. The other photographers, a ratty pair, were only there to invade the turf Philip had carved out for himself, and Philip kept apart from them.

The Thorazine Deb was still perched just outside the service door in the shadows, counting on Kevin to help her.

"Hey, Philip," he called out, hushed but excited, like he just discovered gold in the garbage Dumpster.

He got past the gate and onto the sidewalk, approaching the stalkarazzi where they stood.

"Kevin Doyle, how you doin'?" Philip said, wary.

"I got something for you." Kevin looked over his shoulder, keeping away from the lobby, out of Vlad's line of sight.

"Yeah? What?"

Kevin walked over to the trio and motioned for a huddle. Slowly, Grace leading, they stepped over to him. He waited. One . . . two . . . three.

He could see, over the backs of their heads, the girl in black hugging the darkness of the street, shuffling out of the alley. He waited some more. She came out of the shadows and raised her hand. A passing cab with its "vacant" light on pulled over and stopped for her. She opened the cab door with difficulty.

"I'm thinking," Kevin said very low, to keep the three men bent in around him. "Giants, pretty good spread."

The photographers looked puzzled, then figured it out. They swiveled their heads to see who Kevin made them miss.

"Shithead."

"Asshole."

One of the stalkarazzi spat on the sidewalk.

"Thought we had an understandin'," Grace told him, hurt.

"Yeah." Kevin waved cordially at him. "But I owed you one for the alley."

Cornelia found 153 responses to her e-mail on Dr. Powers's computer.

Sitting in the curator's chair, working at his Mac, she sorted through them, dumping the few delusional types who claimed that Nikola Tesla abducted them in a spaceship or was still living in a *ciudad subterráneo*. One wrote that a week before Tesla had been seated on the living room couch, watching the TV show *Sabado Gigante*.

She filed the more useful responses into "Definite" and "Possible." All told she found fifty-eight people who could be helpful. Many were members of the worldwide Tesla Society, South American division. Of those, some provided information. Others wanted to hear back from her. She formatted her replies, becoming even more excited about the adventure. It was possible that nobody from the United States had ever gone to South America on a similar mission before. The best replies came from Rio and São Paulo in Brazil, and Buenos Aires in Argentina. There could indeed be Tesla papers in all those places.

She also believed it possible, if unlikely, that years of rumor in the Tesla community about a third secret tower in South America could be true. *A lost Tesla Tower.* She felt a chill. Perhaps too good to be true, but she couldn't totally dismiss the notion. History revealed that Tesla's work had turned up in extraordinary places. She knew that the FBI confiscated many of Tesla's papers when he died in New York City in 1943. They delivered them to the U.S. government for use in the war effort. The Russians had taken keen interest in Tesla's particle-beam theory. After a strange "disturbance" in Siberia scorched several thousand acres of woodland, the whispered stories out of Russia said that it was a Red Army experiment using Tesla's formula.

If they could find his papers so could she. Her eyes moistened thinking how Tesla had suffered. He spent his entire life frustrated. She drifted, imagining him in his prime, playing with electricity in his laboratory on Fifth Avenue, creating a blue corona to dance over his head and shoulders to amuse his friends.

Kevin Doyle, of the lovely blue eyes and matching corona, teased himself into her image of Tesla. After the first time she saw Kevin, she had checked for his name on the list of building employees that Chester kept in his study. That first time had only been a glorious tease. But she had glimpsed his corona again tonight. She had never seen, except in her Tesla fantasies, a corona so pure.

Kevin Doyle.

His eyes pulled her in, a magnetic force drawing her gently toward him. Something about his gentle corona reminded her of an afternoon in her mother's arms. They had been at the beach when she was nine. The waves rolled over them, deliciously foamy and salty. They giggled and screeched together, riding the waves to the shore. She felt happy as a dolphin that day, playing in the sea, leaping with her mother in love and trust.

She realized that Kevin's corona matched the color of the sky that day. It had the texture of summer, arching over a world that felt the way life always should.

She shuddered. It was so cold.

That's why she needed South America. A fresh start. In nineteen and one half hours, she would board an Air Brasília flight and escape to warmer, dreamier horizons. Then she could find anything.

She worked on translating the responses to her e-mail.

It thrilled her to realize that, in South America, interest in Tesla had swollen beyond cult status. Rational professors and engineers studied his inventions. Historians glorified his life. In the U.S., Nikola Tesla might be another dead nobody, like so many brilliant people without a knack for business. But in South America, Tesla seemed a mythical hero who dreamed of changing the world with free electricity, until he'd been mugged by the *norteamericano* robber barons. A martyr to his cause.

Perhaps in that mystical continent vibrating with youth and energy, she could finally bring Tesla the worldwide recognition he deserved. A fitting payback to the maestro. And to her mother.

She rubbed her cold hands together. She hated to admit it to herself, but the Electric Girl's anonymity bothered her.

If only she could stand up on top of the museum, scream out her whole story, and let everybody know the truth of Cornelia Lord, faux–party girl.

Perhaps it was selfish, but she couldn't help it.

People were treating her like the wasted debs of song and story. Sad girls like Barbara Hutton, who married enough men to form a conga line. And poor Brenda Frazier, who made her own face up like a clown's in her dwindling years, thinking she was still the toast of the Stork Club.

The Electric Girl would show them once she arrived in South America.

Then she felt a chill through her like an icy finger. What if her plane hit a mountain, as those perfectly normal flights to South America sometimes did? She could be squashed on the face of the Andes and lost forever.

What would people gossip about her then? What would her father think? That she had left this earth with no greater legacy than using her Saks First card and sucking on sake martinis?

She tapped at the keyboard with one finger, thinking. Oh, why not? She owed it to herself to write a little something.

She picked at the keys in earnest now, making a disk. Then she needed to get a few hours rest.

She turned off the xenon spotlights, curled up on Dr. Powers's couch. She could no longer fight the drugs. The energy quickly drained out of her. She wondered if she would find all she was looking for.

And she fell asleep with a glimpse of Kevin Doyle's sky-blue corona.

*   *   *

"Mike, be careful," Chester fumed as the brittle limousine groaned around a corner. "Panda limousines . . . the Koi Tower. As soon as we get that bastard Han Koi straightened out, we're moving Lord & Company back to Wall Street."

Tucker nodded solemnly while Chester seethed, shifting his weight uncomfortably on the slick leather seat.

"Chester," Tucker began, as he played with the laptop he balanced on one knee, the other leg arched as far as it could stretch in the small compartment. "I need to know more about Corny's obsession with this Tesla."

Chester felt his mind empty, suddenly going numb when the name "Tesla" stung his ear. He labored to organize his thoughts about the miserable inventor. Cornelia had shown him his picture many times. He had been a tall, ascetic European with long black hair and a smug grin suggesting deep and hidden knowledge.

Chester began stammering what he knew while Tucker got busy on his laptop. The car slowed and Chester looked up to see lights burning feverishly on the Lord & Company executive floor of the Koi Tower, even now at 4:30 A.M.

Only two years old, the office tower hovered over Madison Avenue like the Colossus of Koi. Chester climbed out of the car and glowered at the Hong Kong–scale office building. He never liked visiting Hong Kong, that chaotic city bristling with gaudy office towers like hostile missiles. The Koi Tower made a spectacle of itself, brassy and raw, housing mostly corporate raiders and their law firms. Old Han Koi spent tens of millions hiring a cast of architects and theme park designers to create the flamboyant structure.

"We do not want a building, we want a happening," Chester remembered overhearing old Han hectoring his architects with a phrase he must have heard in the 1960s, perhaps on some Asian rerun of *Laugh-In.*

Chester's thoughts shifted to his hatred of the Kois, he dimly realized, as a lesser torture than thinking about Cornelia.

He thought of Koi driving him to the Hong Kong racetrack, in a blindingly ostentatious Rolls-Royce they'd actually had covered with gold English Sovereign coins under many coats of clear lacquer. No cheap Panda cars for Han. Now he had been forced to move Lord &

Company to this bronze and gold monstrosity. It made his buttocks boil. This shameless monument to greed and glitz made Donald Trump's buildings look puritan.

The doorway to the Koi Tower's twelve-story glass atrium lobby had purposely been built lopsided, to conform to the principles of feng shui. It always disoriented Chester when he walked through. To the left of the crooked doorway, a theme restaurant called Splendid Shanghai beckoned. Its red-enameled facade reminded him of Mann's Chinese Theater. Chester despised the sepulchral glitz of the lobby and hated seeing the three tiny Panda sedans in red, white, and blue that turned on pedestals on the lobby floor.

The express elevator deposited Chester and Tucker on the executive floor. They headed for Tucker's office, decorated in hard-edged slabs of glass, marble, and hammered steel. His X-shaped desk had once belonged to his teenage hero, a junk-bond king. Tucker had plucked it out of his idol's former office in Beverly Hills, and Chester had gratefully paid a fortune for it.

Tucker stopped by the gunmetal-colored desks where his two secretaries sat within his shouting distance. Both wore dark gray or black as Tucker required.

"Susan," Tucker snapped, and the older blond woman jumped and followed him.

Chester noticed for the first time as he looked at the forty-year-old woman's downcast eyes, how Tucker's few older staff members behaved as though they'd had the stuffing kicked out of them.

Tucker's phalanx of ten young executives stood assembled in his office. Chester entered, briefly and tentatively, to say hello to the group. They were just kids, and reminded him of the wide-eyed, frightening youngsters who worked for politicians. They stood eager as Jack Russell terriers, practically quivering in their conservative shirts and ties and clutching their own laptops, their busy foreheads crammed full of tactical moves. The tireless fury of their youth deflated him, making him feel old and ineffectual.

"Hi," he said, stopping before adding, "kids."

"Hello, Mr. Lord." Their heads all bobbed, unfailingly polite to him. Now Tucker would ask them for something impossible and they would give it to him.

"People," Tucker barked, "you have eight hours to do a world-wide information search. You will prepare me a detailed briefing. You'll also need to find a sophisticated electronics store, get our travel people out of bed and working the phones, and send a shopping team to a number of retail stores that I'll list for you. Problems?"

The energy in the room sizzled.

"Tucker," a red-cheeked woman with short hair said. "Can I ask you what client this is for?"

"No, you can't," Tucker told her.

"Is there a billing number?" Susan his secretary asked.

"Yeah," Tucker sat with a tiny smile. "Tesla 001."

Cornelia arrived at JFK Airport at 7:30 P.M. She'd slept in the museum and stayed there until it was time to leave in the early morning. Dr. Powers, keeper of her secrets, hugged her and warned her one last time to be careful traveling alone. "You can change your mind," he told her, but she was determined.

Early in their relationship, she had worried that Dr. Powers might call her father at some point, outraged at seeing her working anonymously and misunderstood. But he had stuck to his promise to never reveal her secrets. Since the day they met at the event for the Tesla Society, she and Dr. Powers had bonded over the museum. When they flew the Tesla airship together and he taught her the controls, she almost cried to be so appreciated and trusted.

But she never allowed herself to view Dr. Powers as a surrogate father. No matter how exasperating he might be, her real father would one day come to his senses. She believed that.

Cornelia moved rapidly through the big, modern International Terminal at JFK, no Thorazine Shuffle now. Bushberg's drugs, those sly paralytic juices, had mostly evaporated from her bloodstream. The blue and white Air Brasília counters she approached held a row of nutty-brown Brazilians, festive-looking even in their dark blue uniforms.

"Hi," the woman behind the counter said, a caffe latte face under curly hair. "How can I help you?"

"I have a reservation on the 9:30 to Rio."

The night flight to Rio. A delicious thought.

She placed her credit card and passport on the counter tentatively. Could Chester have reported her to the State Department to revoke her passport? No, that was silly. And he knew nothing about her American Express platinum card. He would have no way to cancel it, nor could a detective trail her transactions, she didn't think. But still she held her breath as the creamy Brazilian's fingers flew over the keyboard. The agent studied Cornelia's passport and handed it back with her ticket and platinum card.

"Have a pleasant flight, Ms. Lord. Please use our first-class lounge to wait."

Gotta dance, ran through the Electric Girl's head.

She did a little skip. She wouldn't concentrate now on her regret at leaving her father with his wall-to-wall worry without so much as a goodbye. She would get word to him soon. Perhaps once he knew she was all right, he would even feel relieved that she was gone. He could stay in the cocoon of Cornelia's photographs and his memories of his little girl.

Now she needed to focus on her mission.

She walked swiftly to the lounge, making sure no one was following her. Kevin Doyle, of the sky-blue corona, had joked about her black outfit. She didn't wear black to be stealthy like a ninja, but to simplify her life by reducing time-draining vanity. Wearing all black in New York City attracted little attention.

The cozy Air Brasília lounge was too crammed with noisy, happy-looking voyagers enjoying its bar. Cornelia found a quiet section for business travelers. Like most such areas, this was a masterwork of soulless comfort. Uprooted prisoners of modern business made phone calls, pecked away at laptop computers, and stared dispiritedly out the glass windows at the tarmac. She sat in a leather chair so slick she nearly slid out of it. She relaxed, stretching her legs out.

A man who sat with his back to her, working on a laptop, turned around.

"Hi," Tucker said.

The warm buzz tingling through her turned icy cold now. She started to fling herself up out of the chair.

Tucker touched her arm gently. "Sit, Corny. I'd just like to show you something."

She hesitated, then settled back. How could he have known? Not even Chester knew. The thought of Dr. Powers calling Tucker made her suddenly ill. Then she swallowed, angry at herself for thinking that he would ever betray her. Maybe the thought was paranoid, but even paranoids can have excessively nosy would-be boyfriends who might want to interfere with their plans.

Tucker seemed calm enough, punching a key on his laptop and turning the screen around to her. The pixels crawled into a shape she recognized.

She couldn't believe what he was showing her.

"What I'd suggest," Tucker said, "and only suggest, because you're free to do what you want, is a way to use the two hours before your flight leaves. I want to take you somewhere here in the airport. If you don't like what I show you, I'll bring you right back."

"How can I trust you?"

He smiled and held up two fingers, a parody of a hippie peace sign. "This is a meeting. Not an abduction."

She fretted like Chester. As easy as it was to read Kevin Doyle, whose eyes she could jump in without fearing what she might find, Tucker's were slippery and unfathomable.

But if what he just showed her was real, it would change her life forever.

"Okay," she agreed. "Show me."

Chapter Nine

Kevin slowly climbed the staircase. He bent down to feel the stiff new imitation indoor-outdoor carpet, the Astroturf the landlord had laid right after his mother tumbled down the cement stairs nearly one month earlier. Kevin looked up at the new sixty-watt light bulb in the ceiling fixture. The landlord had paid the utilities this month, too.

Tonight a lawyer was coming by to talk to the family about the accident.

Trudging up past three hallways full of pungent smells in his parents' walk-up building stabbed him with memories. He tried to imagine the way his mother would have seen it as a newlywed full of energy and hope. It was only supposed to be their starter place. Then life dropped by with three kids. No wonder she got lost in the Time Life art books.

When his mother grew up in Bloody Forehead, Ireland, art appreciation probably meant not throwing rocks at the church's stained glass windows. He imagined her discovering Giotto's *Lost Saint Sebastian*. She had traveled to Dublin with her brother Eddie. Waiting for Eddie to arrange two tramp-steamer tickets to New York City, she snuck into the National Museum in Dublin and stood there glued to the painting. Maybe she felt like the saint, looking for meaning in another place. But, whatever she felt, she wanted to share it with Kevin by taking him, not his sisters, to the Metropolitan Museum when the *Lost Saint Sebastian* came to New York.

It was his tenth birthday. He remembered her hands, warm on his shoulders. She made a little gasp when Kevin pointed out the simple lines and shadows that Giotto used to show them Sebastian's character, just from looking through the Time Life art books with her. He told her that he saw Giotto's spark of the divine. From that moment, she treated him as special.

When Kevin got through high school, Uncle Eddie waited with his tight little tyrant's grin for Kevin to ask for a doorman job. No, his mother tapped her finger on Eddie's chest. Kevin would not start a career with the City of New York, or be one of Eddie's doormen. Kevin could work night jobs if necessary, but he would not have to take a real job. Kevin would study art.

This Thanksgiving, his secret plan had been to lead her by the hand to the Stinson Gallery. He would surprise her the same way she had brought him to the Metropolitan Museum. He would show her the Saint Sebastian he made for her, in a real gallery.

That was going to be his gift to her.

Now she would never see his Sebastian, and he had wound up begging Eddie, whose idea of art was *Dogs Playing Poker*, for a steady job to pay his rent.

Kevin tramped up the last flight to the fourth landing. He put his key in the metal door, stepping back when his father opened it for him.

He swallowed. His dad was only fifty-three, but he looked old now, face bleached, chin resting on his shirtfront like a sad, tired bloodhound.

Dennis Doyle had always prided himself on his fastidiousness. Tonight, his neck seemed to have shrunk in his shirt, and a gray stubble covered his raw chin. His eyes had always revealed a little glimmer of the clever boy from Limerick. Now they burrowed in their red rims, lonely and disbelieving, the skin around them pebbly. His dad looked lost. Maybe Kevin should stay at the apartment with him until he found the groove of his new life.

"Hey, Dad," Kevin greeted him with a hug. His father tensed at his touch. They weren't easy huggers, the Doyle men.

"Well, the artist," Dennis said quietly. "Our lawyer, Jon Landau's coming in a half-hour and the girls are here already. Watch your step around the piles of tissues. The girls mean well, but they make me feel worse with Marne ready to smack somebody and Helen all weepy. How's the job?"

"Great," Kevin said.

He kept his smile hitched up while his father took the two bags he carried. He glared at the thin plastic one containing a roasted chicken from the Hamas Deli, dry from twirling on the spit, and a pound of greasy macaroni salad. But he smiled at the brown paper bag twisted at the top, a fifth of Bushmills.

Kevin looked around the apartment expecting, as he always did, some small change to mark the fact that his mother no longer lived there. The mail she sorted through on November 23 remained on the table by the door. Even the scent of her cosmetics lingered in the apartment, probably on the sheets and towels his father would not send to the laundry.

The living room of the Doyles' apartment, sixteen feet square, looked out on Third Avenue through wood-paneled windows half covered with yellowed white drapes. A brown couch and two plaid chairs huddled close together before a gigantic TV set. The day he turned fifteen, they carried home the thirty-two-inch Magnavox and rearranged all the seats to face the tube.

Wall-to-wall photographs of Kevin and his sisters from newborn babies through high school graduation, multilayered with more photos that covered the tables and walls, created a silent documentary of the Doyle family's Big Events.

In the traditional world of the Doyles, Kevin realized for the first time, the next Big Event for each of them would be the disease or accident that killed them.

"Hey, Kevin." His sister Marne hopped up and squeezed him.

Marne got his mother's nice features and auburn hair. She also worked out every day with free weights. When Kevin lightly gripped her forearm through her thin jacket sleeve, it was like he could be holding a length of hard rope.

He sniffed her hair. "You went back to work."

"They gave me three weeks." Marne, twenty-six and single, became a firefighter after two years at City College. Kevin cared about both his sisters, but he looked up to Marne. Not many people chose storming into an inferno, lungs filling with smoke, for the same salary you could earn as a bartender.

And Marne had always backed him up, like his mom. In school, she'd poke guys her age in the eye and make them yowl for picking on her little brother.

"How's your job, Kevin?"

"Great," he said. Flicking a glance to make sure his father wasn't looking, he silently snapped his right fist by his neck and let his tongue roll out of his mouth, to look like he was hanging himself.

She giggled and mussed his hair.

Helen was twenty-eight, but looked middle-aged. When specialists told her she was unable to have kids—at least not without fertility drugs that she worried might give her octuplets—her youth seemed to burn out like the pilot light in a stove. She started to pull her hair back, wear sensible shoes, and take on the rhythms of a municipal-payroll lifer who lived for weekends and vacations. To Kevin, she was serving out a sentence.

While Dennis Doyle took the bags into the kitchen, Kevin went to the sagging shelves over the couch and ran his finger over the old set of *Encyclopaedia Britannica* volumes from A to Z. He pulled out the C volume and read a short section.

"What are you reading?" Helen frowned.

"Nothing," Kevin told her, closing the book, looking around the apartment.

At his mother's wake, this living room had throbbed like an Irish boombox. The rumbling bass sounds came from his mom's people, the Feeneys. They were descended from the Finnachs, the Irish word for fighters. Their faces wore the stamp of craggy western Ireland. They never spoke at less than a bellow. His mom always seemed a mutant in her family, since she seldom yelled and her face never furrowed into dark lines and shadows. His dad's people, the more sociable Doyles, had softer faces with big ears. They came from Limerick, where they sold green beer and plastic shillelaghs to Americans tourists who used expressions like "Top of the mornin' to you" that no real Irish kid had ever heard.

Kevin remembered his childhood as a constant bedlam. Everybody yelled just to make conversation. Kevin squeezed himself into whatever quiet space he could find, sometimes out on the fire escape, even when it snowed.

Now he longed to roil in that old bedlam. His dad would live in this empty-feeling apartment for the rest of his life. He would never remarry.

His father was coming back from the kitchen. He carried a short whiskey on the rocks in each hand, handed one to his son.

"I was just thinking," Kevin started. "Maybe I could move in here for a while."

He didn't say what he really thought, that his father had no life without his mom. But it was true. Dennis Doyle never wanted anything more than to be with his wife. He wasn't like other neighborhood men who snuck out to Riley's Sports Bar and had to be dragged home.

"You'll be lonely, Kevin," Dennis blew him off, sounding phony-brave. "I'm ready to get back to work. By the way, the building residents made a donation to the Heart Association in your mother's name. They didn't get it right, but I suppose it's the thought that counts."

Kevin sat in one of the faded plaid chairs across from his father. He put his drink on the coffee table, alongside a *TV Guide* for the Thanksgiving week when his mom died. He had always believed, when his parents' mortality began to dawn on him, that his dad would die first.

"To Mom," Kevin said. They sipped the whiskey slowly, both drinking to dull the edge, but not get high or drunk.

Dennis got up as though he'd forgotten something. He came back with a copy of the previous day's *Globe*, opened to the "Don't Drop Deb!" headline. Dennis passed it to Kevin and lifted his eyebrow.

His sisters stared at him as though they'd already seen it.

"Yeah, that's me," he told them.

His father frowned. "I could tell by your ears. What are you getting up to in that building? This kind of stuff won't do you any good with the management, you know."

"Her boyfriend called me in the lobby, asked me to help him with her. She has some problems."

"I've read about her before, Corny the Deb," Marne said. "That girl's trouble, Kevin."

Kevin shrugged, not ready to gossip.

"Do you talk to this girl?" Helen asked him, looking worried that the deb and her doorman brother would be friendly.

"She was asleep." Kevin sighed. "She woke up and said, 'Great corona.' Then she passed out again."

"Corona?" Marne asked him. "The beer?"

"Or an electrical arc. We use them making neon. Or maybe a crown. Or a burning star. I just looked up a bunch of definitions."

"Are you interested in the girl or something, Kevin?" his father said. "They have rules against fraternization, don't they?"

"Yeah, but I'm not interested."

"Then why look up what she said?" Marne asked him.

Marne was looking for action, something to argue about. He supposed after chewing over his mother's death for the past twenty-seven days, they were all grateful for another topic.

"Hey, I like that deb for Kevin, Dad," Marne said.

"I don't know if the artist's got time for girls," Dennis said.

"I don't see them making much time for me, Dad."

"Becky Donnelly, she'll make time," Marne said. "She likes you."

Kevin winced at the memory of Becky, a relative of some firefighter. Marne had set them up on Halloween.

"I like her, too," he said to slide it by.

"No, I mean, she *likes* you," Marne pestered. "And she's an artist. She makes sculpture with Reynolds Wrap or something. She just needs a break."

"She's a pinhead." Kevin waved his hand.

"So what are you, Brainiac?"

"No," Kevin explained. "I mean she's got body piercing with pins all over her face and a little gold Cheerio on her tongue."

"A tongue ring's for sex," Marne defended.

"Marne," Helen scolded her.

"She liked me 'cause you told her I had a piece in the Stinson Gallery. She wanted me to introduce her to Jessica Fernandez."

"So?" Marne said. "Help her out, I bet she'll pay you back with her Cheerio."

He should add the little tidbit that Jessica kicked his Saint Sebastian out of the gallery, but hesitated to pile more gloom and doom onto his family now.

"She's not gonna want to go out with a—" Kevin stopped before he said "doorman." He took a swallow of the whiskey instead. It had an aftertaste like smoking metal. How could his parents drink the stuff? He struggled for something to say now. He came here to soothe his father and, after twenty minutes, had already insulted his job. But Dennis Doyle smiled thinly at his son, maybe for the first time since his wife died.

Kevin finally asked him, "You didn't want the doorman job either?"

His father pursed his lips and spoke softly. "I learned the brewer's trade so I didn't have to suck up to people, Kevin. Back then, New York was a blue-collar town. We joked our breweries would close when the Dodgers left Brooklyn." He gave a sad laugh. "Who drank Beck's back then? No, I hated going to Eddie for a servant's job. I could have been a brewer in the West Indies, making Red Stripe with the Rastafarians, all of us living on a beach. But your mother wouldn't have it."

"Why?" Kevin asked.

"She wanted you raised here, for the museums." Dennis started to say more, then looked away.

Marne got up from her seat.

"Well, he's gonna show 'em." She raised her fists in front of her, bobbing back and forth in front of Kevin's chair.

"Marne, c'mon," he laughed, knowing he'd better stand up or he'd get clobbered. She swatted at him expertly but he sidestepped her.

She pounced back in front of him. "Don't make me hurt you, Kevin."

She feinted with her left, then hooked around with her right like a snake and gave him a sisterly kidney shot.

"Ooooof. Two out of three," he gasped.

"Jeez, Marne," Dennis laughed, "go easy on him."

"You're so outclassed." Marne smiled, keeping her eyes locked on his.

"Marne . . ." Kevin dodged a smooth right, feeling the air hum by his cheek.

"That Jessica Fernandez. Tell her you want twenty-five thousand bucks for Saint Sebastian. A saint shouldn't go home with anybody for less, right?"

"Uh . . . Marne . . ." He really ought to fess up about the Stinson Gallery.

But then they heard the downstairs buzzer and a squawking from the intercom after Helen asked who was there.

Marne faked another left, but Kevin caught her right wrist on its way to his chin.

"Good boy." She mussed his hair like always.

Helen let the lawyer in. He was a pale, officious man in his thirties who wore black earmuffs and a herringbone overcoat. His chin stuck out and his glasses were so thick it was like looking the wrong way through a telescope. He carried a bulging briefcase.

"I'm Mr. Hellman from the law office of Jon Landau."

The family all stared at this man who would call himself "Mr. Hellman" with other adults. He didn't shake hands, just took his coat and earmuffs off and dropped them on the couch. Then he flopped down on Dennis's chair without asking permission and snapped open the briefcase, pulling out a yellow legal pad and a form on a clipboard. He looked at the form while he spoke to them.

"Which one of you is Dennis Doyle?"

"I am." His father sat on the couch. Marne sat coolly beside him, folding her hands in what Kevin recognized as self-control.

"These are my daughters, Marne and Helen, and my son, Kevin."

Hellman's eyes flicked up, huge behind his lenses, then fell back to the form as the gold pen he flourished struck paper. "Social Security number?"

"Where's Jon Landau?" Dennis asked.

Hellman gave him a surprised, sour look. "He's a litigator, a trial lawyer. Before I can recommend your case to Mr. Landau, I need to do a screening process. We want to see if your case has merit before we can get you justice."

Kevin could tell by the way he said "justice" that he really meant "money." That was what the law office of Jon Landau had boasted about in its TV ads. He got a feeling from Hellman like the aftertaste from the whiskey.

Dennis merely nodded his head. "We believe that Mrs. Doyle would not have lost her footing on the staircase if it wasn't as black as a coal mine. If our landlord had paid the Con Ed bill on time—"

Hellman held up his hand like a school crossing guard. Kevin guessed that he preferred to hear himself talk than listen to anybody. Kevin looked at Marne. She seemed ready to rip the lawyer's hand off.

"Let's just follow my procedure, okay? I've got twenty minutes here." Hellman's voice snapped like a rubber band at the end of each word.

For the first nineteen minutes, the lawyer asked brief questions to extract financial information. Did his mother work? Did they carry life insurance on her? Finally he came back to the issue of the landlord.

"Did you ever complain to the landlord in writing?"

"I complained five times to the building super," Dennis told him.

"Mr. Doyle, did you put it in writing, yes or no? We need to establish that the landlord created a dangerous condition and he did it in a negligent or reckless manner."

"No, I didn't notify him in writing." Dennis slumped, deflated and seething.

Hellman shook his head. "We'd have to pull his Con Ed records then, show a pattern. We're already talking time and effort on our part."

"I thought that's what legal work was," Kevin said, "time and effort."

Hellman blinked. "We have to assess the value of each death. No offense, but your mother was no kid. Even throwing in punitive damages, pain and suffering, we could only figure on a $500,000 suit. A case like this, we'd settle for half, and our firm keeps a third of that. We're not looking at *Wheel of Fortune* here, folks."

Marne started to breathe deeply but Dennis held her arm.

"Do you think it's right, what the landlord did?" Kevin asked him.

"I can't answer a question like that," Hellman said, putting the papers back in his briefcase and snapping it shut. "But I can tell you we're going to pass on this one."

"Why don't you keep *all* the money instead of just a third," Dennis told Hellman. "Just sue the landlord because he shouldn't get away with it."

Hellman stood up and put his coat on while he thought over Dennis's offer. "Sorry. We've got a state ethics code, and I don't think we could keep the whole award. Anyway, I couldn't make your case convincing."

"Yeah? What's your first name?" Kevin asked him.

Hellman looked up at him strangely. "Mister."

"Your mother named you that?" Marne asked wide-eyed.

He grinned a notch, finally noticing that Marne was pretty. "My friends call me Mickey."

"Mickey," Kevin said, "I bet you could make a jury feel all the pain and suffering our mom did."

Hellman laughed over his shoulder walking out. "I'm glad you're so sure."

"It's easy, Mickey," Kevin said as he hopped up. "I'll just break those glasses you got on and see how far you get down the staircase."

Hellman swiveled toward Kevin and his eyes bulged like basketballs behind the thick glasses. He bolted for the front door and got it open, escaping to the landing.

Kevin followed and stamped his feet, running in place so it sounded like he was chasing him down the stairs. Hellman didn't look back. He just tore down the staircase as fast as his shoes could navigate the oily imitation Astroturf. The Doyles gathered to watch him slip and clutch at the freshly painted wall all the way down.

"There's no railing either," Dennis called down.

"I'll sue you," Hellman shouted back up, almost losing his balance.

"Hey, Mickey, you forgot your ears," Kevin said as he tossed the lawyer's black furry earmuffs down the staircase after him.

Kevin walked east, looking around each corner and alley carefully. The walk home could be trouble in spots. When he reached his neighborhood, he twisted his neck looking right, left, and behind him. Gangs hung out in pockets, so you walked a block, ran a block.

Graffiti plagued his street, beyond any pretense that it was street art. The hostile spray-painted words, most of them unintelligible, covered buildings, sidewalks, and cars.

He saw an Alphabet City regular. She was a disheveled homeless woman who came every night, knelt down on the sidewalk with a knife sharpener, and honed the spikes on a "Severe Tire Damage" grating at the exit of a parking lot.

A man in fourteen layers of raggedy clothes, his face smeared with black, passed close to Kevin on the sidewalk. His red eyes burned with violence. He turned suddenly.

"Vermin!" he yelled at Kevin.

"Demon!" Kevin yelled back, pointing at him.

The street nut pulled back and walked away, dispirited, muttering to himself.

He approached his decrepit building on Avenue B. Had Cornelia Lord ever seen his neighborhood slumming around, going to bars? Maybe she'd excused herself around the crack dealers, dodged the muggers and crazy mutts. In her Uptown way, Cornelia Lord was pretty crazy herself.

He wondered why he was wondering about her.

Because a girl like her who jumped into trouble like a gopher was interesting. And maybe she just *looked* crazy. Maybe she had a reason that the father, the boyfriend, and the weasel shrink couldn't figure out.

He thought about the man he had seen in the coffee shop who flailed his arms around like a lunatic. Then Kevin saw the fly pestering him.

He tried to imagine, if Cornelia Lord had her own fly, what it would look like.

Chapter Ten

*C*orny made a light waterfall noise in her head as Tucker took her hand firmly in his.

She chose to shut out the noisy babble of JFK International Terminal, a multicultural crossroads where all passengers were treated equally as livestock, funneled into the airplanes. Instead, she heard the humming in her head like Iguazú Falls. She could also hear the maestro. *"My preenchaysa,"* he purred to her from his Tesla airship, luffing over the falls.

The Electric Girl inside her practically snapped her fingers in anticipation, wanting to see what Tucker had promised to show her.

"I almost lost it when you left so suddenly," she heard Tucker tell her with much sincerity.

Cornelia frowned.

"I have something else I want to ask you," he intoned with the little tree frog in his voice again. "But I want to wait until you're sitting down."

She watched his eyes as they stepped outside the terminal. They told her nothing. She saw that Lord & Company's gray Koi limousine waited. Chester's driver, Mike, held the door.

"Hi, Mike," she said.

"Ms. Lord." Mike gave her the hint of a smirk. He seemed to get a kick out of whatever mischief she caused that brought Tucker here.

She always saw just the faint outline of a nasty brown corona around the Panda limousine. It was the only inanimate object she had ever seen that possessed one. She peeked inside to make sure that sneaky Dr. Bushberg was not inside with men in white to throw a net over her head. The plush little matchbox interior was empty. She ducked in, settling into the seat opposite Tucker's and placing her duffel bag on the seat next to her, covering it with her arm.

"Tucker . . ." she began.

"Shhh." He held his finger gently to her lips, picked up her hand and squeezed it. "Soon."

This inflamed her curiosity, and she squirmed on the leather seat. But she said nothing. She let Tucker hold her hand, without speaking, for the ten minutes of driving to their destination, watching the rest of the airport go by. When the limousine stopped, the cheap brakes grabbing, she saw through the darkened window that they entered the Fifth Avenue of JFK International, the secluded corner for private aviation. Here business jets sat inside heated hangars with cushions all fluffed up for important people.

This hangar had "Lord" stenciled on the door. She recognized it from many years before as the one where her father kept his company jet.

Tucker held the door open for her.

A Gulfstream V, sparkling white, stood up on its black toes with maroon pinstripes like angel hair and a glossy Lord & Company logo emblazoned on the door. It looked brand-new, but didn't interest her. She looked beyond to the bustle at the far end of the hangar, then headed toward the activity.

A video screen hung on one wall next to a color map stuck with bright red pins. Crates and boxes, bearing red tags, were stacked up on the floor. About ten busy young executives, dressed in khaki bush outfits as though embarking on a safari, hurried around taking inventory of the boxes. Some shouted out the numbers of different items and marked them off on clipboards. Others yelled orders into cell phones.

"Tucker, what is this?"

He motioned her to a fold-out chair set up in front of the video screen. She sat. He carried his laptop, of course, which he plugged into a box that controlled the video screen.

"This . . . is Brazil." His voice was measured, like a Travel Channel announcer.

He tapped his magical laptop, and the same visual he had shown her in the Air Brasília terminal popped up on the giant video screen. It was a detailed topographical map showing the interior of Brazil, focusing on the dense jungle region.

She peered at the insert of an old man. Under the man's picture, she saw the legend, "Tesla Tower Engineer."

Tucker moved his finger on his laptop's mini-joystick, no bigger than a mouse's penis. He jockeyed a red cursor to blink on and off by the capital city of Brasília. "And this is where a ninety-year-old scientist lives who claims he worked with Nikola Tesla."

She studied the insert on the screen, a very old man with skin like carved mahogany, wiry hair, and alert eyes. The image danced with large pixels, like something pulled off the Internet.

"This man says," Tucker paused for effect, "that he worked on a Tesla Tower in South America."

Her pulse fluttered as she stared at the screen. She was more shocked than if Tucker had shown up in a tutu and offered to perform *Swan Lake* for her. But her curiosity about the image on the video screen overwhelmed her.

"Does he say the tower works?" she asked slowly.

"He says it should. According to him, they cracked the code for broadcasting electricity from the tower. It's just like radio waves."

"Tucker, just how do you know about all this?"

Tucker stretched out, taking his time. "There's nothing in this world I can't find out in a couple of hours. I put my team on it, this is what they came back with. Give me a little credit, okay? So here's where the old guy says the Tesla Tower is, deep in the jungle . . ."

She listened distractedly while Tucker talked logistics. Where to land rented helicopters. How to continue a journey on foot. Could the old man be for real?

She looked around at Tucker's bustling young executives. Such an aura of sweaty work and dedication. She saw nothing phony about their zeal to do whatever Tucker told them. But could someone as grounded as Tucker be driven by faith in Nikola Tesla?

Of course not. What mattered to Tucker was an objective, a result. Clearly he was doing all this for her. To impress her. So how impressed should she be?

She stood up and walked to the mountain of large boxes and crates piled in orderly fashion on the floor, picked one and ripped open the lid. She stuck her hands inside, displacing a thousand Styrofoam peanuts, and pulled out a shiny device that looked like a tiny satellite dish, with its own built-in power supply and some digital gauges. She threw the switch and a gauge read, "Set Coordinates."

"That's a remote tracking device," Tucker said, startling her, standing right behind her back. "We can use it to find bursts of electrical energy in the jungle. Assuming there really is a tower."

She looked around at the hangar activity, moving around her like a fast carousel.

"You actually went out and bought all this stuff?" Her voice sounded small, more like Cornelia's than the Electric Girl's.

"I was a Boy Scout." Tucker shrugged. "Be prepared."

"Prepared for what?"

Tucker suddenly turned his head and yelled, "Hey!" That made the people scurrying around the hangar freeze. "Give us ten minutes."

Tucker's team clogged the doorway leaving. She and Tucker were left alone with the provisions and the plane, and ghostly air that was suddenly too quiet.

He followed her as she paced, then suddenly moved close. She stepped back unconsciously and almost fell into a box until he grabbed her hands.

"Corny, remember at the bar when I told you I wasn't good at talking about my feelings?"

"Through a bit of a mist," she admitted.

"Well, I've had feelings about you . . ."

Uh oh. She heard the Electric Girl's metallic warning voice.

". . . but I didn't want to share them with you because I'm not big on losing."

"Losing what?"

"You."

"Me?"

He almost stammered, which disarmed her. "My hopes about you, I guess."

"Tucker, what *is* it?"

"Please. Sit down."

She perched tensely on the folding chair. He sat on a director's chair beside her and moved, squeaking on the floor, inches away. One of his knees lightly touched hers.

"I can only tell you that nothing in my whole life has mattered as much to me as what I'm going to ask you. If you say yes, you'll make me whole. If you say no, I'll be missing out on what I've always wanted for myself."

Leaning in toward her, he looked so earnest and sincere again. So far as she could tell.

"Maybe you'd better ask me," she said.

Tucker tapped a key on his laptop. The big video screen lit up with four words: "WILL YOU MARRY ME?"

Cornelia felt the bright letters burning up and down on the back of her eyes. Her bewilderment began as a numb feeling in her hair follicles and traveled down her nervous system all the way to her toes. She could think of nothing to say.

"What do you think?" he finally prodded.

She tried to overcome her numbness. It made a certain sense that they were sitting in an airplane hangar, given the sudden velocity of Tucker's proposal. But his words made no sense at all. She needed to organize and try to reflect on them.

"Um, I like the typeface," she allowed.

His forthright expression didn't change, but a tiny muscle in his forehead twitched.

"I mean about my proposal."

Could she be imagining this? No. She had slammed into an unseen wall of Tucker and been knocked down. That was all. She tried to return to terra firma.

"You're allergic to monkfish," she pointed out.

"Huh?"

"That's the most personal thing I know about you, Tucker, even though we've been going out to parties together for almost a year. Why do you want to get married all of a sudden?"

"Not all of a sudden, Corny. I've thought this through for a while." His eyes burned with apparent honesty again. "I guess I just never knew exactly the right time to ask you. Because of who you are," he added. "You're smart. You're beautiful. And you're a Lord."

"And what does that mean? That I'm a Lord?"

"It means that our lives are intertwined."

She thought that over. "Our lives or our fortunes?"

"Both." He held up his palms in a gesture of rationality. "Then there's the noblesse oblige part."

"Part of what?"

"Part of being a Lord," he intoned silently. "You have a duty."

"A duty?"

He lowered his head and pinched the top of his nose with his fingers, as though her question hurt his sinuses.

He said finally, "I thought your father would have told you, but I guess he wanted to spare you the worry."

"Told me what?"

"A third party, somebody who we deal with closely, is secretly buying up voting stock in the company. They're planning a hostile takeover."

"Who?"

"Han Koi."

She tried to remember all she had ever known about Han and his son, Han Koi, Jr., whom she had seen socially over the years. At her eighteenth birthday in Southampton, Han Senior had beamed at her and given her a gift. It was so ridiculous, a hot pink boombox, she had found it oddly touching. While Han Koi, Sr., was a gleefully rich merchant, his son reminded her of a not-terribly-nice otter. Sleek and well manicured in Savile Row suits, the younger Han had always seemed mildly contemptuous of her and even her father.

"What would he gain by taking over our company?" she asked.

"Prestige," said Tucker. "Lord & Company is one hundred years old with deep American roots and blue-chip clients."

"Tucker"—she remembered—"weren't you the one who talked Chester into becoming partners with Han Koi?"

"Yes, I was." He nodded, slightly sheepish but also irritated. "And at the time it was the right decision. They were big and hungry for a U.S. alliance. Times change. Now Han Koi is still hungry, but what he wants to eat is us. He's been buying up Lord & Company voting stock. Look."

Tucker tapped a flurry of buttons and Cornelia saw the columns of corporate names and stock lots marching down the big video screen.

"That's the voting stock that's not owned by you or Chester," Tucker explained grimly. "The Kois are using dummy corporations to buy it. They already own 20 percent."

She stared at the screen, like a traffic accident.

"Tucker, they're wasting their money. I own 25 percent of the voting stock. Between us, Chester and I own 51 percent, and that I believe is called a majority because nobody can outvote us. Isn't that true?"

"Technically. But the Kois have been . . . encouraged to think they could pull off a takeover anyway."

"My father encouraged them?"

"Of course not. Chester's a proud man. He's not going to lose the company it took your family a century to build."

She felt like screaming. Trying to pull information out of Tucker was like trying to pull something up from the earth's core. She grabbed his wrist and startled him.

"Then how could the Kois get enough voting stock, Tucker?"

Tucker held his breath and blew it out. His square face seemed to collapse, as though he had tried to keep something awful from her that now hovered over her head.

"Corny, I don't like to think how many times I've taken you off bartops, pulled you out of fountains, with some sleazy photographer around."

"I've seen the pictures. So?"

"So it's not weird the Kois think you're the weak link."

An awful feeling roiled in the pit of her stomach. To think she had acted so badly that business pirates would crank up the Jolly Roger and use her to try to steal her family's company. But how could they if she didn't help them?

"For God's sake, Tucker, I'm not selling my father out."

"I know that, you know that, and Chester knows that," Tucker told her solemnly. "But if the Kois decide to go public with a takeover attempt, they may not have to win you over for Lord & Company to lose."

She squeezed her fists together. "What do you mean?"

"Lord & Company lives by its reputation." Tucker averted his eyes. "The Kois can use all the news stories about you to make Chester look weak. You can figure out their spin yourself: 'He can't even control his own daughter, how can he run Lord & Company?'"

Yes. She could see that. The social vultures had already made up their minds about her. It didn't take much to imagine the same thing happening with the business vultures who hovered over Wall Street.

She sighed miserably. "And that's why you're asking me to marry you now. You want to circle the wagons."

He smiled approvingly, a teacher with a bright pupil. "We'd beat the Kois to the media. A big wedding. News stories like, 'Deb's Crazy Days Are Over' . . . or whatever. But the point is, they'd see us as a united family. They'd have to pull back."

"Why can't you just issue a press release?"

"Corny." Tucker shook his handsome head. "Talk is cheap. Look, I know I've been wrapped up with Lord & Company. It's taken a lot out of me, your father . . ." He waved his hand and let it go. "So what do you think?"

"I think this is a dream," she said. *And not a good one.* She shivered, from the cold inside the hangar and the enormity of what she had to decide.

Tucker Fisk?

She tried to turn him into a personal ad in the back of *New York* magazine. It could read, *"Mogul, 28, full of himself, seeks boss's daughter/heiress for self-interest."* Or she might be taking a simplistic view of him, exactly what she hated about others who judged her behavior. To be fair about it, the ad could just as easily have said, *"Mogul, 28, with intelligence, ambition, and firm grasp on reality seeks flightier partner for fun and profit."* At this moment he appeared humbled, as much as someone like Tucker could be, by what seemed a very real desire to marry her. And there was the trip to South America.

His gift of the Tesla adventure could just be Tucker's version of a young man who hides an engagement ring in a Dunkin' Donut to give his girlfriend, to let her squeal with surprise if she doesn't chip her tooth. In fact, his gesture could be viewed as even more touching. Totally un-Tucker-like. He had done considerable homework about something that mattered to her. Could the Tucker she'd known, that enigma in an Armani suit, turn so easily into this bashful puppy?

Hard to tell. But the Koi takeover attempt, that looked real as acid rain.

She saw a sad, bedraggled image of her father. Sitting at home in his study with disheveled copies of the *Wall Street Journal* and *Barron's* strewn over the floor. Rummaging through snipped articles about the Kois' brutal takeover of Lord & Company, still in a bathrobe and unshaven at cocktail hour, then walking out on the terrace and gazing down over the edge of the balcony.

Enough. This had all been her fault. Not only hadn't she tried harder to reach her father, but she had publicly become a crazed media Ophelia.

"Tucker, why didn't my father just ask for my help?"

He shrugged. "He didn't want to make you feel guilty."

She wiped absently at her eyes with the sleeve of her black sweater. "Okay. I'll cancel my flight."

"I knew you'd say yes."

Tucker moved toward her and she reflexively pushed him away.

"But why do we have to get married? Can't we just get engaged? We'll *look* like we're going to get married and convince old Han Koi."

He seemed crestfallen. "Do you hate me, Corny?" His brow crunched up and the overbite of his large front teeth gnawed at his lower lip while he waited for her answer.

"Of course I don't hate you."

"There's a concept called 'propinquity.'" He seemed proud to have pulled that out of a long-forgotten prep school education, although he mispronounced the word. "If you spend enough time with a person and you don't hate him, you start to like him."

"I think the concept you're referring to is called 'arranged marriage.'"

He smirked. "Don't knock it, it's kept a lot of families together. Look at the Medicis."

"We're not Italian, and I'm not going to carry on traditions that were dead before I was born. Tucker, you don't have a . . ."

"A what?" He waited patiently.

"You don't have a corona," she blurted out.

That befuddled him. "You smoke cigars?"

She felt boxed in, tiny as she was in this vast space almost the size of the Tesla Museum.

What if she just agreed to the engagement? She could always change her mind, after she helped Chester and he no longer felt threatened over losing his business. And he would be so grateful to her, surely this could be the beginning of a thaw in the awful, icy tundra between them.

"Corny," Tucker said. "The way I see it, you've got two choices. You can do what you say you're going to do with my help. Or you can stay locked up in a bedroom at home, sneak out at night, and waste your life. I've got information, the equipment, and the resources and we can stay on top of the situation with the Kois while we're gone. You decide. Either way, I'm keeping all the gear for South America right here in this hangar."

She searched the emptiness around his head again.

An image of Kevin Doyle, and his glorious, sky-blue corona, suddenly popped into her head. She realized that an image of the real Kevin Doyle, not her dreamy fantasy of Tesla, had crept in as her standard for judging the corona of others.

No, she couldn't marry Tucker.

She didn't even know him. And she didn't trust him, at least not yet. But if she *pretended* to agree, at least she could buy time. She would be on her best behavior, and make the Kois believe that the Lords stood together indivisible.

"Tucker, do you swear this is all true?"

"I swear on my mother's life."

She flinched. Could anyone possibly lie about that?

"How long will it take to beat the Kois?"

"Hard to say," he said. "They'll keep buying up shares. When we announce our engagement, that should make them think hard about it. If we get married on Valentine's Day, right before the company's board meeting in Palm Beach, that ought to lock them out for good."

"All right," she told Tucker. "I accept."

She let him give her a hug of beefy but rather soft muscles in fine-suit fabric and noted an ion or two of cologne.

"I knew you'd make the right decision, Corny."

Relieved, she thought. That's how Tucker sounded. Not charged up emotionally or even sexually. But definitely relieved. His hand went into his jacket pocket and a dazzling starburst appeared in her face. It almost blinded her.

Tucker held out her mother's diamond engagement ring. She stared at the sparkling stone in its antique setting, remembered turning her mother's finger to study all the facets of the glorious kaleidoscope of a ring.

"My father gave you that?" How he must trust Tucker, she thought with another sudden wave of melancholy. "I want to talk to Chester about this."

"Sure." He stiffened slightly. "But if you're only doing this for him, don't let him know, okay? Your father's kind of fragile now. I don't think he could handle that on top of everything else."

She noticed that Tucker's face had quickly rearranged itself from the dark, somber hollows of concern to its usual bright and fleshy confidence. "We can announce our engagement at the Lord & Company Christmas party. A lot of people are going to be very happy about this."

"I know," she thought out loud. "I just hope I'll be one of them."

Chapter Eleven

This time, she was a painting of physical beauty. He wondered if she still had underneath what he'd seen before, that moral beauty that Giotto painted.

Kevin watched her walk off the elevator all dazzle and fluid motion, her amazing legs scissoring in high heels with a vital purpose—snip, snip, snip, right toward him. Her straw-colored hair now seemed to flame like a torch, and her clinging dress threw off kinetic energy that hit him from forty feet away. She still wore black, but this time a velvet party dress wrapped artfully to reveal the moves of her body. Her matching velvet coat wouldn't keep a kitten warm. It was the kind of winter outfit that said, "I have a limousine and don't have to worry about getting cold and wet."

She had Tucker Fisk's arm.

Tucker smiled, showing her off. *See my butterfly? Isn't she beautiful?*

Kevin forced the same smile he hoisted up for any other resident. Then he held the door for them.

As soon as she saw Kevin, her eyes fixed at the top of his head. A violet constellation twinkled in her eyes where he had once seen a dingy haze. No more meds. But she looked bittersweet somehow, which made him wonder. When she glided past him, he also saw changes in the hair-and-makeup department. Her hair looked cut by an expert, one strand at a time, and diamond earrings shaped like lightning bolts flashed at her ears. Cosmetics covered a few freckles he had seen across her nose, making her more woman than girl. And her skin tone had blossomed somehow, even under the blush she wore, to a healthy peach-glow.

She looked like, although he hated to use the word, class.

Tucker propelled her out the door, his hair slicked straight back for the evening. Then he stopped suddenly and Cornelia with him. Tucker took a long look at Kevin, finally recognizing him behind the uniform.

"The other night," Tucker asked him, "how do you suppose that photographer knew to hide out in the alley?"

Kevin felt calm even while his sphincter tightened, ready—maybe even eager—to face off with Cornelia Lord's boyfriend. Then he saw, in slashes of red across Cornelia Lord's cheeks and the tips of her ears, her shame over Tucker's accusation. In that perturbed face, Kevin recognized the escapee he'd helped. The perfect deb with her diamond earrings could push his bitch-buttons. The escapee underneath was a lost soul.

To notch back his anger at Tucker Fisk, he looked blankly at a spot over his nose.

"I don't know," Kevin said. "I suppose he thought he was doing his job."

"Well," Tucker flung another spiked glove, "I wonder if you were doing yours."

Now Kevin couldn't help but look Tucker in the eye.

"Tucker!" Cornelia spoke sharply.

Kevin saw Cornelia's gray eyes fill with tiny points of anger.

"If he can't take the heat . . ." Tucker shrugged and left it hanging in the air, grinning at him.

"It's not the heat," Kevin said. "It's the humility."

He picked a large black umbrella out of the stand and held it up so the sharp tip passed not too far from Tucker's nose. Casually, he held the door open.

"After you," Kevin told Cornelia evenly.

The wind almost knocked them down with the winter's first

snowfall, a heavy one. Tucker led her out the door and Kevin popped the big umbrella open to protect them while he walked behind. The flakes pelted him, dripping down his forehead, as he walked what was only a few yards but seemed like a football field from the front door of 840 Fifth Avenue to the back door of their waiting limousine.

"So," Kevin said, with no particular emotion, "you both have a nice evening."

"Thank you, Kevin." She gave him a guilty smile. More than that. Maybe a conspiratorial smile.

"You look hot—uh, nice, Ms. Lord," Mike their chauffeur blurted as he held the car door for her.

She smiled and folded her slender legs to slip into the back seat.

Kevin watched Cornelia and Tucker take off in the cheesy little limousine. The queen of mixed signals, this one. He wondered what condition she'd be in the next time they met.

It wouldn't do to seethe at Tucker with all they had to do tonight.

Cornelia worked to establish a tone of peace and harmony when they popped out of the limousine at Koi Tower. She stood transfixed by the white dazzle of the snowfall.

"It's so beautiful," she breathed.

"It's beautiful on ski slopes and Christmas cards," Tucker said. "In Manhattan, it's just a problem. Everything gets fouled up and takes three times as long."

What a pill he could be. But she let Tucker take her arm and escort her through the crooked portals of Koi Tower. Her high heels clicked across the marble floor to the special elevator guarded by a big, alert Asian man in a blue blazer with a Lord & Company logo patch on the pocket.

While the elevator lifted them to the forty-second floor in one genteel whoosh, she braced herself to make the best of an evening, full of fake laughter and the empty calories of social chitchat. She could also count on much whispering behind her back.

She positioned her mouth in a half-smile. She could wear this expression almost indefinitely, unlike the full *Town & Country* jawbreaker smile that bared all your teeth and gums almost from ear to ear and could wear out facial muscles in a matter of minutes.

"I think you should let me do most of the talking," Tucker said. "These people are vicious."

"Are they?" She made a little O with her mouth, on purpose this time.

He glanced at her. "And I invited the Kois."

"Will they come?"

"I'm sure of it. When we make our announcement, don't be surprised if they're poker-faced. They're good at that."

She paused. "How can you be so sure they'll show up?"

His smile cracked a little. "I just know these things."

"I'll keep that in mind."

He said nothing more until the elevator door opened.

The blast of noise and heat from the party was like an open furnace. Tucker kept a restraining grip on her arm, as if the Electric Girl might escape. But tonight she had agreed to be demure and deliver her engagement lines.

The executive offices of Lord & Company occupied this entire floor of Koi Tower. Floor-to-ceiling glass exposed a full 360-degree sweep of Midtown Manhattan, wrapping glitter around the party guests.

Cornelia hadn't seen the office since she had come to visit her father a year ago. Tonight, the Macho Renaissance of Tucker's interior design amused her all over again, and she had to giggle.

A postmodern entryway had been designed so it seemed to crumble in front of them, creating a giant hole. The floor at first looked like tarpaper, but on closer inspection turned out to be expensive distressed marble. It looked like someone had poured battery acid over it.

The serpentine video wall that Tucker had installed dominated the center of the entire executive floor. It blinked and beeped more like some consumer electronics show exhibit than the hallowed halls of a once-stuffy investment banking firm.

"There's the Winking Wall," she said to annoy him.

The S-shaped granite monolith with holes punched out for television monitors was programmed to scan stock markets across the globe. Tonight, only the Hong Kong and Tokyo exchanges ground out numbers. Other monitors glowed with the TV-Web sites of Lord & Company clients. One screen showed a black-and-white Christmas film, Jimmy Stewart shaking hands with an evil old man, then looking down at his hand as though it had been coated with slime.

She saw a videographer with a ponytail point his camera at party-goers, throwing their manically festive images onto screens of the Winking Wall as well.

She remembered well that last visit to the office, the day the Asian stock markets took a whale-sized dive and sent waves of clammy fear through Lord & Company. Then the granite monolith had looked more like the Wailing Wall, with the fortunes of Lord & Company tied to the Kois. But now the video images blinked almost reverently.

"This floor is definitely a look," she told Tucker evenly, determined to be nice.

"We have to make our people comfortable." He shrugged modestly.

"Hmmm." She didn't argue, but knew that except for a few top slice-and-dicers, the real employees of Lord & Company worked in cramped cubicles downstairs on the forty-first floor.

This floor, Cornelia suspected, was really designed to dazzle visitors with Tucker's need to buy and then discard things that lit up and beeped. He boasted spending millions each year to install new techno-glitz to impress new clients, companies with names like CyberSpend and Firewall Blasters. He spoke of his gift for landing twenty-three-year-old tech-sector geniuses who drank Surge and did interviews for *Wired*, seeming to make up their own language as they went along.

"You have to understand these guys I do business with," Tucker whispered, and it jolted her that he could have read her thoughts. "They're idiot savants, but they've got the savant part down as much as the idiot part. And they've all got egos like football stars." Tucker shook his head. "I get dates for these geeks, take them to Knicks games, that kind of stuff."

So Tucker did understand some people's needs. In the waves of party guests, she saw several of the boy businessmen he talked about with big-framed glasses and funny bowl haircuts. A whole regiment of pouty, giggling models had been hired to fling themselves into the party throng like confetti.

Tucker had brought new life to the somber, if not quite sober, atmosphere that prevailed at Lord & Company when Granddad and Chester ran the show.

A blond girl, about seventeen, in a tuxedo jacket longer than her skirt and black plastic helmet, careened toward them on Rollerblades. She skidded to a stop half an inch from Tucker's toe.

"Champagne?" the teenager asked, holding out a server tray of flute glasses. Tucker took one, but she did not.

"Merry Christmas." Cornelia flicked Tucker's glass with her fingernail and made it chime.

"Merry Christmas, Corny," he said.

She noted a U-shaped bar where young men and women as generically good-looking as daytime TV actors poured drinks furiously. Beyond the bar, a magnificent Christmas tree stood in the epicenter of the room. Tiny electrical candles with glass flames lit the bristly, perfect branches of the tree, this Scotch pine almost too perfect to be bred in nature. Out of habit, the Electric Girl followed the tangled cords from the tree lights to their energy source. A heavy-duty orange electrical outlet on the floor bristled with wires, like a porcupine.

Cornelia removed her gloves, and the diamond of her mother's ring caught the light, reflecting it like a laser show.

As she and Tucker crossed the floor, she felt a giddy rush. Their entrance reverberated, sending ripples. Ice stopped tinkling in glasses. Guests halted in mid-sentence.

The first to clap his hands was Chester Lord, twice.

Then the applause began softly and grew.

She thought the applause was for Tucker, and started clapping. He quickly seized her wrist. And then she looked into the faces of the crowd, lighting on a jowly banker, a hungry socialite, a happy young client whose lip vibrated like a rabbit. It shocked her to her shoes to realize that they were applauding her.

It was the first time she had been applauded for anything since her coming-out party at the St. Regis, before she vanished from that rite of passage and caused a bit of a stink.

But this was a spontaneous and raucous ovation, spiked with cheers and whistles, a symphony of approval. It filled her with the instant happiness she once felt as a child at Christmastime.

But it was even more. She hadn't enjoyed a moment when she felt so overwhelmingly welcome since her mother died.

Her hand squeezed Tucker's. Bathed in the applause, he looked as vainglorious as a cartoon hero, almost shaped like a cone with his big shoulders tapering all the way down in a sleek black suit to Italian shoes like bedroom slippers.

She let him lead her, slipping through the crowd as easily as an eel sliding through oil. She didn't have to say much, other than "Hello" and "It's good to see you."

"I've known you since you were this high," a face in a pin-striped suit with thick white hair said, holding his palm at waist level. She didn't recognize him.

"You look gorgeous, Cornelia," said an older woman in a dress shaped like a trumpet.

"Thank you." She lowered her voice. "Tucker, who are these people?"

"The guy was nobody, the woman was somebody's wife," Tucker muttered back.

"Aren't the photographers horrid?" another woman hissed on her behalf. From her rather feral eyes, she recognized Elsa Innsbruck, a fashion magazine editor.

"She rounded up the models," Tucker explained.

Cornelia smiled and said nothing. She thought of the photographer with the resurrected coat, Philip Grace. She didn't consider him horrid, just a nuisance. Many so-called respectable people, like Dr. Bushberg, were worse predators but seemed to sneak in under everyone's radar.

Tucker gently guided her toward the center of the room where Chester stood. Passing the Christmas tree, she noticed that the sparkling ornaments were miniature versions of the Kois' products.

And then the Kois appeared in front of Chester.

She worked hard to smile, repressing her disgust at their monstrous toadish forms. That's how they looked to her now, knowing their perfidy. For the first time she noted that Koi *père et fils* shared stout, ungraceful bodies. But also the same clever tailor, who draped them in tuxedos made of a midnight-blue fabric so fine and exotic it could have been flown in from another planet. Both had full heads of hair, Senior's white and Junior's jet-black.

Han Senior bobbed his head.

"Little Corny, all grown up. Full of spirit."

"Yes. We always read about you in the papers," Han Junior said with a tight smile, silky and rude.

Then they were past the Kois and Chester stood before her with his arms held open. His eyes were moist and he gently took both her hands in his, protectively squeezing her fingers.

"Hi, Daddy," Cornelia said.

She took him off guard, realizing that she hadn't called him that in years.

"You look lovely," he blurted out, obviously shocked.

Chester impetuously slipped one arm over her shoulders and his other up and around Tucker's, having to stand almost on tiptoe to reach around Tucker's neck. Awkward in his impulse, Chester drew them both close to him, hugged her tightly with stiff muscles, then let them go. His sweet attention lingered with her, even as he turned back to perform his host duties.

She snuck a quick look at the Kois when they thought her back was turned, to catch them with evidence of fraud across their faces. But old Han merely smiled at some guest in the same half-frozen way she did herself. She stared and Han caught her furtive look. He lifted his glass to toast her. Mocking her, she supposed. She studied the corona that wrapped around the head of Han Senior. It was neutral in color, like the airy vapors that drift over asphalt on a blistering-hot day.

Han Junior didn't notice her spying on him. He talked to a model about Cornelia's age with biggish hair. Her sleazy dress exposed cutouts of flesh. She looked awfully obvious for this crowd.

"A sidewalk Cinderella," Tucker whispered to her. "I hired her to keep an eye on the Kois."

She focused herself to make out the corona of Han Junior. It was half-formed—faint but already noxious, with a rusty cast. She could only think of it as a starter corona, taking shape like a twelve-year-old boy's patchy mustache. She shut her eyes and shook her head, to rid herself of the image.

She wondered. Tucker had told her that Old Han kept his middle-aged son on a short leash. How did Chester manage to talk to old Han Koi? He was probably dying to lunge for the old pirate's neck and throttle his turkey wattles.

She made a particular effort to analyze Chester's corona this evening. It had grown so weak lately as to be almost undetectable. Tonight the haze had brightened, a wisp of hopeful light still trimmed with its old outline of sputtering sadness.

His energy's almost gone, she heard the Electric Girl whisper. *Look at how his corona fades.*

She gradually lost her thrill at being a star of the evening. Chester seemed so vulnerable here, surrounded by people of more vitality and less principle. His tenderness touched her in ways recalled from her childhood. She couldn't throw off his sense of fuzzy weakness.

Now she turned her corona analysis to the enigmatic Tucker. She studied the outline of his hair as he threw his head back and laughed at some guest's remark. She could still find no trace of a corona. Not even a dewdrop of light around his powerful head.

Tucker. Early that day, he had actually handed her a page of triple-spaced text telling her what to say when she stood in the spotlight and announced their engagement. It was the sort of large-type, simple-minded creation a political handler would give a not-too-bright candidate.

She had torn up his page while he watched, horrified. Then, for good measure, she yelled "Wheeee!" with a crazed look and threw the little pieces up over his head. As the white confetti of his script fell on his hair and shoulders, she told him sharply that she would manage to put together a few words that wouldn't embarrass him.

Her mantra for the evening, *no drinking, no Tesla,* thumped like a drum in her head.

She weaved through the throng, chatting with guests. She finished sipping her third mineral water. Applause, or not, social chatter was still thirsty work.

"I'm going to the bathroom," she whispered to Tucker, in a huddle with other tycoons.

He nodded, seeming comfortable with letting her go off by herself.

Cornelia smiled her way through the crowd and wound up out in the foyer. Typically, there was a line in front of the women's bathroom and not the men's. In her Electric Girl mode, she might have just slipped in and used the men's room for efficiency. But tonight she felt her duty to be demure.

Instead of waiting in line, she darted down the spiral staircase to the working floor of Lord & Company to use one of their bathrooms.

On this floor, the windows were obscured by a lab-rat maze of small cubicles where the scut work of Lord & Company was performed. Here she imagined a lot of people in short hair and starched shirts plowing through information like pieceworkers in a sweatshop, wearing splints on their arms to avoid carpal tunnel syndrome. The working floor seemed deserted this evening as she walked toward the bathrooms. She marveled at the sterility of the workstations. The employees' only revolt over the corporate blandness seemed to be pinning up Dilbert cartoons and their childrens' artwork. A few chirps of brittle laughter came from a distance.

She walked through a narrow corridor that separated the cubicles from outer offices with doors. Even the real offices had glass walls so the occupants could be closely watched.

As she passed a glass wall, she glimpsed something familiar. This office had been turned into a storeroom full of boxes.

They were the same boxes she had seen in the airport hangar.

Behind them, she saw the big video screen that Tucker had used. All the supplies she had seen in the airport hangar seemed to be here now. She peered in to squint at a sign somebody had scrawled with a Magic Marker, "RETURN TO STORES BEFORE DEC. 30."

A warning noise rustled in her head, like a sheet of aluminum being shaken.

She made her way down the cubicles until she found life. Two men and a woman in their twenties sat drinking New York State champagne in plastic cups, and talking office politics. They had deep bags under their eyes and all wore their hair cropped short. The men had their sleeves rolled up and ties askew.

"Aren't you Cornelia Lord?" The woman stared at her diamond as though it were the Star of India. "Is that an engagement ring?"

"Not yet," Cornelia told her. "So how are you?"

"Great. It's been a killer quarter," the first young man told her.

She nodded appreciatively. "What's all that stuff in the empty office? The maps and boxes?"

"Some presentation for a client, all sorts of travel gear," the woman told her, wagging her head over a fool's errand. "But I guess it didn't work. We have to take it all back to the stores."

"Yeah," the second young man spoke up. "I told Tucker we'd return all this stuff to Safari Outfitters for a refund right after Christmas."

"How nice," she said. "Do you happen to remember a picture of an old man?" she asked. "A South American?"

"He wasn't South American." The young woman rolled her eyes. "I pulled it off the Web myself. I had two hours to find a shot of a guy who looked like a Brazilian over eighty years old. I downloaded it from a Seniors Without Partners site."

The Electric Girl's head rattled again, more vehemently. *I told you so,* she heard the metallic voice in her head say.

"So who was this presentation for?"

"I dunno," the first young man sighed. "We're kind of low on the food chain down here. Tucker Fisk's team ran the thing. We just did what we were told."

The Electric Girl felt a distinct snap somewhere in her head. The clean-cut trio in front of her looked suddenly terrified.

"Ms. Lord, are you okay? Can we get you some water?"

"Maybe just a sip of that champagne," she told them. She grabbed an unopened bottle off the desk and popped the cork expertly. It shot into the cubicle ricocheting off a wall as the young executives ducked. She took a long, sloppy drink, the lusty fizz tickling her throat and running down her chin.

She collected her thoughts as she drank, trying to sort out what to do next. She didn't stop until the bottle was almost empty.

In the downstairs bathroom mirror, when she finally got to it, she noticed that her hair stood on end, frizzing. Her eyes flashed now, Cornelia's soft gray taken over by the Electric Girl's fuses.

When the Electric Girl marched back up the spiral staircase to the executive floor, the party guests made way for her. This time, she saw no admiration.

She approached the center of the party where Tucker stood very close to the Kois. Chester was a few feet behind them talking with a group, playing host.

"Chester . . ." Tucker warned. Slowly, Chester slipped into confusion, then alarm.

"Corny," Tucker stepped toward her with a look of abused innocence. "What's the trouble?"

She searched Chester's face for a strong word, an act of protection. But Chester looked too weak to defend her.

She squinted at the Kois with one eye the way a drunk person drives, because she could clearly see the formation of something she had never seen before. It was a slimy corona that actually moved. It writhed like a spitting swamp creature, slithering a few feet to encircle Tucker's right arm. The ugly current wrapped around Tucker's own like a fuzzy brown snake.

She struggled backward now, losing her balance, trying to connect with her father's eyes.

"Chester," she yelled, but her voice felt so tight and strangled it came out as a puny squeak. She remembered nights when she would scream for her father and he wouldn't hear her. She wiggled free from Tucker as he reached for her arm. Her father approached now, brow lowered, foggy and uncertain again.

"Daddy!" she wailed out loud.

Then Tucker plowed toward her, pushing his way in front of her father. She swerved away from him, maneuvering through the sea of dumbstruck faces. He followed her.

"Cornelia, maybe you should freshen up a little," he called to her in a reasonable voice.

"It's bad enough you lie to me," she yelled over her shoulder. "But taking advantage of Chester? You ungrateful shit."

Tucker shoved through the crowd and grabbed her waist from behind with both his arms. She slipped around in his grasp to face him.

"Hey, c'mon." Tucker actually smiled at her. "What seems to be the trouble?"

She looked for her father, but Tucker held both her arms in check, his big frame blotting out the crowd. The buzzing of the party guests sounded like a dentist's drill.

"I went downstairs and found South America."

"What?"

"You said you'd keep your team working. Why are you returning all the supplies?"

His eyes didn't even flicker. Tucker was an All-Star deceiver. "That stuff from the airport? That was just a demonstration."

"A demonstration?"

"Sure," he spoke earnestly. "We'll get brand-new equipment before we go. I was just dramatizing things for you. I wanted to show you what you'd be missing."

"I believe what I was missing," she said, "was how close you are to the Kois. You made them Lord & Company's partners. You got them here tonight and I saw a . . . connection between you I'd never noticed before."

"You think I'm helping old Han Koi?" He stared at her with eyes as impenetrable as mirrored contact lenses. "That's just crazy."

She summoned the full force of her energy. With a great tug of her wrists, the Electric Girl broke away from Tucker's grip and shoved through guests until she reached the U-shaped bar.

A blow-dried bartender looked her over. "Can I get you some coffee?"

"Never mind." *The Electric Girl works alone.*

She kicked off her shoes, and used both arms for leverage to climb up on the bartop. Thank goodness the dress was short. She worked her knees up on the bartop, then stood up straight. Her toes began to move very slightly on the polished surface of the bar, as though she stood on the bar of Lizards & Ladies, wanting to dance. She made up a little rhythm in her head to help her decide exactly what to say. People turned and gaped. For the second time that evening, conversation dribbled off.

She pulled out her neatly typed announcement, now moist and crumpled in her hand, and waved it in the air.

"Chester," she shouted. "You know Tucker Fisk asked me to marry him."

Tucker, heading through the crowd toward the bar, with the afterglow of the horrid brown corona still circling his arms, suddenly stopped. How peculiar. He should be bullying his way through the crowd to stop her. But he hung back, watching as though he didn't want to stop her at all. He stood there with almost a challenge on his face. *We're all waiting, Corny.*

The Electric Girl struggled to keep her balance as the room veered off in wicked angles.

The videographer had turned his camera on her. It was hooked up to the Winking Wall, and now every screen showed her picture. The Electric Girl made a fearsome sight, her kinetic hair and eyes burning like glowholes.

"But I think it's going to get a little crowded on our honeymoon, Chester," she shouted. "Because I do believe Tucker's already in bed with the Kois."

Chester looked apoplectic as he pushed toward her.

"Get her down," Tucker called out to the bartender.

Now the guests pointed at her like a bearded lady in a carnival. She looked far off at old Han Koi, who smiled into his cocktail glass as though laughing off her false charges.

Chester's face had turned a blotchy raspberry-and-cream. Why had Chester trusted Tucker so? He had given her his mother's ring. Chester clung to Tucker the way a fearful sailor lashes himself to a mast in a violent sea.

She closed her eyes, thought about telling Chester exactly how she saw Tucker and Han Koi in their unsavory alliance. She could imagine his bewildered words, "You saw a *corona?*" Then he would call Dr. Bushberg. This time they might even send her to a place where she would be hopelessly confined.

She jumped down from the bar, grabbed her shoes, and ran.

A man stood in front of her, grasping to stop her. She hopped from foot to foot to confuse him, then sprinted through the postmodern crumbling foyer to the elevator. She jabbed the elevator button and the door opened for her. Once inside the car, she jumped up and down to fool the elevator sensors into closing the doors.

Tucker appeared at the door to the car. But the elevator closed in his face and the Electric Girl was alone.

When the doors opened with a chime, the unsmiling Asian security man in the corporate blazer beckoned her with his finger. His face looked like an angry fist, as though he took great enjoyment in hurting people and had the skills to do it.

"C'mon," he said. "Everything's okay."

She put her head down and charged the man's stomach like a bull. His belly had gone soft, and when she rammed it she felt a squishy movement of organs shifting.

He lost his breath in one long whoosh like the elevator and fell backward onto the floor, landing on his well-padded rump. He sat looking confused, legs stretched out like a Raggedy Andy.

She ran for the lobby's side door, which opened to the crosstown street. She turned the bolt lock and pushed the door open. It flew back with a gust of horizontal snow.

The snowflakes had turned into a blizzard.

She slipped on her shoes with the spiky heels, bent forward, and ran out into the storm, leaving little black holes like deb tracks in the snow.

Chapter Twelve

She made it halfway up the first block, crunching and sliding in the snow, before she realized she had left her coat behind.

Well, it wouldn't matter much now. Her shoes buckled in the lumpiness of the sidewalk. The snow she had admired a few hours earlier now threw chips of white against her face, pricking her before they melted.

She felt unsteady from the liquor. Even though the sidewalk was perfectly level, she leaned forward to plow ahead as though she were fumbling uphill. And she felt horribly cold, wearing only the short velvet dress with a deep décolletage and no back. The plunging neckline that exposed the hollow of her breasts so glamorously when glamour had been the goal now bared her flesh cruelly to the elements. Nothing had worked as planned. Tucker had lied. Something loathsome linked him to old Han Koi.

And her father would never listen to his crazy daughter if she tried to warn him.

Her ankles twisted sideways until she was running on the side of each flimsy shoe. She would like to stop and take the shoes off, knock off the heels and go on with flats. But she knew that if she stopped moving ahead, she would lose her balance and fall. Maybe to freeze and die here, to end up an Old Electric Woman who once had a mission in life but was now cast out to drift away on an ice floe. She plunged on. Through the sleet, she could make out Fifth Avenue and the distant shape of the Plaza Hotel. A right on Fifth Avenue, six long blocks, and she'd be home.

But where exactly *was* home, now that Tucker seemed to have snuck in and gained control over her life?

Chester looked angrier than Tucker had ever seen him, stumbling out in the snow and snapping his arm away from Mike the driver, who tried to steady him.

"I hope you have a plan B," Chester growled at Tucker between his teeth.

You just saw Plan B, Tucker felt like saying.

Tucker thrust his hands into his jacket pockets against the cold. It took truckloads of self-control to bear the awesome weight of managing Chester's company, Chester's indecision, Chester's regrets, and now Chester's daughter. He used that discipline to force his mind into hyper-diplomacy before responding.

"Chester, we can't both leave the party. Go back and I'll find her."

"Damn the party," Chester yelled at him. "I'm going to find Cornelia."

Chester climbed into the back seat of his Panda limousine and slammed the tinny door. "Drive up Madison," he told Mike. "Come back down Fifth from 67th to see if she's headed home."

Tucker watched the car crunch away in the slush, fishtailing. As usual, Chester blamed him for Corny's behavior. It made him feel, just for a second, hot indignation even with the cold and sleet against his face. To Chester, it would look as though he had fumbled the ball, and Cornelia had sent him sprawling in the mud.

Funny, he thought, how he could get his pride hurt even when he was the one who had just passed the forty-yard line with the ball.

All Cornelia had done was make the game more interesting. Now Chester would be forced to send her away for treatment. Confinement. Isolation. Treatment by a psychiatric staff. Tucker knew only one thing about doctors, they loved money. But with the insurance companies putting the screws to them, a lot of doctors weren't raking it off the table the way they used to. He knew that he could find a psychiatrist he could persuade to see things his way, once he found out who the players were.

Tucker blocked a stooped-over businessman slogging toward him, throwing the older man off balance and propping him up just before he fell.

"Did a blond girl with no coat go by you?" Tucker shouted into his face.

"I remember her." The man's teeth chattered. "I think she called me a 'fucker.' "

No, that would be me, Tucker thought, releasing the man to slide on the ice. There weren't any cabs and she didn't have much of a head start. So he plunged ahead, jogging into the blizzard. By the end of the block, he could make out a shape some distance ahead, frail and unsteady. She would be going home. She had no money, no other place to go.

But this time it would be a short stay. He would get Chester to pack her off in a matter of days.

Who could argue against that now?

Roni Dubrov wore a uniform for her job, and it made her look like an old English chimney sweep from Oliver Twist's time.

She always dressed in a long black wool coat with peaked lapels, her long, curly black hair spilling over the shoulders. In her black top hat, her height exceeded six and a half feet and awed the tourists on Fifth Avenue. Now her hat and the shoulders of her jacket were dusted in a coat of white, piling up steadily even as the wet snow evaporated.

Roni worked seventy hours a week as a horse-carriage driver. She squired tourists through Central Park in one of the few hansom cabs that offered the cover of a landau roof. Her carriage had been constructed back in 1903 when craftsmanship mattered. White lacquer and red-leather seats made it the showiest of the numerous carriages that usually lined Grand Army Plaza, where Fifth Avenue met Central Park South and haughty old buildings like the Bergdorf Goodman store and the Sherry Netherland Hotel still reigned.

Most impressive of all, the famous Plaza Hotel looked as grand to Roni as a European palace. Tourists dressed in baseball caps and running shoes flocked to get a look at this great hotel they'd all seen in movies. And the most romantic tourists took horse-drawn carriage rides through the park.

She had just driven two young couples, Plaza Hotel guests, for three hours from Central Park to Gramercy Park and back again. But then they got caught in the blizzard, and she had barely managed to bring them back to the Plaza through the slush and wind-driven snow. She neatened up the cab, getting ready to take her horse, Peggy, back to the stable. The only people left on the sidewalks were the ragtag homeless. She called them "scarecrows" because they wore tattered clothes and scared the hell out of the tourists, yelling in their faces demanding money.

Other hansom drivers went home when it snowed. Roni stayed on. At home, she had served as an officer with the Israeli army. She could abide discomfort. If she held her position in the snow, she could always expect some crazy couple to want to ride through the park cuddled together under the heavy wool blanket she kept in back. That's why Roni bought the hansom with the roof. She was maximizing her utilization of the cab, exactly as she'd learned studying management for a year at Technion University in Jerusalem.

Peggy wore blinders, because Roni believed that Peggy thought more like a car than a horse. With the blinders on, he would stay in one lane, stop for red lights, and stay exactly one car length behind other vehicles, as though he had studied the New York Motor Vehicle Code. True, Peggy revealed a mean streak now and then, and nipped Roni. But they got along. She gave him the name Peggy after a song by Little Peggy March called "I Will Follow Him," a private joke to cheer her up when she first moved to New York.

It was perhaps the loneliest city on earth for a single woman. With all the beautiful, successful women and so many gay men, it left a girl with few prospects.

"Home, Peggy," Roni ordered from her high driver's seat. The chestnut horse jerked gratefully and started from the curb, heading west toward his stable.

Then she saw a single, pitiful scarecrow staggering against the blizzard on Fifth Avenue. The shape of the stumbling creature got her attention. Usually when she tried to help scarecrows, they just screamed at her to go away. But this one looked different. She peered through the snow to see a young girl trying to run on the sides of her shoes, her legs buckling. She wore a short dress. And she had no coat. Oh, well.

"Cluck, cluck," she repeated. "Home, Peggy."

Then she saw the girl collapse on the sidewalk. She could die there. Roni heaved a brooding sigh because it would take time and make Peggy difficult. But during the holiday season especially, it wouldn't kill her to help.

"Peggy, whoa," she ordered.

Westward bound by habit, the horse turned toward her in disbelief.

"Whoa!" Roni told him sharply.

Peggy stopped with an irate snort. Roni stepped down from her driver's seat into the snow, and took long strides in her stovepipe pants. In the gutter of Fifth Avenue at 59th Street, the scarecrow was trying to pick herself up.

"Are you all right?" Roni shouted.

The scarecrow lifted her head, and Roni saw a frightened young woman who didn't belong on the street. The girl's delicate features and skin, now raw, looked well cared for.

"Upsy daisy," Roni said, scooping the girl up. Her ruined dress probably cost what Roni made in four months. "Where do you live?"

"I can't go home." The girl's light blue lips quivered. "They'll put me away."

With good reason, Roni thought. But maybe things weren't as they appeared. Perhaps her husband beat her and she was running away from him. The girl looked desperate enough.

"Do you want me to call the police?" she asked.

"Oh, no. Look, I'm sorry," the girl's white teeth clattered. Then she began crying, her skin slowly turning from red to a more disturbing blue.

"Listen to me," Roni barked in her army officer's voice, pitched sharp enough to startle arrogant young Israeli men. "I will drive you home and we'll see what's what. Where do you live?"

"Eight-forty Fifth, at 65th Street."

Roni knew the building, a very rich person's building. More than just rich. A classy building. A lost slip of a girl who lived in a magnificent building. Then she saw the diamond ring as big as a crab apple reflecting from a streetlight. She thought of other people who could find this girl, rob her of the gem without any shame at all, and leave her to freeze on the street.

She used her lean muscles to heft the girl, and carried her across the street. Lifting her into the back seat of her carriage, she bundled her up in the heavy plaid lap robe.

"I'm going to drive you home," she yelled, deciding to take Fifth Avenue against the traffic. She might get into trouble if a cop stopped her. But this was an emergency.

"Peggy, turn," she shouted. The horse balked at first, but Roni yanked the reins, a battle of wills.

Peggy started the wrong way up Fifth. Roni imagined how troubled Peggy would be to see the long stone wall of Central Park now on his left, when he knew it was supposed to be on his right. He would perform this senseless duty for her, but might pay her back with a nip delivered days later when she didn't expect it. When they returned to the stable, she would make amends and give Peggy a sugar treat as well as a hug around the strong muscles of his neck. He would deserve it.

Lifting his ears peevishly, Peggy worked up to a steady trot.

The Panda limousine spun out a few feet at the corner of 67th Street, heading downtown on Fifth.

"Slow down, Mike," Chester shouted, the glass partition muffling his voice. The Panda drove atrociously in snow, bucking from side to side like a covered wagon. Fifth Avenue seemed especially treacherous.

Chester stewed in misery. Thanks to him, Cornelia had broken down in a way he could not have believed possible. He tormented himself with her display of anger and, well, insanity. No other word described it. His little girl broke his heart as, clearly, he had broken hers.

His chest suddenly heaved with difficult breaths. An anxiety attack? No. His brain signaled a physical danger ahead.

Through the windshield covered with sticky white frosting, a black apparition came at them, something from another time. Chester pressed his face against the glass. A horse trotted toward them and, behind the horse, a crazy woman stood on the prow of a hansom carriage. Yes. A woman with curly hair that flew out from under a top hat. She steered the horse directly at them.

"Mike, for God's sake, watch out."

"Yes, sir." He slowed down. Then headlights lit up Chester's back window.

They veered over as a yellow taxi, driving much too fast, barreled past them.

Mike hunched over the wheel honking the horn. He flashed his brights, trying to warn the cab driver about the horse carriage. Then Chester saw the taxi's red taillights brighten, the driver obviously jamming on the brakes as the yellow cab lunged toward the horse.

Chester's heart banged in his rib cage as he saw the horse rear up, front legs windmilling, trapped in the taxi's headlights. The driver of the carriage seemed unable to control him.

The Panda limousine swayed. Chester tried to grip on to something, sliding across the rear seat as the car weaved on the ice. He saw the taxi barely miss the body of the carriage, but its steel, bull-bar bumper tore through both of the wooden wheels.

He heard the terrible shrieking of metal splintering wood. The tearing of the fragile wooden wheels sent kindling-sized pieces flying into the windshield of Chester's limousine.

They had sped past the accident now, Mike trying to brake in the slush, while Chester looked back to see the carriage tumble on its side, throwing up a massive wave of white like a snowplow. The driver's gangly black frame fell off into the snow and seemed to somersault, like a paratrooper landing.

As the carriage scraped along the ground spraying sparks in the haze of flying snow, Chester could make out a bundle of horse blanket rolling onto the street from the carriage.

"Shit," Mike yelled. He stuck his head out the window. Ahead, the taxi stopped and its driver threw open his door and ran back to the scene.

Chester grabbed at the car door, something awful overcoming him. The hansom driver struggled onto her feet and looked at her broken carriage. He focused, for a reason that he could not explain, on the odd bundle in the street that looked like an old Scottish plaid blanket, like one he used to share on the beach with Elizabeth and Cornelia, those comfortable old picnic blankets covered with sand and smelling faintly of tuna sandwiches. But this, he felt with a vile tug on his chest, was a very bad blanket indeed. He needed desperately to see what was inside it.

"Mike, go back."

As Mike obediently shifted into reverse and gunned the engine, the car began fishtailing.

"Oh, God, be careful." Chester stared out the rear window, transfixed at the bundle in the snow that now glowed in his limousine's backup lights.

Time slowed for Chester, unbearably so, as the bundle began kicking like a giant beanbag. His limousine was skidding backward toward it. Whoever struggled inside would be run over by his vehicle.

Then an arm stuck out of the blanket.

"Cornelia!" Chester yelled.

Chapter Thirteen

*K*evin held the big black umbrella to protect Mrs. Stern while he helped her out of the back seat of her Rolls.

The car smelled musty, a curvy black-over-burgundy sort of antique with cloth seats and bud vases. Mrs. Stern's chauffeur held the car door while Kevin gave the scowling matriarch his arm, so he could drag her up and out like a heavy sack of sable and diamonds. Her fingers were strong, a wrinkled condor's claw seizing his arm. He lifted her up onto the patch of sidewalk he'd swept free of snow, then escorted her toward the lobby, angling the umbrella to keep the blizzard from knocking her down.

He heard a horse snort, a car horn. Then brutal sounds of destruction, metal on wood, from Fifth Avenue. He gaped out through the snow. Taillights lit up a horse in red. It reared up before an old carriage lying on its side.

Then his eyes came to rest on a bundle lying on the street. His heart skipped as a woman's arm shot out, grasping to find purchase in the slush. He sensed that it would be Cornelia Lord. The flaky Cinderella had smashed her own pumpkin. Then he saw a limousine careen through the slush, ready to back up over her.

He shook off Mrs. Stern's claw and began running toward the body in Fifth Avenue. Hitting a patch of ice, he took a skipping dive on the curb, landing on the icy street scraping his hands. A face stuck out from the bundle only nine feet away, and it was Cornelia's tiny nose and straw-colored hair. The backup lights from the limousine sickeningly lit her face and the snow around her. She tried to pull herself out of the heavy blanket twisted around her and inch toward the curb.

"Stop," Kevin yelled at the limousine. He tried to stand up but couldn't, and began scuttling toward her on his knees in the slushy street.

Cornelia's eyes bulged like a trapped puppy's, terrified but unable to act.

He hauled his body up off his knees and lunged for her outstretched arm, felt the cold flesh of her fingers, pulled her forward. Her bare legs kicked back at the tangled blanket. But not fast enough. The limousine, out of control, plowed directly toward her. He could actually see the tread of the spinning tire that would crush the leg now flailing helplessly from the blanket.

Kevin's lungs exploded as he bent way forward, grasped the blanket that held her, and lunged backward.

He'd done it.

Not exactly a heroic save, Kevin thought, seeing her body lying in a jumble beside the car lumbering past, but it worked.

Then something cold and hard as a steel hammer whacked Kevin from behind. He heard the sound of slapping meat, and his ear and shoulder suddenly felt as detached from his body as if they'd moved to some other borough. He saw the limousine's side-mirror rip off on his shoulder and go flying over his head, landing in the snow. Blood roared and pounded in the artery in his neck.

His shoulder might have come off, too. He wasn't sure. He stayed on his knees, looking for his arm, and found it right where it belonged, but with pins and needles jabbing through. He saw Cornelia Lord wriggle out of the blanket. It dragged behind her like a bridal train as she ran toward him.

Everything seemed otherworldly now. The limousine swung away after sideswiping him, and plowed broadside into the street sign on the corner of 65th Street. When it hit, the center of the stretched-out sedan cracked on impact. He watched the limousine snap exactly in half against the pole, like a child's toy.

The front end of the limousine threw sparks and stopped first, with its hood jacked up and headlights turned up illuminating the snowflakes. The rear half kept running, like a detached nervous system. Then it dug into a mound of slush and stopped dead.

Kevin heard cursing, astonishing in its venom. He turned to watch the carriage driver yelling and banging on the front half of the limousine.

Cornelia Lord's fingers clutched at his sleeve. She was trying to help him. Her velvet dress looked grubby like a refugee's, her pantyhose torn on her legs. She cried as she touched him, her hands frozen and her lips open and fearful. But not for her, for him. Kevin struggled up and they helped each other to the sidewalk. He tasted his own blood. She seemed to move well, not limping.

He wondered if she would walk inside and leave him bleeding.

He saw Philip Grace and, in the totally irrational way of accident victims, focused on the reporter's new coat of pewter leather. It zipped across his mind that Cornelia Lord had bought it for him, in an indirect way. Philip led three other stalkarazzi on a charge toward them. Camera lights went pop, pop, pop. Flashes and floating blobs filled his eyes from the white explosions.

"You guys okay?" he heard Philip shout.

Kevin squeezed Cornelia's hand tightly and led her toward the front door. They held each other up, panting. Philip and the stalkarazzi followed. Now under the awning of 840 Fifth, Vlad the Self-Impaler appeared. He gently took Cornelia's arm and tried to draw her inside the lobby door.

"Wait," she told Vlad.

She squirmed away from Vlad's grip and turned to Kevin. "Are you all right?"

His ear throbbed mercilessly; it felt like a searing knife tearing through his rib cage and right arm.

"Yeah," he said. "What about you?"

She looked at his ear and tears appeared on her cheeks. She reached down and scooped up a handful of fresh snow from the sidewalk, rolled it into a snowball. Then she touched his ear with it, very gently.

"Kevin Doyle," she spoke softly.

The pain and shock gripped him. "I used to be."

He stared at the girl's liquid eyes and his heart skipped. The tender way she treated his wound made his chest feel full, until he felt the pain very little. He wanted to put his arm around Cornelia Lord, deb escapee, and try to protect her some more.

"Miss Lord, come inside and get warm," Vlad the Self-Impaler begged. He took her arm again with his white glove.

She shrugged it off. "No, thank you."

Kevin used only his right arm, which didn't seem hurt, to slip his doorman coat off and wrap it around Cornelia, now trembling violently in her skimpy wet dress.

Life began to turn red and blue, with sirens.

The first police car swerved into the curb and some officers jumped out in a hurry. Then more blue and white cruisers slid in behind them. He heard whoop-whoops and hi-lo bleats, saw grim-looking men and women in uniform.

"Where's the woman you called about?" a police officer asked Vlad.

"Here," he pointed.

"I'm fine, but this man's hurt," Cornelia told the officer, still holding the melting snowball to Kevin's ear. "He needs a doctor."

Kevin felt as remote as a spectator in the very last row. His vision had turned into a single wobbly lens thrown out of whack and unfocused. A red film formed over the circle. He began to see people around him as more horizontal than vertical. Philip Grace grabbed him before he could fall down, then Philip and Cornelia held him up between them and moved him toward the police car.

"Officers," Philip spoke like the police were derelict. "Get these people to a hospital. This here's Cornelia Lord. And this young man just threw himself in harm's way to save her life."

"Okay," the older cop said, "get in the car."

The back seat of the police car released a blast of previous-perp body odor, strong as animal fear. The police officer packed Cornelia and Kevin carefully inside. Then Grace hopped in, closing the door behind him.

"All accounted for," Grace announced.

"Where do you think you're going?" Kevin asked him.

Grace banged on the Plexiglas partition. "Our hero's rantin' and losin' consciousness back here."

The officer behind the wheel whipped the car out of the nest of blue and white police cruisers onto Fifth Avenue, siren wailing. As they sped down the avenue, weaving around the hulking remains of the carriage and the limousine like some war-torn city, Kevin saw Tucker Fisk jogging in a tuxedo, his face and hair dripping wet.

"There's your boyfriend," he weakly told Cornelia. "Looks like he missed the carriage. You want to tell him you're okay?"

"Oh, no," she said. "Thank you so much for what you did, Kevin."

She took his hand in both of her palms, now warm, and smiled directly into his eyes, only glancing occasionally at the top of his head while they sped to the hospital.

He wondered why, jogging through the storm in a tuxedo to find his runaway girlfriend, Tucker Fisk had been grinning.

In his traumatized funk, Chester clung with both hands to the hand grip in the rear half of the broken Panda. He looked out the ragged cave mouth made by the destruction of his car, which had torn away the facing seat along with the driver's compartment.

"Jeez, I'm sorry, Mr. Lord." Mike the driver stood just outside the cave looking in, trying to coax him out. Then police officers pushed Mike aside, bending down to throw their flashlight beams in to see Chester. The lights blinded him. The carcass of the half-limousine shook as two officers climbed in to help him out.

"Where's Cornelia?"

"She's on her way to the hospital," a young cop told him.

He let go of the hand grip, and began sliding down, until the officers grabbed him and frog-walked him out so he wouldn't bump his head.

"How badly is she hurt?" He felt a shivery pall settling over his soul. At every misstep in this horrible debacle, Chester believed that he could never be more afraid of what was to come next. But this was the coup de grâce, hitting his daughter with his car. Or had he? Had his car hit her? Hadn't the doorman appeared, seemed to whisk her away?

"Don't worry, sir. We'll take you to see her," an officer said.

Odd sounds assaulted him as he stepped out of the broken limousine. He heard snorting. The horse, a sturdy beast, had got up on all four legs, pawing the snow with his hooves. And he heard a female voice yelling. It was the woman in the black suit, the driver of the carriage. She yelled at him in what sounded like a drill sergeant's parade-ground snarl.

The overbearing woman must be insane. She'd carted his daughter the wrong way in a blizzard. Perhaps all female lunatics had a secret understanding like Freemasons and helped one another, a subculture running on scrambled brains and estrogen. Thanks to him, Cornelia had officially joined them. Chester felt a deep sucking wound in his stomach, and not a physical one.

The fault line between Chester and his daughter had stretched so far apart it had finally snapped, like his stupid Panda. Now it would take more than words or good intentions to put her back together again.

Outside the emergency room entrance of Manhattan Hill Hospital, in the confusion of the ambulances and snow, Cornelia and Kevin were gently extracted from the police car. Placed in wheelchairs, they were quickly rolled off to separate destinations.

A top-heavy team of doctors and a few nurses crowded around Cornelia Lord on her way to the Lord Pavilion. This special wing of the hospital had been donated by Cornelia's grandfather Chester II to treat VIP patients, who could recover in teak-paneled rooms with sweeping views of the East River. Chester II was its very first patient.

Nurses gingerly removed Cornelia's clothing. The highest-level staff doctors examined her closely for unseen wounds, internal bleeding, hard-to-detect injuries. While the medical team scrambled, a woman with thin hair and a nervous rash who worked as the hospital's staff attorney monitored her treatment.

"Her leg is fine," a doctor reported. "Basically a turned ankle. No head trauma. A few bruises, but nothing serious."

"Keep testing her anyway," the lawyer said.

Philip Grace hung back in the emergency room. He assumed, correctly, that he would be ignored as he hunkered down in a plastic chair between a minor gunshot wound and an ulcer. Then he took off his coat and rolled up his sweater sleeves like a hospital employee. Pressing as close as he could to the doors leading to the Lord Pavilion, he slipped out the Minox spy camera he kept in his pocket for emergencies.

All he managed were a few candid shots of a dismayed Chester Lord and a stoic Tucker Fisk.

Chester and Tucker were escorted by police officers who pushed away other reporters yowling like mad dogs. A senior-looking official met them at the doors to the belly of the hospital. Then two hefty security men stepped in front of Philip Grace, preventing him from following them into the Lord Pavilion.

"You need some tests, Mr. Lord," the head of emergency services insisted.

Chester waved him away. "No. Just a conference room, please."

They led him to a mahogany-paneled, plum-carpeted staff room. The moment Tucker sat Chester down, Dr. Bushberg rushed through the door. Cornelia's psychiatrist fumbled in the pockets of his Burberry raincoat and Chester felt an odd twinge of satisfaction to see that Bushberg had forgotten his pipe.

"Cornelia was riding in a horse carriage," Chester icily told Tucker. "To get away from us, I imagine."

A doctor with a short gray beard popped in the door without knocking. He shook Chester's hand with a surgeon's careful squeeze.

"Cornelia looks like she's going to be fine, Mr. Lord. It doesn't appear that the car even touched her. We're running tests to be on the safe side."

Edgar Chase, Chester's lawyer, bustled in after the doctor. Edgar's intimidating presence always reassured him. Even when Edgar had little to say, as was often the case. The tall, barrel-chested attorney wore a well-tailored dinner jacket and white scarf as though he had been interrupted at a tête-à-tête of great splendor.

"How is she?" Edgar Chase's baritone rumbled, as he peered over tortoiseshell half-glasses at Chester.

"So far, so good. No injuries, apparently," Chester answered, his voice trembling. "A building employee saw the accident coming and pulled her out of . . . harm's way."

Edgar settled into the conference table and took a legal pad from a slim leather portfolio. Chester saw the note he wrote.

Bldg. Emp. involved: Will he sue?

A shrill whistle tortured Kevin's eardrum and he couldn't remember the past few minutes clearly. Now some people were picking him up and putting him on a gurney. A woman in white asked him about his blood type and whether he was allergic to any medications, then put a Plexiglas mask over his face.

His gurney was being wheeled through swinging doors marked "Trauma Bay" that banged open at his feet, into a trauma unit where several gunshot victims, a sad club, lay bleeding. He felt a little light-headed. It was exciting to be in the middle of all the life-saving activity—orders being shouted out in jargon and quickly followed. He admired the sense of life-or-death importance.

A stout nurse listened to his heart with a stethoscope. She took his fingers in her hands and turned them over, then poked at his shoulder. "Can you feel this?" she asked.

"Oh, yeah," he told her through clenched teeth.

A young Asian doctor in designer glasses appeared. He started firing orders as he spread both Kevin's eyelids wide and looked into his pupils with a blinding penlight. "Hang a bag of Ringers . . . start a unit of O-packed negative cells . . . prepare to intubate . . ."

"Open your mouth wide, Mr. Ramirez," the nurse told him.

"Huh?" Kevin said, as she began to probe his throat with a plastic tube that made him gag. His gurney was suddenly wrenched into motion. The young doctor, looking down at his chart, walked along beside him.

"Okay, Mr. Ramirez, you lost some blood. We're going to stabilize you, clean your wound, and get you into surgery to take the bullet out. No problem."

"What bullet?" Kevin yanked his head away. "My name's Doyle."

The doctor shuffled through his charts. "Oh."

"Who's Ramirez?" Kevin asked weakly.

"Ramirez is a chest wound," the nurse explained. "You don't want to be Ramirez."

Kevin believed her. At the moment, he barely wanted to be himself.

"Edgar," Tucker got down to business. "Cornelia had a severe nervous breakdown tonight at the office Christmas party. I asked her psychiatrist, Dr. Bushberg, to meet us here. It seems she ran off through the blizzard without a coat and somehow got one of the Central Park carriages to drive her up Fifth Avenue. A taxi hit them before Chester's car . . . arrived on the scene."

Chester noted the craft of Tucker's phrasing. "Edgar, she's taken a turn for the worse and it's my own fault. I came within inches of hitting her with my car." He glowered at Tucker and Bushberg. "I let you people deal with her and now we're all to blame."

Dr. Bushberg backed away.

"You," Chester glared. "You were supposed to be treating her."

The psychiatrist's face drained. Nobody spoke while Chester shook, until Edgar Chase tried to fill the silence with nostalgia.

"I remember that night I saw Cornelia in her first party dress."

And now she's ready for her first straitjacket, Chester thought.

"She's become a danger to herself, Edgar," Tucker said with cool certainty. "Chester, we probably have no choice but to get her into a hospital for treatment. Dr. Bushberg?"

When Tucker whipped his eyes at the psychiatrist, Bushberg jumped like one of Pavlov's salivating dogs.

"In practical terms, she's not living in the real world," Bushberg said quickly. "She's delusional and self-destructive. I would recommend treatment at the Sanctuary in Westchester. It's the best private psychiatric facility in the country. Don't fiddle while Rome burns, Mr. Lord."

Chester's shoulders jerked, but he said nothing.

Edgar Chase nodded. "I believe I've heard of the Sanctuary."

Yes. Edgar's wife had probably dried out there, more than once. Chester felt angry at all of them, a burning in the tips of his ears.

"Dr. Bushberg can push some buttons," Tucker said in his maddening business voice, wiped free of all emotion. "He can get her admitted tomorrow. What if she resists, Edgar?"

"Well, it's a bit more complicated," the lawyer said. "There's a very unwieldy legal procedure for involuntary treatment in New York state."

"Then get a judge on our side," Tucker ordered, then hurried to add, "Her life is at stake, Edgar."

"She'll go voluntarily," Chester said with finality. At least she'd be well looked after. Perhaps he would talk with the new psychiatrists there himself, a fresh start, to begin behaving like a real father even at this late date.

Then the lights went out in the conference room.

Below the Lord Pavilion, Kevin Doyle underwent a CAT scan on his head that was pronounced normal, and X rays of his shoulder.

Then they gave him painkillers. The side of his head still pounded, but it no longer bothered him. He felt a remarkable sense of well-being. He beamed while an intern sewed up the gash in his ear.

The doctor with the designer glasses nodded over a series of X rays of Kevin's shoulder that he slid onto a wall-mounted lightbox. He could see little white dots and dashes like Morse code on the X ray.

"Those are your stitches," the doctor explained.

"I feel okay."

"For man versus limousine, you did pretty well, Mr. Doyle. Your head looks fine. Your shoulder is not dislocated. You'll hear a noise in your ear for a few days, and we already gave you Percocets for pain." He wrote two prescriptions on her pad. "Take the antibiotic every twelve hours, two painkillers every six hours as needed, and stay out of traffic."

Because Kevin had entered wrapped in the arms of VIP Cornelia Lord, formal hospital procedures had been slighted temporarily. Now he was retrofitted into normal hospital policy, told to take a chair beside a small desk, twisting his body painfully to talk to a bored clerk who stabbed away at her computer. Her nails fascinated him, little mini-murals, over two inches long with glitter and rhinestone studs.

"How are you paying for this?"

In his painkiller euphoria, Kevin recalled his Brotherhood of Portal Operators union health care benefits. He clumsily found the plastic card Eddie had given him in his wallet. The admissions clerk punched its code on her computer. Then her tired eyes popped open like an astronomer finding a new planet.

She stared at him admiringly. "Your health plan gives you 100 percent coverage for everything. We never see plans like this anymore. Where do you work?"

"Eight-forty Fifth. I'm a doorman."

"Honey," she handed him his card back, "you ever get a job opening there, you call me."

Kevin heard a commotion.

"We lost our light in the ER waiting room," somebody shouted.

He heard spurts of confusion from beyond the double doors.

"Generator's on," a voice yelled. "We've got lights again."

Then he recognized a wail that could only be Philip Grace.

"Who the fuck took my new coat?"

Part Three

Code Green

Chapter Fourteen

No comment," Kevin told the feral-looking stalka-razzi waiting outside.

He left the hospital glowing from the painkillers, which acted to block the nerves. Real linebackers, these pills were. His head began to congeal as if wet cement were pouring in and hardening. A ringing like a chorus of crickets began in his ears, canceling out the yowl of the photographers and a rap version of "Silver Bells" playing somewhere on a boombox.

"Kevin, you sure you're okay?" Marne had come to meet him. Now she pointed him toward the curb, and stuck her fingers in her mouth to whistle for a cab.

Kevin stared out the window of the rattling taxi. New York at Christmas could be beautiful, like a fairy tale with sparkling lights. Trust welled up inside him. Everything was good. Everyone was fine. He turned to his sister, that Joan of Arc in her Fire Department Athletic League team jacket, who saved infants and old people from burning buildings. He gave Marne what he imagined was a beatific smile. Her green eyes scanned his face in the half-light, while waves of neon darted across the inside of the cab as they wormed through traffic, then reeled down Second Avenue.

"Dad came off work and waited in the ER for you as long as he could. He had to go back, but I called him to say you're fine. Helen, too. Kevin, what happened?"

"I helped a girl, that's all."

She sighed and looked past his face at the street. "A screwed-up deb. Kevin, she's not somebody you ought to be doing for. She's got serious problems."

"What? She's got money, so she can't have feelings?" He surprised himself, letting Marne push his buttons. Especially when the Percs made him feel as charming as a game show host.

"It's not money," she told him. "It's class. Like Dad says, Old Money comes from a different planet. I'll give you an example, you tell me if I'm wrong. I'm working a fire at the old Ivy Club, trying to get a guy out of his guest room. Sweet old man, barefoot in his bathrobe, face full of soot with the eaves falling down around him. So I'm helping him through the burning timbers and putting my coat down so he don't burn his feet, and I yell to my partner, 'He don't have shoes.' And the old guy stops and looks me in the face and says, 'He doesn't.' I say, 'sir?' He corrects me, 'He doesn't have shoes.' He was looking down his nose at me while I'm saving his life, Kevin. He doesn't, he don't. Two different worlds."

"Marne," Kevin said. "I'm not interested in her."

"Yeah?" Marne chuckled without humor. "Well, good. 'Cause if you'd gotten killed, she would have stepped over your body and gone crying home to Daddy."

As she spoke, he felt the sweet party of the painkillers wearing off. His ear felt like it had expanded to the size of a cantaloupe and his shoulder throbbed. They alternated, like parts of a toy man, swaying mechanically back and forth to punch him.

Marne let him off in front of the black-streaked facade of his tenement building. All the windows were either gated or boarded up. Nobody walked on the streets here, they only darted in and out of doorways.

"Nice," Marne commented on Casa Kevin. "You want me to go up with you? Throw out the burglars?"

"No, go home." He gave her a little hug. "Thanks for picking me up."

The cab lurched off with his sister.

*   *   *

Chester left the hospital surrounded by a small knot made up of Edgar Chase, Dr. Bushberg, Tucker, and two security guards. Their route took them through the emergency room.

Suddenly a curtain was pulled back to his right, and he stared into the coal-like eyes of the crazy woman carriage driver. Her tattered black suit coat reminded him of Abe Lincoln, if Honest Abe had tousled black curls that fell over his shoulders. With one hand, she had yanked the curtain open, obviously seeing him pass. A young, balding doctor was still trying to stitch a cut on her other hand. The procedure looked painful, a giant needle threading in and out of her flesh.

"Mr. Lord," she called, as though the pain didn't bother her. "Just a minute."

Edgar Chase tried to keep him moving. "Don't say anything. She'll want money. I'll deal with it."

"Excuse me," Roni Dubrov told the doctor working on her wrist. She stood up and reached Chester in a few sprightly steps. God, her legs were long, like a person on stilts. Her grip on his arm felt firm, but not aggressive. "I have something for you."

She's going to hit me, he thought recoiling, trying to throw her arm off, but her fingers held him in place. She reached into the pocket of her black coat.

"Mr. Lord, this belongs to your daughter. She said it was for breaking my carriage."

Then she pressed Cornelia's . . . his Elizabeth's . . . diamond engagement ring into his hand. Chester looked at the dazzling heirloom, trying to puzzle out her motive.

"I don't know what to say," he told her truthfully. "Your carriage, do you have insurance? If not, call me. I can help."

"Help your daughter first," she leaned in and whispered, so people around them couldn't hear. "She's just a child."

Chester could only mutter a feeble thanks before Edgar and Tucker pulled him away.

Kevin opened the door to the filthy foyer of his building. All three locks had been forced open by sledgehammers and crowbars at various times, so he didn't need his key.

He checked his mailbox, which had also been pried open, then walked up the three deserted flights of grimy stairs. His ear and shoulder hammered away, an efficient factory churning out pain.

He spotted a pattern of shadows on the wall that wasn't usually there. He sensed somebody up on his landing. A mugger, probably. Or a robber looking out while his partner ransacked his apartment.

"Get out of there, you pinhead junkie fuck," Kevin screamed up the stairs.

He waited. Nothing.

Kevin climbed the last few stairs cautiously and peeked around the balcony.

Cornelia Lord sat on the dirty floor of the landing outside his door. A giant gray leather coat covered her body like a tent. Philip Grace's new coat. Underneath it, she was dressed in a green hospital outfit. On her feet were hospital sock slippers, ruined from the slush outside. Her arms locked around her knees, one hand holding her other wrist, and she swayed forward and back. She looked up at the top of his head. Her face shone, very fresh and young without makeup, the freckles showing across her nose.

"Hi," she said.

He helped her to her feet.

"How'd you find me?"

"Your address was on the list in my father's study. I came to thank you again, Kevin."

He didn't think she would have fled the hospital and braved her way to Alphabet City in flimsy hospital booties to tell him that.

"Just doing my job," he said and wondered how stupid it sounded.

"May I use your bathroom?" she asked politely. She seemed to be having a hard time keeping still, moving from one foot to the other.

He worried that she could be getting him into another jackpot, this flaky deb he had just ten minutes ago defended to his sister. She had the staying power of a flea jacked up on Tabasco, running from everything, leaving broken carriages and limos and probably people. Plenty of blood on the trail behind Cornelia Lord. But she also had that way of looking at the top of his head.

"Sure," Kevin said. "But keep your coat on, okay? It's colder inside."

He found his keys and opened his new lock, one that had not yet been plucked out of his splintered door. He let her go in first. Before he could turn on the light, she gasped in the dark.

"Oh, Kevin, your corona!" she squealed.

When Kevin switched on the light, he could see that her eyes had locked on to the top of his head. Like the first night he found her passed out in the limousine.

"What do you see up there?"

"Sorry. Nothing." She walked into his kitchen looking right at home, past the rusty steel bathtub, studying the battered cabinets he'd painted several coats of white, with a few lumps where he had accidentally trapped speeding roaches under the wet paint.

He sat in his living room and didn't move while she used his bathroom. He heard her flush the toilet. Then she came into his living room, her face poking out of the gray coat, taking in his rat hole like an explorer discovering the New World. All the furniture had been stolen from his living room except for two webbed lawn chairs with some missing strips. The only remaining light was a floor lamp from some kid's room about thirty years before, its yellowed shade displaying pictures of spaceships.

She stopped at his wall where he had hung a print of Giotto's *Lost Saint Sebastian*.

"Oh, you have Sebastian," she breathed.

She touched the gold-leaf disk Giotto created around the man's head and Kevin's ear and shoulder stopped thudding in his shock.

"Do you know the story?" he asked her.

She didn't take her eyes off the halo. "He was an officer in the Praetorian Guard. When he became a Christian, the emperor ordered him killed."

Kevin's heart skittered. "Are you Catholic?" he asked her.

"No," she whispered. "I saw this painting in Italy when I was a little girl."

Naturally. He felt a familiar stab of resentment at this rich girl, bombing around Europe checking out Giottos while he put in his time at a New York City high school that couldn't even afford an art teacher. But, strangely, his envy felt like a useless appendage now. She looked so impressed at Giotto's *Lost Saint Sebastian*. And that was just a warm-up. Her eyes moved to the Polaroid shots he had stuck on the wall with red pushpins. This was the step-by-step saga of how he created his own neon Saint Sebastian, from his first sketches to pictures of the sculpture at different stages of completion.

"Kevin, what's this?" she asked him breathlessly, touching the blue halo on the picture.

"I made a neon Saint Sebastian. It's in a gallery . . ." Kevin hesitated. What the hell, she wasn't doing much better in her life than he was with his art. "Was in a gallery."

She stared like a maniac at the Polaroid.

"I love what you did around his head. Why did you use blue?"

"You can't do gold neon. I figured, he's looking up at the sky, so maybe it's a reflection. But I need to fix his halo. See how it's crooked? It ruins the piece."

"I don't know about that. I've never seen a neon saint before, Kevin, but it seems like a lovely halo." Her voice was so hushed. "Is this a school or something?"

Kevin exhaled. Even tonight, it seemed especially bizarre to have Chester Lord's daughter standing with his paint-trapped roaches and used lawn furniture, giving critical commentary on his art. How could he even start explaining to a Girl Who'll Always Have Everything what he went through to make the saint?

"It's no school," Kevin told her. "Unless maybe you're thinking about the Ashcan School. That's the only place it's headed right now. The subject matter, it's kind of a personal thing with me."

"I don't want to pry." Her eyes finally moved on to the last Polaroid shot stuck up on his wall. "Oooh. What's this?"

"An experimental piece I did," he told her. "I called it *Open Heart*. It didn't go anywhere."

She studied the roughly heart-shaped squiggles and wobbles, "Why not?"

"My teacher said it was too ephemeral or something. I made it by mixing a special set of neon gases. Krypton, argon, and xenon. Then I electroded the mix to get a plasma effect."

"Well, it's nice ephemeral."

"Thanks."

"It's more you than Sebastian, isn't it?" She peered at the blob on the Polaroid. "But I think you need to make it glow a little better, Kevin."

"Tell me about it." That casual insight stung and thrilled him in roughly equal measure. "I can't do anything else until I get Sebastian perfect."

"Why?"

"I just do."

"What more can you do for him?"

She pressed on innocently, like a curious ten-year-old. He knew she wasn't really asking about the noble gases and ribbon fires. She was worming into his deep tissue.

"Sebastian was my mother's favorite saint," Kevin finally said. "She died the day before Thanksgiving."

"Oh." Her hand flew up to her mouth. "I'm sorry."

"She loved Renaissance art," he told her. "She took me to museums."

"Of course," she nodded with matter-of-fact wisdom. "You won't do anything else until you've made things right for her."

He stared dumbly at the girl like some farmer might look at an extraterrestrial. She reached out and took his hand in both of hers, like she had in the cab.

"What's the matter with him, Kevin? He looks like a perfectly good neon saint to me."

"Well"—he still felt spooked, but tingling and inspired, too—"I have this teacher named Max, and he makes his pieces glow."

"Really?"

"Yeah. Max's work kind of shimmers. Mine still looks like a beer sign."

"Then I'll have to see Max's work," she told him, her enthusiasm beyond intense. "Where do you work on your saint?"

"On 14th Street. It's at my school. NYIAT."

"Gnat?"

"It's called the New York Institute of Art and Technology."

"Let's go over there right now," she told him, pulling her coat around her, ready to leave.

"Ms. Lord . . . Cornelia . . ." Kevin spoke slowly. "I can't help you anymore. I need my job."

He stepped back trying to get out of her space, an instinctive grasp at survival.

"No, Kevin, I can help you. Do you know who I first thought our doorman was? When I was little?"

She totally flustered him, always coming from different angles. "I give up."

"Santa Claus," she said. "One Christmas my father came home with gifts. The doorman had brought them upstairs from the car. The man came through the door on Christmas Eve with a mountain of presents, so I thought he was Santa Claus."

He wondered whether she made that up on the spot, to make him like her. He didn't think so. But if that's what she was doing, it was working.

"Anyway," Kevin said, "my school's closed for Christmas. I can't get in. Not legally, anyway." He forced a laugh but she still looked serious.

"This Max, is he a very good teacher?"

"He makes perfect bends." Kevin shrugged, a little helplessly. "And he told me to become a better liar."

"What?"

"Art is a lie that makes us see the truth," he told her.

"Picasso."

"I'm sorry?"

"Picasso said that. Your teacher was quoting him."

For the first time, Kevin felt his awe of Max slipping.

"How much do you pay the New York Institute of Art and Technology? If it's not too personal."

She got the school's formal name right on the first try. He was impressed. Most people didn't bother.

"About seventy-five an hour, and it's a three-hundred-hour course."

Her eyelids darted up, opening like parachutes and gliding back down. "What do they teach you?"

"Neon flameworking's kind of technical. You put on a space suit and work over a fire, bending tubes. The tubes are conductors. After you get all the bends right to make your figure, you shoot neon gas through to give it color. Then you wire your piece to a transformer and plug it in. The electrical current makes the gas shine."

She watched him, fascinated, breathing deeply and looking like she needed to compose herself. "Seventy-five dollars an hour. I think that kind of money should buy you visiting rights to your saint. Especially at Christmas."

That was the second time he saw her gray eyes explode into a violet constellation.

"Maybe. But we can't just break in."

Chapter Fifteen

Kevin wished he'd taken two more painkillers.

Now he leapt up in the air, grabbing the ladder of the fire escape with his good arm, his ear and shoulder both throbbing.

Growing up, he had perfected scaling fire escapes. He had needed that skill to get in and out of the apartment at night to meet his friends and do nothing. Now he felt he was definitely going to do something here at the deserted New York Institute of Art and Technology building. The not-knowing-what part kept him interested. He caught the bottom rung and pulled it down.

They scrambled up the fire escape, then over the roof of the building. Kevin twisted the lock on the metal door. If he could force it open, they could go down the staircase. He kicked the door around the lock but only made it whang defiantly while he worked up a sweat. The lock dented, but wouldn't loosen.

"Don't hurt yourself." She watched him work, tiny in the oversized coat.

He gave the door a savage look, partly meant for the school that had taken his money, and partly for Max, who wouldn't share his neon-glow secrets with him. Kevin looked around the rooftop and found a cinder block that weighed about thirty pounds. He came back and raised the cinder block over his head with his good arm like Thor, then smashed it onto the doorknob. It snapped off and the disabled door fell open.

They went down the cement stairs together, down to the empty NYIAT studio floor.

She sniffed the air like a rabbit, her nose with its freckles wriggling. "Did they have a fire?"

"Every day. Look at the worktables. Those pipes with the nozzles on the end that look like periscopes? That's where the fires come out. We bend the tubes over them."

He hadn't noticed it since his first day, but the school resembled a bombed-out building from all the soot. Nobody ever scrubbed or even dusted the place. He felt embarrassed by his school. A small reflection of city lights peeked through the filthy windowpanes of the skylight, but failed to illuminate the coat of dinge over the workstations. A single dull night-light burned in a corner of the huge, blackened floor. Kevin took her by the hand to Max's workspace and showed her Max's pieces, still softly glowing on the table, mocking him.

"Look how Max's stuff shines," he pointed.

"Oh?" she picked up Max's pieces and studied them.

"Neon only lights up when you plug it into an electrical source. But his pieces glow all by themselves."

"I see that."

Kevin guided her to the storage closet. They found Saint Sebastian covered with soot where he left him, next to the neon Fat Elvis.

Together they carried the saint out of the closet and placed him on Max's worktable. Kevin took a cloth and dusted the white tubes carefully, revealing it to her a little self-consciously.

He watched her touch the curves of Saint Sebastian's face, and the thin arrows that stuck out from his torso.

"Ouch," she said appreciatively. "So what do you have to do to his halo?"

"Bend the tube into a perfect circle," Kevin explained.

"I'll help."

He took two Mylar space suits out of Max's supply closet and helped pull one of them over the hospital greens she'd borrowed. Then he placed the shiny black Pyrex safety mask over her face, tightening the strap around her hood. The black eye mask and suit made her look like a junior astronaut. He could see her trembling a little, even through the suit.

"Are you cold?"

"No. Just excited."

He reached for Max's suit to put on himself. He'd be the teacher today. Cornelia helped him slip it on so he wouldn't hurt his tender shoulder or ear. Then she strapped on his mask for him, which he kept flipped up so he could talk.

"I like music when I work," he said.

Kevin searched the cabinet where he kept the only two discs he ever listened to when he worked, depending on his mood. He reached for Portishead first but changed his mind. Instead, he found his Rossini CD by the opera diva Cecilia Bartoli.

As the singer filled Max's studio with her voluptuous mezzo-soprano, he led Cornelia to the flameworking table. Its charred surface now inspired him with the residue of Max's perfect, glowing work. Kevin fired up the burner, keeping Cornelia slightly behind him where she could watch closely.

"With neon, you've got three common fires," he explained to her. "This is called a ribbon fire."

She grasped his good arm as he lit the burner, a blue spurt hissing, then a blast of hot orange flame exploded from the pipe. He put her mask down over her face, and the flame reflected in the Lucite, a ring of fire on the glossy black surface.

"Now I'm going to start. I'll try one long, smooth bend to make the halo arc over his head. I need a perfect circle."

She tightened her fingers on his arm. He felt a surprising heat from her, even through their fire suits.

"I use a thin tube to get a perfect arc." He explained his main problem. "But a thin tube like this breaks easily when you bend it. I have to keep my moves real fluid. Cornelia?"

"Yes?" Her voice was small and muffled under her hood.

"This halo, it's what you call a corona, isn't it? An electromagnetic field."

She said nothing.

"Did you see a corona around my head the first night you saw me?"

"Yes. It's around your helmet now."

Uh-huh. Kevin felt a small seizure of panic, a thought that maybe it wasn't a good idea to come here with this girl and, even in his space suit, let her hand stay on his when he was working with fire. But he wouldn't be here with her at all if he hadn't trusted her. He just needed to go with the flow. So she saw a kind of halo around his head that nobody else could see. Like the guy in the Waldorf-Estonia coffee shop swatting at the fly. Maybe she was the new art concept he had left to simmer on a back burner.

He listened to Bartoli begin a languid aria. It crept under his skin, keeping his nerves taut the way they should be, especially with Cornelia's body pressed so close to his, as the fabric of their suits slid together.

"I never did a perfect arc," he told her, his voice muffled through the mask. "It's like finding a black orchid, Max said. The hotter the fire gets, the better the bend. But heat makes the glass more brittle."

He held the flame of his torch to the glass tube. It stuck straight up next to the saint's head, like a skindiver's snorkel.

"I'll bombard the glass now. The trick is to go with gravity."

Her fingers rested on his glove. What was she doing?"

"Uh, be careful . . ."

"Don't worry. I'll help."

"I'm starting the first curve now," he said. She seemed to caress his hand inside the glove. Just a tingling, but definitely something.

"I have to feel the bend now," Kevin's voice rasped. "Pivot with me toward the table . . . good."

Her suit seemed to melt into his arm, her fingers guiding him.

He felt her energy race under his suit with Bartoli's voice, and didn't want her to remove her hand from his after all.

The arc took shape, the molten glass the tube only an eighth of an inch thick. Now it swelled dangerously, the way it did before snapping, so he'd have to start over.

"I'm slowing it down," he told her, "working with gravity. There. That's the first curve. I have to be careful not to let it wobble. Now I let it cool."

His back felt prickly. The fire coming from her suit pressed up against his burned like the fire from the table. He felt as though her body had completely molded into the shape of his back.

"We can't force cold tube into the fire now," he rasped. "Okay, slow. Maintain the curve . . . let it warm . . . Oh, Jesus."

"Yes?" she exhaled through her mask.

"It's a perfect arc. I've got to stop."

He started to pull the half-finished halo out of the fire.

"No," she told him. "Keep going. Finish the circle."

Together, her gloved hand helping his, they continued the arc encircling Sebastian's head.

"We can finish it," Kevin yelled through the black Lucite face mask. "I can feel you with me . . . just hold it in the fire now . . . help me . . ."

He felt her hand guiding his through their space suits. He finished. No, *they* finished the halo together. He inspected it.

"Oh Jesus!"

"Is it perfect?" she asked him.

"Yes!" he yelled.

"Yes!" she yelled with him, their screams muffled by their suits. She clawed at the fastener of her mask, and then his.

She opened up his face mask and kissed him in a frenzy. The tip of her tongue crept inside his mouth and touched his gums, sending shocks through his body. Her fingers held the hair at the nape of his neck.

She pulled away from him. "Wait a minute. You have to trust me, now, Kevin. Close your eyes."

His heart, his ear, his shoulder all pounded together like an anvil chorus. He closed his eyes and heard her run off, swishing in the Mylar space suit. Then he felt her hands on his waist, guiding him.

He waited.

"Open."

Kevin saw the face and halo of Saint Sebastian glow between the girl's hands, like Max's work. The face shimmered in a luminous flesh tone like a living thing, not a bar sign anymore. The halo radiated in saintly fashion, perfect as any of Giotto's gold disks. The change was subtle, but it made art out of his tangle of white tubes.

He touched the sculpture.

"Fiber optic coils, thin little threads. I saw them on Max's workbench. They're called freestanding coils because they light up by themselves. You can only get them in Europe."

"How did you know about them?" he croaked.

"A museum curator showed me."

Naturally. Kevin felt hot, and not in a completely good way.

"That's how Max illuminates his work," she said. "Didn't he show you?"

"No. I can't believe you did that."

"You made Sebastian," she said modestly. "I just gave him a little charge."

"It was so easy for you, making the bend, lighting it up." Kevin kept his voice down. "Let's see. I've been working on this two years, trying to get it right. I guess you figured it out in, what, two minutes? I brought you here to show you what *I* do . . ."

She owned his eyes, he realized. She burrowed into them and found his vanity, then his heart.

"I only wanted to help."

"Yeah, I know," he breathed out. "Cornelia, how do you know this stuff?"

She crossed her arms in the space suit, raised her chin up. "Do you know who Nikola Tesla is?" she asked.

"He made the Tesla coil."

She shut her eyes as though patient but slightly exasperated.

"He did a little more than that. If you really want to know."

"I want to know."

"Well, how about in the morning? I wouldn't mind staying here, if you want to go home."

Leave? Kevin felt as attached to her now as a magnet to a refrigerator door. Should he invite her back to his place? He fumbled with that idea, which could mean a slog through the snow, maybe running into a police car, and in the pisshole of his apartment groping with the question of sex.

Now she looked tired enough to sleep. Her eyelids were at half-mast. "Let's stay here, both of us." But he wouldn't touch her.

"You're sure I'm not keeping you?"

"No, I'm single."

"Of course. Saints have to stay single."

He reddened. "I mean . . ."

She touched his cheek, warming it.

"Maybe next time, you'll show me your heart."

Chapter Sixteen

Kevin woke up first, Cornelia's hair in his face. He peeked over her head. The wall clock read 9:37 A.M.

He didn't immediately feel the aching despair that had been his wake-up call for the past three weeks. His first sensation was the scent of her hair. He imagined a meadow in Florence, Italy, where the Renaissance artists painted. If they had meadows in Florence.

He also failed to notice, for the first few minutes, the rousing anthem of pain now pounding away in his ear and his shoulder. He realized that he hadn't filled his prescription for painkillers.

Then he remembered that he was supposed to work the 8:00 A.M. shift this week with Andrew.

He slowly disengaged from her body spooned into his. They'd slept in their clothes, to keep each other warm on the narrow, ugly sofa in the director's office. They were outlaws, he remembered. They'd be looking for her. He just hoped they wouldn't be looking for her with him.

Carefully, he leaned on his elbow and surveyed her. Her smooth shoulders, a little bony under the fabric of the hospital scrubs she had stolen, were striped with broken light from the snow-covered skylight. The hair on her arms sparkled like tiny silk threads. He felt her breath on his hand.

He traced his finger lightly across her profile. He studied her small waist that dipped under the flimsy green, rumpled hospital scrubs, her slender legs and the calf that stuck out where the pant leg rolled up. They were finely proportioned, so aristocratic. He looked at her slightly freckled nose, her flat, peach-colored belly just visible under her green top. There was no part of her that wouldn't drive him crazy. This could be an infatuation, mostly based on looks and some lust, just like high school. But he was older now, so it had to be a *mature* infatuation.

Her sculpted forearms were still wound together under her cheek.

He had to laugh at himself, then carefully inched off the sofa. He found Philip Grace's gray leather coat she had worn to his apartment and laid it gently over her, tucking the bottom around her toes.

He padded through the untidy office to a telephone, and punched in his number to pick up messages.

Beep.

"Hey, Kevin Doyle. This is Philip Grace, gimme a call, man . . ."

Beep.

"Fran Lerner, Action News, I saw . . ."

Beep.

"This is Eddie . . ."

Maybe he'd been fired for not showing up at work. He played it back.

"This is Eddie. Call me at my building . . ."

Eddie greeted him with a gruff curiosity. "Kevin, where you calling from? You alone?"

"I'm about to call the building," Kevin said, "and tell Gus I can't come in."

Gus Anholdt was the building manager at 840 Fifth. He reminded Kevin of a school principal who really wanted to be a hermit. Gus's motto was, "My door is always closed."

"Forget about it. Gus already called me," Eddie said.

Kevin felt unease flopping over in his stomach. "Oh, yeah?"

"Some lawyer for Chester Lord called Gus, told him to take you off duty. They're giving you two weeks sick leave. He said to tell you, thanks from Mr. Lord. Maybe you got an extra Christmas bonus. You want me to pick it up for you?"

"Thanks," Kevin said. "I'll get it."

"Where are you, Kevin? You with anybody?"

That was the second time he'd asked.

"Some welfare hotel. I wanted to get away. My phone was ringing."

"Telephones these days, you're allowed to take 'em off the hook," Eddie offered. "Get well, Kevin. There's other residents in the building still have to give you Christmas tips. 'Tis the season to have money, you hear what I'm saying? You owe me for this job, kid."

Kevin climbed back onto the sofa carefully. When he saw her, he felt giddy, and brushed her hair with his hand, seeing little flecks of gold.

She definitely wasn't crazy. Not the way Philip Grace wrote about her, and Marne wrote her off, and the workers at 840 Fifth gossiped about her. But there seemed to be two Cornelia Lords. There was the Girl Who'll Always Have Everything, and the one who could look into his soul and know things. He wondered which one would wake up and greet him this morning.

He dozed lightly, jumped when he felt himself going to sleep. He didn't want her to wake up first and run away. For all her good points, she was still a flight risk. But he seriously doubted she would run away from him, since she promised to show him something that meant a lot to her that concerned the inventor Nikola Tesla. Hard to believe a girl like that would care about a dead inventor.

But it was even harder to believe that she cared about Kevin Doyle.

He wouldn't be a total idiot, getting twisted up in some romantic fantasy. Maybe he was a fling for her. If he tried to make anything more out of it, the social class curtain would come crashing down on his head. This was New York City, not one of Vlad's fairy tales. But right now he felt safe and warm with her, scrunched up together.

His ear and shoulder hurt, but curling up with Cornelia Lord gave him a better false sense of well-being than the Percocets. His eyes closed again and he slept.

Cornelia saw 10:06 in red numerals. Her eyes darted around the studio, as she collected her thoughts.

She felt Kevin's arm around her, deliciously warm. She felt tingly, as she had from the moment she had first seen his corona. Kevin Doyle had plenty of hurt under the splendid corona. She could understand his sorrow over his mother, and his need to make Saint Sebastian perfect for her.

She admired that.

For the first time, she also realized that Kevin Doyle was handsome. His face spoke of both wildness and decency. The tender mouth and chin that sprouted morning whiskers looked noble, like Sebastian.

He thrilled and disturbed her. She could connect with Kevin Doyle. She could feel his grief; terribly new and raw, and quite familiar. But caution should forbid, shouldn't it? He had swept her off her feet—off the street if she wanted to be literal about it—in such a display of bravado, it would be easy to make a misstep here. His corona, his decency, excited her. But she could be taking a risk, confiding in him about Tesla.

She had just trusted Tucker and look where that had gotten her.

She sat up suddenly. Oh, God. She had to warn her father that Tucker had become entangled with old Han Koi. That ugly double corona that snaked from the Kois to encircle Tucker, that was the sign. Coronas couldn't lie. Or could they?

She bit her lip, trying to recall exactly what she had seen. She had, after all, chugged most of a bottle of New York State champagne on an empty stomach. That could have been enough to cloud her perception of things.

What did the blackish brown corona really tell her? She tried to imagine convincing her father of what she believed to be true, without the supporting evidence of the Koi corona. Tucker had definitely lied to her about the South America business. The old man on the screen was fake. Tucker's people had returned the supplies. There would be no grand adventure in Brazil with Tucker.

But *why* had he duped her? Perhaps just to enlist her help with the voting stock. Maybe he would be the one who couldn't wait to dump *her*.

Who could tell?

Tucker still revealed no corona of his own. Maybe he just sort of used other people's coronas, like other people rented cars. Maybe the Kois had only *tried* to ensnare Tucker. She needed a second opinion desperately. But nobody advertised a "Corona Hotline" in the Manhattan Yellow Pages.

Now quite sober and blissfully snug on this cramped couch where Kevin Doyle wrapped his warmth around her—like the little wicker love seat on the Lords' sunporch that she shared with her mother—she couldn't be so sure about Tucker and the Kois.

What she knew for certain was the joyous charge of being with Kevin Doyle.

She regretted his hurt at her discovery of the fiber optics. It seemed so obvious to her, but of course he didn't have Dr. Powers showing him new developments in electricity. *He wasn't of her world,* Chester would say.

And snobbery could work both ways, couldn't it? She felt his resentment of her for being rich. On the other hand . . .

No. Too many hands. A clumsy octopus of doubt. She would tell Kevin Doyle about Tesla and be very careful not to compromise him for helping her so many times now. No matter what, she wouldn't make him lose his job. And she wouldn't waffle, flipping back and forth like her father. She would call Chester and tell him her suspicions about Tucker, and that would be that.

She gently stroked Kevin's face with her fingertips until he opened his eyes.

"Good morning," she greeted him. "How do you feel about museums?"

"She's not with her friends. Not at any of her haunts," Chester told Edgar Chase on the telephone. "I think we might have to get the police involved, discreetly."

"You don't get the police involved discreetly," Edgar explained. "Even if we speak to the commissioner, there's no assurance."

Chester listened but didn't hear, worn and preoccupied. Tucker had slept in a guest room, after sitting in Chester's study all night making telephone calls. Tucker had already dispatched his people, that busy, well-scrubbed youth gang, and even some private investigators to check Cornelia's friends, her acquaintances, anywhere she could possibly have run to hide.

His daughter had vanished.

Rubbing his nose, he thought of her trudging through the snow somewhere alone. He desperately hoped she would stay in a reasonably good neighborhood. Thank God New York City had a mayor who cracked down on street crime.

"Mr. Lord." O'Connell appeared at the door to Chester's study. "There's a gentleman to see you who claims to have information."

"Goodbye, Edgar." Chester hung up with a clatter and took the business card O'Connell handed him. He recognized the card with its double-door logo of the International Brotherhood of Portal Operators. It read, "Edward J. Feeney, Delegate," a man he had met representing the doormen of 840 Fifth in their labor negotiations with his co-op board.

Feeney entered the study. His too-small suit was rumpled, and there were small stains on his hand-painted tie. He had random gray whiskers that had eluded the razor jutting out from his rough, reddened jowls. They gave him a seedy look, like a small-time gangster ready to be gunned down in a barber's chair. Chester watched him as he tried to balance his bulk on the smallest chair, then finally gave up and moved to a larger one. Feeney's lumpy face seemed oddly pleased. His eyes actually twinkled. He leaned forward, resting his elbows on his knees, clutching a rolled-up newspaper in his fists.

"Can I call you Chester?"

Chester clenched his hands in his lap. "If you promise to get to the point, Mr. Feeney."

"You seen this morning's *Globe*?"

Chester saw Feeney smirk, just enough to make his blood rush to his head. He steeled himself.

"No. Only the *Times*," Chester told him. "There was an article about . . . the accident in the Metro section."

Eddie Feeney pursed his lips and nonchalantly unrolled the newspaper.

"Doorman Saves Deb from Dad," the front page screamed.

Chester flinched at the sad, grainy image of Cornelia twisted in the horse blanket in the snow, being plucked by the young doorman named Doyle from the jaws of Chester's own car. Naturally, the photographer had captured the exact moment when his car struck Doyle, recording the full measure of the young doorman's agony. He imagined it would prove useful for some personal injury lawyer.

Chester focused on Feeney. He had a bulldog's jowls. Yet Chester recalled that Edward J. Feeney, delegate, had never, in his negotiations on behalf of his Portal Operators union revealed even a trace of that breed's loyalty. Feeney looked out for himself, first, then his men. "Your point, Mr. Feeney?"

"This guy is my nephew." Eddie tapped a stubby finger twice on Kevin Doyle's likeness. "I got a feeling your daughter's with him."

Chester tried to visualize Cornelia with the doorman. Anything seemed possible now.

"Why would you think that?" he asked.

"I'm just saying, I got a hunch. If I helped you out—"

Chester cut off this unsavory whiff of a money demand before it could leave Feeney's mean little mouth.

"Thank you for your time," he told him. "We'll discuss compensation if this proves true. Please keep it to yourself."

"Keep what to myself?"

Chester frowned before he realized the man was joking. While O'Connell swept Eddie Feeney out to the foyer, Chester walked upstairs to check several guest rooms, and finally found Tucker. He shook the boy awake. While Cornelia slept like a little girl, Tucker sprawled across the small guest bed in his boxer shorts like a monstrous Gulliver, snoring loudly.

"Chester," Tucker squinted at him. "What?"

"Do you think it's possible that Cornelia is with the doorman?"

Tucker didn't take long to collect himself. "You mean that guy Doyle?" He yawned. "I checked him out. Lives in a slum. I sent somebody to look at his apartment and there was nobody home."

"He behaved well at the hospital," Chester remembered, "refused to talk to the media. But if he's taken Cornelia . . ."

"Chester," Tucker said with a sigh. "That guy's a loser. He couldn't get her to go with him unless she wanted to, and trust me, she wouldn't want to."

This was definitely Corny's place.

He saw the look of almost religious rapture that made her skin flush and her eyes seem to glitter.

Kevin looked around the New York Tesla Museum and its few visitors.

"We aren't open to the public yet," she explained. "Just the students and Tesla Society members who drop by. And people who need to get inside."

Some he figured were students, busy peering at signs and taking notes. And some homeless people wrapped like mummies in their layers of ragtag clothes and faces streaked with permanent dirt. During the winter months, chased out of Midtown where they might annoy the tourists, they went anywhere they could warm up. He had to admit that even the homeless drop-ins looked curious about the exhibits. Some other people, whose eyes burned with the fire of true believers, drifted in and out. Did Tesla have groupies? They were mostly young, dressed neatly enough, but some had their shirt collars buttoned up all the way to the top and buzzcut hair that could have been styled by Black and Decker.

Kevin looked up. The museum was a knocked-open space four stories high and half a block square, full of exhibits. There were old-time inventions and photographs of the wacky inventor.

In the middle a steel-girded tower shaped like a stainless steel mushroom with a bulbous head shot up almost to the roof. Directly over the tower, a massive skylight had been installed in the ceiling. It was made up of two huge glass panels set on tracks.

"Does the skylight open up?" he asked her.

"Sure. When we want to raise the tower."

She stared at the tower and spoke in the same hushed voice she had used for his Sebastian. Here he felt a sinking feeling that Cornelia Lord was a little too devoted. A self-made nun in the Church of the Wrong Assumption.

"You paid for this museum?"

"Some of it. I spent nine months helping to convert this space. I found the curator, came up with some of the exhibits. But the owner of the building leases it to us for a dollar a year. He belongs to the New York Tesla Society, too."

She gripped his good arm in excitement. Around the tower objects dangled on wires. Kevin saw that they were models of odd airships, tent-shaped with aluminum wings that looked like they couldn't get off the ground in a tornado. Scattered among the models, he saw silvery disks with lumps in the middle. Uh, oh. Flying saucers.

Coronas. Tesla Towers. Flying saucers. Cornelia had definitely made good on her promise to show him something he'd never seen before. Anybody else, he would have written this stuff off. But he couldn't deny that her exuberance was catching.

"How'd the tower work?"

"It didn't. His investors pulled the plug too early. It's a long story." Her eyes took a detour through sadness, then came back. "He designed it to broadcast free electricity through the atmosphere so anybody could use it. Like radio waves. If he had his way, the whole world could run on free electricity. Houses. Factories. Cars. Even boats and planes. After he got the little bugs out, of course."

"Bugs?" Kevin studied the tower and the hanging plane models. Electricity didn't work like that. Tesla must have had the balls of a brass monkey. "He was way ahead of his time, I guess."

"That's what they said about Leonardo da Vinci, Kevin. Watch."

She moved over to the control panel, flipped a switch underneath, and fiddled with a button and a joystick.

He heard a rumble from the ceiling like a subway train, and looked up to see the big glass and steel panels in the roof begin moving apart. She flicked another switch and the platform groaned and lifted the giant mushroom of the Tesla Tower. It lumbered up toward the roof in a whine of pneumatics. Then the tower's head poked through the roof, jutting through the opening as light poured in from the sky.

Kevin stood awed as licks of blue electric current began to shoot around the top of the tower. Suddenly, the little licks burst into a spider's web of huge blue bolts that danced and crackled over this dingy old rooftop in the crummiest part of the West Side of Manhattan.

"Hello," somebody greeted them from behind.

A man with thick, silvery hair and a trim beard appeared beside them. He wore a charcoal suit and silver tie. His skin looked ruddy, like images he had seen of nineteenth-century Englishmen. Kevin expected him to speak with a British accent, or whip some snuff out of his pocket.

"We missed you." The man flashed his teeth at Cornelia. His accent sure wasn't British. Pure Brooklyn, maybe Flatbush. The man gave Cornelia a bear hug. Then he shook Kevin's hand with a kind of reverence. "And you're Kevin Doyle. I'm Gene Powers, the museum's curator. I saw your picture in the *Globe* today. I know a lot of people who'd thank you, if they only knew what this woman did for this museum. She's too modest."

Cornelia shrugged. Powers looked at her, then at Kevin.

"Well, I'll be in my office if you need me."

"Nobody knows you helped build this museum?"

"Nobody but Dr. Powers. And now you."

"What got you into this?" Kevin asked.

She evaded him. "Tesla started out as a penniless immigrant in America, digging ditches. Then he went to work for the Edison Electric Company and invented modern electricity."

"Not Edison?" Kevin asked her.

"Edison invented DC, direct current, but it was limited by wires. New York City in 1906 was a rat's nest of electrical wire. So Tesla discovered AC electricity."

"What we use today."

"Yes, but Edison got the credit, didn't he?"

He waited. She hadn't really answered his question.

"What's this?" Kevin pointed to a small open airship. It looked like a helicopter some kid would make. It had a boxy frame with a tufted seat for two, a propeller on top and one in back, and a rudder. A row of big batteries was stuffed between the seat.

"It's a Tesla airship design."

"Where's the engine?"

"Under the propeller mast," she told him proudly. "It's an electric engine to run the propellers. I had it designed to run on AC current."

"That looks like a box made out of Tinker Toys," he pointed out. "You sure it can fly?"

"Dr. Powers and I flew it once in Connecticut. It's called a gyro-copter."

She placed an almost maternal hand on the airship, beaming. She didn't look like a crazy nun anymore. The fact was, she looked like a real person with a spark of the divine.

"Cornelia, all you've done, I mean, I've never known anybody who could even dream up something like this"—he waved his arm at the exhibits—"and you made it happen."

"I just helped."

Like she had just helped with his Sebastian.

Cornelia Lord could spend her whole life on yachts, eating caviar with little flecks of gold. But she didn't. She had spent her time and money on a dead inventor, more like a half-nutty artist than an engineer.

She'd shown him her secret world. And he liked it. But why, of all people, had she turned her candlepower on him? How long could a mortal man cling to a goddess?

"Kevin?" she giggled. "Hello in there. Let's go work on your saint."

Chapter Seventeen

The dense snowfall, driven by a cold wind, swirled over the city for a second day of stung cheeks and school closings.

Cornelia wound her arm into his and rested her head on his good shoulder. Like explorers or penguins, they helped each other navigate the icy streets, crossing half the West Side on their way downtown to the New York Institute of Art and Technology.

As they tramped through the street slush, Kevin noticed that it hadn't had time to turn gray. New waves of powder kept falling to bleach the old. They kept their heads down and hugged the buildings, just in case some hawk-eyed *Debwatch* reader might recognize Cornelia Lord.

As they crossed by the rent-controlled tenements between West 42nd Street and Chelsea, Kevin noticed that Cornelia Lord never looked wrong anywhere. Her creamy skin belonged to the world of Fifth Avenue. But she seemed right at home among the hangdog buildings on Tenth Avenue. At street level, she seemed enchanted by the flower shops run by broad-faced Koreans, and happily sniffed pungent smells from the Greek luncheonettes. On the second floors of the old tenements, she pointed out the young mothers with kids and elderly Medicare patients crammed into tiny rooms waiting for doctors and dentists.

They were walking just like a couple through his New York, not hers. And she was having fun. He nudged her. "That's where I used to go to church, when I was a kid."

On the corner, even the arched roof of St. Agatha's Church had been covered with a layer of snow. The gray stone, dusted white, made the stained glass shine brighter than a fire in an oven. This sprawling urban church, where Kevin had taken his Communion and they'd held his mother's funeral, never looked less oppressive. Today he saw grandeur in the twin spires instead of boredom and authority, maybe the way a peasant like Giotto was inspired by the medieval churches.

The two big oak doors to the church opened suddenly. Children in white angel gowns with gold-braided necks roared out, shoving and yelling at one another, carrying white candles.

"That's the Christmas pageant," Kevin said. "I was in it when I was eight. I still don't see Round John Virgin."

"Who?"

"From the Christmas carole, 'Round John Virgin, mother and child.' I got the words wrong, looking for some fat kid."

She laughed, then pulled away from Kevin, stretching her arms out to each side in the oversized leather coat.

"Snow angels!" she yelled.

She fell backward, thumping into a pile of snow, and waved her arms back and forth. She leapt to her feet.

"Look!" She showed Kevin the outline she made. "Come on!"

Her angel looked more like a melanic snow moth in its patch of city grime. His arm and shoulder still throbbed, and he hesitated. But she'd already got him into the spirit. He closed his eyes, stretched his arms, and fell backward too. He worried, falling like a toppled tree, that he might get hurt when he hit the ground.

"Oooof." He blinked, looking up at the sky. He felt fine. The fresh layer of snow he had landed on cushioned him like a velvety mattress.

"See?" she squealed. "Nothing hurts as much as you think it will."

Then without warning, she ran off into the alleyway beside the church, gray coat flapping, and disappearing around the corner. Kevin ran after her. He puffed through the alleyway onto the crosstown street looking both ways, but didn't see her. He ran in the direction of the Hudson River. He couldn't find her.

"Cornelia!" he yelled.

He ran a long city block in the other direction and looked up and down Ninth Avenue, then all the way back to Tenth Avenue until he couldn't run anymore. He stood bent over, hands on his knees.

Whatever kept him from getting too attached to her failed him now.

Then he felt cold hands over his eyes.

"Gotcha."

He turned around and saw the red tip of her nose. She laughed, catching her breath. Then she slipped on the ice with a gleeful whoop, and he leaned over to help her up.

"Are you okay?"

"I think I twisted my ankle," she said.

He bundled her up in the pewter-colored coat and carried her the last ten blocks to his school building, as carefully as he'd held Sebastian. The throbbing in his shoulder didn't bother him at all now. Finally he got the door to the school building open with his foot and it closed behind him.

Neither of them saw the two New York City police officers who spotted them from their car.

They had followed the young subjects discreetly in their white and blue cruiser for the past few blocks. Now they pulled to the curb across the street from the school.

The officer in the driver's seat, an antsy male sergeant named Cantwell with gray-flecked hair and a painfully inflamed prostate, took the duty clipboard and flipped it over. He stared at the photo on the faxed and photocopied handout, a muddy blotch of lines and smudges. He squirmed uncomfortably. His black leather jacket squeaked against the car seat. The car's blasting heat made their close space feel like the inside of a tank.

"I can't tell." He shook his head. "Lemme see that *Globe*."

He scrunched his forehead, analyzing the picture on the second page under the headline, "Where's Corny?"

"It's her," said his partner, Officer Diaz, a compact woman with muscles like pistons and very long hair pulled up under her cap so the visor sat slightly high on her head.

"Better call it in as a possible abduction," Sergeant Cantwell instructed his partner.

"You sure about that?" Officer Diaz said. While Sergeant Cantwell possessed many useful police skills, she believed that his prostate condition made him overly eager to find something physical to do to take his mind off the burning gland.

Cantwell gave her a sidelong look. He was a sergeant and she wasn't. She took the radio and checked their clipboard again for the special code name they'd been given at their shift briefing.

"1348," Diaz spoke softly into the radio, so she wouldn't break the dispatcher's eardrum. "We've got subject Charlie Oscar Romeo, corner of 14th and Ninth. Possible, I repeat, *possible* 802. Requesting instructions."

"Copy 1348," the short crackle came back.

They watched the old loft building, then watched some more. They sat in dead silence, as only partners on surveillance can, except for Cantwell's leather jacket squeaking on the seat. Each had started to wonder what the hell was going on when the dispatcher's voice squawked out of the dashboard.

"1348, secure the location. Blue Dog is responding."

"The captain. Do you believe this?" Cantwell said, rolling his eyes.

Officer Diaz turned the rearview mirror her way to check out her uniform. "This debutante's supposed to be a mental subject."

"Maybe she's dangerous," Sergeant Cantwell said.

Officer Diaz could tell that her partner had taken a personal dislike to the girl for bringing their captain into the picture. Now she'd have to make sure Sergeant Cantwell, prisoner of his angry prostate, didn't accidentally shoot some debutante for running at them with a lipstick tube.

"That sly old Max," Cornelia chuckled. "Watch."

In the institute's vast blackened loft floor, she lit up Sebastian's halo again with the freestanding fiber optics.

"So how many do you use?"

"Less is more," she said. "The light has to be subtle, just barely luminous. There. You try his face, Kevin."

He struggled to slip the tiny coils carefully into the thin, brittle tubes.

Freestanding fiber optics.

In a way that he admitted to himself was stupid, he hated the little glowworms. Max, the sneaky bastard, had kept this technology from him.

But they were hard to work with, thin little threads that slipped away from his fingers like silverfish. Then she guided him just slightly and he implanted two of them in Sebastian's face. The glass-tube profile sputtered into life, shimmering. He didn't even have to plug the transformer in.

"See?" She clapped her hands. "All Max can make is little circles and squares. You're a genius, Kevin. You should start working on something new."

"Like what?" He asked her, staring at Sebastian's face. The fiber optics gave off an amazing light.

"I don't know. A heart. A dance of light."

"What about you, Corny?" He used her nickname for the first time. He realized that little slip broke through the last thin membrane of his resolve to not get involved, so he might as well go on.

"What about me?"

"I mean, your Tesla Museum's done. What happens next?"

"I go to South America."

A very bad feeling. "Why South America?"

"Because it's possible that Tesla did some work there."

"Okay. But what are you going to do after the whole Tesla project gets finished?"

She looked startled, and sounded slightly defensive. "Why, nothing. That's what I do."

"What I used to do," Kevin reminded her, "was make a saint that looked like a Bud Light sign. You showed me something better. Now maybe I'll move on. Don't you ever want to move on?"

She bit her lip. "Answer me honestly. Do you think I'm crazy?"

He took her chin and drew it up close to him, gently touched her lip with his.

"I think you have this thing my mom called the spark of the divine. But nobody around you knows what to do with it."

Officer Diaz, watching Sergeant Cantwell's back, poked around the first floor of the industrial building on reconnaissance. It was a dump, old and badly maintained.

She peered at the tenant registry. So many different typefaces, it looked like a ransom note. The six-story building housed a nest of marginal businesses, and she took no special notice of the New York Institute of Art and Technology. She determined that the building could be accessed through one front door, one back door, and a door on the roof.

"We just got backup," Sergeant Cantwell said in his low business voice.

She looked outside to see another cruiser from her precinct running without lights or siren. It turned next to the building and crunched down an alley in the snow to block off the building's back door. A third unit skidded to a stop at the curb. Two officers got out and hustled into the lobby to join them. They huddled.

"Nobody in the super's office. I think we ought to check the roof," Officer Diaz said. "The staircase is locked up and so's the elevator."

So the four officers went outside, stayed close to the building to be invisible to anybody upstairs, and entered the lobby of the building next door. They found a superintendent's office where a young man tried to run from them. They caught him by the back of his jeans. He explained in Spanish that his name was Carlos from Tegucigalpa, Honduras, and he had a family here. And no Green Card, Officer Diaz finished for him, also in Spanish. But they would develop amnesia about his being an undocumented alien if he quietly helped them check out the building next door. Carlos from Tegucigalpa took the four officers to his building's roof where they could just look down a few feet and see the rooftop of the subject building. Officer Diaz immediately spotted the broken knob on the door to the staircase.

"Burglary," she pointed out to Sergeant Cantwell, who grunted as if he'd told her so.

"Hey, Diaz, you make the report," one of the officers standing by the wall told her, pointing down at the street.

Officer Diaz leaned over the wall and saw a gray sedan with red and blue lights on its front grille pull to the curb below. A big dark-skinned man in a captain's uniform got out wearing a blue greatcoat with stripes on the sleeve and white gloves. Captain Washburn, a hard-ass. He had obviously been plucked from some formal big deal to bail out this flaky debutante with connections.

Washburn's scowling face looked up at the grimy, cast-iron subject building. Then he caught Officer Diaz looking down at him from the adjoining roof.

This better be important, he told her by moving his lips clearly enough to read from six stories up.

They stood in the dark looking at Sebastian glow. Kevin realized they were studying it the way people contemplate real art in a museum. It made him feel giddy.

"How's your ankle?" He touched it, a little black-and-blue.

"Watch," Cornelia said. She hopped up on her feet and jumped up and down.

Then she grabbed a glowing fiber optic coil in each hand and began to dance.

She started spinning in circles. Kevin saw that she could really dance. She's probably taken courses like ballet or modern dance, because she sure knew how to be delicate on her feet, even with a twisted ankle. She executed the same little leaps dancers did on PBS, skipping around him, twirling around to make spinning circles of light with the fiber optics, having fun putting on a show for him. The little dancer with the perfect, sculpted calves still wore her hospital scrubs and slippers.

But she looked like a heavenly dance of light.

Officer Diaz joined Captain Washburn on the street.

"Sir, the rooftop door's got a hole in it and the doorknob's gone. Minimum we got a break-in."

"Secure the lobby," the captain ordered.

This was shaping up as more than she expected. Maybe Captain

Washburn was seeing it as a kidnapping now. She started thinking about extra Christmas gifts she would buy with her overtime before the FBI took over.

Then she remembered her glimpse of the debutante's face in the male subject's arms. No, This didn't feel right. She avoided Sergeant Cantwell and spoke directly to Captain Washburn.

"Captain, I got to tell you, this girl didn't look like any kind of victim to me."

Cornelia's limbs felt the rapture. The blond hairs on her arms stood up. She was a child again, twirling toward the window.

She loved her dance in the falling darkness with only Kevin for an audience and the fiber optics she spun for light. Then, as she started her turn right in front of the window, her eyes suddenly locked on to the street below.

She saw, in that microsecond, police cars with black numbers on their hoods. They were stopped right in front of their formerly deserted building. A gaggle of police officers stood on the street, pointing up. Not exactly toward where she spun by the window, but close enough.

Without breaking her turn, she twirled back to Kevin and dropped into his lap.

"I'm famished." She gave his cheek a kiss. "I think I'll go out to get us something to eat. I can cook on Max's sculpting fire."

A look of concern passed over Kevin's face. "I'll go with you."

"Oh, no. You stay here. Do Sebastian's torso. I'll just be a minute."

She threw her arms around his neck and squeezed his mouth to hers. She recorded the memory of the gorgeous blue corona that surrounded his hair.

"Are you sure?" His look was heartbreaking.

"Look, Kevin, you have to trust me sometime," she told him as she opened the elevator and stepped in.

It groaned all the way down. Before she reached the bottom, she took off the stiff new leather coat that belonged to Philip Grace and folded it neatly, leaving it on the floor of the elevator car so Kevin could return it. When the elevator stopped, she opened the door and crossed the shabby foyer in measured steps. Then she walked out into the cold.

A stocky gray-haired police officer in a black leather jacket stood outside with his back to her, scratching the seat of his pants.

"I beg your pardon," she said.

He spun around like a madman, pulling his gun out of his holster and leveling it a few inches from her nose. His eyes looked wild over the black hole of the gun.

"Freeze," he yelled at her.

"I'm frozen already." She held her hands up and out, unsure of what to do with them.

"Hey," a serious-looking woman officer with a cap that sat very high on her head moved beside him. "Cool it."

"I'm very cool," Cornelia trembled.

A giant officer in a long blue coat like an admiral stepped up to her. Even as she stood shivering in the flimsy hospital scrubs with her bare arms stretched out, she felt protected by the man's authority. His coat sported gold stripes on the sleeve. He scowled, then put his hands in the white gloves behind his back and inspected her.

"Ms. Lord, I'm Captain Washburn," his voice rumbled. "Are you okay?"

"I'm fine, thank you."

"We had a report that you might have been abducted."

"Well, I haven't."

"If that's so," he said, "why don't you just let me escort you home."

Then he held his arm out with the white glove, as though asking her to waltz. She folded her own arms and kept her distance.

"Do you promise to leave that building alone?" she asked.

"Ms. Lord," the captain sounded a little bemused. "I don't have any orders concerning that building. If you swear to me there was no criminal activity going on in there, we'll just leave quietly before anybody notices you're gone."

He held the door of the gray sedan open for her.

And from above, Kevin watched the straw-blond head duck into the back of the car and vanish in silent waves of white and blue.

Chapter Eighteen

*C*hester, listen to me," Cornelia told the lapel of his charcoal suit, as he hugged her close to him in the study.

Chester pulled back. She observed from his sad eyes that his melancholy had joined with something new. A sharp glint of resolve.

"No, darling, this time I have to insist that you listen to *me*. You need to confront these Tesla issues."

"Forget about Tesla. Tucker's the problem here." Her voice sounded a little wild, even to herself.

"Tucker?" He stood dumbfounded. "No, I've decided that a time-out will be good for you now. I've made all the arrangements."

O'Connell arrived in the doorway clutching two of her suitcases. *Uh oh.*

"Time-out, good idea." She made a frantic T with her hands. "Stop the clock and listen a minute. Tucker lied to me about things. He told me you needed my help to stop the Kois from taking over Lord & Company."

"He wasn't lying, darling. It's true."

She felt poorly organized, at an awful disadvantage. "I know, I mean, about other things."

"About what?"

"I believe that Tucker is involved with Han Koi in this takeover."

Her father sucked his breath in. "Why?"

She needed to fight for both of them now. And quickly, with her luggage already in the hall. *Sent away.* That inevitable fate of Electric Girls who knew disturbing truths. She grasped for facts, but they seemed slippery and inconclusive at best.

"Tucker promised to take me to South America if I'd marry him. He claimed that he'd found a Tesla Tower and . . ."—*the old man*— ". . . an engineer. But the engineer turned out to be a senior without a partner. I found that out because all the supplies for the trip wound up in your office . . ."

This wasn't helping. Chester looked baffled.

"Darling, I take full responsibility for anything that Tucker may have told you. He asked my permission, I gave it."

Tucker's planning had tied her up in knots, leaving Chester to administer the last little nips and tucks. It made her stomach boil with injustice that her father could trust him so implicitly.

"I suppose you told him to behave suspiciously with the Kois."

"Suspicious in what way?"

"There was a distinct connection between them." She gave up and tears burst onto her cheeks. "Please, Daddy. I have to ask you to take it on faith. Keep an eye on Tucker. Look at his motives."

"*You* look, Cornelia." His exasperation had smoldered like firewood. Now it snapped at her. "Tucker brought the takeover to my attention. If he was involved, I wouldn't have known about it until it was too late. And it wouldn't have gone well for us after that, I assure you."

"Tucker warned you?" She tried to process that new information."

Chester turned one palm up, continued his grating reasonableness.

"Cornelia, contrary to what you said in front of my business associates, Tucker did not lie to you or make underhanded deals with Han Koi. Tucker had every intention of taking you to South America, he assured me. Now he's more concerned, as I am, with getting you help. O'Connell, please put Cornelia's bags in the car."

"Wait, O'Connell," she pleaded. The butler stood frozen in the doorway. "What kind of help?"

"A more residential sort of help than Dr. Bushberg can give you.

There's a place in Armonk called the Sanctuary." He paused. His palm spun in a circle while he searched for words. "We'll come up to visit . . ."

" 'We' should be you and me, Daddy."

Chester winced but didn't budge. She felt a sudden cold shudder.

As bad as this was, it could get worse. What if she kept protesting, and Tucker began snooping into her past thirty-six hours? He would certainly uncover Kevin Doyle. Poor Kevin, so innocent under his beautiful corona. Tucker could hurt him, if he found out, in ways that might not end just with Kevin losing his job.

"Darling," her father intruded. "Tucker's waiting for us in the car. All I'm asking is that you take an evaluation for thirty days. The Sanctuary is practically a resort."

"Oh? Do they let you leave?"

"Not immediately. You'll take some tests first, talk to the doctors." He softened a bit. "Tell them whatever you can't confide in me."

O'Connell stood firm, becoming better acquainted with his heavy shoes. Her father had folded his hands stiffly in front of him like a parson.

The Sanctuary.

Her thoughts drifted to soft foods and even softer walls. She would need to get word to Kevin, and to Dr. Powers, to let them know that she would be away temporarily. But what else could she do? Chester didn't believe her.

It dawned on her that she would be more likely to find a sympathetic ear at the Sanctuary than here at home.

Kevin lay on his bed in the dark bedroom, staring at his telephone.

He had slept fitfully, trapped in that netherworld of people in crisis, where spasmodic dreams solved all problems. The painful throbbing in his shoulder had woken him. He felt punches in the shoulder over and over again, imagined a burly Irishman slamming his shoulder with an overgrown fist. And his first thought was about light reflecting on blond hair that vanished in the back of a car.

You have to trust me.

When she had left the studio, he disciplined himself to not go to the window and look. He finally decided to take just a small peek, not because he didn't trust her but because he just liked to watch her. All he could make out, pressing his mouth and fingertips against the cold glass, was the halo of bright golden hair in a dirty back window. Then he felt panic, the need to take action.

He had steeled himself to act cool, phoning Andrew to see what he knew, just pretending he wanted to stay in the loop of building events while on sick leave. Andrew told him nothing except that they whisked Cornelia Lord away in a brand-new Mercedes limousine, her father and Tucker Fisk, less than an hour after the police brought her home. And the driver loaded the trunk with two suitcases.

Kevin pulled the covers up over his head. His ear and shoulder pounded, drowned out by the wailing in his chest.

Suddenly, feeling like the whole floor buckled under his bed, Kevin understood why he'd never fallen in love before. Who would want this hollow longing, to feel ripped open from inside out? And the lust part. He'd been lonely and disillusioned for so long, he'd almost forgotten about the lust part. After she'd gone, he realized she'd awakened that in him, too.

He rolled over, twisting in his sheets.

Just when his hands and eyes had seemed shriveled and useless, she'd brought him back from his Art Death. Soul mates were the elusive wonder of the world. He'd always worried deep in his gut that his real soul mate might be someone so unappetizing he'd never get to know her. Like the nasty waitress with the bleached arm hair in the coffee shop. But Cornelia Lord? She was so unattainable, he might as well fall in love with the Pope. Still, he desperately needed to find her. He climbed out of bed and looked at the print of *Saint Sebastian*.

Lucky Sebastian with only a few arrows to think about.

His body felt so wretched, he wished he could just check out of it like a cheap hotel room. This would not be a temporary loss if he let her run away.

This would be another permanent one.

A deadly, freezing loneliness crept over him. This time, he wouldn't just take the hand he was dealt. He'd turn over the table if he had to.

This was the time for performance art.

*　　*　　*

Kevin marched to Gus Anholdt's little building manager's office, with its shabby aura of punishment.

"Back two weeks early?" Gus had a high forehead and small wire-rimmed glasses that pinched his nose. He looked unhappy. "I'm supposed to tell you, Chester Lord's very grateful to you."

Gus handed him an envelope.

"He said thanks for not talking to the media, exploiting the whole thing. If there's anything more you need, doctors or whatever, he said you ought to call the phone number on the note."

"Thanks," Kevin mumbled to Gus, whipping out of his office for the staff room. He opened the envelope and pulled out a card. It was a "Season's Greetings" card, designed only for giving cash tips to low-level service employees. The cut-out pouch contained a check, drawn on a Lord & Company bank account at AmeriCorp.

The check was made out to "K. Doyle," with a blue and red check protector imprint, in the amount of "$5,000.00 EXACTLY." A little notation in the lower left corner said, "For Services." The typed signature on the card read, "Per Chester Lord IV." It gave the office number for Lord & Company.

He studied the typed data. Not even a handwritten note. Kevin put the envelope in his jacket pocket.

He sat alone in a corner booth at the Waldorf-Estonia Luncheonette, trying to stomach a club sandwich, when Philip Grace arrived. The photographer shook the snow off his old camel-hair coat, not half as nice as the gray leather one. Grace untied his white silk scarf and tossed his aviator-style sunglasses on the table between them.

"Hey, Philip."

"Our reluctant hero," Philip greeted Kevin. He rubbed his hand over his shaved head, wiping off the wet snow. "Threw yourself in harm's way out of valor, a rare jewel in our time. 'Course that was two days ago, and the *Globe* ain't exactly a historical publication. You got something new for me?"

"Maybe. First, I was hoping you could tell me where she is."

"Well," Philip Grace fooled with the sugar packets on the counter, stacking them in a pile. "Let's say I slip you tomorrow's story today, and tell you Ms. Cornelia Lord's presently residin' in a luxury rubber room in Westchester County. I'd need a little quid pro quo from you before I go into more details."

"Like what?"

"Help me get a shot of her in the funny farm."

"Say you were in a hospital, drugged up," Kevin asked him. "You'd want people taking your picture while you're drooling on your bathrobe? I can't do that."

Philip smiled and settled back in his booth. "You know, I miss these *ethical* discussions. You never get into talkin' philosophy after college."

"I never got to college. You?"

"Ivy man for one semester, Columbia. Till they kept dunnin' me to pay the tuition." Philip chuckled, flicking his pile of sugar packets over with a snap of his finger. "Problem is with what you're askin', that'd be a whole mountain of quid for you without even an itty-bitty thimbleful of quo for me."

"Are we off the record now?" Kevin asked him.

Philip laughed and wheezed until he almost choked. "Off the record? What you think, this is *60 Minutes*? I'm wearin' a camera inside my eyeball?"

"Well, are we?" Kevin said, not smiling. "Off the record?"

"Okay, Mr. Doyle. You go ahead and give me something on background, like we say, me and Diane Sawyer."

"I need to see Cornelia," Kevin said. "I don't care how."

Philip frowned and stared at Kevin. "That's pretty tall money and power you're up against. Chester Lord and her fiancé, Mr. Tucker Fisk."

"Fiancé?" The blood roared in Kevin's ears.

"What I hear about Mr. Fisk," Philip blabbed on, "he may not always go strictly by the rules, he sees somebody wants to take his little ball away."

"Tucker's not even her boyfriend," Kevin tried.

"You need to keep in touch with current events. Tucker Fisk put the word out they got engaged. Would she be playin' with your head, Kevin Doyle?"

"No. I'm just surprised."

Like if the earth stopped spinning around the sun and they all got flung into infinite space—that kind of surprised. That was exactly the reason he needed to talk to her one on one, without people like Tucker Fisk and Chester Lord and his lawyers and butlers to confuse things.

"I'm not saying it's easy," Kevin said. "But you act like a pretty slick guy. I'm just wondering if you can handle a problem that takes a little more strategy than hiding behind a garbage Dumpster."

Kevin took the $5,000 check out of his pocket and handed it to Philip.

"I don't know much about checkbook journalism," Kevin said. "But this is yours if you give me the name of the hospital they put her in."

Philip took the check and studied it. "She's in the Sanctuary. Up in Armonk, New York."

Kevin stood up again. "I have to call you tomorrow after I check some stuff out, ask your advice."

"Hey," Philip said sharply. "Checkbook journalism means we pay you. You best get that straight, you gonna be foolin' around with the media."

He dangled the check out in the air with two fingers and Kevin took it.

"Thanks, Philip," Kevin said.

"Seems to be the pattern of our relationship, man, like a slot machine." Philip put his hands up in the air, shaking his head at his own foolishness. "I keep givin', you keep takin', pay me off just enough to keep me interested. Don't know why I do it."

Kevin considered that. "I guess you need a lot of hope, the business you're in."

He picked up the plain brown shopping bag from under the table and placed it on Grace's seat, watching him for a second while he walked away. Grace pulled out the gray leather bundle and unfolded his new coat, frowning.

Kevin felt the Debwatcher's eyes on the back of his neck as he walked out of the luncheonette.

"Uncle Eddie? Kevin. I'm feeling kind of bad since the accident. Like I need to see a doctor. How good is my health plan? I mean, can I use any doctor I want?"

"You can go to Dr. Kevorkian if you want to."

"Unlimited hospitalization?" Kevin asked.

"Yeah, any hospital."

"Dental?" Kevin breathed in and held it. "Psychiatric?"

"Yeah. Jesus, Kevin, what's wrong with you?"

It took only one more brief meeting with Philip Grace the next day, same booth, same luncheonette, same waitress with the attitude. But this time she said she read about him in the paper and asked him to autograph her order pad. Then Kevin sucked up his strength to call Helen.

Helen and Harold lived in Stuyvesant Town, a project in the East 20s developed by an insurance company for middle-income people. In a city where new high-rise buildings were built as high as the city would let them and used windows as big as possible so they looked like giant ice cube trays stood on end, the low-rise mottled brick buildings of Stuyvesant Town looked like a village of brownies.

He heard Harold's reedy voice over the intercom and got buzzed in. Harold wasn't a bad guy, Kevin thought, once you got beyond the frizzy hair that stood up from his head and ears.

"You look terrible," Helen greeted him at the door.

Harold sat him down on the Naugahyde living room couch. Kevin politely looked through a Kodak packet they handed him full of photographs taken on their last vacation, a photo safari in Africa. One picture showed them standing with their tour guide, a tall Masai. Harold said the guide was a fan of *Seinfeld* reruns who had to give his fiancée's father five goats as a dowry. Kevin studied a picture of a monkey stealing Helen's sunglasses from their jeep. Then a picture of a hippopotamus drifting in brown water. When he ran out of photographs in the yellow packet, he put them back and slowly folded it over.

"There's no easy way to ask you for this," Kevin said. "So I'm just going to do it."

They looked both clueless and curious.

"I think I can help this girl I know. She's got some issues . . ."

"That crazy debutante?" His sister bounced on her seat in horror, like he'd thrown a bucket of paint on her couch.

"Harold," Kevin pressed on, "how do you diagnose people when they come into Bellevue?"

"We take the diagnostic process very seriously," Harold said. "We give each patient a comprehensive battery of tests. We always try to interview family members to give us background and context. Several different staff members talk to the patient—"

"What do you want from us?" Helen interrupted him.

"I have time off and insurance," Kevin said. "Lots of it. I can get any kind of medical care I want. Cornelia's father sent her to the Sanctuary in Westchester."

Helen's face turned a blotchy red, and she spaced her words out. "I hope you're not going to ask my husband to help defraud a psychiatric hospital."

Kevin nodded. "And an insurance company, if you want to be negative about it. I can't explain this in a way that's going to make total sense to you. If I can be with this girl, one on one, I can help her. But I need to do this, Helen. I've never asked you for a favor like this in my life."

"That's the most self-serving excuse I've ever heard," Helen told him. "Your mother would be ashamed of you."

"Why?" He leaned over toward them, resting his elbows on his knees, ready for a siege.

"It's totally dishonest," Helen snapped. "And it's despicable to ask my husband to coach you. He could lose his license."

"I don't expect Harold to open his mouth. All I need is a look at the diagnostic tests. Just an idea of what the questions are."

"Kevin," Harold spoke up. "Psychiatric diagnosis isn't like a civil service exam. The Sanctuary? My God. You're talking about fooling some of the best psychologists in the world. You can't cheat the diagnostics. They give you a whole battery, five or six tests, and they cross-check to weed out malingerers. They'll know you're faking. Even if you got referred by some psychiatrist, even if you got *admitted*, you'll be under observation every day. Psychiatrists weren't born yesterday."

"What about Bellevue, Harold? You admitted some guy who claimed he was Robin Hood. So Robin Hood robbed the hospital pharmacy. You think he gave his Class A narcotics to the poor?"

"That was a fluke," Harold mumbled.

"Come on, Harold, who's going to get hurt?"

"The girl," Helen said.

"How?" Kevin asked her.

Helen looked blank and turned to her husband.

Harold obliged her, warming to his task. "You want to manipulate your way into a relationship with her when she's most vulnerable. I've always liked you, Kevin. Maybe you're no hard-charging guy, but you always tried to do the right thing. If the girl wants you when she's better, she'll look for you. But I couldn't let you do what you're saying, even if I wanted to help. It's selfish and irresponsible."

He turned to his sister. "Is that what I am, Helen? Selfish and irresponsible?"

She said nothing.

"Okay. I respect what you're telling me. I just want to say something. Hey, sit down," he barked when Harold started to get up. "This is for you, too."

Harold fell back into the cushion of the Naugahyde sofa, hissing like a tire losing air.

"Helen, when you were at CCNY having an affair with Harold, you weren't even eighteen yet and he was married."

"That was different," Helen said.

"It's always different when it's you. Mom and Dad were raising hell. Marne was going to report Harold to the college, screwing around with an underage student. But I said, maybe it's not ethical, maybe it's not legal, maybe it's crazy. But it's Helen, and she loves the guy, right or wrong. Let's wait, see what happens." Kevin took a long pause. "All I need is a shot at it, Helen."

Uh-oh. He'd gotten a little carried away. He hoped he didn't hurt her feelings. But somewhere along the way Helen seemed to have lost her ability to feel either pain or pleasure.

She set her jawline tight as a vault. "You'd better go."

Kevin stood up and walked out of the apartment. He didn't slam the door behind him, but clicked it shut very politely to make more of a statement.

He heard Harold through the doorway. "You know, he guilts pretty good, for a guy who isn't even Jewish."

* * *

He took the subway to the Columbia University library.

Philip Grace, who had actually attended Columbia for one semester, had kept his campus ID card and given it to Kevin to customize. Using a matte knife, he had inserted his own photograph taken in a booth. Then he changed the dates carefully with a stippling pen. Finally, he put his creation in a plastic laminating machine and became Kevin Doyle, Columbia student.

The security guard at the Columbia University library entrance barely glanced at the doctored ID when he walked past.

He started in the room where they kept the psychology stacks. Carting six volumes to a table, Kevin suddenly felt desperately tired. Not just physically, but from a kind of hopelessness. He looked around the table at the Columbia students with piles of books open in front of them, taking notes on pads and laptops. They would go on to be doctors, captains of industry, lawyers.

It reminded him of all the money and power that would be against him in his struggle. Not just Tucker Fisk, and Chester Lord, but the entire Establishment, whatever that was, down to his own pathetic municipal lifer brother-in-law Harold.

On Kevin's side, he had Uncle Eddie's health plan and a half-baked reporter with a bunch of temporary restraining orders.

"How can I lose?" he snarled out loud.

A few people at the library table took unnecessary zeal in shushing him. Kevin opened a fat book called *The Diagnostic Manual of Psychiatry* familiarly known as the *DMP*, and a companion book, *DMP for Dummies*.

He knew these books from his work at Bellevue. They gave mental health workers a way of classifying the weird things candidates for admission did, like confusing their spouses for empty milk cartons and trying to squeeze them into trash compactors. The categories were coded in the *DMP*, and an admitting psychologist would check off boxes.

Kevin plunged through the diagnostic codes for different conditions. He studied 1003.1 with care, "Delusional Disorders, Grandiose." It came with a list of symptoms like a menu.

Kevin sampled other books, paying close attention to *Treating the Delusional Adult*, by Dr. John Blackwell. Philip Grace had given him

Blackwell's name, a Park Avenue psychiatrist with society credentials. If Kevin could fool Blackwell, the doctor would refer him to the Sanctuary and think he was practicing medicine. The problem, as Harold pointed out, was the lie scales on the psychiatric tests.

The main diagnostic test was called the Maryland Mental Questionnaire, or MMQ. It had trick questions to trap people who were faking mental illness. If he couldn't get his hands on the MMQ test manual, he'd be snared by the random sneakiness of the lie scale questions.

When he finished with the psychology section, he moved to history. He studied Gibbon's *Decline and Fall of the Roman Empire* for a time, then returned to the psychology stacks.

After fifteen hours, the horrible, turgid writing in the textbooks finally got to him. Now he could clearly see how easily he would fail. *Doctors could actually read these books and understand them.* He'd never beat the doctors at their own game.

What would really happen was, Cornelia would get beaten by the system, too, just at a much higher level. She would become Mrs. Tucker Fisk. In a couple of years, Kevin would touch his hat to the happy couple every day. Or at least Tucker's half of the couple would be happy, as they breezed past him in the lobby of 840 Fifth with a nanny pushing a baby carriage. The swift, sure injustice of it all finally whizzed down on his neck and detached his will to go on.

He left the reference books on the table. In a few minutes, he was falling asleep on the subway home.

His own slumlord paid Con Ed every month, but the light fixtures had been stolen from the building again.

He looked at the walls, ripped out by junkies for the copper wires inside. For the first time, rage tore through him as he saw the violated walls. He ran upstairs and slammed his hand against his splintered wooden door. It flew open, unlocked. Somebody had been there.

He kicked his door frame, tears welling up, and lunged into his apartment. He didn't care anymore. The crack addicts could throw him against the wall and gun him down like a dog.

"Come on, you bastards," he bellowed.

Nobody answered, but he kicked something small with his foot.

A black rectangular box sat on his floor with a note underneath it. He stared at it without picking it up. Maybe Tucker Fisk had left a bomb inside his apartment.

It would probably be an exploding nail bomb. A thousand nails would fly into his body. He would bleed to death from all the holes. He would never see his family or Cornelia again. At least Saint Sebastian would survive, back at the school.

Then he looked more closely at the writing on the note. It started "*Kevin, take this MM . . .*" The rest of the note was obscured by the box.

Kevin bent over and squeezed the sheet of paper carefully between his two fingers. He gently held the box so it wouldn't slide. Then he slowly pulled the paper out along the floor until he could read it.

"*Kevin, take this MMQ and use the guidebook. You must return it to me by tomorrow morning.*"

It was signed, "H." He knew it wasn't Harold.

His heart pounded. The Maryland Mental Questionnaire. His heart raced as he leafed through the secret User's Guidebook, found the L scale for trapping liars. He ran his finger down the top of the long row of cards packed in the black cardboard box, each card asking a question requiring a yes or no. Kevin seized one card at random. The statement read, "In real life, I am a messenger from God."

Things were finally starting to look up.

Chapter Nineteen

*A*re you sitting down, Kevin? I'm about to make you flavor of the month," Jessica Fernandez of the Stinson Gallery told him over the phone.

He had been waiting for this call all his life.

Now, in his apartment at ten in the morning, sluggish after staying awake memorizing the MMQ on the brink of his mission, he pictured Jessica in a short black skirt with her slinky legs crossed, her long fingers with blood-red nails playing with the telephone cord. Her eyebrows, those little peaked roofs, would be raised while she spoke to him.

"Jessica," he managed, "why now?"

"The minute I saw the story about you on the front page, getting hit in the head by the limo? I took out my Rolodex and called seventeen clients," Jessica said. "I told them you were a method artist, that you needed to hurt yourself badly to perfect your neon saint. My client Jack Bremer, he owns that custom plumbing company, Mr. Bidet? He ate it up, Kevin. He's going to buy Saint Sebastian."

"Jessica, I made Sebastian glow," he began to tell her.

"Yes, darling, it's neon."

"I'm using fiber optics now. You have to see it."

"Okay, I can see it clearly, Kevin. You had an epiphany, getting hurt in the accident. I'm building on the marketing strategy already. The important thing is, you've got to get working, fast. I need more product, much more product, as fast as you can make it."

He tried to think of some way to explain to her.

"Kevin, why aren't you answering me? You're up in a bubble right now, but it's going to burst anytime. I need to build momentum for you. How soon can you make more pieces?"

"The thing is, I have to go away for a while. Maybe a couple of weeks, a month . . ."

"Kevin," she snapped at him, "you will not be salable in a couple of weeks or even a couple of days. Are you listening to me? I found a buyer *now*."

"But what I have to do, it's very important to me."

"Kevin"—she sounded wary—"did you sign with another gallery?"

"No."

"I want you to meet me for lunch today. I'll bring a contract. Schrappnel at noon."

"Thanks, Jessica."

The abrupt disconnect buzz came. Definitely Jessica Fernandez. Not a dream. He suddenly collapsed onto his knees, clutching the phone to his chest.

But why now?

For months, he had rehearsed how he would handle the glorious news of a sale if and when this call ever came. The truth was, he would have just yelped and done a wild goat dance of victory. But now all that had changed. His new mission directly conflicted with the glossy world of Jessica Fernandez, actually shrunk it down from the galactic importance it once held.

He could still have lunch. He deserved just a taste of the sweet fruit, to sun himself for maybe an hour in the new Art Life that would end as suddenly as it had begun.

Calling his sister at the fire station where she worked in the rump of Brooklyn, he could practically hear the water from Dead Horse Bay lap at the station door while she came to the phone.

"Marne, I need a favor, bad. It involves wearing something you might put on to go to church and meeting me on Park Avenue. You can't tell anyone."

"Why?"

"I can't tell you. I just need to know if you're in."

"I dunno. Is it about that debutante?"

"Maybe." Silence. "Marne?"

"This better be good, Kevin."

Crossing over the threshold of Schrappnel gave Kevin bumps on his arms.

The heavy-duty art, film, and music people ate here in TriBeCa, the epicenter of Art Life, the volume of their chatter careening off the hard surfaces. Languid models looking for jobs served their food with adoration. He had read that a syndicate of dentists from Long Island owned the place, and they hired the metal sculptor Xavier Schrapp to decorate it and used his name to give it tone. Schrapp was one of Jessica's clients. She had pushed him to an oeuvre of tortured metalwork she called "Schrappnel." Brand names were key to Jessica's artist-marketing strategy.

For the restaurant, Schrapp had chosen a theme of danger. It forced Kevin to be careful squeezing to his table, to avoid being pierced by the sharp metal projectiles sticking up and out from the floor and walls. He'd bet that Schrapp executed the design in one day by setting off dynamite in some Bronx auto graveyard and dumping the result in the restaurant, then playing the artiste by forbidding the owners to move a single jagged piece.

Meeting Jessica Fernandez, here at the Valhalla for New York artists, to talk about the sale of his work. He wished his mother could see him now, being led by a stunning sylph with a permapout to a corner table. Jessica looked even slinkier than he imagined, a little black dress over her golden brown exuberant body, the sulking red lips.

He wished, brushing by a metal spike, that Cornelia could see him, too. But should she see Jessica? Would Corny get jealous over him? He wondered if Cornelia even had a jealous bone in her body. Somehow, she seemed beyond that. He had to add that question to others he had formed about her since she had followed his corona to his apartment.

Jessica stood up and gave him both sides of her face to kiss. A waiter hustled over with a champagne bucket and made a fuss of pouring them two flute glasses with perfectly equal crests of fizz. The man performed with his own topspin, like a wannabe actor. He held the bottle in such a way that Kevin could read "Krug" on the label before it got crunched back in the ice bucket.

"To those baby-blue eyes and all the green they'll make us," Jessica toasted him, wrinkling her nose at the ugly black stitches in his ear.

Kevin drank the champagne and felt the merry bubbles tickling his nostrils. After a moment, they struck his brain.

"Your hair doesn't match your eyes," she said. "Are you really Irish?"

"Black Irish," Kevin said.

"I'm Cuban, you know." She smiled at him like Salome contemplating John the Baptist. "What I was thinking, I have a house in East Hampton with a studio. We can get it fixed up for you and you can turn out, say, one piece a week."

"One piece of what?"

She seemed flustered for a moment, leaving an imprint of her red lips on the champagne glass. "You know, what you're doing. More neon saints."

"Jessica, I don't want to do any more saints. Somebody showed me how to work with freestanding fiber optics. I'm ready to move on."

Jessica Fernandez looked as stung and betrayed as though he'd stabbed her with his bread knife.

"Kevin, *no!*" Scolding a dog. "You will not do any little artsy-fartsy departures on me. You will only do art that people will buy."

"It's not creative unless it sells?" He sighed. The attractive qualities he once saw in Jessica Fernandez were falling away now, like shedding skin. Well, he only came to bask in the moment. He might as well have his fun with it.

"I guess I could do Saint Catherine next, spread-eagled and spinning on a wheel in the fire. Make the piece move with light, use red and yellow, some kind of burnt-flesh tones."

"Like crème brûlée," she agreed. "Brilliant."

"Then maybe Joan of Arc. Whites and blues. I can make her feet dance in the flames. I can do a whole series, call it *Rhythm of the Saints.*"

"Astonishing. You're a genius, darling. How long does it take you to make these saints?"

"Sebastian only took two years."

Jessica's smile dropped below the horizon and her face lost its creamy luster. "We're going to have to speed the process up. Can't you do something smaller? Maybe something we can merchandise in volume?"

He thought it over.

"I guess I could start with a Saint Sebastian pencil holder."

Her eyes sparkled again, and he realized that Jessica had also begun turning them on him in a new, heavy-lidded way.

Her eyelids reminded him of a reptile's the way they closed from both top and bottom. Her hand casually dropped below the table to touch his leg. *Just you and me together on this rock, sunning ourselves, and don't let the fact that I'm all coiled up and ready to strike bother you.*

Unless he struck first. "Jessica, have you ever been in love?"

"What are you asking me?" Her eyes smoldered.

Kevin stood up. "All I can tell you is, I fell in love with somebody. She went away and it's like losing a leg or something. It changes your priorities about life. No more saints. I'm sorry. Maybe some other time."

She looked so damaged. "Did I offend you, Kevin?"

He took a last sip and saw in the flute glass his career circling the drain.

"Thanks for the champagne. I really have to go."

"Kevin, just remember," she recovered, calling loudly after him as he worked his way through the tables and sharp points. "You have until five o'clock to change your mind and call me. Or you can stick that mall art up your ass, darling."

The lunch crowd turned around to watch him. He was only punctured by one of Schrapp's twisted fenders before he made it out the door.

His breath made a circle that appeared and went away on the window of the Hyperkinesis Gallery on Greene Street.

He stared inside at a metal-and-light sculpture in the window with a red "Sold" tag on it. The red tag seemed almost larger than the sculpture, the way he concentrated on it. He thought about "cognitive dissonance," a concept he had run across in his four-day crash course in psychology. It said that once you make a decision, all of the negatives about it pop up like demons in your brain. The psychologists said you should ignore it.

But looking at the red "Sold" tag in front of him, Kevin thought that maybe cognitive dissonance was a bullshit concept. People made decisions that ruin their lives every day. Like Romeo killing himself, believing Juliet was already dead. Or Kevin pissing off Jessica Fernandez when she was ready to ignite his Art Life.

He wondered. He had begun walking toward his apartment at some point, in what felt like a low-level coma. Was it possible to create a *Twilight Zone* kind of reverse ending, to turn the clock back by just one hour? That's all he would need. Jessica would show up at the restaurant feeling good about him again. He would just drop down on his knees and ask for the train schedule to East Hampton. He glanced down. Unconsciously, his feet had actually started moving a little faster.

No.

He slowed down again. Cornelia had changed him. Before Corny, he just crept around the idea of love, too timid to really go after it. Like golfers on television who walk around the hole fifty times measuring and pointing with their clubs because they don't really want to take the shot. Cornelia was a catalyst for good things. But, at the moment, she happened to be Tucker Fisk's catalyst.

His plan was so insane that maybe he really did belong in a psychiatric hospital. He could probably just tell the Sanctuary doctors what his plan was, and they would look at one another and open their doors to him. Any struggling artist who blew off Jessica Fernandez was a certifiable lunatic.

He shook his head to try to throw off his fuzzy paralysis and think. If a sane young artist had done something like that by accident, by some tragic misfire of the brain, he would still have time to call Jessica and beg. He stepped up in his pace again until he was trotting. She had definitely said "by five o'clock."

Then he was flat out running, working his legs like pistons, his breath hoarse as he thundered toward his apartment.

It was 4:47 with only four blocks to go.

He rounded the corner of Avenue A at 4:51, zipping around the pinheads and junkies. His arms didn't pump anymore, they flailed around in front of him so people moved away as he sprinted toward his building.

He counted on his building's front door still being broken, and it was. He tore into it at ramming speed, rehearsing his apology to Jessica, a story about some new virus that invaded the brain and shut it down for only twenty-four hours, then went away.

At 4:57, he was clattering up his staircase with three glorious minutes to spare.

Then he saw the envelope sticking out of his mailbox. It looked expensive and tasteful, even from a distance.

He stopped.

Slowly, he started back down the stairs and plucked it out of his box. The address was handwritten. But there was no stamp, and no postmark.

Somebody must have delivered it by hand. And recently, because it hadn't been stolen yet.

He opened the envelope carefully and extracted the note. The paper had the texture of linen napkins. Under the embossed initials "CJL," it read:

> *Dear Kevin*
>   *I feel badly that I could not properly say goodbye to you.*
>   *Since it is my sad belief that we are unlikely to see each other soon, I wanted to thank you for the world we shared for thirty-two and one half hours.*
>   *I'm sorry that I must put down my pen now, but my medication makes me quite sleepy and I feel another nap coming on.*
>   *Love,*
>   *Cornelia*

Kevin read the letter standing in the dark foyer of his building. Walking upstairs to his apartment, he read it six more times. When he finally noticed his watch again, it was 5:26.

But he didn't care.

"And when did your brother first present these symptoms, Ms. Doyle?"

The psychiatrist had straight silvery hair and a winter half-tan, probably from hopping to islands and ski resorts. His suit looked expensively rumpled, to signal that he was no coarse Wall Street money-changer, but a keeper of the intellectual torch passed by Freud and Jung.

For Kevin's purpose, Dr. Blackwell had the perfect combination of impeccable credentials and bad judgment. He had clout not only to refer him to the Sanctuary, but to bump him up to the front of the waiting list. Philip Grace had identified him. But Philip also had his doubts about Kevin's plan.

"Problem is, you're nobody," the reporter summed it up.

"Then maybe I'll have to be somebody else," Kevin decided.

Now he sat mute in a chair beside Marne, dressed primly in a blue suit with her hair neatly combed. She folded her hands in her lap and planted both feet on the floor. Kevin thought of her as a pretty pilgrim amid the pre-Columbian sculptures of fertility goddesses with jutting breasts that cluttered Blackwell's office. Marne kept her mouth shut, for the most part, exactly as Kevin had begged her. She looked up at Dr. Blackwell from under her bangs, and they discussed Kevin as though he had left the room.

"He's been a little flaky all his life, Doctor, but he got worse after the accident. He got hit on the head, you know."

"Yes. I examined him, and I looked at his neurological tests from the hospital. He seems fine physically, Ms. Doyle, but I'm afraid that I see a red light here."

"Excuse me?"

"A red light signals a need to stop. In your brother's case, to take time out from his life and get help."

She flashed Kevin a "Jackpot" kind of look. "Stop how?"

"I believe that he would benefit from in-patient care. Perhaps at Manhattan Hill Hospital . . ."

"Doctor," Marne's eyes burned with righteous fire. "Is that *absolutely* the best private hospital in the area for . . . what Kevin has?"

"Hmmm." Dr. Blackwell pondered that. "Actually I happen to be on the board of the Sanctuary, a hospital in northern Westchester County . . ."

Marne's eyes flicked at Kevin. Philip Grace had already turned up that little morsel for them.

"It's considered the premier facility on the East Coast. In your brother's case, there's a very interesting pattern of delusion. Quite fascinating, really, from a psychiatric standpoint." Dr. Blackwell glanced at a copy of *The New England Journal of Medicine* on his desk. He licked his lips, as though contemplating how his name would look on the cover.

"I'll recommend an open-ended inpatient program there, although I'm afraid that it also would preclude working at his job of . . ." he struggled to recall.

"Doorman."

"Yes, doorman. Unless, of course, he works in the Roman Catacombs." The doctor's body jiggled a little, laughing to himself.

"Pardon?"

"Oh, nothing. But my office has checked your brother's health plan, an excellent one, and I would urge you to let him take a thirty-day observation at the Sanctuary. It could be a very pleasant break for him. No responsibilities except to get well."

Marne put on a nearly over-the-top show of a Ping-Pong match going on in her head, working her fingers in a fret. "I just don't know what we're supposed to do with him now. I can't get Kevin into a place like that, with waiting lists and all."

She pouted and crossed her buffed legs.

He smiled charmingly. "I don't believe in waiting lists for my patients, Ms. Doyle. I can get him in this evening, if you can get him packed."

She frowned deeply. "So soon? I don't have transportation."

"Oh, I'll put it on his plan."

Chapter Twenty

Kevin examined the hi-fi and air conditioning controls above his seat in the stretch Lincoln Town Car. He had never ridden in a limousine before.

Heading north, he watched the four-acre zoning part of Westchester County whip by at night, outlines of mansions on vast stretches of woodland. It seemed like a time warp. Just half an hour before, the limousine had sped through the South Bronx, like firebombed ruins of World War II he'd seen on the History Channel.

The driver, Majik, wore a black suit and white turban. A six-pointed brass crown had been attached to the dashboard. Close to Kevin, a brass statue of a multi-armed Hindu goddess sat glued to the plastic-walnut bar.

A dark-skinned man with a neatly trimmed black beard, Majik tried more than once to engage Kevin in conversation. But Kevin had already resolved to say as little as possible.

"What is your occupation?" Majik asked twice.

Oh, well. "I was an officer."

"Ah! A military man," Majik pronounced it the British way. "What branch of the service?"

"The Praetorian Guard."

"I am not familiar with this branch." In the rearview mirror Majik's dark eyebrows rose. "Where are you stationed?"

"In Rome."

"Of course, you guard the Pope in the Vatican." Majik spun his head around. "Such a coincidence! My family's caste is Rajput. For centuries we were India's warriors. Oh, yes, my grandfather drove the official Rolls-Royce for Lord Mountbatten."

Kevin listened to Majik but followed a wire mesh fence along the road. Far behind it, he could make out a great stone building.

Majik turned off at an exit, spinning gravel under the tires.

"This . . . is the Sanctuary," Majik said with reverence.

No signs identified the hospital. Kevin could only see, on the high wire fence, a sign posted "Danger. High Voltage. No Trespassing." The limousine stopped at an unmarked guardhouse where uniformed security guards peered in the car.

Majik handed one of the guards an envelope. Kevin's admissions note from Dr. Blackwell. As they waited, another limousine passed in the other direction. It was a shiny new stretch Mercedes with blackened windows that roared off onto the unlit country road.

"Take him to Admissions," the guard told Majik.

Kevin scanned the property, not brightly lit like a penitentiary, but with discreet security lights planted just where they were needed. He counted two pairs of security guards patrolling the property in golf carts.

Philip Grace had told him that the Sanctuary was the "Canyon Ranch of psychiatric hospitals." It sure didn't look like any ranch. Despite the large grounds, the space felt closed in. Kevin saw a footpath resembling a dog track, open and circular with no privacy. Kevin thought of Cornelia, so small and helpless. If she tried to escape from here, she'd be manhandled by security men who probably knew the body's pressure points and smiled when they used them.

How could her family treat her this way?

Majik pulled onto a twisting driveway. Lumpy speed bumps jolted the limousine, threatening to loosen the Hindu goddess from her perch.

They reached the main house, a dark gray stone mansion with elegant French windows and shutters. But the double doors looked solid as a dungeon's, and the windows displayed the same kind of wrought iron security bars that covered the street-floor windows at 840 Fifth Avenue. Behind their wrought iron, the rich started out eccentric and went crazy.

A male aide dressed in white with a very blond crew cut answered the doorbell. He took Dr. Blackwell's note and gave Kevin a doorman's forced smile.

"Hi, Mr. Doyle, I'm Tim. I'll take you from here."

The black Mercedes stretch limousine that had passed Majik's smelled of old wood and new leather. Chester slumped into the plump, biscuity rear seat next to a console full of Sony, not Koi, components. Tucker used the space to spread his legs just as Kevin had in the Lincoln, while he made Chester a drink from the mini-bar.

"She's in good hands," Tucker told him. "We can visit her again next week."

Chester nodded, looking idly out the window.

"We can probably skip that family therapy stuff," Tucker told him smoothly. "It's just bad for everyone's morale. The best thing we can do now is focus on the wedding plans. I can get the invitations sent out this week for February 14. A Saturday wedding right before our board meeting the end of next week."

"Jumping the gun, aren't we?" Chester took the drink from him. "She only agreed to an engagement."

"We still need to be practical," Tucker said, and Chester noted that even he sounded tired. They had all made such an effort to get through the visit. "She can always call it off, but the announcement is the important part. It's what the Kois think that counts."

Chester sighed. "Keep it very small. Just a ceremony and reception at the apartment."

"Good idea." Tucker smiled. "We'll cut it down to four hundred people. We don't want to put too much stress on Cornelia."

We already have, Chester thought.

"I'm doing this for you," she had whispered to him at the hospital, nodding in Tucker's direction. "All of it."

He'd felt the awful anvil of shame and doubt settling in his chest again. This hospitalization could be a horrible mistake. He wondered what Elizabeth would have thought about it.

Tucker played with the laptop.

"The Kois are buying up eighteen thousand shares a day now. Here's an odd lot." Tucker squinted, then his face broke into a big appreciative grin. "Ha! It's the same number as the Chinese Year of the Rat. He's got some stones, old man Koi."

Chester slunk even lower into the pillowy leather of his plush rear seat.

"We should invite the Kois," Tucker suggested. "It'll be a hoot."

Chester felt the anvil sink into his stomach. How could Tucker keep a sense of play about this catastrophe?

Only a few minutes inside the heavy doors, Kevin felt a wave of class anxiety. He could handle a snake pit. This place came at him from a different angle entirely.

The admissions area looked like an expensive hotel lobby. An antique desk had an inkwell perched on top. An inkwell? A discreet sign read "Concierge." What did that mean? Some kind of specialist who screened for malingerers?

The cheery aide named Tim led him to a chair beside the desk. Then a woman appeared in a tailored black suit with blond-gray hair and chin angled up. She sat down and gave him an X-ray look. It lingered over his battered clothes and, he supposed, working-class face. She frowned as she read the letter from Dr. Blackwell, and asked briskly to see Kevin's health plan.

He set his Platinum Health Care card on the desk. She tapped out numbers on her desktop computer, and looked entranced. Then her face rearranged itself from guard dog to hostess mode.

"Well, Mr. Doyle," she flashed a sunny, approving smile. "It's a pleasure to have you with us."

She dipped a gold fountain pen into the inkwell and scratched a notation on his admission form, "Code Green." He hadn't heard about this code at Bellevue, or read about it anywhere in his library research. He should find out what it meant.

"Tim will see you to your room. You'll spend your first night here in Reception. Tomorrow you'll begin your tests, and you'll be assigned to a wing." She didn't say *ward*, but *wing*. "I hope you enjoy a beneficial stay with us."

Tim picked up Kevin's cheap duffel bag and invited him to walk ahead, down a jade-carpeted corridor off the lobby.

"Room 10. This will be yours for the night," Tim told Kevin. He used a plastic key that punched up a green light over the door latch to admit them. Tim opened his bag and began to unpack it, but stopped when he examined Kevin's clothing. He pushed the grungy clothes back in.

"We'll get you some new clothing from the Sanctuary Boutique tomorrow," Tim said. "There's a brochure on the side table to help you get acquainted."

Kevin looked around the room. A built-in wall TV so he couldn't get at the electrical cords and strangle himself. The thick carpet matched the emerald walls, with one framed print of brown and white ducks on each wall. There were no windows.

Kevin entered the bathroom. He laid his toothbrush on what he assumed was a marble-covered vanity. A bar of soap carved with an S lay in a gilt dish. When he touched the top of the vanity, he realized that the marble was actually painted rubber. He tapped the mirror that stretched to the ceiling and discovered plastic, not glass. The rooms were psycho-proofed.

"You'll be here overnight," Tim said. "We'll wake you up early for breakfast. Whichever wing you're assigned to, you'll be quite comfortable. Sleep tight, Mr. Doyle."

Tim shut the door with a firm ker-chunk behind him. A deadlock.

Kevin bounced up and down on the cushy bed. Somebody had left a gold-foil-wrapped piece of chocolate, also carved with an S. In the closet, he found a fluffy white terry cloth bathrobe with a pink and green logo on the pocket. He undressed and put on the bathrobe.

Kevin lay on the bed feeling clean and imagining Cornelia's lovely lips curving around her piece of Sanctuary chocolate.

The lights suddenly cut off. He lay in darkness, fumbling for the lamp beside him and knocked it onto the floor. It fell with a thud, probably made of rubber.

"Good night, Mr. . . ." cooed the recorded voice coming from the air vent. It changed tenor slightly as it personalized, ". . . Doyle."

The rigorous test battery fell short of Harold's warning.

They had put him in a small white room with a table and two chairs similar to the Stinson Gallery. The psychologist had stringy hair and was named Rudin. She looked bored for an hour while he answered her MMQ questions, with all the appropriate responses a "1003.1 Delusional Disorders, Grandiose" type of patient would make.

After a lunch of chicken salad sandwiches on thin white bread with the crust removed, an aide escorted Kevin back to the white room. His doctor was a smartly dressed, oval-faced woman in her forties with warm red lipstick and an almost motherly concern. She greeted him with a husky, soothing voice that made him glad to be with her instead of a colder, more clinical kind of doctor. Or a self-serving ferret like Cornelia's therapist.

"Hello, Kevin," she smiled. "I'm Dr. Lester, and I'll be your therapist. Tell me what brought you here."

"The Raj Limousine Service. But my name is Sebastian."

"I see," Dr. Lester reached into a thin briefcase by the side of her chair and took out a stack of cardboard sheets, holding the top one up so Doyle could see an inkblot.

"Kevin, please describe what you see for me. There aren't any right or wrong answers."

The smear looked like two men with swords.

"Gladiators."

She made a brief note on a pad. "American Gladiators?"

"Whatever. They fight to amuse our citizens."

She jotted another note, and tried a general-reality question. "And how many citizens are we talking about?"

"Since we crushed the Goths, about one million."

She stopped writing and looked up at him, then put her pen down.

"Sebastian," Dr. Lester asked evenly, "what year is this?"

"295 anno Domini."

Dr. Lester stuffed her inkblots back into the briefcase. "Do you have any questions you'd like to ask *me?*"

"What's Code Green?"

Her mouth almost turned up into a grin but she restrained herself. "Let's just say you'll never have to worry about leaving us before you're good and ready. The Sanctuary is set up on a system of rewards. If you work hard in our therapy over the next week, you'll earn the right to go to activities. Classes, walks outdoors, evening socials with the women patients."

"Socials with women?"

"Do you like women?"

"Yes. I feel better when women are around."

"The women patients stay in separate wings from the men."

"Why?" Kevin tried not to look too anxious.

"Those are the rules," she told him firmly. "But we'll have an agreement. If you cooperate with the staff and work hard on your therapy with me, I promise you'll get to go to evening socials very soon. Just remember one important rule; no physical contact. You can't touch another patient. Now, tell me, are there any times when you're *not* Sebastian?"

"I'm tired now. Can I go back to my room?"

Chapter Twenty-one

After two weeks in the Sanctuary, exasperation had worn Cornelia out more than the drugs or the mind-crushing tedium of her daily routine.

Eat. Therapy. Eat. Watch *All My Children*. Meds. Eat.

They served all the patients on pink plastic plates in the small dining room of her wing, Astor II. The food was too high in caloric value for a sedentary lifestyle. Her daily menu card boasted of "quenelles" and "boeuf nouvel," but proved to be a pretentious guise for institutional food heavy on macaroni and cheese, Swiss steaks, and tapioca dolled up in fancy molds. She had already developed a minor potbelly.

She couldn't drag herself, much as she wanted to, from the mirror. Her face looked wan, and slightly greasy from the institutional food. Tonight, when the meds had ground down and she felt more able to lift her weighty arms, she would do some jumping jacks. Then she'd have the small satisfaction of a task completed.

At least she had not completely lost her work ethic.

Corny tried to tie the sash around her bathrobe but couldn't find it. Giving up, she decided to shuffle out with her robe open, revealing her black bikini underwear, her breasts, her small belly. Or maybe she should just go back to sleep. It was what they all wanted.

No. A line must be drawn.

Struggling, Cornelia tied the robe, slowly and carefully, in a running bowline knot recalled from her sailing lessons so long ago, and walked to the dayroom to sit with other patients. She had a friend, of sorts, nicknamed Creamcheese for the white pallor of her skin.

The women of Astor II, diverse in age and behavioral quirks, shared little in common other than the imminent risk of falling completely off the planet.

Her own thoughts, while infinitely slower than usual, still managed to pierce the veil of her medication. She thought about Chester and Tucker occasionally.

But she thought about Kevin Doyle at least once every ten minutes.

He wanted to shout "Corny" through every doorway he passed.

Instead he joined the patients chanting about a "yellow brick road" as they marched through the tunnels, inspired by the bright yellow bathroom tiles that covered the walls.

Located beneath the Sanctuary, protected from the elements, the tunnel system served as the asylum's highways and byways. Staff could move around the hospital easily, and high-security patients could be transported through the passageways using locked metal doors at each crossing.

Kevin bounced along with two other patients from his new wing, Vanderbilt II. He had already been moved up from Vanderbilt I, considered a step up on the hierarchy of sanity. Two beefy male aides escorted his group.

Kevin watched his wing mate Richard, who had zipped his massive layers of baby fat into a tight-fitting, all-cotton jogging suit. Kevin resisted the staff's attempted makeover for him using country-club style outfits from the Sanctuary Boutique, which they added onto his Platinum Health Plan. They had bought him a green blazer, pleated flannel slacks, some button-down oxford shirts, and several ties with the S logo. Instead, Kevin dressed in his old jeans with the patched knees, sweatshirts, and turtlenecks.

He watched Richard march ahead, oblivious to the others, tossing a Maalox bottle high in the air almost to the yellow ceiling, just far enough ahead that he could catch the plastic bottle easily without modifying his speed or gait. He looked into middle space, his big round face placid. Today, as usual, he recited airframe specifications in a monotone.

"Messerschmitt 262, first jet fighter . . ."

"Richard, what did you do on the outside?" Kevin whispered to him.

"Aeronautical engineer," Richard snapped in a higher-pitched voice, annoyed to break his recitation.

"You do any commercial planes?" In case his plans ever called for air travel.

Richard smiled enigmatically. "I was a bad boy," he cackled.

The aides steered Richard and Kevin into the group therapy room. His pulse quickening, Kevin scanned the group of eight or ten people making a fuss settling into a circle of chairs.

The group consisted of ten men and women in various stages of disturbance, many dressed in a severely wardrobe-challenged style. The men wore what looked like expensive clothing, no grunge or real shabbiness, but mixed and matched badly. One older patient, with a pink face and small nose like a rabbit's, wore only one sock but a perfectly knotted tie under his green Sanctuary blazer. The women, most of them young, favored mismatched sports clothes, tops, and slacks. Neither the men nor the women, no matter how loony, wore anything other than textured wools and cottons—not an ounce of polyester.

He studied the patients carefully. They displayed various facial tics and other traits which Kevin knew to be a sign of either their problems or a reaction to the drugs used to manage their problem.

But none of the patients was Cornelia.

Kevin's therapist, Dr. Lester, was in charge of group therapy. She already sat in the center chair.

"Good morning, Richard," Dr. Lester spoke soothingly. "Hello, Kevin."

Some of the group muttered greetings, tense and wary.

The door opened again and Cornelia entered with an aide.

She stood with her perfect legs in tight blue jeans and a black turtleneck sweater. Her blond thatch fell over her forehead artlessly, and her skin looked slightly pasty and transparent from being kept indoors. Kevin thought that tiny flaw made her even more beautiful. Her eyes seemed washed out, the sparkling points of violet submerged in the gray as she tried to smile.

Then she saw him and reared back. She looked so startled, he worried that she would fall over backward. Her gray dull eyes blinked. When they opened, the little violet stars made a round bouquet for him.

"Hi, Cornelia," Dr. Lester greeted her.

She walked very slowly to a chair directly across from Kevin and sat carefully, not taking her eyes off him.

"This is Kevin. He prefers to be called Sebastian," Dr. Lester watched them. "Cornelia, do you know Sebastian?"

"Not personally," she replied slowly, as if considering the possibility for the first time. "He looks like a painting I've seen."

Kevin sat in the dayroom of Vanderbilt II, his medium-security wing.

It was decorated in the hospital's plush green and pink motif, like country clubs he'd seen in movies. The only way he could identify it as a hospital ward was by the glass nurses' station. It jutted out into the room like a giant tollbooth with a young nursing staff in white uniforms bustling around inside.

Tonight, a "Happy New Year" sign had been hung carelessly across the nurses' station. Patients were rounded up from their private rooms and corralled into the dayroom to socialize. Most looked as though they'd rather be sleeping off their meds. They stared blankly at their party hats, tried to open their baby-proofed party poppers.

Kevin tried to wrap his mind around the New Year spirit with the rest of his only moderately disturbed wing mates. He declined a funny hat out of a sense of dignity, but accepted a plastic glass of bubbling nonalcoholic champagne.

"Hail," he toasted the other patients and the staff so new or despised by their supervisors that they drew shift duty on New Year's Eve. Then they all sang a ragged chorus of "Auld Lange Syne."

When the staff retreated to hold a glum party of their own inside their glass-wrapped room, one of the student nurses named Ms. Babcock approached him. Kevin liked Ms. Babcock. She had regular, pretty Irish features like Marne, and wore dark hair pulled in a tight bun under her cap.

"Happy New Year, Sebastian," she said to Kevin. "You have a visitor."

Kevin followed Ms. Babcock to the visitors room. His visitor hadn't arrived yet. The windowless room was empty except for the floral print couch facing two chairs and a still-life print of flowers on the wall. Flowers were supposed to be soothing, he had heard, but they overdid them and the result was more like jungle rot.

He would have to stay in character. He quickly stripped to his underwear, so he looked more like Saint Sebastian, naked except for his white loincloth. He stood bravely and looked toward the ceiling like a martyr searching for a sign.

He heard a harsh laugh as the door closed.

"Cute," Marne told him. "But it's only me."

Kevin sat down in a plump chair next to his sister.

"Where's Dad?"

"Couldn't come. He had a double shift. He said to tell you, he's proud to have a saint in the family."

"I left him laughing his ass off, Marne. It's like he finally got one over on Eddie."

She shrugged. "He's not upset at you or anything. But he won't say the psychiatrists are wrong either. He thinks you're crazy for doing this."

"You think maybe Dad has too much faith in authority figures?"

"Somebody's got to."

"What about Helen?"

Marne said. "She doesn't ask, I don't tell. So do you see Cornelia tonight?"

"She's on her wing. I start socials next weekend."

"Wing? Socials?" Marne rolled her eyes. "So now what?"

"Now I have to spend some time with her, just the two of us. No relatives, lawyers, boyfriend." He still couldn't handle the word "fiancé." "She's not really crazy. It's just that nobody tries to understand her."

Marne snorted, sat back, and gave him her buzz-saw look. "I dunno. They've got a whole staff here for therapy."

"She doesn't need therapy," Kevin said. "She's aware. She's kind."

"She talks to electrical poles."

"No, Marne. She just puts her heart into things."

She stared at the ceiling, with a very Sebastian-like why-me look. "She could blow you off anytime, Kevin, like 'excuse me, time for my pablum, I'll have my doctor call your doctor.' "

"That could happen, but—"

"But what?" Marne turned up her hands, genuinely baffled.

Kevin let his breath out. "But I feel like I've been praying for her all my life and didn't even know it."

He expected a snicker. Instead, Marne looked startled, then her eyes moistened. She took out a tissue.

"Kevin, that's the dumbest thing you ever said."

"I just need time," he told her. "At work, they don't know I'm in here yet, right?"

"All they know is you're on sick leave for two weeks," she said. "They won't find out until the union gets the hospital bills. Make it count, Kevin."

"Okay."

She got up to leave. "And put your pants on. Martyrs don't wear jockey shorts."

"I hear you."

For his first escorted tour of the grounds, Kevin wore a hospital-issue down coat, puffy and white like the Pillsbury Doughboy.

He drew in the air, not minding the cold sting on his face. Against the roiling gray soup of winter sky, the Big Circle shone with ice. In the distance, a thin black clump of reedy, denuded trees threw long shadows over the snow like a film noir setting. Beyond the trees, he saw the electrified fence, a jarring note in the wintry postcard. And, behind the fence, he saw the road that led to the parkway he'd driven up with Majik.

He looked around for her and, as always, became fascinated with the other patients. What is it about rich people's faces, he wondered, that made them look so undamaged no matter what happened, the confidence that they'd always be looked after somehow.

"Come here often?" She appeared suddenly.

A wine-colored scarf covered her to the chin, and her hands were stuck in the pockets of a simple black coat. Her cheeks were flushed, her blond hair driven back by the wind over her small, perfect ears, the tip of her nose a little red from the cold. He felt both cleansed and agitated when he saw her, like going through a washing machine and coming out happier.

He swallowed. "You look . . ."

"Fat?"

"Oh, no. Definitely in the top one percent of mental patients."

No physical contact, he had to remind himself.

They walked, side by side, as the patient body shuffled forward around the Big Circle like a giant, quivering Jell-O mold, residents of three or four moderate-security wings clumping together.

A female aide walked ahead to pace them briskly, an impatient trail boss. While the wind lashed his face, Kevin sunned himself in Cornelia's company.

"I got your note," she whispered, pulling out the pink napkin he had sent her, a scrawled note written with a stolen nurse's pen. "A girl on my wing sneaked it to me. How did you ever send it?"

"I gave it to a guy. He gave it to somebody else. An underground."

She beamed, clutching the crumpled napkin as though it were the most precious gift anyone had ever given her. "Did you mean what you said?"

"About you being a dance of light? No, that was for some other patient."

She chuckled merrily, then leaned in and whispered, "Before you came, I was about to go AWOL. See that electrical fence?"

Kevin looked in the direction she pointed, to the malevolent wires strung close together eight feet high in the distance behind the trees. The red and white "Danger. High Voltage" signs posted every few feet along the wires could be read from the Big Circle.

"Please tell me you wouldn't even touch it. That's really dangerous."

"Not for an Electric Girl." She gave him a wicked grin. "Tesla used to let a million volts of current flow over his suit and hair until the electricity created a blue halo. As long as he kept the frequencies high, it couldn't hurt him. That fence is high frequency, too. It wouldn't hurt you too badly. But you're here now and I don't want to go anywhere. Kevin, how *did* you get in here?"

"I think the medical term is Code Green. I was wondering, if you're not busy tonight, maybe we could have a date."

"I thought you'd never ask."

The Sanctuary's Retreat Club could be a hundred other executive dining rooms, Tucker thought, except that everybody jumped up to answer pagers like dogs on a leash.

Medical degrees hardly intimidated him. He had never wanted to be a doctor, a glorified mechanic wrestling with body parts. A doctor's only real power was the life-or-death thing, which you could only use on one person at a time.

It was their third weekly visit, and Cornelia had greeted Chester with her usual sad disgust, and Tucker with sullen apathy. It was time, Tucker decided, for dinner with the Sanctuary's chief administrator, Dr. Burns, and Cornelia's therapist, Dr. Loblitz.

They sat at a corner table. Through a window, he looked at the bleak Westchester scrub outside. Dr. Burns was a celebrity psychiatrist in his late fifties with a full head of gray hair and the lion's face a Supreme Court justice should have. Dr. Burns obviously didn't know much about Cornelia's case, but made plenty of soothing noises to Chester. Tucker suspected that visions of a new "Lord I" and even a "Lord II" wing danced in Dr. Burns's head, from his smart little nods whenever Chester spoke.

He regarded Cornelia's therapist, Dr. Loblitz. He knew the type. An intense young techno with curly black hair, Loblitz fought to steer the conversation to nuts and bolts without stabbing his boss with his fork. Loblitz was doing all the work. And Tucker knew that talking to Chester might be the hardest work the shrink had ever done. In this little world, Tucker sniffed out, Dr. Loblitz wore the unmistakable mantle of rising star. Burns had all the patience in the world with Corny's psychiatric meter ticking at $3,500 a day. But Tucker sensed impatience in Dr. Loblitz, which created an opportunity. Tucker suspected that the young doctor didn't believe in coddling family members. Loblitz had his own agenda.

"You need to be aware," Dr. Loblitz skated on the brink of lecturing Chester, "of the time-consuming nature of talking therapies."

Chester dug in. "I just have the feeling that if I listen to Cornelia, try to reach her . . ."

"That's admirable," Dr. Burns cooed. "I wish all family members had the same desire."

Loblitz pressed on. "Dr. Bushberg talked to Cornelia for how long?"

"A year," Chester replied.

"I've talked to her now for several weeks, and I can tell you that her delusional system is intact. She's angry, she's confrontational, and she's not going to leave this hospital until we switch to a more aggressive treatment." Loblitz held his course, Tucker was pleased to see.

Chester looked at Tucker, pleading for help. Tucker held Dr. Loblitz's eye.

"No," Chester insisted. "Just try to reason with her."

"Well, that's a conservative strategy, sir." *You rich idiot.*

Chester said. "She's very precious to me."

"And to us." Dr. Burns gave Chester's arm a manly squeeze.

Chester stood up, raising the two doctors like marionettes. While Chester and Dr. Burns shook hands, Tucker smiled and motioned privately to Dr. Loblitz, telling him to stay put.

"Chester, give me a minute. I'll be along." He waited until Chester and Burns left the Retreat Club.

"Why don't you call me Tucker," he smiled at Dr. Loblitz. "And you're . . . ?"

"Ken." Loblitz appeared flattered at this intimacy with Tucker, a mogul no older than he was, whom he might have read about in the *Wall Street Journal*.

"Well, Ken, that was definitely the right way to handle Chester Lord. We both care deeply about Cornelia's recovery."

Dr. Loblitz shrugged. "Cornelia presents nonspecific symptoms. But you can waste a lot of time trying to diagnose people."

"I understand your specialty is shock treatments," Tucker said.

Dr. Loblitz acted surprised, warming to Tucker's interest in him. "Why, yes. A lot of us who trained more recently like shock. We call it ECT, electroconvulsive therapy. It's faster and cleaner than talking therapy or even psychotropic drugs. There's some memory loss, but memories are what disturb the patients. I just give them a clean slate."

"A clean slate," Tucker nodded. "I like that. You know, Cornelia and I are getting married on February 14."

Dr. Loblitz looked stunned, as though seeing Tucker for the first time.

"I'm afraid that's impossible," Dr. Loblitz said. "I could *only* recommend her release if she undergoes electroconvulsive therapy."

"So? I'm convinced."

"Mr. Lord is her responsible party. He has to approve my treatment."

"I know it's a burden." Tucker lifted his laptop onto the table. He opened it up and punched two keys.

"Mr. Lord isn't a burden exactly," Dr. Loblitz said tactfully.

"No, I mean your student loan," Tucker told him.

"What?" Dr. Loblitz's face reddened.

Tucker turned his laptop toward the psychiatrist. The screen flashed "LOBLITZ, KENNETH R." on and off with the number $122,900.00" in blazing red.

Tucker smiled broadly. "You haven't made a payment on your student loan for six years."

Loblitz wet his large lips. "I bet Chester Lord wouldn't like whatever you're suggesting."

"All I'm suggesting is that you use your best skills to help Cornelia," Tucker said solemnly. "I'm just afraid that Chester's irrational fears are getting in the way. You're going to cure Cornelia sooner or later anyway. If you do it on my time line to help me, I'm ready to pitch in and help you. Look. Here's your bank account."

Tucker tapped one key and "UNITED BANK OF WEST-CHESTER" appeared on the screen with Loblitz's checking account information in clean lines. The last one read "Balance: $13,560."

"And here's your bank account with Cornelia on shock treatments." Tucker tapped again and the last line changed to "Balance: $250,560."

"Oh my God," Loblitz said, watching the screen.

"I'm only asking you to do what you know is right, Ken. If you *did* choose ECT, how long would the treatments take?"

"Probably two weeks." Loblitz's upper lip began to sweat. "But I can't guarantee anything. Dr. Burns hates to rush people out of here."

"I'll handle Chester. I watched you, and I know you can handle Burns."

Tucker smiled winningly at Dr. Loblitz, who nodded in agreement. Their eyes met again. But their roles had changed dramatically. Now they were brothers-in-arms tackling a mess created by older, obdurate superiors.

"There's only one detail." Tucker reached into his pocket and pulled out an ordinary-looking tie clip. He slipped it onto Dr. Loblitz's muted tie and smoothed it out. "I want you to wear this to your staff meeting when you talk to Burns."

Loblitz looked confused. "What is it?"

"Just to keep a record, so we'll know we're on the same page. If you run into problems with Burns, we'll listen to the tape and I'll help you solve them. That's what I do, Ken, solve problems. Fair enough?"

Dr. Loblitz's eyes let his jaw drop watching the screen where $250,560 blinked as though medieval magic occurred there. "I can't give you any guarantees."

"I'm not asking for any."

"I just give it my best shot?" Loblitz said. "That's all?"

"Hey, you're the doctor."

On the Big Circle, Kevin shuffled in a desultory way with the other sheep from his wing, wearing his Poppin' Fresh winter coat.

Cornelia's group had arrived without her. One of the female patients, a wild-eyed girl with straight hair cut sharply inward at the chin like one long ingrown toenail, whispered to Kevin that Cornelia had two visitors.

"Her father and a hunk," she whispered.

That would be Tucker, Kevin sulked. He kicked up a sparse layer of gray gravel on the Big Circle pathway. He measured his life now in short moments with Cornelia Lord, and the long hours apart. Not seeing her brought a crushing disappointment.

Soon their exercise period was over and the aides called out, "Vanderbilt II!"

Kevin hung his head on the winding path back to his wing. They passed the vast stone building where the Sanctuary's administrative staff worked. Kevin imagined that it looked like a European prison. Maybe the Tower of London looked like that.

On their route was the parking lot where the senior staff kept their cars.

Kevin always studied this display of expensive metalwork, marveling at how the designers created little fantasies for the buyers. There were substantial-looking Mercedes 600 and BMW 740 sedans, those slab-sided Autobahn cruisers reeking of power, their taillights notched in like stylish lapels. He wondered what psychiatrists thought, streaking down the parkway in those Teutonic big rigs. He admired the curvier Jaguar sedans from England, lacquered in royal-looking maroons and deep greens, their front grilles a little fussy with serrated chrome. A silvery Porsche 911 looked racy but oddly bulbous, like a potato car made of liquid mercury.

Walking with his herd around the lot now, he heard the soft throbbing of the big Mercedes limousine before he saw it. The wisp of exhaust from its pipe formed a cloud in the cold. The charcoal gray limousine had been stretched, with even bigger slabs and blackened windows added to the body. Twenty-five feet long with dark windows, it looked like Darth Vader's car.

Too late, Kevin saw the driver leaning on the front fender closest to him with his arms folded. He wore a familiar gray flannel chauffeur suit and had taken off his cap, so Kevin recognized him instantly.

He was Mike, Chester Lord's driver. And Tucker Fisk's.

Their eyes met. Even from fifty feet, Kevin could see Mike squint to figure out who Kevin was. He didn't have to read lips to see Mike's beefy mouth, seared like a steak from the cold, form the words, "Son of a bitch."

Kevin thought about darting behind another patient, getting lost. But Mike had made him. End of story. Now the driver's face twisted, wondering why he had just spotted Kevin Doyle, doorman, at the current home-away-from-home of Cornelia Lord.

Kevin's brain reeled around, trying to pull together all the facts and impressions he could stuff into the category "Mike the Driver."

He knew Mike didn't always look when he was backing up in the snow. The healed-over gashes in Kevin's ear and shoulder still hurt in damp weather. Before that night, he had only spoken to Mike maybe four times. Mike spent half his life waiting, but didn't talk all that much when Kevin had tried to strike up a conversation.

But from the grunts and gestures and half-smiles he recalled, his instincts made him pretty sure about a few things. Mike was unfailingly loyal to Chester. For whatever reason, he also seemed to get a kick out of Cornelia. And there was that one morsel of hope Kevin could still cling to. Mike had never seemed to like Tucker Fisk. The night Tucker called him to meet in the alley, Mike had wanted to help them carry Cornelia inside. Tucker had told him to shut up and do what he was told.

He studied Mike's expression. The driver held his eye with a tight little smile that could be saying either, "You're mine now, asshole," or "This I gotta hear."

It was too close to call.

So instead of avoiding him or looking guilty, Kevin smiled back. Then he checked the position of the two aides from Vanderbilt II who were supposed to be herding them. Neither one was watching him. Kevin lowered his head and duck-walked through the herd toward the parking lot. The aides would do a head count when they reached the door, but he had a minute.

He approached the driver. "How you doing, Mike?"

"Can't complain," Mike said. "You?"

"Hard to say. You'd better ask my doctors."

Mike glanced at the other patients. "That's what you're doing here, Kevin? Getting help?"

"So they say. My union's got a great health plan."

Mike grabbed Kevin's arm and stuck the beefy face inches from his nose. He could almost feel the bushy brows that stuck out in all directions like quills.

"Listen, Kevin, I didn't see you that night. It was a mess, snow flying. I was just trying to help. You know that, right?"

"Sure, Mike."

"You here 'cause you got brain damage? I heard the side mirror hit you, sounded like whacking a side of beef with a hammer."

Kevin shuddered. "Yeah, that's what it felt like."

"Kevin, answer me honest, okay? Are you going to get a lawyer, sue me for what happened?"

Kevin paused, as though he were considering it. "You know what I'm thinking, Mike? I'd hate to have anybody know I'm in here. I don't want their pity."

Mike thought that over for what seemed like a week. Then he nodded sagely. "I got you covered. What do you hear about Cornelia?"

He shrugged. "I never see her. Separate wings, two different worlds."

Mike gave a hard, sincere nod. "She's a good kid. Saved my job. Chester was about to fire me. She made him promise to keep me on."

"Yeah," Kevin nodded. "Sounds like her."

"A good kid," Mike said again, shaking his jowls for emphasis so they waggled like saddlebags. "It pisses me off, the stuff I hear Tucker Fisk saying about her . . ."

Mike's eyes, already moist from the cold air, grew more watery as he looked away.

"What did he say to you?"

"To *me?*" Mike snorted incredulously. "Nothing. Tucker Fisk thinks I'm the part of the steering wheel that says 'yes sir.' He forgets I'm there when he's on the phone."

"We're invisible to guys like Tucker, Mike," Kevin pointed out. Then he waited as long as he could. "So what did he say about Cornelia?"

"Calls her flaky . . . impetuous, that's the word he likes to use. The only time he ever looked happy talking about her, he was yakking on his cell phone to the Chinese guy. Said he'd only deliver Cornelia if he could be thirty by thirty."

"Thirty by thirty? It doesn't sound like a fun size to be, Mike."

The driver shrugged. "All I know is he was grinning like a real shithead when he said it."

Kevin had been mulling something over, looking at the driver who thought Corny was a good kid and felt guilty about Kevin. "I got the letter from Cornelia Lord at my building. No stamp. Somebody had to bring it there. You know anything about that?"

Mike looked at the snow, the little smile spreading across his big jaw again.

Then suddenly Kevin felt big cold hands like bear paws on both his shoulders. He didn't have to turn around to know that Luke, the better-natured of the aides on his wing, had been the one to nail him. That was lucky. Luke was a big man with a gentle way about him. He had grown up in the Bronx and studied at City College. Now he gave Kevin a look of mock concern, deep cracks in his forehead.

"Hey, Sebastian, man, you gonna miss the Punic Wars, you don't start haulin' ass back to your wing." Luke turned to Mike. "Saint Sebastian bothering you, sir?"

Mike looked vacant. "Nah. This guy don't bother me at all."

Chapter Twenty-two

*I*n Vanderbilt II, Kevin dressed for his first social in a spiffy WASP ensemble from the Sanctuary Boutique.

He slipped on a green wool blazer over a pink cotton shirt with button-down collar and a Sanctuary tie. This would be the closest he'd ever come to an old-school tie. Looking just right mattered. This would be his first actual date with Cornelia, where they had made plans to meet in a social setting.

Sweaty palms deluxe.

He felt the mix of anticipation and dread he recalled from his first real date at fourteen, dressed up to take a girl from the neighborhood to a party. He'd gone to Marne for advice. His sister was strikingly pretty at thirteen and already fielding guys.

"Put your tongue back in your mouth," Marne had told him. "Stop looking at the girl and find the person."

Good advice, but he always found the *wrong* person. He also realized, from the oily street-corner Romeos and neighborhood psychos who showed up to take Marne on dates, she wasn't doing much better. Nobody really knew anything when it came to dating.

In high school, blinded by his heat-seeking Cyclops, he'd ignored Marne and jumped into heart-pumping infatuations with any girl who encouraged him. Other guys could do that and move on. He couldn't.

He wasn't raised by his mother and two sisters to hurt girls' feelings. So he spent his high school years in a luckless pattern of spending three days in every new relationship and six months trying to break up. Twice he thought about changing schools.

After he'd gone out in the world and discovered neon, he only wanted women who had a BoHo way of looking at things. They tended to look and act spooky, which he wrote off to having an artist's way of viewing the world, an artist's eye, and not being appreciated. But most of them turned out to actually *be* spooky. None of them had an artist's eye, but they did have probation officers or jealous boyfriends on Rikers Island who carved homemade tattoos on their arms and sometimes their foreheads.

The more he worked on his neon at NYIAT, the more his art took out of him. It was like having a bitchy girlfriend who was never satisfied. Then Cornelia Lord came along.

Could he form a total mind meld with Cornelia and take up Nikola Tesla as his cause, both united in amperes? Maybe. Could he honestly help her search for an electrical tower South of the Border? The truth, no. The problem was, he had studied just enough electricity to know how it worked. A utility like Con Ed fed electricity to people through wires. What Tesla was trying to do, build a tower to broadcast electricity to everybody through the airwaves, that was a story only Vlad the Self-Impaler could get behind.

Despite what he had told Marne, Corny's ideas didn't always add up.

He picked up the book about Nikola Tesla he had checked out of the Sanctuary library and glanced through the pictures of Tesla's inventions. Some of Tesla's ideas belonged in cloud-cuckoo-land, funky Victorian helicopters like Corny had in her museum and *Star Trek* particle beam machines. Why Cornelia Lord chose to pledge her soul to this man was the puzzle of the decade.

Then he turned to a page of his Tesla book and stared. It was a copy of an old letter. He read it twice, then read it again. This musty historical document, he believed, was Cornelia Lord's personal fly.

He closed his eyes. *You have to trust me sometime*, she had told him, then kissed him. He still tingled thinking about it. She had sacrificed her own freedom to keep him safe when she vanished of her own free will into the police car. He owed her a leap of faith. If she wanted to believe in Tesla, maybe he shouldn't discourage her. He just had to make sure he knew why.

Knowing her, really knowing her, would be his gift to Cornelia.

On Astor II, Cornelia dressed in one of the black cocktail dresses O'Connell had packed for her.

Since her hands were a little shaky from the meds, and from the jitters of her first date with Kevin, she let an aide apply makeup. She brushed her own hair. Then she slipped on her shoes. Not high heels. They were illegal here. No doubt because she needed steady footing so she wouldn't keel over from the meds that kept her body unstable, as though she balanced herself on a long spring that swayed back and forth. She settled on flat espadrilles.

She felt completely Cornelia tonight, just as she had tried to be the evening of her father's office party. But there was a huge difference. Now she didn't need to talk herself into anything. With Kevin, she never had to fake calm. She *was* calm.

And now he had done the impossible, breaking into this dungeon of psychiatry to rescue her.

They were protected here. As long as they were both discreet, they would be able to explore what they had, within certain limitations. And maybe that part was good, too. The constraints made them free, in a funny way, like school uniforms.

With thorny issues of sex and status on hold for the time being, they would be only Cornelia and Kevin.

The Electric Girl might want to work alone, but Cornelia had grown so tired of that lonely vigil. The risk was that Kevin might get to know her too well. The longer her father knew her, the less contact he had with her. If your own father didn't want to be with you, who did? Tina French and other trust fund delinquents. And for his own murky reasons, Tucker Fisk.

Kevin came from another world where, even though he was too kind to say so, a Cornelia Lord was distrusted. She felt the sting of his wariness, sensed he was afraid.

She bit her lip. Her own fear nagged, like being nibbled to death by ducks. One day, when she became the girl in Penthouse A again, would he still follow her like she had followed his corona?

Evening socials are planned by our staff to provide social interaction in the comfort of a chaperoned setting.

Kevin had read that in his Sanctuary brochure.

He stood in the club room for evening socials, the Abraham Maslow Room. In this fine, old mahogany-paneled hall with vaulted ceilings and wire-gated glass, patients abided by a strict Dress and Conduct Code. Men needed jackets and ties, with the added stress of matching socks. Women were supposed to wear party dresses and flat shoes, but no sneakers.

And no physical contact.

Kevin looked around the room, admiring the patients who'd given it the old college try. Male patients who ran naked and snarling through his wing now held chairs for female patients. It didn't seem that different from the outside, where guys left alone tended to act like crazed apes and only pulled themselves together to meet girls.

This would be his first upper-class party. He expected plenty of slack, because some of the guests who stared into space or snapped their fingers continuously probably didn't have a heavy social calendar on the outside.

Cornelia waited alone on a couch. He followed her stare dreamily out the bay window with only a thin mask of wire. It had begun to snow, trapping the white flakes in outdoor spotlights. Holiday lights twinkled on all the tree branches. It reminded him of probably the most bucolic place he had ever seen at Christmas, the Tavern on the Green restaurant in Central Park.

Over the sound system, a scratchy old record played on a turntable. His mother and father had actually danced to the same record album, *South Pacific*, about twenty years ago. It had brought out his parents' sappy, romantic side that, in hindsight, was pretty nice.

He maneuvered in front of Cornelia and she slowly turned, first looking up to the top of his hair.

"Is it just me, or is this a good song?" he asked her.

"It's called 'Bali Ha'i.' Someone's idea of paradise." She smiled and patted the seat for him to sit down. "You're not looking much like Saint Sebastian tonight."

"I'd strip down to my loincloth, but I'm afraid they'd take me off socials."

"It's a fine line," she agreed slowly.

His anger kicked up at how heavily they had medicated her.

"Now tell me from the beginning," folded hands in her lap, "how did you ever get in here?"

"I did my homework, used a couple of connections."

No physical contact, Dr. Lester said. He kept physically apart from her but left his pinkie close, a half-inch away from hers.

"Corny," he said, "I have to ask you something before I get too comfortable. Do you really love Tucker?"

Her mouth turned down. "It's messy."

"Does he love you?"

"He's undoubtedly in love with the prospect of marrying Cornelia Lord. You have to know my family." She stopped and Kevin waited for her. "When my mother died, Chester fell apart. Worse than I did. He was running Lord & Company very badly."

"So he hired Tucker?"

"My father hates confrontation. Tucker loves it. He fired all the troublemakers and terrorized the rest. Tucker saved Lord & Company once, and now it's in trouble again. A business partner of my father's named Koi is plotting a hostile takeover. Tucker told me my father needs my help. I own shares of voting stock. He wants to make sure we keep it all in the family."

"By getting married?"

She slowly smoothed the wrinkles from the lap of her cocktail dress. "By showing the world the Lords and Tucker are all sticking together."

Kevin pushed on. "So Tucker wants you to settle for a . . ."

"I guess you'd call it a marriage of convenience."

"It's not so convenient for you," he pointed out, "marrying a guy you don't love."

"Tucker had his plan, but I had mine, too. We were going to *announce* that we were getting married, to discourage the Kois. I never intended to marry him, Kevin. Not even when he promised to show me a Tesla Tower. I just wanted to help my father."

"A Tesla Tower?"

"Yes. Like the one I showed you at the museum, but bigger of course. Tucker swore on his mother's life that he'd take me to South America. He knew that would really get to me, and I'd have to believe him."

"Well maybe Tucker and his mom made a pact," Kevin said. "They could swear on each other's lives."

"Perhaps. She's an attorney. Anyway, we were going to announce our engagement at the office Christmas party. I assumed I could go through with it. But two things threw me off a bit. I saw that he lied to me about the trip to South America . . ."

She hesitated.

Kevin wondered how she knew, but he didn't want to stop her now. "And?" He waited.

"And I thought I saw a corona between Tucker and Han Koi."

"A corona?"

"A very bad corona."

Kevin thought hard about whether he should bring up what Mike the driver told him. Neither of them were in a position to do much now, unless he came up with something more concrete. She needed his support, not more things to worry about. So he changed the subject. "You know, the first time I saw you was a picture in the *Globe*."

She closed her eyes and flushed slightly. "I bet I was standing in a fountain at the time."

"Yeah, but I could see you were trying to escape. How come you always run away?"

"Maybe I don't like confrontation either."

"I don't know about that." He gestured with his hands, making emphatic shapes in the air. "You believe in things."

"I owe Tesla, personally." She seemed to withdraw from him slightly. Deep concern had clouded her lovely face, tightening her mouth, causing little white lines around her eyes.

"Okay. He was a genius. But he's everybody's genius, Corny. Why do you owe him personally?"

She folded her arms. "It's a family business thing."

Our business, not yours, she seemed to be saying. "I'd say your family's business could use some minding, the way they treat you. Corny, talk to me. I've been reading about Tesla. I saw things."

"Kevin, you can't just take a broom and drive all the bats from the Lord family belfry. We have rather long-term issues. One hundred years, to be exact."

He held up his arm and looked studiously at his wrist where a watch should be. "I've got at least thirty days."

She curled up on the couch, tucking both her legs under her body. It amazed Kevin the positions women could work themselves into to sit comfortably, especially if they had incredibly sculpted legs and perfect feet.

"Okay," she drew a deep breath. "One hundred years ago, my great-great-grandfather Chester Lord founded Lord & Company. One of his big investments was the Edison Electric Company."

Kevin helped her. "Nikola Tesla invented AC electricity. But Edison got the credit for Tesla's invention and made a fortune out of it. Tesla just wanted to broadcast free electricity. He built his Tesla Tower on Long Island after he got J.P. Morgan to finance it. Until a guy I figure as a relative of yours sent a letter to Morgan."

Kevin reached into his jacket and unfolded the page he had ripped out of the Tesla book. It was a reproduction of a letter written in 1903, with all the formality of that day. He handed it to Cornelia, who took it and, with a flash of recognition, read it over very slowly:

To the Immediate Attention of J. Pierpont Morgan

My Dear Friend:

   I am astounded to learn that you have backed the inventor Nikola Tesla in his endeavor to create a Tower of Free Electricity, which he is now constructing at Wardenclyffe on Long Island.

   I do not join those naysayers who scoff behind your back that the invention may fail. To the contrary, I am deeply troubled that the experiment should succeed. My God, man, consider the economics.

If everyone on Earth will be able to receive electricity
through the atmosphere, where will you hang the meters?
Let us meet at The Player's Club to discuss this soon.

Your Servant,
(Which you know damn well I am not!)
Chester B. Lord

"You found this?" Her voice was high and reedy, as though strained through something that hurt.

"In a book. I couldn't help notice that line, Corny. That's what J.P. Morgan told Tesla. *If everybody can get electricity through the air, where do we put the meters?*"

"Yes," she nodded once, numbly. "That's how my great-great-grandfather ruined Tesla. He did it to protect his own investment in Edison."

He moved to take her hand, but she pulled it away.

"No physical contact, remember? Afterward, nobody took Tesla seriously. He was so far ahead of his time, not even other scientists would support him."

And now he'd seen her fly.

He nodded. "So you come along a whole century later, trying to right the wrong."

"Yes."

Silence.

"Well, I'm glad you told me, Corny. I was worried, maybe it was irrational."

She couldn't seem to speak, but rubbed her eyes with the back of her fingers.

"I don't think I can talk any more now."

Something had gone wrong in his plan to swat her fly. She looked more miserable than before, sniffling, tears running down both cheeks. He longed to touch her and settled for holding her finger, but she took it away again.

"Okay," he said. "Are you free tomorrow?"

She rubbed her nose, composed herself. "Well, maybe I could make time between *All My Children* and my Magic of Watercolors class."

Chapter Twenty-three

*T*hey trusted accomplices now, other patients on Kevin's wing and hers. Their allies passed their notes back and forth. And they created a diversion when needed.

On the Monday after their Saturday social, Cornelia's friend Creamcheese distracted the aides. Kevin's group passed hers on a Yellow Brick Road, both being herded to activities. Creamcheese screamed uncontrollably with no warning. She raised such a fuss that aides from both wings had to gang up to surround and quiet her.

In the confusion, Kevin scooped Corny up in a bundle for a sprint up the stairs, closing the door behind her.

They had a good ten minutes of stolen Sanctuary time before sneaking back.

She settled on a landing and Kevin kissed her. He took the nape of her slender neck in his hand, and they touched lips as gently as butterflies. Her lips tasted of sweet Necco Wafers and trembled slightly. She put her arms around him and kissed back. Her tongue darted furtively, circling his teeth, a sweet invasion that made his nerves skate on dangerously thin ice.

But he had promised himself to be extra scrupulous about not getting into the lust part, however much his body ached, before he could have his talk with her.

He had to sneak up on her passion for Tesla, which sent her skipping off into the ozone. She took on the dead inventor's cause too zealously, like trying to use her fingernails to tear down a brick wall. He understood why she'd have a bad aftertaste from what her great-great-grandfather had done to Tesla. But it didn't explain why she made Tesla her whole life.

He pulled back from her kiss.

"Don't stop."

"Corny, who told you about Tesla?"

Her eyelids, lazily drooped, snapped open. "Pardon?"

"I think you heard me."

"My mother."

"And she died."

"Yes."

"Can you tell me how she died?"

"She was killed."

"Killed."

"In a helicopter accident. A system failure."

She licked her dry lips, becoming quiet. Her fingers found a strand of hair that clung to her neck and twisted it.

He kissed her forehead again. "What kind of a system?"

"An electrical system."

"Do you, uh . . ."

"Think it's a conspiracy or something? Of course not."

Good.

"Corny, isn't it possible you think it's like some kind of . . . karmic boomerang? Your ancestor, this Chester I, screws Tesla out of his tower. Nobody gets free electricity. A century later, your perfectly innocent mother dies because of an electrical system failure."

"I think that's rather far-fetched." Her fingers felt stiff in his hands. "I mean, that I'd try to—"

She stopped.

"Make it right and bring her back somehow?" Kevin finished for her very slowly, looking into her eyes, searching her soul. The points of violet in them had turned hazy. "Remember what you told me about getting nuts over Saint Sebastian? You said, 'You won't do anything else until you've made things right for her—my mother.' Think about it. It's not really Tesla you want to save, is it?"

She looked away from him.

He tried to lighten things a little. "Corny, in a few years, nobody's really going to *need* Tesla Towers anymore. We'll all have freestanding fiber optics."

She twisted her hair with her fingers and started to say something. She shut her eyes, pulling her hands from his and crossing her arms.

"It's cold. I'd like to go back now."

On Saturday evening, they planned to meet for the social. But an aide tugged Kevin out of line by the sleeve of his Sanctuary blazer.

In the visitors room, Philip Grace lounged with his feet up on the coffee table. The sole of one loafer had a hole. His beat-up camera bag sat on the couch beside him.

"How you doin'?"

"Pretty good, Philip. How'd you get in here?"

"Told 'em I was your brother-in-law Harold. They asked me for ID, I said, 'Shit, you wouldn't ask me if I was white,' so they backed off."

Grace frowned at Kevin's outfit.

Kevin sat across from him and crossed his leg, getting comfortable. He had worked to adopt the casually disciplined way he'd seen the nonpsychotic men on his wing sit. They were the ones who'd come for rehab. Good posture was buried so permanently in the WASP genes that those people whose faces had been collapsed into bulbous veins and creases by booze or worse still managed to sit like they owned the world.

"Man, what are you wearin'?" Grace shook his head, looking at Kevin's paisley tie like it was a platter of worms. "Who still makes ties with them little amoebas?"

"I think the label said Brooks Brothers."

Grace sniffed. "Ain't a brother in the whole world who'd wear that."

Kevin noticed Grace resting his hand on his camera case. Getting him used to the camera. It reminded him of the way the salesman at

NYIAT laid his pen on the contract the day he signed up for school, trying to get Kevin comfortable with the idea of having it around.

"I was thinkin' I'd check up on you," Philip said, "see what kind of progress you're makin' in your treatment'n all."

"Pretty steady, Philip."

"You seen my missin' deb?" Grace tried to sound offhand.

"Yeah. Thanks again. I couldn't have done it without you."

"That's why I'm gonna ask you to tell me where to find her, get a candid shot."

"I thought we agreed, no story at all until we're both out of here."

Grace shrugged helplessly. "Truth is, it's been a slow news *year* since she's been up here. Didn't know the worth of the girl till she was gone, know what I'm sayin'?"

"So you're thinking, quid pro quo again?"

"Yup."

"Okay." Kevin nodded. "Tell me what thirty by thirty means."

"Huh?"

"Let's say I heard Tucker Fisk tell a guy he was going to be 'thirty by thirty' if something happened."

Philip Grace gave a laugh so cold and bitter it sounded like it came from a dead person. "Wall Street guys say that. Means they expect to make thirty million before they turn thirty years old."

"Oh, yeah?" A concept from another planet.

"You and me, we gonna be lucky to make one million by ninety between the two of us, the rate you helpin' me out here," Philip grumbled. "Gimme some Corny dish, I'll get you some cash for the commissary, whatever they call it here."

"No," Kevin said.

"I could tell Chester Lord."

"Take your best shot, I don't care." Kevin leaned over, resting his arms on his knees and his palms up. "Something's going on with Tucker. Give me a little time, that's all I'm asking. Please."

"Man, I'm dyin' out there on the street."

Grace stretched out his hands, his forehead knotting. Kevin felt ambivalent about the guy who'd lost his meal ticket, Cornelia Lord. Philip looked more frazzled and needy than Kevin had ever seen him.

"Look," Kevin told him sincerely, "I'm working on a plan right now."

Kevin thought that sounded better than just admitting that he badly *needed* a plan, and soon.

She was still on intravenous meds, a handicap, but Kevin was not. He got his orally, tongued them, and spit them out when nobody was looking. So they divided up tasks.

Today his friend Richard helped them sneak away by dropping his plastic Maalox bottle and shaking himself into a phony seizure on the Yellow Brick Road. Cornelia clutched a pink tablecloth wrapped up and tied like a hobo's bundle under her top. She had slipped it off her table in Astor II's dining room, then filled it with stolen bread and cheese.

They had ten minutes today. In delicious Sanctuary time, that could be a picnic. They stormed up the staircase they called their "Stairway to Heaven," because they could never stay longer than the length of the song.

"Do you think we're using people like Creamcheese and Richard, getting them in trouble?" he asked.

"Not on my wing. We're their Designated Couple."

On the upstairs landing, Kevin slammed his elbow against a window frame at the top of the stairs and it sprung open easily. He helped her through the opening.

They settled down on a five-foot slab outside the window, hidden from the view of guards patrolling the grounds. She pulled the hobo bag apart, taking out bread and two types of cheese and spreading it neatly on their slab.

"We're like bandits," she said, "hiding in the rooftops of Notre Dame."

She watched him break off a piece of yellow cheese for her, then stop. "No. You like the white one, don't you?" he said.

She felt gratitude swelling up through her whole body, just because he knew those tiniest factoids about her. He fed her a gooey morsel of Camembert.

"You see everything." She kissed him, a tear on her cheek.

He smiled, not quite understanding, but put his arm around her and squeezed.

"I've been thinking," she said. "How are we ever going to get ourselves out of the hospital?"

"You mean go AWOL?" He looked worried.

"Our checkout time seems up in the air, Kevin."

"You could do it the old-fashioned way. Just show everybody you're okay." He looked serious. "I've been thinking about your family business thing. How old is Tucker Fisk?"

"Twenty-eight." She moved to tickle him.

He held her fingers back. "Is he going to make thirty million dollars as soon as he saves your father's company?"

She sounded surprised. "How could he? He doesn't even make a million dollars a year, I know that much."

"How about if your father gave him a bonus."

"A *bonus?*" she picked up and nibbled another bit of Camembert to keep from giggling. "Kevin, I wouldn't call my father miserly by any means, but he wouldn't give Tucker a thirty-million-dollar bonus. And WASP families don't believe in big dowries, even for crazy daughters."

Kevin had a thought.

"What about the people behind this hostile takeover . . ."

"Han Koi and his son."

"Yeah. Would they give Tucker thirty million dollars if he, uh, 'delivered you'?"

She almost choked on her Camembert. He pounded lightly on her back while she coughed and her face turned red.

"Are you okay?"

"I'm fine. Who gave you that idea?"

"Your driver."

"Mike?" She recovered, breathing hard.

"I saw him here." She tensed. "But he won't say anything to your father. He says Tucker was talking on the phone to 'the Chinese guy.' I think he was asking for thirty million, but I don't have any proof."

"Neither do I," she said, coughing again. She sat stiffly. "Kevin, we have to tell my father, but he won't believe me."

"You'll make him believe you."

"How?"

"Well, I've been doing an electrical count."

"A what?"

"I counted how many times you've mentioned electrical stuff to me the past three days," he said, putting his cheese down. "Zero. You used to be two people. You and—"

"I called her the Electric Girl."

Called. She spoke slowly and carefully, like the thought had to crawl up from somewhere. She wanted to be certain she heard no warnings, none of the Electric Girl's signals to protect her.

"You're okay, Corny. Call your father. Tell him to come up without Tucker."

"Why would he listen?"

She watched him brush the breadcrumbs off his hands.

"Because," he told her, "you're all Cornelia now. He'll see that. What are you grinning about?"

"Because I can't see people's coronas anymore," she told him. "But I can still see yours."

In a stroke of ego, Tucker Fisk had taken out a whopping mortgage for one of the apartments on the top floors of Koi Tower.

He bought it sight unseen, bragging that he was too busy to take the elevator upstairs and look at it himself. Now it mocked him, his little glass and steel one-bedroom squirrel hole that cost him $2 million and change. He had learned, too late, that it was the cheapest apartment in the building because it had been designed as a fancy servants quarters for the $15 million three-story palace next to it. Before the sheik who was supposed to buy it reneged.

Now he hated his dark quarters. He had expected to lord over the skyline of Midtown Manhattan from an eagle's nest. Instead, his floor-to-ceiling windows commanded a total loser's view of the office building right across the street. All he could see was its reflective mirrored glass. To prevent the workers across Madison Avenue from spying, he was forced to leave blackout shades down day and night. They gave his living room, crammed with his oversized leather and steel furniture, the feeling of a luxury coal mine.

He felt scalded by the indignity, and saw it as a sign to push even harder. He had plenty to do, keeping Lord & Company storming ahead at 25 percent annual growth, while having to shoulder all of Chester's family burdens besides. He performed these marvels as a salary serf, not even a partner in the company he had led to greatness in spite of Chester Lord—the only CEO in America who refused to lead or follow or get out of the way.

But he wouldn't waste time feeling sorry for himself. He practically had the Cornelia problem solved. Assuming that his butt boy Loblitz—of course, the arrogant young doctor wouldn't like to think of himself that way—had done his job at the hospital staff conference.

Tucker tore open the manila envelope that had just arrived by messenger. Concealed in bubble wrap was the tie clip microphone he had given Loblitz—a marvel of Koi microengineering. Recorder and mike were both built into the little tie bar, a miniature of the 1939 World's Fair Trylon and Perisphere. Now he would find out for sure how Loblitz performed under pressure, and how useful the young doctor would prove to be as offensive end during the last moments of Tucker's game.

His muted lights reflected off the shiny tie bar. He took the little eavesdropper to the blinking sound system built into his wall and attached the recorder to its adaptor. The recording, made on an ultrathin wire, would now play through his twelve Bang & Olufsen speakers.

He kicked off his sleek black loafers, sprawled into his ergonomic egg-shaped listening chair, and flicked his remote.

The novelty of it tickled him, listening to what psychiatrists would say about Cornelia, now that Chester couldn't hear them.

He first recognized Dr. Burns's measured voice. *"Next, Cornelia Lord . . . Dr. Loblitz? Where are we?"*

"Stalled." Loblitz's voice sounded a decibel too high. *"She came to us hearing voices and believing that a dead inventor named Tesla is some kind of romantic hero. If we accelerate to ECT now, we can get her back home in two weeks."*

Then a woman doctor's voice. *"What's the rush?"*

Tucker scowled at his sound system, blinking red and green in the near-dark.

"Not to put too fine a point on the family's interest," Dr. Loblitz said, *"but they want her out for a wedding date in February."*

"Are wedding planners writing our treatment procedures now, Doc-

tor?" The woman doctor again. Tucker's chest heated up with acid. Who was she to question his plans?

"*That has nothing to do with it,*" Loblitz sounded wobbly, obviously not expecting this counterattack. "*She's resistant to therapy, she had a hell of a tolerance for chlorpromazine, and her defense mechanisms are hardening.*"

"*Maybe they should just postpone her wedding date.*" The stupid woman again.

Dr. Loblitz took a needling tone. "*This isn't some feminist thing, Joanne.*"

Then Burns. "*All right, start ECT next week, we'll see what happens. Let's move on. Joanne, what about Kevin Doyle?*"

Tucker smiled broadly. His finger moved to switch off the button, but hesitated at the mention of that name, Kevin who?

"*Doyle's showing all the cues of a spontaneous recovery,*" the woman said. "*He manages to control his Sebastian delusion around other patients. I'd say he's even been a positive influence on Cornelia Lord.*"

Tucker jumped out of his chair and stood facing his audio player.

"*All right,*" Burns told her, "*but don't be in too much of a hurry to rush him out . . .*"

". . . out the door." The words bubbled from Tucker's lips. He saw the doorman Kevin Doyle, the runty mutt with sullen eyes giving him backtalk. No. It was cunning that had lurked under the black visor.

So, Kevin Doyle, doorman of Slack City, had executed a clever end run around Tucker. How had he pulled it off? Absently, Tucker destroyed the little tie-pin recorder with his fingers, ripping it apart to calm himself down.

Well, it didn't matter. He'd seen that kind of play before, and knew how to stop it.

In the Abraham Maslow room that night, the Designated Couple managed to slink out the locked door behind an aide.

They ran as fast as Cornelia could, and she yelped with the fun of it, holding hands as they raced into the wind with her hair flying.

"Five minutes," he breathed in her ear. "I just have to show you something and we go straight back."

They hugged the double line of trees along the circular driveway, checking for guards. Then they broke into a run again. They rushed toward the tall, barren clump of trees at the end of the property, scuttled around the spiky, leafless woodland, poking their way carefully until the outline of the electrical fence loomed ahead.

"You've got to watch closely," he told her. "I can only do this once, or the guards might see."

"Okay," she promised, taking deep breaths.

"Ready? Watch the fence right there."

Then he stepped back and threw a small object, as though skimming a stone across a pond.

The buzz of the fence made a hiss. She felt the electrical surge through the ground from fifteen feet away.

The curved lines and squiggles of tube were attached to the electrical wires. They lit up a brilliant red as light scampered through the shape of Kevin's heart.

"Kevin, your *Open Heart*. You finished it. How did you *do* that?" she cried, happy and bewildered.

"In Artistic Expression class. I got the teacher to order some plastic for me, nothing sharp or breakable, you know? Then I snuck out and attached it."

She bit her lip. "Weren't you afraid of bringing the Electric Girl back?"

They held each other like close dancers.

"I don't think we're going to see that Electric Girl around here anymore." He slipped both arms around her and pressed the small of her back.

They kissed almost violently until the glare of a flashlight found them.

"I'm fine, really," Cornelia explained. "Kevin helped me tremendously. I'm ready to leave the hospital now, and so is Kevin."

Dr. Burns and Dr. Loblitz had left her alone with Chester. Her father sat in a large chair, uncomfortably. He crossed his leg and played with a sock, pulling it up so it wouldn't expose a white flash of his leg. She'd never seen Chester undone by his executive-length socks before.

"Dr. Loblitz doesn't agree," Chester finally said, not happy about it. "They'll need to change treatment now to repair whatever damage this Kevin Doyle has done to you."

"Damage?" Her eyes exploded. "If you'll recall, Chester, what Kevin did involved pulling me from under the wheel of your car. I just want to get to know him better on the outside. I realize that he's not exactly at your social level—"

Her father waved with his hand, frustrated.

"It's not that he's a doorman," he told her. "If it made sense otherwise, I could learn to live with the social difference. I could even help him if he had the right material."

"He has more material in his little finger than Tucker Fisk—"

"Cornelia," he told her, "I didn't just take Tucker's word for it. I checked his background myself and made every effort to find some redeeming value. All Kevin Doyle has ever achieved is to talk his way into this hospital. Why would he do that?"

"To be with me where you couldn't blow him off as a nobody. And Tucker couldn't manipulate him."

"I don't think so, Cornelia," her father said with a mulelike shake of his head. "In the worst case, he's a fortune hunter. But even if he's not, I couldn't bear to see you marry a man whom you ultimately won't respect."

"Because he wants me? You think that someone would only be interested in me for my money?"

Her father put his chin in his hand and looked down at the floor.

"You don't even know me, Chester, and it breaks my heart."

Kevin found him in the visitors lounge, toying with a shiny computer the size of a thin-crust pizza slice on his lap.

"Have a seat, Kevin." Tucker didn't get up. "Or is it Sebastian today?"

"No, thanks," Kevin told him, standing. "I sit all day."

"Suit yourself." Tucker shrugged. "I just wanted to show you something."

He angled his laptop around so Kevin could see the screen clearly. It was a page from some encyclopedia. The title of the page read, "Saint Sebastian." The dense type under it was illustrated by the lost Giotto painting of Sebastian in a corner of the screen.

"The funny thing is," Tucker told him buddy-to-buddy, "Sebastian didn't die from the arrows like everybody thinks. A woman nursed his wounds and he lived. But, you know what? It didn't matter. The emperor found out and sent the soldiers back to beat him to death. The poor guy couldn't win. Not after he took on the emperor."

Tucker smiled sadly and waited for Kevin to speak. Kevin let him wait.

"I just wanted to share that with you," Tucker went on. "The difference in your case, Kevin, is that I haven't forgotten you saved my fiancée's life."

"And you're thinking, quid pro quo."

"I don't speak Latin." Tucker shrugged. "I'm just telling you, there's an upside to this. I found out something that might interest you. There's a program at the Benito College of Art in Rome for young artists."

Kevin watched Tucker punch up a new screen with one line, "Scholarship: $100,000."

"They don't have dorms at this school," Tucker continued, a little more slowly, polishing up every word. "So you get a furnished apartment near the Spanish Steps on a little street where they do art shows. I've been there. I don't know much about art, but I can tell you about the women."

Kevin said nothing.

"Just sharing that information," Tucker said.

"Thanks," Kevin said. "You know, you had Corny right there, no obstacles or anything. All you had to do was care about her. If you were a half-decent guy, I might let her go for her sake. Just sharing."

He studied the mogul, whose jaw looked so pink he must carry an electric razor around and shave three times a day. Tucker said nothing to contradict him. He smiled like it was a joke on everybody else.

"So how're you going to do it?" Kevin asked him.

"Do what?"

"Make thirty by thirty. Chester won't give it to you."

Tucker looked startled, a rat with a twitchy nose caught in a flashlight's glare.

"What are you talking about?"

"I'm just thinking, thirty million's a lot for Chester Lord to give you. So you've got to be getting it from somewhere else. The Kois, I think Corny said, trying to take over Lord & Company."

Tucker closed his laptop with a sharp click like a cricket.

"You seem like a guy who looks out for number one, Tucker. I figure maybe they've got you covered."

But now Tucker Fisk moved like a lion, all lazy power. He flung his blond head back and stood up.

"I remember when I played football, liking the pain a little," Tucker told him man-to-man with a hint of pity. "But the game you just decided to play, Doyle, it's going to hurt all the time."

Part Four

White Doves Falling

Chapter Twenty-four

*T*he small plaque on the door read only "ECT."

She forgot more and more lately, but never the ice in her stomach whenever that plaque appeared. She tensed as her aide escort, a powerful woman, steered her inside.

"Hello, Cornelia." Two unfamiliar nurses greeted her, one stout, the other with a knobby chin. They moved efficiently about the small room, bare except for a single hospital bed. The bed was surrounded by stacks of electronic equipment, piled up like hi-fi components, with lots of multicolored wires dangling down.

The stout nurse helped her to take off her clothes and helped her slip on a flimsy hospital gown. The other gave her pills and a paper cup of water.

"What are these for?" She obediently gulped them down. They left a bitter taste.

"To make you feel a little dreamy," the nurse recited, as though she had to repeat it too often. "You'll be more comfortable during the procedure."

"Thank you. What procedure?"

"ECT, Cornelia." They helped her onto the hospital bed.

A pretty black doctor entered the room.

"Good morning, Cornelia."

"Hi. Who are you?"

"I'm your anesthesiologist, Dr. Love." Like the nurses, the doctor sounded mechanically patient in her response. Was she the only one missing something here? The doctor rested her hand on Cornelia's arm in a familiar way. "I'm going to give you a short-acting anesthetic after the nurses prepare you."

"Prepare me for what?" Now the nurses secured her to the bed, fastening some sort of restraints onto her limbs. "Is this a gynecological exam? I don't see any stirrups."

"No, dear," the stout nurse explained again. "This is ECT."

The confusion reigned, an awful feeling of living in an eternal present where she couldn't recall events from even moments before.

"Haven't I done this already?"

"Several times, Cornelia. Now we need to do it again." The nurse with the chin touched her bare flesh with a sticky goo, and attached the ends of several red and white wires.

"Lie on your side, dear. Good. We're going to monitor your blood pressure and heart."

She felt her scalp being cleaned. Wires dangled in front of her eyes. She felt something attached to both sides of her skull.

"That's not my heart up there."

"No, the wires are for the procedure, dear."

"Cornelia, I'm giving you something to relax you now," said the pretty black woman in the white coat and blue nameplate. Hadn't she just introduced herself?

"What is it?"

"It's a combination. Part anesthesia and part muscle relaxant."

The machine that looked like hi-fi components came to life now. She heard beeping and bleating, saw red and green numerals, a line that made sharp peaks and valleys on a monitor.

"ECG and pulse-oximeter leads are in," she heard. "Methohexital . . . midazolam . . ."

Her body in the thin gown slipped away from her. She felt naked and out of control.

"Why?" Cornelia asked her, trying to blink back tears. "Why are you doing this?"

"Doctor will explain, dear," the nurse told her.

A young man with curly hair entered the room. He looked quite familiar, but not at all comfortably so.

"Good morning, Cornelia. Do you know who I am?"

She saw the white coat. "Dr. somebody."

"Dr. Loblitz. What's your home address?"

"Eight-forty Fifth Avenue." That remained clear to her. She had lived there all her life. More recent memories—the past days, months, even minutes—could not be summoned so easily.

"Cornelia," the doctor asked her, "who invented electricity?"

She thought it over. She had been asked and answered that same question more than once, she believed.

"I'm sorry. What did you say?"

"Who invented electricity?"

"Nikola Tesla," she told him.

"Prepare her," the doctor instructed the nurses. "Run a monitor strip."

A nurse checked the goo and wires on both sides of her head.

The chin-nurse told her. "Open." She opened her mouth and the nurse stuck in a piece of very hard rubber.

"Mmmrumph?"

"This is so you don't bite your tongue." The nurse pulled the bed-side rails on either side of her into the upright position.

"Give her thirty seconds," the black-haired doctor said curtly.

A clear mask came over her nose.

"This is just oxygen." The woman doctor's voice.

She closed her eyes, and felt the shock. A wavy one, oscillating, lifting her up, then dropping her as her muscles contracted.

Black. And a terrible dryness.

When she awoke, a clammy sweat enveloped her and saliva trickled out of her mouth. Her head ached horribly. Her thoughts were jumbled. When she tried to organize a question, her thoughts flew hopelessly out of her control. She made a waterfall sound in her head to protect herself. Through that rumble, she heard snippets of hushed disagreement.

"Again? But Doctor . . ."

"Just do it."

"It's awfully high, Doctor."

"Airway . . . suction . . ."

Blackness again.

The waves ended, crashing. She believed someone spoke to her. But she couldn't talk. She labored just to breathe. A heavy, prickly heat fell over her as someone wrapped her in blankets and removed the flat, stiff object from her mouth.

Several minutes passed before she heard a man speak.

"Cornelia, who invented electricity?"

She squeezed her eyes shut. Such an odd time for a quiz. She thought she was lying in the school nurse's office, with a god-awful headache.

Her mouth felt woolly and full of a funny odor, like animals lived inside. "Alexander Graham Bell?"

"Electricity. Who invented electricity?"

"Oh. Thomas Alva Edison, wasn't it?"

"Good, Cornelia. I'd say we just achieved a major breakthrough."

"Break through what?" She slurred her words. She felt ashamed, afraid that she must be drooling.

"Let us worry about that." The voice sounded so arrogant and smug. It came from the male doctor with curly hair who scribbled notes on a chart. "You just concentrate on getting better."

She felt so weary and hopeless. As though her whole being collapsed into herself and she was left alone in a black void.

When she opened her eyes, she was sitting on a couch, dressed in a robe. She was in a room surrounded by strange women. A few of them greeted her by her name, Cornelia. How did they know her?

So tired. She slouched down into the folds of the green sofa, studying the terry cloth bathrobe she wore with a T-shirt underneath. Three girls sat around her, dressed just as oddly. She would really like to leave. Immediately.

"Creamcheese," one of the girls whispered to another so she could just hear her. "Give it to her."

A porcelain-pale girl with inky black hair leaned over.

"Corny, I have a note for you." She pressed a folded pink napkin into her hand.

She tried to smile. At least she could be polite in her disarray, until she sorted this out. Slowly, she unwrapped the napkin. Someone had written on it with a pen in black letters. She moved her lips over the words, four times, before folding it and handing it back to the pale girl.

"I'm sorry," she said. "I don't know anyone named Kevin."

He waited in the therapy room of Astor I for Dr. Lester.

Now his notes to Cornelia went one way and vanished. Since he had been transferred to this maximum-security wing, the only information about her came from hospital gossip. That shaky grapevine told him that Corny's doctor gave her shock treatments regularly, and she wasn't remembering a lot.

The door opened. A young doctor with a half-bored, clinical look and curly black hair plopped down in the chair across from him.

"Where's Dr. Lester?" Kevin asked him.

"Dr. Burns took her off your case because she wasn't tough enough with you. It's time for a new regime, Sebastian. I'm Dr. Loblitz. I'll be your therapist from now on."

Now Kevin recognized him from Cornelia's description. He crossed his leg in a sprawling way so that his ankle rested on his knee. He had a nervous tic. His heavy brown shoe shook up and down.

"I have good news for you, Kevin. I've cured your friend Ms. Lord. She's made a complete recovery."

Kevin felt the hairs rise. "A recovery?"

"Yes," the young doctor worked his unpleasant, wet lips. "I helped her forget all her disturbances. Her delusions about Tesla. Her irrational reluctance to marry Mr. Fisk. And her flirtation with you."

The doctor sat back. Maybe he wasn't exactly enjoying this, but he sure wasn't hating it either. "I'm discharging Cornelia Lord tomorrow. But I'm afraid your prognosis isn't so clear."

"Meaning?"

"You're still manifestly disturbed, suffering from—"

"Code Green," Kevin guessed. "I'm covered by my health plan, as long as you want to keep me."

The doctor looked surprised. "Very good, Kevin, but even the best medical plans come to an end sometime. We have about a year left to work together. Let's make it count."

He actually smiled now, a mean little "gotcha" smile that made him look more like a prosecutor than a psychiatrist. No, more like a torturer warming up. Kevin scorched his brain searching for what could work to change the doctor's mind.

"Look, aren't you supposed to 'first do no harm'?"

"Kevin, am I harming you? I'm here to help."

"I faked my way in here. You can kick me out for malingering, do whatever you want. But you can't keep me in here when you know I'm okay."

He was very nervous about this doctor's smile now, the way his blubbery lips curled.

"It's not just me you're up against, Kevin. We have your referring doctor's diagnosis. We have test batteries. You can't fake those."

"I was only *acting* crazy for Cornelia."

Dr. Loblitz chuckled. "And you did a fine job, Kevin. Why don't you just settle back and enjoy it. Working people like you never get to stay at the Sanctuary."

A growl began deep in Kevin's stomach and worked up through his throat. He leapt up from his seat, lunging at the doctor's stringy neck.

"Aides!" Dr. Loblitz yelled.

Then he could recall only a noisy red fury. He almost lost consciousness with one beefy aide's arm around his neck, the other twisting his own arm behind his back. They wrestled him into the most feared room in the entire hospital. The one with no plaque on the door.

The staff called it "Seclusion."

The patients knew it as "The Rubber Room" or "The Wet Room," depending on their doctor's orders.

The floor and walls were padded with foam rubber. They had been smeared with something unsavory by the last patient. It smelled like a monkey cage treated with disinfectant. One foam mattress was placed against the wall. It was there to be walloped like a punching bag to work off anger. Another mattress lay on the rubber-padded floor for resting. There was no other furniture.

"Cold-pack him," Dr. Loblitz snarled, straightening his tie. Kevin's wild efforts to strangle this doctor hadn't even mussed his curly hair.

The aides stripped Kevin's clothes off. They wrapped him in pink bedsheets soaked in ice-cold water, and secured them tightly around his body with fabric belts. Kevin pressed his face against the mattress on the floor. He began to shiver, his teeth clattering together.

He lay there for what seemed like hours yelling into the mattress. He couldn't stop thinking of Cornelia standing politely at the big oak front doors of the Sanctuary, ready to go home.

Chapter Twenty-five

Chester swung the door open.

"Where are my bridesmaids, Monsieur? Bring them to me." The woman's voice cut though the elliptical foyer of Penthouse A like a haughty foghorn.

"Good afternoon, Madame."

"Eh, bien." Madame honked, then sneezed in Chester's face without apologizing.

Chester swallowed his dislike. He greeted the frail woman heartily and took her by her brittle arm. Carefully, he escorted Madame Marie-Claude, Manhattan's oldest wedding planner, across the foyer under his glittering chandelier. She shook off Chester's arm and hobbled away, stabbing her walking cane with a top ornament like a Fabergé egg into his floor.

This was the woman who would reign over Cornelia's wedding. In his heart he suspected that Madame had peaked about half a century ago. Then she had served as one of the royal wedding retinue for the movie star Grace Kelly, soon to become Princess Grace of Monaco. "Happily ever after" had seemed quite attainable to Elizabeth's generation of debutantes, with the right selection of husband and wedding planner.

So Elizabeth had chosen Madame Marie-Claude to spin their

own fairy-tale wedding—had it really been twenty-five years earlier? Chester had found the old tyrant insufferable even then. But when Cornelia went through the photographs of her parents' wedding and asked about the old crone, Chester encouraged his daughter to hire her. Even this fragile connection to Elizabeth proved irresistible.

Chester followed Madame into the living room. He tuned out Madame's hectoring of Cornelia's bridesmaids, Tina French and other childhood friends huddling around his daughter.

"Hey, Madame," Tina greeted her, deadpan. "Torquemada called you. He wants his personality back."

Chester regarded smirky, quirky Tina of the cylindrical body wearing a "Models Suck" T-shirt under a man's dress shirt.

"Venez vite ici!" Madame barked.

Chester marveled that each of the bridesmaids who slouched around his living room in a fairly unappealing collection of sloppy, street-chic get-ups understood Madame's command and dutifully jumped up to gather around the old fascist. Respect for wedding planners must be burned in these girls' genes, Chester mused, the way they leapt to her authority.

Except for Cornelia.

Cornelia sat before the hearth, frowning at the flames.

"C'mon, Corny," Tina screeched at her.

His daughter finally smiled and stood up to join Madame. Though she seemed warm on the surface, undeniably calmer, Chester keenly felt the dullness in her eyes as though it were his own emptiness.

How her sparkle had gone.

She no longer ran away. She never bothered to argue. Sometimes she hovered near her father in a tentative, almost fearful way, as though he were the only person in a precarious land. And that had been his wish.

Be careful what you wish for, Elizabeth would have told him.

Most of Cornelia's memories would return in time, Loblitz promised. He felt a simmering of anger at the doctor. Loblitz neither realized nor seemed to care about the passion that seemed lost, perhaps irretrievably.

Dr. Loblitz had brushed aside his concerns. He had immediately begun with the jargon. Something about anterograde memory loss. Once Chester had cut through the hokum, Loblitz had admitted that Cornelia would be confused and possibly suffer some minor loss of memory. But Chester felt ill-prepared for the depth of her funk. When she tried to remember her past, even some of her fondest recollections of her childhood remained pockmarked.

The great positive, he supposed, was that Cornelia seemed to view Tucker as a new person in her life. At least she didn't reject him, or bring up her conspiracy theories. It was good that she could start with a "clean slate," as both Dr. Loblitz and Tucker had taken to calling her evacuated memory banks. Fortunately, she recalled nothing at all about the Tesla business or the doorman.

Chester had sat her down several times and talked to her. He had omitted some thorny topics such as Kevin Doyle, shaded others. He told her that she needed help dealing with painful memories of her mother's death and had received it at the Sanctuary. He belabored the loyalty Tucker had shown her. With a hazy and rather tragic gratitude, she had accepted Chester's abridged version of events. Sometimes she even seemed to fake recalling things to make him happy. Her genuine recollections, notable by the glint in her otherwise full eyes, came infrequently. Each recaptured true memory seemed a small treasure.

Yet in the coldest and most practical terms, their plan—or he should say Tucker's plan—had worked. In her halting way, Cornelia seemed to enjoy occupying center stage as the bride-to-be in Manhattan's Wedding of the Year.

He had defeated Corny's rebellion, but at a terrible cost. And now his heart punished him.

Chester left Madame with Cornelia and slumped off to his study. At the door, he was taken aback to see Tucker working at his English desk, a trophy plucked from the Rothschild banking house. The boy was treating Chester's private sanctum sanctorum as his own.

"Should I look into getting a partners desk?" Chester asked dryly.

Tucker looked up, startled. He pulled some papers together and tapped them on the desktop to smooth out the pile.

"Cornelia and I signed these yesterday in Edgar's office. We're going to beat the Kois, Dad."

Dad.

"Don't look so depressed." Tucker slapped his arm. "Loblitz told me an interesting mind thing. The closer you get to a goal, the more you see the negatives."

Tucker rolled his eyes playfully at the mysteries of the mind.

Chester's heart skipped for some reason. "I didn't realize that you and Dr. Loblitz were so close."

Tucker cocked his head. "Close? Why would you say that, Chester?"

Suddenly he felt too queasy to stay in his own study. "I think I'll step outside for some air."

In the lobby, Andrew, the doorman, tipped his hat. "Congratulations, sir."

"Thank you." His own voice sounded high and tight.

Chester couldn't walk through the lobby and see his own doorman now without the apparition of Kevin Doyle flitting through his mind.

Doyle had been a hero at first. No question about that. Then, in the way of young people today, he had taken advantage of the situation, forcing himself on his daughter. No better than a surly, overpaid professional quarterback who makes one good play and—

Quarterback. No. It wasn't Kevin Doyle whose image leapt in front of him, but Tucker's. Why had his grim doubts all turned in Tucker's direction lately? Perhaps Chester had overreacted to the boy's sitting at his desk. But he had physically *recoiled* when his future son-in-law had called him "Dad" and touched him.

Was it possible that, although Chester had always known the awful fire of shame that burned the tips of his ears bright red, he had never really felt *guilt* before? On his daughter's wedding day, when he would get to keep Lord & Company, all of his troubles would be over. So why did his world seem ready to collapse like a . . . what did they call those stars that imploded into themselves, becoming dead, cold little raisins in the universe?

White dwarfs.

Why did he feel like he would turn into a white dwarf?

Walking south on Fifth Avenue, he looked back at 840. For the first time, Chester found a hint of the Bastille in the limestone tower. It had always been just "home," familiar and unremarkable. Now it looked old and ugly. *His daughter's prison.* He turned abruptly into Central Park. The cold should bite his skin, but didn't. He felt suddenly inured to sensation, as though his body had turned to salt, like Lot's wife, and could blow away in the wind.

Chester followed the path toward the entrance to the Central Park Zoo, looking up at the big stone gate. He saw the bronze animals at the top, the bear ringing the bell. He had loved that bear as a small boy. Now it looked as grotesque as a gargoyle.

His bench-made English shoes kept moving toward Grand Army Plaza. The Plaza Hotel sparkled, fresh from its latest sandblasting renovation. If only one's spirit could be sandblasted, he mused, to rise up so tidy and renewed. The fountain in front had been shut off for winter, perhaps just after Cornelia's incident. Limousines huddled together under the hotel awnings in loud colors that could only be commissioned by sultans and rock stars.

He felt so cold and alone that one of his worst childhood memories came back to him.

During his fifteenth summer, his dad arranged for him to crew on a competition sailing boat. Shivering below in the dark, swinging in a net hammock under a skimpy blanket made of silver foil, he dreaded his first shift as night's watch. The boat pitched and brine swept over decks with only a six-inch-high railing, with nobody else to notice if he should go overboard and drown. His crewmates laughed and shoved him on deck, then locked the door behind him. He slid across the bow as if it were slicked with oil, and clung in terror to a cleat with his eyes closed until he was finally relieved . . .

"Oh, sorry." He was clinging to the back of a park bench, a woman bustling her children away in fright.

He moved on, gathering speed. His feet found a groove, did his thinking for him. Everyone who he had trusted with Cornelia . . . Tucker . . . the psychiatrists . . . had given him queasy waves of uncertainty lately, cold pockets of dread. With one exception. Only one person in his recent memory had unburdened him with an act of goodness so pure and comforting, it still glowed inside him, pulling him forward.

Chester found what he had come for across the street from the Plaza. There were already sparkling lights on in the trees at the rim of the park, and the hotels along Central Park South shone full of comfort and celebration. He could see the couples bundled up under lap robes in the backs of the horse-drawn carriages, black coaches with gold fittings and red tassels, driven by men and women in stiff white shirts and top hats.

The carriage stood out from the others, spanking white. What ambition it must take to sit up there. He walked toward Roni Dubrov, towering over her black-leather driver's seat, the black curls spilling around her shoulders. She wore round wire-rimmed sunglasses with glossy black lenses today, a bit intimidating on her sharp cheekbones. As he approached, he noticed that her skin kept its bronze warmth even in this thin winter sunlight. He breathed in the comforting horsy scent.

"Hello," he called up to her.

She looked down in his direction, located him.

"Chester Lord," she called happily. "Do you like?"

"Very much." His eyes rested on her face.

She laughed raucously like a soldier in a barracks, a surprising sound from her womanly lips.

"No, Chester, the carriage."

"Oh." He admired the freshly painted black frame and patted the maroon leather, old but well oiled. "It's quite magnificent."

"Good. You paid for it. That was a nice thing. How is Cornelia?"

"Back from the hospital." He tried to strike an optimistic tone to match her own. "And getting married."

He expected her to gush a bit like everyone else, to offer some congratulatory bit of fluff. Instead, she removed her sunglasses. Her eyes made him wither. They were as coal-black as the lenses she had just taken off, and full of distrust.

"What do you mean, getting married?"

"Well, just that. Actually, I came here to ask you to the wedding."

"To drive the carriage?"

"No, I thought as a . . . guest."

She looked so formidable up there, her tangle of hair in the light like a burning bush, judging him. "Mr. Lord, did you honestly come to bring me a wedding invitation?"

"Uh . . ." Chester fumbled.

"You don't look so right to me."

"Listen," Chester said. "Do you suppose I could hop up there and just talk for a while?"

She put her sunglass frame between her teeth and nibbled on it, unconsciously, her eyes drilling into him.

Chester froze in her stare, intimidated. But he did not feel like walking away.

She spoke crisply. "Do you remember what I told you about Cornelia, when I saw you at the hospital?"

"You said to help her."

"I said that she was only a child." Roni pointed her glasses at him, shaking them.

"We did. We found her professional help in a . . . uh, residential facility."

"A mental hospital?"

"One with a lovely grounds and swimming pool."

Suddenly he felt the enormity of his burden come rushing up like something bilious from his stomach.

"And she had shock treatments," he blurted. "She's lost her memory."

Roni Dubrov's forehead plunged into angry furrows under the mass of curly hair. "She's getting married in this condition? Have you gone crazy, Mr. Lord?"

"It's complicated."

He wondered if he looked as lonely and exposed as he felt.

Finally, she gave him the look he now realized that he had come seeking, the one he had remembered every day since the horrible night at Manhattan Hill Hospital.

"I think you'd better tell me about it."

Kevin pressed his fingers and nose flat against the glass of the nurses' station, reading the *New York Globe* headline upside down. The staff held a daily conference inside, with their backs turned to him. The newspaper lay on a table just inside the booth.

"Corny: Crazy in Love?" The headline read.

And Kevin saw Philip Grace's byline underneath the headline, trying to make out the words while his heart pumped so hard, it almost shook the glass.

Grace's story said, "*. . . private afternoon nuptials at the Lord penthouse on February 14 . . .*"

Valentine's Day.

He turned around and crumpled into the closest chair. The patient sitting next to him rose up and walked away in quick, robotic steps.

The nice student nurse, Ms. Babcock, stooped down to look at him, concerned. "What's the matter with you, Kevin? Your face is all red."

"I'm trying to see if I can die if I hold my breath long enough."

"Kevin, you stop that." She helped him up. "You have a visitor."

A visitor, good. He would pull himself together. Push Mr. Shit Out of Luck back on the shelf and take out Mr. Last Pitiful Hope. He could beat this. It was only Chester, Tucker, and the New York Establishment again. He had already climbed into the ring once. And he'd snuck into this hospital, sucker-punched them all. For a while, anyway.

And just when she was really getting better.

He flashed on an image of Cornelia as one of those tortured explorers he had seen at Bellevue—patients who had shock treatments and lost their memories, looking for their lives in every corner of the ward. Were they married? Were their parents still alive? He felt shattered for her, ached to be with her while she began to pick up those broken shards of her past. It could be months before she would really be Cornelia again.

If ever.

Anyway, she couldn't save herself now. It was on him to patch together his thin armor and go after her.

Thinking about the "nuptials," that almost obscene-sounding word, he felt suddenly drained of all energy and hope.

Who was he kidding?

If she stepped into her world again, they could flick a finger and be rid of him forever.

An aide approached him, warily. "You've still got a visitor."

He slumped to the visitors room in his bedroom slippers.

"Jesus, Kevin," Marne greeted him. "You look like you've been chewing the rug. What happened to you?"

"They gave Cornelia shock treatments and released her."

"Shock?" She blinked. "What kind of shock?"

"Right out of the Middle Ages. They use them to zap somebody's brain if they're really disturbed or suicidal. I can't believe her father could do that to her."

Marne involuntarily flexed her biceps under her jacket. "So what are you gonna to do about it?"

"Do about it?" He looked at the wall, as if the secret hung on a light fixture. "Marne, they're holding me until my health plan runs out. If I act crazy, they're happy. If I act normal, they say I'm manipulating them and they drive me crazy all over again. It's a beautiful system."

She scowled. "Can they do that? I mean, they got laws in New York State. Look at all the nuts on the street. Maybe I should call the ACLU for you."

"The ACLU?" His eyes stung with a hopeless fury. "I need the 101st Airborne. She's getting married on Valentine's Day. Oh, Jesus. What's the date today?"

"February 7."

He tried to get control but felt his eyes rolling like pinwheels. "A week. I have to break out of here, get past building security at 840 Fifth, sneak into the Lords' apartment, and convince her she ought to take a chance with me. Marne, you've known me since I was two. You really think I'm up to that?"

"What I think," Marne said after a hard look at him, "is that you rescued that girl once, all on your own. You earned her, Kevin."

Vlad's stupid story about the Doorman Prince had lodged in his brain. Now it crept forward to mock him. He felt that life had just swallowed him up.

Doorman Prince, my ass.

Hope had driven him into the hospital. Hope gave you that dumb ambition that spits in the face of reason. But sometimes hope failed. You get outsmarted, outspent, life comes at you thundering like a bullherd, and you get trampled.

Maybe real wisdom came when you realized it was smarter to give up.

His voice was only a whisper. "Maybe you were right all along. It's not the end of the world just being a doorman, is it?"

His sister flashed him the defiant glare of the Feeneys, the fighters.

"Being a doorman may be okay for some people," she told him. "But not for Kevin Doyle."

Chapter Twenty-six

To the father of the groom!"

"To Sloopy, hear, hear!"

She obediently stood and hoisted her champagne glass. Forty-eight relatives and close friends selected for this intimate dinner at Binky's, a jewelbox of a private club, bobbed up like a line of dominoes jerked on a string.

The man from the *New York Times*, the only society reporter permitted into their dinner, ticked off photos of Cornelia as she smiled at Tucker. She widened her jaw until it showed all her teeth and gums. She lifted her own glass to clink onto his.

Now the whole table stared at Tucker's father. Sloopy Fisk flapped his fluffy eyebrows in Cornelia's direction. Amazing that his friends still called him Sloopy, his nickname from Yale. But not quite as amazing as his marriage to Tucker's mother.

Perhaps they found each other in a marriage of convenience. Sloopy's family had the name, but was shabby genteel. Tucker's mother, Elise, wore the pants and made the money. She stood as far apart from Sloopy as seating permitted, clutching the stem of her glass too tightly.

Her new in-laws. Harmless Sloopy and intense Elise. Her future mother-in-law's heart pumped so much adrenaline, her fingers almost broke the stemware. But she wasn't marrying Elise, was she?

Now it was time for sweet Sloopy's toast, and she stifled a giggle at his stuffy formality.

Sloopy began luffing at length. "It's good to finally be in the 'family way' with my old college roommate, Chester Lord. We've always been close, but as Chester's dad used to say, 'Nothing wrong with inbreeding . . . works for racehorses, doesn't it?'"

She heard echoes of polite laughter.

A flickering candle caught her attention inside the glass of the candelabra in front of her. Like a firefly, casting little stars and shadows, shapes like . . . *that face in uniform.*

A uniformed officer of some kind, with his ear bleeding.

Her father had just explained *that face* the day before. It was a man who used to work at her building. He had done something and been fired. When did he work there? she wondered. Surely when she was a child. She couldn't recall his name, but he saved her from a terrible accident. It was a trauma, Chester told her, like her mother dying.

Oops. All the guests stood up around the table, looking at her.

She shifted her attention back to her well-wishers. Sloopy had finished his part. Now they all waited for her.

She smiled apologetically. "Thank you," she said, lifting her glass. "I have a toast, too. To my fiancé, who I'm sure you've all read about in *New York* magazine as the city's number one bachelor. What more could I add, except that we'll be putting an end to that foolishness soon enough."

Relieved laughter bubbled from the table.

Kevin whaled against the old Beautyrest put up against the wall of the Seclusion Room.

Dust particles flew as he skinned his knuckles red. He raged, screeching and muttering, yowling and cursing. He no longer cared how he sounded. It didn't matter, anyway.

Loblitz had downgraded him even further, a unit so hellish they didn't even call it a wing—South One, an apt name for this lowest level of pit, for patients with random bursts of aggression and bad table manners. There were so many problem patients, the South One Seclusion Room often became as overbooked as an HMO's waiting room. Kevin often had to share it with other patients.

He tensed for trouble from one of the real psychos when the door clicked and slammed open with a squish against the rubber. Then he relaxed.

"Hey, Richard," he said.

The aides wrestled his pudgy old pal in, pink-wrapped in a cold sheet, and dropped him onto the floor mattress. The aeronautical engineer rolled his eyes up so high Kevin could only see the whites like two cueballs.

He felt sorry for Richard, but at least it wasn't his turn in the freezing sheets.

Then the door opened again and Loblitz's curly head popped in.

"Cold-pack Doyle, too," he ordered.

They sat shivering together.

Kevin tried concentrating on a plan. He had heard about prisoners of war who survived by building houses in their heads, down to the last nail. He was constructing his plan. But now Richard was interrupting, blowing big holes in his plan so it kept collapsing. Richard was whining in one of his high-pitched monologues that lasted hours, sometimes days. He recited aircraft specs in a voice so incredibly high-pitched and singsong there was no way to keep it from intruding on his thoughts.

"Richard," he finally asked him, "what are they punishing you for?"

"My doctor had me taken upstairs," Richard told him, teeth chattering. "I went for it."

Richard had a rare but very real mental disorder Kevin had heard about at Bellevue. Richard was an obsessive personality who, if he went above the first floor, would look at a window and feel the compulsion to fly. Now Richard had been cruelly denied both the thrill of flight and his plastic green bottle to throw up in the air. He needed more than ever to recite the specs of every aircraft ever built, to bring order back to his world.

"If you had a plane in the Wright Brothers' day, Kevin," he babbled in the high-pitched whine, "it was probably a Curtiss . . ."

Kevin sighed and gave up on constructing his plan. Instead he tried to imagine puffy clouds and Richard's old planes. The tiny germ of an idea started, but Richard's voice chased it away.

He fell fitfully asleep. He dreamed of a cobalt sky and a flock of white doves soaring into the sun. He woke sharply and saw only the white room.

Richard lay next to him, snoring.

Cornelia waited for Tucker in the Oak Room of the Plaza Hotel.

She read her daily checklist for the third time. She had forgotten to do a bridal registry at Bendel's, Tina's suggestion. But she did remember that she and her parents had always brunched in this lovely, archaic room when she was a child.

This would be her last chance to really talk with Tucker before the wedding. And she did have some questions.

Now Tucker threaded through the room toward her, beaming, clearly the star of his world. His presence excited one tableful of businesspeople who smiled and nodded as he passed. With his shiny blond hair combed back and his crisp white shirt and wine-colored tie, he seemed practically anointed for power.

She tried to organize her thoughts. They were so hollowed out somehow, like craters of the moon.

"Hi," he greeted her. "Rough morning. Am I late?"

"Only an hour."

Over these past few weeks, she had definitely learned Tucker's sense of priorities. Her handsome young man smoothed out his tie, a silky Armani, and swept his hair back with his hand to strike a leonine pose.

Tucker Fisk, King of Beasts.

But much of his story needed to be repeated to her. She could recall so little of their time together. She remembered the feeling of high pressure, being jostled around in a small plane. Then some incident by a fountain where he appeared to look after her. They seemed to have shared some rough moments, which of course could glue a couple together. What seemed to elude her in her recollections were the giddy, carefree times that they must also have shared to be so in love that they were now heading for the altar.

"Tucker, what exactly did we do when we dated? I hate having to ask, but I can't help it."

He shrugged and patted her hand once. Whether it was from tenderness or a hint of impatience, she couldn't tell.

"We saw friends, went to parties."

The nice waiter appeared. He had already brought her five cups of coffee while she waited, and joked with her so she wouldn't feel so alone.

"We'll both have kippers and eggs with coffee," Tucker told him.

"Tucker, don't I hate kippers?"

"Oh. What do you want?"

"Just the coffee. And maybe a mimosa would be nice."

The waiter started to move away.

"Waiter," Tucker called loudly. The man returned without flinching. "No champagne in her mimosa."

She glanced out the window toward Central Park. The morning had been bright and cloudless. Now a thundercloud drooped north of the park. She watched it darken and saw light flash through it.

A lightning storm—rare for February. It made her tense. No, severely troubled. She sensed a vague memory through her body, stirring her nerve endings.

In the distance, a white bolt crackled out of the thick cloud. She jumped in her seat.

"What's the matter?" Tucker asked her.

"I don't know."

The lightning had startled her with what she recognized as traces of forgotten feelings, important ones. They slid across her face like fingernails on a blackboard, sharp, intrusive.

"Then what's bothering you?" Tucker asked.

"An electrical storm."

A single line of worry appeared on his forehead.

"No," he told her firmly. "It's just a storm."

Chapter Twenty-seven

*C*ornelia lay in the half-world between sleep and waking.

She slept for so long, a crust of sandpaper had formed between her eyelids. She opened one eye and looked around her.

The pillows and bedsheets sandwiched her among layers of lavender silk and pink chenille.

She opened the other eye. The room looked almost exactly as it had when she was a child. She was sure she recognized the hand-painted bed table. It was a pastoral scene of maidens in togas frolicking in a yellow field, their faces like peaches over ample arms and legs. All that exquisite brushwork, just to decorate a drawer that contained her hairbrush and Excedrin.

A piece of Lalique crystal on the table had also been shaped into a maiden—maybe the White Rock girl bending over and pushing her hair back. Simple maidens cavorted everywhere in this girl's room, dewy virgins, milkmaids. Like the young girl in the poem "Maud Muller."

What was the phrase about Maud?

> For of all sad words of tongue or pen
> The saddest are these: It might have been!

Why did she remember this room as having been simpler once?

She had the nagging sense that it had been quite stark. Yes. And she was certain that a fish tank once occupied the space where a huffy Louis XVI armoire now stood.

She slipped out of her bed and walked nude to her closet, threw open the door, revealing a rarefied fashion warehouse full of dresses and sportswear and suits. Hanging in the center was the giant plastic Baggie that held her wedding gown.

She took down her extravagant dress and held it up to her neck, studying herself from all angles in her three-way mirror.

She swayed her torso left and right, the elegant wedding dress flowing with her. Perhaps one hundred yards of silk, tulle, and taffeta, gathered and draped, puffed into a fantasy, crowned with a few dozen yards of lace to be swept back over her head and shoulders. Her blond hair folded itself neatly around her head now, snipped into a debutante's understated haircut.

She hung up the dress. She would adhere strictly to schedule. Madame timed this day as precisely as boiling an egg.

Cornelia pulled a terry cloth bathrobe tight around her and headed out to the corridor.

She passed the sconces that her father told her were from Napoleon's castle at Waterloo. Ironic that he should be so proud of them, since it was hardly a lucky castle. As she crossed the foyer, she glanced at the miniaturized portraits of the Lord men.

She paused before the picture of her great-great-grandfather, Chester I, who had founded the Lord & Company investment bank that supported them all. His eyes sunk far back under the ridge of his forehead, unreadable, hinting of villainy. But she supposed it took a bit of the robber baron to succeed in his day.

Capitalism in the rough, her father had called it.

She started away from Chester I, then felt suddenly weak and anxious. She looked back at the painting. Were his eyes following her? No, but something about him fascinated her, and not in a nice way.

She separated herself from her forebear's small head and drifted across the foyer to the living room. Every inch of the apartment seemed choked with flowers, their scents overpowering. White silk swept the living room from the floor to the high ceilings. She felt immersed, no, almost mummified in Madame's silky gauze. She swept the fabric that hung like flypaper with her arm and made it billow as she passed. At the far end of the room, just before the French doors leading out to the terrace, the Wedding Bower stood twined with roses. In this delicate gazebo, she and Tucker would vow to love each other to the end of their lives.

She turned into the round alcove where she and her parents used to eat breakfast together. The table shone with bright yellow linens and gleaming silver. O'Connell removed the shiny cover from a platter of warm scones. Her father turned to her, stood up, and smiled in his rather sad fashion. He dressed casually, for him, in an old blue blazer and flannel slacks. His eyes looked red, as though he hadn't slept well.

"Happy birthday, darling." He pecked her on the forehead. "Let's have our last breakfast alone together, shall we?"

"Yeeooow," Kevin yelped, clutching his jaw.

The two aides pried his arm away to grip him, one on each arm, as they prepared to escort him off the unit. The bigger aide used his key ring to unravel the maze of deadbolts on the metal door of South One.

"Right to the dentist, no stops," the charge nurse instructed them. "Stand right by him while Dr. Brooks does the examination. It's probably just an abscess."

Kevin began counting when they hit the Yellow Brick Road. He counted the tiles, 136 to the first right turn, then 182 to the doorway, then up the staircase that would take him outside. There would be twenty feet of outdoors between the door to his building and the door leading to the dental clinic.

Both South One aides were built like wide receivers. Between them, he felt about as big and strong as a prepubescent girl. The key aide opened the door. The other kept a firm grip on Kevin's arm.

Showtime.

Kevin raised his foot as high as he could, slamming it down on the aide's shoe. The aide screamed and bent over double, releasing Kevin's arm.

"Sorry," Kevin yelled.

He didn't look back as he sprinted. He could use his arms to pump ahead, since they hadn't restrained him. The aides shouted and cursed. But following hospital policy, they didn't chase him. That would be a job for the security guards.

Kevin bolted for the trees surrounding the Big Circle, the path that he and Corny ran down that last night together. The thought of her jolted his heart alive and propelled him. His stiff muscles shrieked. Pain tore at his lungs as his feet pounded on the frozen ground.

In his peripheral vision, he caught a flash of sun glistening off metal. He turned to see a white Jeep Cherokee with blue stripes and a bar of orange lights flashing on the roof. That would be the first wave of security guards. He had expected one of their golf cars, not a sport utility vehicle.

Fear pumped through him.

They wouldn't hurt him too badly so long as he had his Platinum Health Plan. Worst case, they would capture him with handcuffs of the plastic-Ziploc variety. He had seen them used on patients here. And maybe treat him to the zap of a stun gun to lay him flat, twitching like a chicken, and take the heart out of his resistance. He had heard that they'd just gotten the new-technology foam to spray around a patient's legs that he'd seen used on *Cops*. It would quickly harden and turned to glue, so the quarry would collapse on the ground in a sticky, humiliated pile of defeat.

He used the fear to squeeze his adrenaline, force more juice into his unused muscles.

He gauged the distance to the trees, then beyond the trees to the perimeter of the Sanctuary grounds where the electric fence stood waiting. Its slack wires strung at the top between the posts seemed to smile, "C'mere, we're ready for you."

He suddenly veered right and the Jeep zigged right along with him. Then he straightened out for the hundred-yard dash. Hey, they only had a couple hundred horsepower under the hood, and none of his motivation. If they failed, they'd catch hell from their boss. If Kevin failed, his whole future, and maybe his life, would end in the Sanctuary.

Seventy yards away now. His nerves leapt to see that the Jeep Cherokee had gained on him.

Fifty yards and the Jeep made a long lazy curve around him. It was over. They were just playing with him now. He plowed ahead, his breaths nothing but loud, ragged grunts.

Thirty yards. He saw them smiling through the window, taunting him. What does a cornered animal do?

He threw both arms to the side and howled like a werewolf, suddenly racing not toward the trees anymore, but directly at the Jeep. The guard on the passenger side changed his expression from playful to uncertain. The driver sped up so that Kevin wouldn't slam into the side of the Jeep and hurt himself.

He had found his edge.

"Hey, guys? You can't hurt me," Kevin taunted them. "I still got a year left on my health plan."

The driver jerked the Cherokee to a stop. The guard in the passenger seat opened the door and jumped out, hunkering down like a Dallas Cowboys defensive end.

"C'mon, man," the chunky guard with no chin yelled at him. "No problem, we're just gonna take you back."

Kevin feinted left, confusing the guard. But a second white Jeep with orange lights on the roof suddenly came rumbling over the Big Circle. They'd catch him now, no question.

Twenty yards to go.

He crashed through the underbrush around the line of trees. The brush clung too thick for their vehicles to penetrate. Now the guards would have to get out and follow him on foot.

Ten yards.

The eight-foot electrical fence, that malevolent wire grid with its red "DANGER" sign punched up with illustrations of lightning bolts, loomed dead ahead.

Well, he'd just have to trust her on this one. And if she was wrong, what had she said the day they made snow angels in front of St. Agnes Church? Nothing hurts as much as you think it will.

Please be right about the current, Corny.

As he flung himself up against the side of the fence, a force like a vibrating power drill tore through his body tissue. He barely smelled the burning, dimly saw the flames.

He only saw, in the periphery of his vision, a tickle of blue fire dancing on his shoulders. His hair must be on fire. His mouth filled with the noxious taste of metal, like eating aluminum foil. His dental fillings, he guessed, conducting the electricity.

That was his final thought. He used his body's last adrenaline spurt to pull himself over the top wire.

Kevin fell like a crash-test dummy over the top of the Sanctuary fence. He landed with a nasty thud on the freedom side.

His eyes twitched once toward heaven. Then he lay as motionless as an empty sack.

Chester watched his daughter's hand slip on the glass she held. He thought she had a small seizure.

"Is everything all right?" Chester rose from the chair, his voice shaky.

"I just felt . . . nothing. I'm fine."

They sat over the English silver coffee service, the warm scones covered with Devonshire cream and plump strawberries. Chester tried to clear his mind, to savor their last moment of peace before the stress of the wedding.

"It's all a bit of a stressfest, isn't it, Daddy?"

"Well, yes," he had to agree.

Cornelia wore her black terry cloth robe, as she had two months before to interrupt his co-op board meeting. On that day, her gray eyes filled with sharp pinpoints of pink and amber, her skin flushed with indignation as she snapped at him because he had locked her closet.

This morning, she hunched in her robe, withdrawn. Her hair now lay demurely to the side of her head instead of falling over her forehead like an unruly hayloft. Her eyes revealed no luster, just a cloudy gray.

She set the glass down on the linen of their breakfast table and looked out onto the terrace.

Chester followed her eyes. Around the perimeter of their wide, ninety-foot terrace was a profusion of life in white, red, yellow, and lavender. He imagined the floral waves as the Elysian Fields, re-created by Madame Marie-Claude. The old tyrant had done an inspired job.

He cleared his throat. "Well, this is our big day, isn't it?"

His daughter sipped fresh-squeezed orange juice from the crystal glass, and ran her tongue over her lips. They always looked dry now, pale and slightly cracked. Dehydration, Loblitz had warned him. Yet another side effect of the ECT.

"Daddy, do you think Tucker's nice?" she suddenly asked him.

The question disturbed him—both the fact that she would feel the need to ask it now and the realization that he stumbled for an answer.

"How do you mean? Tucker certainly has loyalty and stick-to-it-iveness, as my sixth-grade teacher used to call it." His laugh sounded hollow. "He's a gentleman."

"Do you mean socially correct?" Cornelia's voice sounded crisper. "Or a gentle man?"

Tucker and gentle. Chester pondered those two concepts.

"Well, compared to whom? He treats you very respectfully. He has been patient with you during your recovery, hasn't he?"

"In his way. Compared to you, Daddy, is he nice?"

"I guess I don't know how I'd score myself on that issue."

"You don't?" She sounded dumbfounded.

"I try to do the right thing, certainly. Your mother, well, she never doubted herself. I'm afraid I can't claim her moral certainty. Life can be something of a maze, darling. I spend a lot of my time just trying to feel my way through. What you're about to do, Cornelia, it takes courage to . . . to . . ."

"To get married?"

"Well, no, to do what's necessary."

"Necessary?" Her eyes grew more muddied. "For who?"

"Well, for you and Tucker and . . . all of us." His voice became stern and his face had turned red and blotchy.

She lifted her coffee cup hesitantly, unsure what had fanned her father into this rather frightening display of tics and bluster.

"Cornelia. What I'm trying to point out is that life can be terribly complicated and sometimes you need to take a plunge."

"Plunging into marriage." She made an odd shape with her mouth. "I would think people could walk around and stick a toe in first, to make sure."

"Well, of course you already did that." He felt desperate. "Unfortunately, your therapy made you forget all the walking around part, and now here we are, you and I, at the plunge, aren't we?"

He realized that he half-stood now, hunched over toward her, and had raised his voice.

"Calm down, Daddy, please. I'll get you through this."

My God, had he allowed their world to turn so upside down that he needed his poor, beleaguered daughter to take charge of him on her wedding day? She took his hand across the table and held it protectively.

Chester's heart felt the dreaded anvil again, sinking deeper into his chest and soul.

Kevin lay like a snow angel without wings.

"No, he's not moving," a guard explained through his radio. "The last thing we saw, he was vibrating like a fork with his clothes on fire."

The Emergency Medical Services ambulance, a square van, squealed up in less than five minutes. It arrived slightly before the carload of medical staff from the Sanctuary.

Dr. Loblitz hopped out of the Sanctuary car. He ran to where an EMS team squatted in orange suits, juggling their lifesaving gear. Loblitz could see, before he even reached the group, the bare foot that stuck out from the emergency technicians' huddle. Shouting at each other, the EMS techs used shears to snip off Kevin Doyle's shirt.

The woman tech holding the paddles suddenly yelled, "Clear."

They lurched back and Loblitz saw the body hop up off the ground and fall back.

"Again. Clear," the EMS tech shouted.

Loblitz heard another ker-chunk from the electrical paddles. So much like his own specialty. But he felt a shocking sense of dread when the charge brought no response at all from the patient.

His patient.

Loblitz felt sickened. He would not announce himself as Kevin's doctor now. All his instincts told him to retreat, write a memo. It would be better to keep a low profile and explore his legal position.

He slunk back toward the staff sedan, wondering whether the family of Kevin Doyle would sic some mad-dog personal injury lawyer on him. The unfairness made him tremble. He had shaved a few therapeutic corners before like anyone else, but he never kept a patient he knew to be normal in the hospital for his personal gain. But the nearly $250,000 honorarium from Tucker Fisk would give him away.

How could he have been so stupid?

He wondered how much of that money he would need to spend in legal fees to save his license.

He watched the Emergency Medical Services team slow their efforts down around the fallen man and finally halt. Then they began packing up their gear before placing the limp body on the gurney, sliding it into its track inside the ambulance. No technician stayed in back with his patient to administer life support.

That eliminated his last flicker of doubt. Now Dr. Kenneth Loblitz braced himself to go to Administration. He wondered how he would report this final discharge status of his patient Kevin Doyle to Dr. Burns.

He didn't believe the Sanctuary even had a form to fill out for anything this horrible.

Chapter Twenty-eight

*E*ight-forty Fifth Avenue, that sooty dowager, rustled its awning petticoat as guests began arriving for the afternoon Lord-Fisk wedding.

Andrew and Vlad, both with a bounce to their steps and a special snap to their white-gloved salutes, greeted the First Families of Manhattan. The blinding gold Rolls-Royce which Old Han Koi had shipped from Hong Kong to Manhattan jolted to a halt in front of the building.

"The Kois," Andrew sniffed to Vlad. "Man, no taste at all."

Other Rollers and Mercedes and Aston Martins formed a cavalcade of imported luxury cars that snaked around the block. The trendier women arrived draped by Marc Bower and Vera Wang, leaving Chanel for the starchy doyennes. The men wore tailored dark suits with white shirts but not morning coats and striped trousers. Madame had harangued Chester to enforce that formality, but Tucker Fisk had scrawled her a terse note that cowed her into silence, "No monkey suits or you're fired."

The lobby staff funneled the guests through the building's narrow foyer and packed them into the two creeping passenger elevators bound for Penthouse A.

In his ancestral co-op, Chester Lord assumed the mantle of Father of the Bride with less inner gaiety than his guests imagined.

He held court standing in his big living room, wearing a midnight-blue suit and an expression of bland geniality. The stew of old friends, socialites, and businesspeople gushed and brayed. He could, if he chose to, overhear whispers about Cornelia.

Even as Chester mumbled through the motions, he was stricken by how his "set," as they called it in his father's time, had grown profoundly tiresome over the years. That included even the new members, youngsters like Cornelia's school friends Tina and the two Roberts who stood in a fierce little huddle pointing and giggling at the other guests. Watching them, Chester realized that freedom from financial worry had only doomed this aging posse to a life lived with a casual malice toward others.

"Look what the woman's *wearing*," one of the two boys called Robert snickered at Lily Stern's dress. "Valentino meets Norma Desmond."

Then the Amazing Stone Heads of Fifth Avenue appeared. He braced as the three members-for-life of the 840 Fifth co-op board, Lily Stern, Chip Lindsay, and Tom van Adder approached.

Old Chip Lindsay, dressed in the same musty pin-striped suit from the 1950s he had worn to the board meeting in December, led the phalanx. Their expressions looked dour even on his daughter's wedding day.

"We have some new business," Chip said taking Chester by the sleeve.

"Can't it wait?"

"No," Lily Stern barked, reminding him of Madame Marie-Claude's foghorn voice. The old crone was in Cornelia's room dressing her now.

"What is it?" Chester snapped.

"We thought you'd want to know, before you read about it on the *New York Times* society page," Tom van Adder's eyes twinkled in merriment, "that we've approved Cornelia and Tucker Fisk for 20B."

Chester nodded and took Tom van Adder's gnarly hand. At least that formality was out of the way. He had wanted to surprise the couple with the apartment two floors below as a wedding present, a modest seven-room but with a view of Central Park. This starter home would do until they had a family and growing pains.

Then, in a few years, it would be time for Chester to turn the reins of Lord & Company over to Tucker, and hand over the keys for Penthouse A to his daughter and son-in-law. The kids would keep O'Connell, if he were still useful. This rite of handing down the ancestral co-op from generation to generation that so thrilled his grandfather and father left Chester with a stuffy feeling, almost a sinus headache.

Where would his own home be after that? Probably Palm Beach. He saw himself as an old man in a wheelchair, sitting on the sunny Addison Mizner–designed terrace looking out over the Atlantic Ocean through his cataracts, and shivered. At least he would feel relieved to conclude his lifelong duty, at long last, to Lord & Company. In the meantime he would try however possible to address his duty to his daughter. Perhaps now he could begin to pay her back, in baby steps if need be, for the damage he had done.

Then he brightened as a new guest arrived, drawing rapt stares from the men and narrowed eyes from the women. Roni, the carriage driver, entered wearing a form-fitting dress. It exposed her firm shoulders, draped with an explosion of jet-black curls. Her eyes were lightly made up to accent their almond shape, resembling exotic characters he'd seen in storybooks.

"Excuse me." Chester left Chip Lindsay muttering some hollow pleasantry.

". . . her father's date," Tina whispered to the two Roberts as they passed Roni, seeing Chester on his way toward her. "Chester has that fifth-grade-crush look, doesn't he?"

And the Pack stopped to gawk at Roni. All three of them had to look up.

"Who are you?" the meaner Robert, No. 2, asked her.

"My name is Roni."

Robert No. 2 put his hand out, glanced to see that Chester was still out of earshot, and leaned up to whisper in her ear. "How about meeting me on the terrace for a drink?"

Roni took his hand and squeezed it slowly until it made little crunching noises and Robert's mouth turned down in painful stages.

"If I see you outside," she promised Robert, "I'll field-strip you like a cigarette."

As Roni led Chester away, Tina tried to shake some pink back into Robert's fingers.

"What did he say to you?" Chester asked her when she let him take her arm.

"Nothing."

He could only nod, feeling somehow vital in this woman's presence, feeling her warmth through her sleeve.

"So, Chester," she said, "did you really talk to your daughter? Listen to her?"

"Ah . . ." He had tried at breakfast, but she had gone off in an unexpected direction.

Her almond eyes begged him. "You have a little time still. These people don't need you now. She does."

Two blocks away on Lexington Avenue, the Emergency Medical Services ambulance pulled to a stop, double-parking on Madison Avenue.

Marne Doyle, still wearing her borrowed EMS uniform, stepped out of the passenger seat and ripped large strips of sticky-backed black tape off the sides and backs of the van. The words they obscured, "City of New York," would have given them away at the Sanctuary. The back doors opened up from inside and Kevin Doyle stepped out, muscles stiff and sore.

"Thanks again, guys." Kevin jumped out of the back door and shook hands with each member of the EMS team his sister had mustered from Brooklyn. He hugged Marne. "How do I look?"

"Not bad for a dead guy," she told him, stripping off her EMS vest. "How'd you get over the fence?"

"Corny told me it was high-frequency current and wouldn't do much damage."

"You still took a big chance." Marne gave Kevin a look.

"First time for everything."

Marne checked her big watch with twenty dials and gauges. "Guess you better get to the church on time."

"Marne," Kevin said as he kissed her cold cheek. "I owe you."

She mussed his hair and whipped him a kidney punch just hard enough to take his breath away. "You watch yourself."

He kissed Marne and jogged off for the front door of 840 Fifth. His getup of jeans, EMS work boots, T-shirt, and cheap nylon jacket smelling of mothballs and emblazoned with "New York Bets" across the back, an old nickname for New York City's off-track betting parlors, was hardly impressive. A fine figure of a prince, galloping up to save Cornelia Lord on her wedding day.

At the door, he squeezed in front of a couple with mahogany tans. Kevin caught a whiff of what he imagined as golf course gardenia about them.

"Hey, Andrew. How's it goin', Vlad."

Andrew clutched.

When he planned this out, he'd carefully weighed how the other doormen would take the shock value of his just showing up unannounced. He counted on Vlad to nurse his old romantic fantasies. Andrew, sworn keeper of the status quo, was the wild card.

Vlad's eyes bulged and Andrew's forehead crumpled into confusion. Neither spoke for a moment as Kevin started past them.

"Guess I'll just head on back, get changed. Thought you could use a little help today, the wedding and all. Me, I'm feeling great. Really needed the rest."

Andrew stepped directly in front of him.

"Son," Andrew said, as kindly as he could manage. "It's good to see you back in one piece, but we'd better talk. See, you are what we call persona non grata around here, meanin' you're about as welcome as a rat in the wedding cake."

Kevin raised his hands in a wide shrug. "Hey, I've just been on sick leave. I left a message for Gus, told him I was punching in today."

He had Marne call the building manager earlier, believing correctly that Gus Anholdt would make himself scarce on a busy day. She got his answering machine.

Andrew took out a white handkerchief and mopped his forehead.

"Vlad, watch the guests." His watery eyes searched Kevin's. "Son, Gus said you were fired. He sent us a memo."

"Why?"

"He didn't say why."

Vlad whispered in Andrew's ear, loud enough for Kevin to hear. "The boy defies authority. Is that so bad?"

Andrew spoke solemnly and stubbornly. "All I know is, you're through here. It's no good, son. Chester Lord himself left standing orders, we can't let you in the building."

"Chester Lord doesn't cut it." Kevin folded his arms. "This is a union thing."

"Say what?"

"Go back to the staff room, check the bulletin board. International Brotherhood of Portal Operators Regulation 247. 'No Union employee shall be discharged except by due process. Wrongful discharge shall be cause for a Job Action.' They can't fire me. Let me get my uniform on, and I'll talk it out with Chester Lord myself."

"He's a little busy today, Kevin." Andrew gave him a minimal smile.

Kevin planted his EMS boots a foot apart and crossed his arms again. "I think when you tell him I'm down here, he'll find the time."

On his way to see his daughter, Chester found Han Koi, Sr.

The Hong Kong pirate popped out of a huddle of businesspeople misted in cigar smoke and planted himself in Chester's face. He grabbed Chester's hand and pumped it violently, his droopy wattles shaking in mirth.

"Congratulations, Chester. We are so happy for you."

Han showed his teeth, revealing lots of his receding gums. The studied absence of any malice at all in the old predator's face was too much for Chester to abide.

"Are you?" Gimlet-eyed, he withdrew his hand and spoke softly. "You lose your run on Lord & Company now, you two-faced son of a bitch."

And Han did seem to have two faces now, sucking in and out like an aquatic plant, moving between stunned and bellicose.

"Chester," old Han finally wailed, "how can you insult me?"

"Insult *you?*" Chester labored to keep his voice down. "For God's sake, I got you into the Hamptons Bath & Tennis Club when they tried to blackball you."

Han glowered. "And I took you to the races in Hong Kong, our special box. You didn't even have a top hat. Typical ignorant American."

Oh, the venom would come on now if he let it. Instead, Chester drew his shoulders back.

"Enough. This is my daughter's wedding day."

Then he noticed O'Connell tapping him on the arm.

"Mr. Lord," the butler whispered, rolling his r's. "It seems there's a problem to sort out with the building staff."

Chester fumed. They were circling him like buzzards, on what should by all rights be a day of bliss. "I can't handle that now."

"I do think you might wish to address it personally, sir." O'Connell insisted, holding his head down to avoid eye contact with the Father of the Bride.

The phone rang in Chester's study, but Tucker ignored the soft jangle. He ushered his guest into the room first and locked the door behind him. Tucker motioned him to one of the wing chairs across from Chester's desk.

Tucker removed from the pocket of his shantung-lined black suit Cornelia's power of attorney and placed it on the desktop near the picture of Chester, Elizabeth, and Corny at age nine.

"This," he pointed out, "gives me control of Cornelia's voting stock the minute we finish the marriage vows."

"Very good," Han Koi, Jr., nodded, glancing over the document.

No, Chester won't need to buy a partners desk now, Tucker chuckled, recalling his mentor's unease. Chester's business career just ended. He settled into the well-worn burgundy leather chair, pulled open Chester's humidor, and removed two of his cherished Romeo y Juliet robustos.

"Han," Tucker offered. "Have a cigar on me."

"Ah." Han Koi, Jr., took the fat Romeo y Juliet. He leaned toward the heavy gold table lighter that Tucker held for him and puffed hard.

Tucker lit the tip of his own cigar and put his head back to stare at the mahogany paneling on the ceiling. He released dense rings from his rounded lips to create a cloud cover inside Chester's sanctum sanctorum. A good cigar, he believed, forced others to gag in his presence.

Han Koi, Jr., sat back across the desk from him, ramrod straight, holding his own Koi laptop. Bringing it to wedding, for God's sake. Tucker had to smile. Maybe there was some good in him after all. If anybody should consider himself even luckier than Chester Lord that his father had come before him, it was Han Koi, Jr. No wonder the old man never let him make any decisions. But Han Junior had discretionary power over just enough Koi cash to buy up Lord & Company voting stock without old Han finding out.

And partners without much ability needed Tucker to make their decisions for them.

"Good time to congratulate the groom," Han Junior smirked, as Tucker punched him playfully in the arm.

"Fuck that, Han. We'll get on the front page of the *Wall Street Journal* on Monday morning. You and me. We pulled it off, buddy."

Tucker hauled up his own laptop from beside the desk and fired it up, his fingers sprinting over the keyboard. "Today we consolidate Cornelia's shares in Lord & Company with the lots you bought. That's us in the column that says '51 %.' Here's how bad we just kicked Chester Lord's ass."

Han Koi, Jr., studied the screen that Tucker turned proudly in his direction. His face became a happy jack-o'-lantern's.

"Your father's going to be proud of you when he finds out." Tucker blew smoke at his new partner. "He'll complain a little, but he's a businessman."

What a joke. Tucker believed the elder Han would view his son's actions as sneaky and underhanded. In the best-case scenario, old Han might blow an artery in his shock when he found out what Han Junior had done behind his back and drop dead. In the worst, Tucker would force a split in Koi Industries. The father would be blackmailed into swallowing his son's deal whether he liked it or not.

Whatever.

This would be only the beginning. He'd met his first goal of thirty by thirty. On Monday, as Cornelia Lord's husband with her power of attorney, he would make the board of Lord & Company change the name on the door to Fisk & Company. Next goal, push the elder Han Koi out of Koi Industries so young Han and Tucker could take over.

Tucker blew a perfect smoke ring into the air.

"Let's go give Chester his big day," he told Han.

"What will happen to him?" Han asked.

"After we throw him out and seal up his office?" He chuckled. "He'll survive. Useless rich guys always do." He didn't add "present company excepted," even though he could clearly see Han's future.

He stood up as Han rose, came around, and slapped his much shorter partner's toadlike back. "Congratulations, big guy."

Tucker sauntered out of the room, adjusting his tie. He rubbed his hands together.

Poor, forgetful Chester.

Chester hadn't noticed recently that Penthouse A was put in Corny's trust for tax reasons. Corny's power of attorney would even give Tucker this co-op once they were husband and wife. Would he automatically become chairman of the co-op board? Outside the study, he bumped into a parchment-skinned woman who wore a sequined dress and tiara on her head. Lily Stern, a widow who got lucky with a husband about ninety years ago.

"I love to win!" Tucker blurted out to Lily, full of executive helium.

"Of course you do, dear," she cooed mechanically.

He swept through the guests, making small talk over the strains of three string quartets. In the dining room, the catering firm Fête Accompli bustled around an eighteenth-century English hutch that groaned with treats. Waiters dressed in white tie moved in a smooth glide pattern.

Tucker saw the mayor and his wife talking to the police commissioner. The mayor had married an editor of the *Daily Globe*, but the newspaper still stuck it to City Hall anyway. The *Globe* was owned by another guest he saw bullying his way around the room. He was a fireplug of a man with a shaved head who looked like a professional wrestler in a business suit. He yelled something to Tucker over the crowd about condos or condoms, it could be either.

Another media lord, a silver-haired mogul who owned several square miles in a pristine stretch of the Andes called Patagonia, stopped to pump Tucker's hand. "You coulda used my spread for your honeymoon."

No, he didn't want Cornelia anywhere near South America.

"I appreciate it." Tucker tried to smile like a man in love. "But I took a place in the Bahamas."

He had booked a whole private island in the Caribbean with a pristine beach and a fully staffed estate. It cost $35,000 for a week, but the seclusion would be worth it. All hell could break loose on Monday when the law firm he had hired in secret, that Park Avenue shark tank, took Corny's power of attorney and their marriage certificate and padlocked Lord & Company. Although he would never admit it to Han, he didn't want to face Chester. He hadn't wanted to ruin Chester necessarily, but his mentor had left him no choice.

A player plays, Chester.

A week on the beach would give him time to make long-term plans for Fisk & Company. Then, at the end of the day, he'd have Cornelia's body to explore. It was new to him. Maybe to anybody. He'd never asked, she'd never told. He genuinely looked forward to sex with Corny, showing her his best moves. She seemed a little flaky still, but it would be worth it.

He had already decided that he would stick with her for as long as it served his interest. Why not? Controlling Corny would be like molding putty. He could put his own spin on his Lord & Company takeover. *Good for your dad, he's been so stressed lately.* Her memory was totally blown out. And he believed that good-hearted Cornelia would make a fine mother. Family values really did matter. At least until they worked the bugs out of cloning.

As he crossed the foyer, he found Chester on the antique French phone, his face a crimson blob.

"He's off-limits," Chester was muttering into the telephone. "Call the police if necessary. Mr. Doyle is fired."

Tucker's stomach flopped over in a brand-new way. For the first time in his life, he actually felt it knot with a tiny glimpse of the F-word.

F-F-F-Failure.

"Chester," he kept his voice low, "what's going on?"

Chester covered the receiver. "Andrew the doorman called up to say that Kevin Doyle is downstairs. He's demanding his job back and he wants to speak to me."

The little dick. But he needed to calm down. Doyle must not get into this apartment.

"I'll take care of it," he growled.

Chester wagged his head. "This could spiral. He's citing some union regulation, claims he's entitled to work."

"The police commissioner's here," Tucker said. "We'll arrest Doyle for fraud, mayhem, who cares? By the time they let him go, Corny and I will be in the Islands."

"No." Chester seemed calmer than he ever had during a crisis. "I've met his uncle, the union delegate. Get back to the guests and let me handle this."

Well, Chester taking charge. Tucker smiled thinly. "As long as you have it under control, Dad."

He smirked at how the old man winced when he called him that.

In the staff room, Andrew stood over Kevin while he called Eddie Feeney.

"Don't count on him to back you up, son," Andrew prophesied, looking glum at this social breakdown at his workplace.

"Eddie!" Kevin talked fast into the phone. "I just reported back to work, and Chester Lord says I'm fired. Listen, I'm covered by Regulation 247, right?"

The pause felt like sudden death at the other end. Then Eddie came back.

"You listen to me you little son of a bitch. Whatever you're trying to pull, I'm not helping you."

"Forget it's me, Eddie," Kevin said. "I'm a union guy. Just do the right thing."

"The right thing?" Eddie sounded mean and spiteful as usual, but with a rehearsed quality. "Your old man's a lout and a layabout, without me he couldn't even provide for my sister. And you're worse. No union rule's going to cover you, lad."

Kevin held the receiver away as Eddie's bile spilled out. He knew.

"So what did Chester Lord offer you?" He slammed the phone down. "Andrew, I'm not going to rant and rave or anything. I'm just going to lay out the facts, let you decide for yourself. Uncle Eddie got bought off. He says the union rules don't matter here. He's not going to help me."

For once, Andrew didn't seem certain.

"Something stinks about that." The doorman's forehead remained marbly. "The rules are pretty clear. You still got a job here, till the union says you don't. Chester Lord can't change that. Fact is, Eddie never did shit for the guys, 'less we leaned all over him. Hate to say this, but I don't see no real cause to fire you, Kevin."

"There isn't, Andrew. Right now, I just want to put my uniform on and go to work. Anything wrong with that?"

Andrew mulled it over, the kind eyes seeming to flare with resentment of Eddie. "Don't see how that's out of line."

Good, Kevin thought. "If Chester Lord and Eddie can pull this on me now, they can do it to you or Vlad next week, right?"

"Maybe." Andrew studied his white gloves. "You gettin' at something?"

"If I ask you to take a side, would you go with me or Eddie?"

He saw the embryo of defiance in Andrew, disturbing his years of keeping a positive attitude. "I dunno, son. Just get your ass in gear, suit up and get to the lobby."

"Andrew, maybe you could send Vlad in for a second while I get dressed. I just want to talk to him."

"Cornelia, is everything all right?"

Her father's voice crept through the bedroom door like an anxious fog.

"I'll be out soon, Daddy."

This stubborn need to sit alone and collect her thoughts interfered with her duty to Tucker and the rest, but especially to her father. She felt a damp itch in the small of her back. The perfect folds of her dress seemed as hot and cumbersome as an astronaut's suit.

"Where are you, child?" the French-accented foghorn rumbled through the door.

Dear Madame, that frail tyrant, would probably want to crucify her at the Wedding Bower if she could see her bride, sitting on her bed in her dress, no doubt creasing the taffeta.

"Cornelia! Everyone's waiting." Her father's worried wail broke through and nearly jerked her stocking feet to respond, but she would not allow herself. Not yet.

Something needed remembering.

Or not really some *thing*, since she had taken inventory of all her essentials. Only her lacy white shoes still lay on the velvet-cushioned hassock like lovebirds, waiting to be slipped on.

No. Some *one* needed to be remembered, she felt certain.

Cornelia held the framed photograph of her mother tight and closed her eyes. She imagined her mother saying "I do" to her father. Then a blizzard of rice and good wishes as he swept her away in . . . a carriage?

A horse-drawn carriage came to mind quite suddenly. White with a black landau roof.

"Daddy, how did you leave the church on your wedding day?"

She endured the long silence.

"An MSG," she thought he said. *Monosodium glutamate?*

"A what?"

"An MG. A car, darling. A little English sports car. Someone stuck white ribbons all over it. Cornelia . . ."

"I'm almost ready."

She sounded more reassuring than she felt, her fingertips pressing white on the silver frame that held her mother's picture. She kept her eyes closed tightly. It seemed so necessary to finish the image she tried to make out of the faintest traces and shadows.

Something to do with a heart, hers or somebody else's.

But that would be Tucker, wouldn't it?

The three doormen stood alone in the lobby, now that all the wedding guests on their list had been deposited in Penthouse A. They formed a huddle. Kevin argued and cajoled while Andrew, arms behind his back, pursed his lips in mighty conflict, and Vlad the Self-Impaler cleared his throat for an announcement.

"Da!" The Russian doorman brandished the old newspaper from December with the headline, "Doorman Saves Deb from Dad." Kevin had kept one copy of it in his locker and another cuddled under the pillow of his bed in Alphabet City.

"What?" Andrew asked him, cranky from inner turmoil.

"It's the downtrodding of a young worker," Vlad barked to Andrew, summoning up all the phony communist party platitudes ever hammered into him. "The boy has been trampled by the owners. Eddie Feeney is a traitor. We must stand together."

"Vlad." Andrew blew out air, frustrated. "Even if Kevin got screwed, what do you expect us to do about it?"

Kevin answered, "I think we ought to go see Eddie up at 2000 Fifth."

"Yes! No one will watch the door!" Vlad stood at attention, his chest stuck out. "We will make our stand and fuck the owners!"

The three strode out the bronze doors of 840 Fifth Avenue, Vlad and Kevin holding their chins high and propelling Andrew forward with them. For the first time in the seventy-five-year history of 840 Fifth Avenue, the lobby stood unattended.

Out on 65th Street turning uptown on Fifth, Philip Grace hurried toward them, his battered leather camera bag slung over his shoulder.

"Kevin Doyle! Got your call, man." Philip looked at the three doormen, then peered into the empty lobby. "Seems to me, two of you oughtta be on duty. You leavin' 840 Fifth to the workin' press?"

"I told you, Philip," Kevin said. "You want a real story, come with us."

She could only feel around the fringes of her memory, stringy and peripheral. There was definitely a person in uniform, then the vague image of a picnic enjoyed with a man, perhaps the same one but out of uniform, on the rooftop of a big stone building that seemed a little like Notre Dame. Or someplace. But in all these images, never a face to match.

"Corneeee!"

The reedy uncontrolled shriek tore through her bedroom door, collapsing her structure of half-captured memories.

"Corny, you're making us crazy out here. If you don't come out this minute, I will shave my head."

Uh, oh. She realized how critical the wedding situation must have become for her father and Madame to pluck poor, delicate Tina from the line of bridesmaids to intercede. Well. She sighed her father's familiar sigh of obligations heeded, hearing it like a strange voice trapped somewhere in her soul, and got to her feet.

She slipped her feet into the lily-white shoes. Then she opened her maiden's bedroom door for the last time.

Eddie Feeney, in a uniform too long for his legs and too small for his arms, glowered as he spun the revolving door of 2000 Fifth Avenue.

New Money must have moved into this building, Kevin noted. The shoulders of Eddie's new maroon uniform had epaulets to match the glitz of the renovated lobby. The light of an oversized chandelier bounced off the gilded walls and shiny marble surfaces. This ornate room had once been old and stuffy. For fifteen years, Kevin's father had worked the door, sorted mail, and called each resident by name.

"Where's my dad?" Kevin wanted to know.

"On a break." Eddie's eyes shifted uncomfortably seeing Philip Grace. "What's this asshole doing here?"

"Capturin' the real you, fool," Philip told him, yanking his camera out of his bag and pop-popping off pictures of Eddie covering his face with his arms like a crook.

"What the hell are you up to, Kevin?" Eddie yelled. He didn't call him Dumbo now, Kevin noticed. "Andrew, what do you think you're doing?"

"I'm with Kevin," Andrew said with his jaw out, nodding so hard his hat slid back and Kevin could see the base of his "I Love Jesus" skullcap.

"Chester Lord fired me without cause." Kevin fished in his pocket and pulled out the page ripped off the staff room bulletin board. "Here's the regulation."

"Two forty-seven." Eddie Feeney didn't bother to glance at it, running his tongue over his lips, his eyes drifting in every direction. "That's bullshit. You're a mental case."

"We're going on strike, Eddie. With or without you."

"A strike. You tellin' me how to do my job, now?"

"You learn something new every day."

Eddie's chest bunched up under his coat, his fists tightening. And then Dennis Doyle appeared from the deep corridor of the rear lobby. Dennis looked like some banana republic colonel in his new uniform.

He looked stunned to see his son. For the first time Kevin could remember, Dennis embraced him in a hug as fierce as a wrestling lock.

"It's good to have you back in uniform, son."

"Dad, we need your help."

"What for?"

"Job action!" Vlad the Self-Impaler held up the *Globe* page with the photo of Kevin and Corny and shook it in the air. "Wrongful firing at 840 Fifth. The workers unite."

"Eddie sold us out, Dad. Chester Lord fired me in violation of R247. Eddie won't do anything."

Kevin kept an eye on Eddie while he spoke. Not a pretty sight. He could smell his uncle now, the heavy musk of a trapped animal. He watched him seem to devolve, before his eyes, from *Homo sapiens* doorman into the essential brawling Eddie. His forehead jutted over his eyes, ancient resentment forcing his mouth open with what looked like roast-beef gristle caught between his teeth.

"So it's you or Kevin I have to believe, Eddie?" His father gave his uncle a stare of royal contempt Kevin hadn't seen since Charles Barkley played for the Suns.

Eddie looked slick and sweaty as he appealed to his father, for the first time ever. "I got you your job. Your kid's so full of crap, he can't even fart straight."

"Let's go, men," Dennis said.

Eddie growled, his fingers flexing in their gloves, and started to block their way. Dennis and Kevin looked at each other, grabbed him up together and shoved him against the wall.

"Don't make me tell the union management on you, Eddie," Dennis said. "You can get fired easier than any of us."

The delegate looked away defeated, no longer meeting Dennis's eyes.

"Hey, Eddie," Kevin said.

Eddie turned back to scowl at him.

"Ping!" Kevin snapped his uncle's left ear with his finger.

The doormen walked out of 2000 Fifth Avenue, wheeled left, and started downtown from 95th Street. Fifth Avenue sprawled before them with neat rows of expensive co-op buildings on the east side,

Central Park on the west. Their first stop was next door, an elegant prewar building.

Dennis stuck his head in the lobby. "Charlie . . . Humberto," he told the two doormen on duty. "Let's take a walk."

"Huh?" An elderly man in a dark blue overcoat and cap with silver trim squinted at them. "We're on duty here."

It took Kevin, Dennis, and Andrew only five minutes to talk the first two doormen into joining them, with Vlad holding the *Daily Globe*, and pointing to Kevin's picture for effect. Then it became a movement. In the next ten minutes, the squad of doormen had grown to ten. They strode at a military clip, taking the full width of the sidewalk, with Philip Grace leaping beside them like a border collie. Kevin felt a stirring in his chest. As they greeted the two men tending the next gilt-edged doorway, he felt that he spoke with the voice of legions.

"Guys," he yelled, "the doormen are walking."

Kevin had never led anyone before. Now a brand-new and giddy confidence glowed from inside out. They were walking down the glorious stretch of Fifth Avenue known as Museum Mile, bordered by the Museum of the City of New York to the north and the Frick Collection to the south. In the middle, just twelve blocks down, stood the Metropolitan Museum of Art, where Kevin's mother had last shown him Giotto's *Lost Saint Sebastian*.

They worked each door they passed steadily and with conviction. By the time the gathering storm of doormen reached the elegant Cooper-Hewitt Museum at 91st Street, their ranks had swollen to thirty men falling behind him.

"The doormen are walking," they yelled. But it wasn't just a walk now.

It was a March of the Doormen.

From every filigreed doorway, men from the ranks of New York City's private guard enlisted. The polished black brogues began to tramp on the sidewalk like military boots. The working faces—Irish, Puerto Rican, black, Polish—took on a fresh purpose, with shining eyes and chins held higher.

"The Artist," Kevin's father beamed at him.

They passed the flamboyant Guggenheim Museum on their left. Kevin had walked up the heady, winding aisle of the Guggenheim many times. He had never agreed with some critics who sneered that the slab addition behind the flared white cylinder made it look like a toilet.

The *artist*. He was definitely doing something now, pulling these men together in common cause, but was it art?

Well, why not? Nobody ever did it before, and it would offend some people. But if it worked, that was what mattered.

As they marched one hundred strong past the big intersection of 86th Street, spilling out into the street and disturbing traffic, the word spread down Fifth Avenue as though Central Park were on fire. On this boulevard where the rich, the mighty, the royalty of New York City looked out their windows at the commotion, none of them would dare face down these marching men. If sanitation workers struck, the doormen could pile up the garbage on the streets. If the police staged a call-in-sick action, the doormen would be extra vigilant for burglars and muggers. But each marcher knew in his heart that, once the doormen walked, neither Old Money nor New Money would open their own doors or whistle for their own cabs.

All the wealth and power and majesty of Fifth Avenue would collapse like a house built of RSVP cards in the face of an organized doorman strike.

Gently supported by her father's arm, Cornelia stepped carefully in the outrageous sweeping dress, lace flowing behind her. Two tiny blond cousins lifted the ends in their small fingers, giggling as they tried to match the bride's steps.

Ooooh.

She heard the guests in genuine throes of appreciation or envy as she rounded the corner and revealed herself. She saw family friends and neighbors. Lily Stern, haughty and mildly disapproving. Old Chip Lindsay, leering. The two Roberts, her old friends, nudging each other and smirking like schoolboys. Don't men ever grow up? Especially Robert No. 2, who stared at her gown with a fascination that went beyond admiration. Envy seemed to roar from his face. Robert No. 2 had always been overly fascinated by his sister's clothes closet. And Tina, her maid of honor, crossing her eyes to make Corny laugh. Memories had begun to flicker as she walked down the aisle, with so many familiar faces.

Madame had coached her in each step. She moved forward, head held high and unwavering as though a stack of twenty volumes rested on her forehead.

She glanced sideways toward her father. No poker player, her father, his eyes reflecting doubt. He stood near a woman she dimly remembered, at least six feet tall in a slinky dress, with prominent features and an explosion of hair like a burning bush. Her eyebrows were dark and arched, her lips wide and somehow comforting.

And now she reached the Wedding Bower where Tucker stood. He stood so proudly and threw off such absolute confidence. Her father released her arm with a little squeeze, then angled off to the side and left her to the bower, bequeathing her to the groom.

Tucker steered her gently toward him with his strong hands. She stepped into the fragrant gazebo and the minister greeted her, bobbing his bald head and several chins.

"Dearly beloved . . ." the minister began.

By the time Kevin steered them the last block to 840 Fifth Avenue, the March of the Doormen had grown to over two hundred men thundering in close formation.

Pedestrians stood aside and gawked. Yellow taxis and black Town Cars, locked in that yellow and black checkerboard of New York streets, screeched and piled up in a jumble of stopped traffic.

Vlad the Self-Impaler marched on point, arms swaying and legs lifted high up in the old Red Army parade ground style. Andrew had fallen in lockstep with him, eyes gleaming with the gentle fury of the righteous. And even Dennis Doyle was a firebrand today, his nostrils flaring in defiance as he marched beside his son.

"I won't forget this, Dad," Kevin said, squeezing his father's arm.

"Nor will I." Dennis winked at him.

The minister's chins opened like an accordion as he began to speak.

He looks like a frog, Cornelia thought. She had to bite her lower lip to keep from laughing out loud.

" . . . in the state of grace and this holy company . . ." the minister croaked. In the shafts of light seeping in through the French doors to the terrace, his gray hair took on a silvery haze around it, a halo of light.

"A corona," Cornelia blurted out. The minister stopped speaking, causing Tucker's face to spin toward her with a look of sudden horror.

"Excuse me?" the minister asked, perplexed, and she could hear the faintest murmur in the room.

"Nothing," she apologized in a small voice. "Sorry."

The odd vision of the halo had gone away. A cloud was passing over the sun outside, and she could see only the minister's slicked-back gray hair in the winter light.

Kevin squinted down Fifth Avenue, his chest thrust out against the cold. The unmanned awning of 840 Fifth Avenue came into sight just as the bleating of police sirens grew louder.

Four blue and white cruisers pulled up to block the entrance to 65th Street. The officers piled out, meeting a crew of eight police officers who suddenly came huffing around the corner from the side street. They carried yellow "Police: Do Not Enter" sawhorses to create a barricade in front of the marchers. Kevin saw that Uncle Eddie hustled along in front with the befuddled building manager Gus Anholdt and a harried police supervisor holding a megaphone.

Kevin didn't break the march of his men toward 840 Fifth now as the police supervisor, a heavyset officer with deep caramel skin, raised his megaphone in their direction.

"This is Lieutenant Simms, NYPD. You've got no permit to march," his voice reverberated. "Turn around and go back to your jobs."

Philip Grace ran ahead, waving his press pass high in the air, to prance in front of the lieutenant. "Hell, no! Workin' press here, plus a whole mess of pissed-off union men. Why you strike-bustin' for the owners, Lieutenant?"

As the March of the Doormen kept its cadence like a drumroll, advancing on the police line, the officers who manned the barricades looked uneasy. Kevin put his hand over his eyes to look up to the terrace of Penthouse A. He could see white silk billowing in the wind, like banners on a parapet.

He threw his white-gloved hand up in the air, and was shocked when the first ranks of the doorman actually halted at his command. The movement rippled through all the rest as the mass slowed down and finally stopped, men spreading out across the entire intersection of 65th Street and Fifth Avenue.

Kevin walked briskly to the police lieutenant, who projected an air of authority with no clear idea of how to use it at this moment.

"Officer, if it's okay with you, I just need to borrow your megaphone for a second."

"Are you kidding me?"

One of the police officers tapped their lieutenant on the shoulder and leaned close. "Sir, I'm tellin' you as your PBA rep, I think you ought to look at the big picture here."

The lieutenant, looking ungrateful for his rank today, covered his mouth as he huddled quickly with the Policeman's Benevolent Association union man so Kevin couldn't hear what they were saying.

Andrew moved in, speaking low to the lieutenant. "Get on the right side of this, brother. We've got a peaceful situation here. Keep things steady."

The lieutenant's eyes went back and forth unhappily, trying to look at a big picture that had just changed with the new element, Kevin realized, of a swelling crowd of pedestrians around them. Civilians were running and jogging from every direction for a better view of the March of the Doormen. Traffic stopped on the street, bumper-to-bumper like rush hour. Horns honked. Drivers shouted.

Kevin took a breath and took action. He grabbed at the megaphone the lieutenant held loosely in his hand.

The lieutenant gripped it and pulled it back, wide-eyed. "What the hell you think you're doing? That's police equipment."

"C'mon," Kevin pleaded. "Just for a second."

The lieutenant looked at his megaphone like it was giving him an ulcer, and let Kevin take it.

Kevin spoke clearly into the megaphone, shouting up to the sky. "Chester Lord! I need to talk to you. Now." His voice reverberated with a righteous calm. "And I really need to speak to Cornelia."

*   *   *

The minister was in no hurry, a man in love with his own fine baritone.

He made eye contact all around the room as he mouthed the vows of marriage as "the most joyous covenant."

Tucker had begun giving the minister hard looks and gestures to speed things up a bit. Guests had begun coughing and swishing their clothing as they sat on Madame's too-petite gilded chairs.

Cornelia thought about the most joyous covenant. She felt glad that she had finally insisted they change the "until death do you part" thing. Perhaps a needless break with tradition, yet somehow the phrase made her claustrophobic. But at the rate the minister was going, it would be a good long time before it came up.

She heard a muffled call from outside. It sounded vaguely familiar.

Then a furious commotion began to disrupt her wedding.

She glanced behind her to the terrace.

Looking out the French doors to their huge penthouse balcony lined with white fabric and a profusion of flowers, she was surprised to see that a few of her guests had actually left the ceremony to gather at the parapet. They looked down at the street, then stared back inside at her.

Telephones suddenly began ringing and chirping all over the apartment. Emergency pagers began beeping and others quietly vibrated in the pockets of the mayor, the police commissioner, and the owner of the *Daily Globe*.

Chaos reigned.

"Music," Tucker loudly ordered the string quartet in the living room. He took Cornelia's hand and held it tightly to keep her with him in the Wedding Bower. But the guests were starting out to the terrace in droves now. Finally Chester himself walked out one of the open doors to the terrace, and peered over the balcony, with the tall, curly-haired woman on his arm.

"Who *is* that downstairs?" Cornelia asked Tucker.

"A disgruntled building employee. He was just fired, now he's back causing trouble."

"A building employee?" She couldn't grasp why he would be yelling her name.

"People!" Tucker shouted. "Let's get on with it."

Startled and guilty to be caught straying, the wedding guests wandered back to the ceremony like errant sheep.

"Go on," Tucker told the minister. "And pick it up."

The minister stubbornly looked to the bride. This was her day and she would dictate its terms.

"Yes," Cornelia told him firmly. "Please, let's get on with it."

The minister began in a halting voice.

"Cor-nee! Cor-nee!"

She heard the chant from below, and broke off from Tucker's grip.

The guests followed her as she went out the doors to the terrace choked with flowers. A young man dressed in white tie and tails under bright yellow hair stood near the wall with bird cages. He would be the dove wrangler, ready to release a dozen white doves to circle overhead as soon as he received his cue from Madame. Now the restless doves sat on their perches, picking at their feathers and darting their heads in quick gestures.

She looked over the wall to the street below. Spread across the entire corner of Fifth Avenue in both directions, a crowd of men stood in uniform. Police, she thought at first, or army officers. But the uniform looked wrong.

No, they were doormen.

Hundreds of them were looking up, focused on her terrace for some reason. And beyond the doormen, a large crowd had gathered almost like a street festival. But they were all looking up at her, too. She saw a van from Channel 7 Action News pull up, and a crew of people with cameras and sound gear spill out.

It must be an event, a march down Fifth Avenue like the St. Patrick's Day Parade. But they weren't marching and they looked agitated, as though penned up and ready to be released. Should she know what it was? Her memory had become so untrustworthy. Perhaps it was some new occasion, a Running of the Doormen on Fifth Avenue, like the bulls of Pamplona.

Then she saw that the doorman who seemed to be their leader, who looked as though he wore the uniform of her own building, was breaking off from the rest and hopping into a yellow cab. The taxi peeled out, honking, maneuvered out of the traffic mess and turned into the roadway that crossed Central Park.

The taxi kept honking, passing other cars, as it careened toward Central Park West.

Dr. Gene Powers, curator of the New York Tesla Museum, looked unhappily at his computer screen, reading the disk Corny had made.

He felt responsible for Cornelia Lord. On one hand, he wished her whatever happiness could come out of this wedding. On the other, he had never heard her say anything good about Tucker Fisk, and worried about her long absence from the museum. It wasn't the Corny he knew, this girl who flashed her gums from the society page of today's *Times*.

What schmucks her father and this fiancé had to be. He desperately wanted to forget his promise to her and let her father know what Cornelia had accomplished here, all on her own, without a scintilla of credit. He loved Cornelia Lord with a fierce protective quality that made his bowels boil at the injustice. But a pledge was a pledge. Cornelia Lord had honored her word to the museum. Could he go back on his? He pondered the ageless dilemma of love versus honor. Why did those two kinds of good always have to butt heads?

A million miles deep in his own thoughts, he felt air moving in the entry to his office and looked up.

"Kevin Doyle?"

Chapter Twenty-nine

$\mathcal{D}$o you, Cornelia . . ."

Her big day, her father called it. She strained to tune out the sound of "Cor-nee, Cor-nee." That chant wafting up from the streets baffled her.

She would steel herself and go on. A Lord does not complain or explain. A Lord maintains her composure in the face of total peculiarity.

The minister had just begun the phrase leading up to her cue, and she would filter out all the noise and respond properly.

Tucker held her hand tightly now and worked his jaw rather ferociously, seething at the handful of guests who still stood out on the terrace.

The guests seemed to be looking up at the sky.

". . . take Tucker to be your lawful wedded husband," the minister droned. "To have and to hold from this day forward, in sickness and in health . . ."

But what could be happening on the terrace? She saw the guests' hair blowing in a strong wind. They looked up and pointed as though aliens were invading Fifth Avenue. The rows of flowers on the terrace waved together like grain in a windstorm, and the billowing white silk blew back, plastered over the terrace furniture. Even the dove wrangler in tails threw his arms around the small cages with the birds inside. A tornado seemed to have landed on her terrace.

". . . so long as your love shall last?"

As both Tucker and the minister looked to her, she caught sight of the rickety airship through the glass doors. It sailed down the entire length of her long terrace, resembling a quaint, open-air Victorian helicopter. One propeller twirled on top, another spun on the rear. Two men sat side by side on a bench seat, clearly visible through the skeletal frame.

Tucker grabbed both her arms.

She shook herself from the tight grip on her sleeve, and ran to the door, flung it open, and stepped out.

The muffled noise of the airship seemed so familiar. Except for the gentle whop-whop of the propeller blades, it made no engine sound at all. Weaving over the terrace to land, it bounced onto the terrace on two of its four wheels. She laughed out loud. Guests screamed and scattered getting out of the way. Dresses and suit jackets billowed up crazily. A man's toupee flew through the air.

She squinted at the men in the flying machine. The older man looked awfully familiar, his eyebrows huge and fuzzy over a ripping smile.

And now the airship wriggled to a stop, leaning forward, then settled back down. The spinning propeller still wreaked havoc, blasting her guests with gusty waves of confusion. The younger man leapt out of the open airship, a bit shakily. He ran directly toward her. His face had been hit by a couple of insects. And his lips were forming words. She took in the black hair and clear blue eyes in the uniform. A doorman's uniform.

She felt a tight glass box shatter inside her head. Her memories began cascading like a waterfall. A horsy-smelling bundle in the snow. A neon Saint Sebastian. A red heart that lit up the night sky.

"Kevin?"

"Corny." His smile dazzled her, the light blue eyes.

Kevin Doyle.

He approached her slowly, his arms opening. The guests, with few rules of etiquette to follow for such an incident, simply got out of his way.

And they met, the debutante in her taffeta and the doorman in his dress grays. Without a word, each understood what they would do.

As Kevin began to whisk her over the windswept terrace, Tucker leapt in front of them. He grabbed Kevin's neck to strangle him.

"No!" she screamed at Tucker. "Don't touch him."

She shoved Tucker in the chest. He stumbled backward clutching at air.

Amid a crunch of guests now pressing around them, her father suddenly stood in front of her on the windy terrace. "Cornelia, what in God's name . . ."

"Chester, talk to her," Tucker said. His smoothed-back hair blew straight up like a troll's from the helicopter squatting in the middle of Madame's wedding flowers, her friend Dr. Powers grinning at the controls.

"Back off," Kevin told Tucker. "Mr. Lord, Tucker Fisk sold you out for thirty million dollars from the Kois."

A wail behind her. "That is a lie!"

She swiveled around to see Han Koi, Sr., his ancient head wagging so violently she was afraid it might pop off like a champagne cork. Then Han Koi, Jr., appeared at his side, hissing frantically in Chinese, trying to drag his father away. Han Junior, that sleek otter, now looked as frantic and humbled as if his trousers had just fallen down around his English shoes.

"A lie! A lie!" old Han chanted, a sclerotic mantra.

"Get your father out of here," Tucker yelled at Han Junior.

"All of you shut up!" Chester suddenly thundered in a rip-roaring bellow, as though possessed by the spirit of General Patton.

Cornelia turned back, stunned. The crowd around them abruptly hushed. Even Tucker's mouth hung agape at her father's fury. Chester the reticent. Chester who had never raised his voice above what was necessary to bid "two hearts." Now the only sound to be heard was the rhythmic whooshing of the electrical airship's propeller.

"What's this about?" Her father now pointed his finger in Tucker Fisk's face.

"Chester," Tucker stammered, not at all coolly persuasive now. "You can't listen to some escaped mental patient."

Chester stared briefly at the spindly gyrocopter that had landed on his terrace. Then he turned to Kevin.

"Is that what Cornelia told you in the hospital?"

"No. I found out from your driver."

"My driver?"

"Mike your driver. He heard Tucker talking on the phone."

"What do you think you know?" Tucker shouted in Kevin's face. "You're a *doorman*. You don't even know what business we're in."

"When you came to see me at the Sanctuary, you were in bribery and extortion." Kevin dropped his voice an octave to mimic Tucker's. "'The way I see it, Kevin, you have two choices.'"

He turned to Chester, whose face had wrung itself into a knot.

"He did the same thing with Dr. Loblitz. That's why Corny got shock treatments. That's the only way Tucker could get her to marry him."

Chester's face began to unknot itself, reddening in shame.

"Just look at the two of them, Mr. Lord." Kevin turned and pointed at Tucker and Han Koi, Jr. "There's your wedding couple."

And as the two betrayers shouted their denials, caught as surely as bank robbers soaked with red paint from a trick money sack, Chester understood. He turned his back on Tucker, and took both Cornelia and Kevin by the hand.

"You warned me," Chester told his daughter softly. "Cornelia, I look at you today and see your mother. Tucker wouldn't have fooled her."

"Mr. Lord," Kevin stood with an officer's confident brace of the chin over his doorman's epaulets. "I came for Cornelia. We have some things to talk about."

Chester watched his daughter wipe the tiny insect wings off Kevin's lips. "She and I have some, too, son. What in God's name is that contraption you flew in on?"

"A Tesla airship." Kevin waved at the open-air cockpit. "That's Dr. Powers over there with the beard. He'll tell you all about it."

She saw the brilliant blue circle around Kevin Doyle's head all over again. But now the corona was in his eyes, too, as they searched her soul.

"Corny, he just taught me enough to help you fly it."

"Fly it?" Cornelia stared at the Tesla airship. She stuck her finger in the air. A light crosswind. Yes. She could do that. She closed her eyes and could see the rudder pedals. Throttle. Clutch. Lead-acid electrical batteries good for two hours of flight time. She flung her arms around Kevin's neck and clutched him so tightly she almost choked him.

"Are you okay?" he asked with a laugh.

She took Chester's hands in hers and kissed the Father of the Bride. "Thank you, Daddy. I believe I'm good to go now."

"Not—not to South America," Chester stammered.

"South America? No, with Kevin. We just need to get away for a bit."

"You aren't taking her anywhere," Tucker's strangled yell hurt her ears. The mean, red, sweaty face of a spoiled child revealed itself in full flower now.

Kevin leaned calmly into Tucker's bursting-tomato face. "Hey, you aren't the only thing out here that blows. We're taking off before the wind changes."

Tucker lunged for Kevin again. It took Chester and O'Connell to hold him back.

"Excuse us." Kevin swooped her up in his arms. The bundle of rustling, itchy taffeta felt delicious against her skin now. He carried her like a real bride toward the waiting airship while the stunned guests parted.

"Go, Cornee!" Tina French screeched.

"Dr. Powers, thank you," she said, hugging the museum curator.

"Watch your head," Dr. Powers yelled as he scuttled out of the tufted velvet bench seat, handing off the controls. She took the now-familiar stick and throttle in her hands. She examined the simple dashboard with two gauges, one for "Airspeed" and one that read "Batteries."

"You've got the aircraft, Corny," Powers told her. "Do you remember everything?"

"Enough," she said, grabbing the stick as she and Kevin sat at the controls. "Kevin, take the clutch and the throttle. I'll do the rest."

Kevin took the quaint hand controls, the clutch lever and rheostat throttle knob. He pulled his own harness on and helped tighten hers.

"Ready?" Kevin shouted.

"Full throttle," she told him.

He turned the throttle knob full ahead. As the electric engine spooled up faster, it twirled the propeller blade into a frenzy. She tested the foot pedals that controlled the rudder with her wedding slippers.

She kissed his cheek, let out her breath, and toyed with the stick. The airship vibrated on the terrace, as eager to leave as they were.

"Thank you all for coming, but there's been a change of heart," she shouted to the guests crowding the terrace in their path.

She nudged the stick carefully. The round gyroscope on top of the center mast tilted the propeller forward. With a lurch it thrust them ahead. The small wheels rolled and they began to hurtle down the long, narrow runway of her terrace, scattering the guests, who shrieked and threw themselves out of their path as they charged the far wall.

"Uh, Corny . . ."

The brick wall of the terrace raced closer.

"Pop the clutch," she told him.

He disengaged the clutch lever and the rickety craft hopped up like a rabbit. Then, just as abruptly, it fell back onto the terrace, plopping down hard on its small tires. They raced faster toward the terrace wall, yawing from left to right. She could clearly see the bricks, then the mortar between the bricks.

"Pop the clutch again."

And the ship lifted up a few feet before the wall. She felt glorious wind sting her eyes as the gyrocopter pointed to the sky and hovered, then felt heavy and shuddered. The lumpy drag held them a few feet off the terrace as though they were being pulled down by a giant hand. They would smash against the brick wall like two dolls in a matchstick toy.

"Corny . . ."

"I've got it!"

She bit her lip and angled the propeller just right. A rush of air swept underneath them, scooping them up and flinging them into the sky. They cleared the wall. Then, in a huge gulp of lost altitude, they dipped sharply down toward the street.

"Something's wrong," she shouted. "We feel too heavy."

Kevin looked behind, then under them. "That's because Tucker's hanging on down there."

"I'll kill you, you little prick," she heard Tucker scream. "Cornelia, help me."

She leaned down. Her ex-bridegroom hung on to her airship's axle by his elbows. She had to laugh at the figure in the wedding suit, caught in the severe crosswind that whipped past the tall buildings of Fifth Avenue. Tucker's legs spread wildly in the smart trousers and his blond hair peeled back from his skull.

"Oh, keep still," Corny yelled at him. "It's just a little wind buffet."

"What do we do with him?" Kevin asked her.

"Well, we certainly don't want him along with us, do we?"

She whooped with the thrill of the wind in her face and shoved the stick. The little gyrocopter tore almost straight down into a dive toward the crowd, now fifteen stories below. While Tucker screamed and cursed, she looked back. His shiny black wingtips were visible wide apart behind the tail.

They plunged toward the doormen in uniform, the police, and a crowd of pedestrians who now pointed and shouted. They were one hundred feet over their heads . . . fifty . . . the crowd below gasped and ducked, making a human wave. She feathered the rudder pedals with her slippers and jolted the stick.

The airship made a wobbly dip onto its side and started up straight again, hovering twenty feet above the crowd.

She pointed behind them. "Kevin, look."

The wedding doves had left the terrace and made a V-formation. All twelve doves, the downy little aviators, spread their white wings and swooped down to meet them.

"The dove man must have thought this was part of the ceremony," Kevin said.

"Where shall we go after we get rid of Tucker?" she asked.

"How about the Palisades?"

"That sounds wonderful."

She worked the stick and they whipped into a sharp left over the crowd. They passed over the stone wall separating Central Park from

Fifth Avenue. A little low, they skimmed over the trees, scraping the ends of the tallest branches.

"Owww," Tucker yelled below.

She leaned over. "I thought you loved aerobatics."

Then she executed a nice, smooth banking maneuver toward the Central Park Zoo. Busy New Yorkers with their skates and boomboxes and baby carriages, and strolling tourists with their Walkmans and tote bags, stopped on the cobblestone path below. They looked up in shock, pointing at the quietly whomping little helicopter. Then they began to applaud. Who had sponsored this giddy, impromptu airshow? This soaring deb in her bridal gown with her doorman in uniform. Not to mention the guy in a suit dangling below.

"Tucker," Corny yelled down, "you'd better let go when I tell you."

She peeled off and made a snap turn to approach the zoo. Dipping down to twenty feet, she hovered briefly over a large round hole built into the ground.

"Goodbye, Tucker," she yelled.

She lifted the nose sharply and the airship sprang up. They felt so much lighter now. There was a rude shout below. Then a splash and a round of barking.

"What was that?" Kevin asked her, busy with his rheostat.

"The seal tank. I'm glad they left some water in it."

She made a lazy, confident bank west, and they climbed to five hundred feet. Beyond Central Park West, across Manhattan and the sparkling Hudson River, they could see the thin winter sun beginning to set over the cliffs of the Palisades. She pointed the airship at the rosy haze.

And as they cleared the skyscrapers of Central Park West and soared to one thousand feet, the Tesla Tower replica poked up from the roof of Corny's Museum. She stared at the proud steel mushroom, blue light darting around the bulbous top in a spidery electric ribbon. So what if it didn't broadcast electricity, and probably never would? It was a tribute, not some crazy experiment.

She looked at Kevin.

"Great corona," they said together.

Chester Lord stood with his right hand gripping the railing of his terrace, as though afraid to let go.

Roni was at his side now, her arm around his back. Together they watched Cornelia and Kevin become a white speck somewhere above Central Park West and vanish into the cobalt sky.

"I'd say she looked very happy on her wedding day," Roni told him.

He nodded dully, and felt something in his left hand. He still clutched the small disk that the gruff, bearded man from the helicopter had pressed into it.

"Corny recorded this before she planned to leave for South America," the man had said. *"I think you ought to see it."*

He looked around for the bearded man, but he was gone now. So he stared at the silvery disk again, shiny and alien as a tiny UFO.

"Roni, would you come inside with me?"

They found Tucker's laptop sitting on his desk. Chester approached it gingerly at first, circling the enemy. He picked it up for the first time. It felt heavier than he expected, the tungsten case solid as a safe door. He tried to open the lid, but the clasp was locked.

"We'll fix that," Roni told him.

She removed a book from Chester's shelf. It was a musty, leather-bound copy of Margaret Mead's study, *Coming of Age in Samoa*. She looked at the spine and gave Chester a heavy-lidded, bedroom glance. "I read this once. Very sexy."

Then she brought the heavy volume crashing down hard on the sweet spot of Tucker's laptop case, breaking the clasp. It sprung open like a Jack-in-the-box, sprawled flat on Chester's desk to reveal the mysteries of its wafer-thin keyboard and silvery diode screen.

"I could never figure out how to work these things," Chester admitted.

He tried jabbing at a few keys. Nothing. They were tiny, the letters miniaturized for a younger person's eyes. Squinting, he found the button that made a little compartment slide open. He inserted the ultracompact disk that the bearded man had given him. Then he located another small button and pressed "Play."

The words faded up hazily on the screen.

To Mr. Philip Grace, Debwatch, The New York Globe.

He read Cornelia's words slowly. Then he turned the screen to Roni to show her.

"In January, the New York Tesla Museum will open to the public. I was one of its founders, although nobody knows I helped to build it. Not even my own father.

"No history book really does justice to Nikola Tesla. He invented modern electricity, discovered radio and television waves, X rays, and even the particle beams that will become this century's lasers. He lit the world's darkness.

"I think you're a real reporter at heart, Mr. Grace, even though asking me to 'back up' into the Plaza fountain the other night was rather paparazzo. Since I'll be away and you'll be seeking a new subject, I wanted to invite you to visit the museum and possibly encourage others to do the same.

"On a more personal note, I am not some wild debutante.

"I probably earned a reputation for being flaky. But I learned from watching my father that a person must take their responsibilities seriously, even when it becomes quite lonely. And my duty was to the museum.

"So I have dedicated my part of the Tesla Museum to my parents, Elizabeth and Chester Lord IV. There's a small plaque near the Tesla helicopter.

"I hope it brings some brightness to my father's life, which I'm afraid you and I have made rather glum lately just doing our jobs as Reporter and Electric Girl.

"Regards from Rio, Cornelia Lord."

Chester felt a rush in his chest. But it wasn't the dreaded old anvil rising up this time. This was a feeling so unfamiliar in its absence of burden or remorse, so kaleidoscopic in its sweep of pleasure and possibility, he actually laughed out loud, ferociously, for the first time in a decade.

Roni stared in amazement. "Chester?"

He settled down just enough to tap the laptop screen proudly with his forefinger. "Roni, this is my daughter."

Acknowledgments

Stealing from one person is plagiarism.
Stealing from many is research.

Many people contributed their ideas to this first novel. I would especially like to thank:

My literary agent and friend, Robert Tabian, the real hero of this book, and those literary lions of song and story, Howie Sanders and Richard Green at UTA.

Discerning publishers Larry Kirshbaum and Jamie Raab at Warner Books. My unsung co-author through three revisions, Executive Editor Rick Horgan at Warner Books, as well as Executive Managing Editor Harvey-Jane Kowal, Creative Director Jackie Meyer, Deputy Director of Publicity Jennifer Romanello, Associate Editor Jody Handley, and copyeditor Fred Chase.

Lithe gourmet Lynn Harris at New Line Cinema, screenwriter Robert Kamen, and producers Mark Johnson, Elizabeth Cantillon, and Tiffany Daniel.

Stephen Fischer, for his guidance at the very beginning.

Sandi Gellis-Cole, wickedly accurate with her creative prodding and Glock nine, for her Boot Camp in fiction writing.

My earliest ally and muse Mandy McDevitt, who turned my handwritten swamp creature into a manuscript. Her *belissima* typing is, as advertised, A-1.

For their creative and professional support, those wild romantics

Christopher Gilsons I and III; my singularly gifted assistant Debie Klein, with special thanks to Cynthia and Kacie; the world's best-loved in-laws, Greta and Louis Zuckerman; the inimitable Caron K; Beryl Echlin; Gene Powers; George Pammer; Sue Barton; Joyce and Chuck Beber; Lieutenant Dan Hollar; James Degus; Avanti de Mille; Allen and Cheri Jacobi; Bob Gordon; Richard and Dina Nicolella; Peter Rodriguez; Stenya Lipinska; Kerry and Susan Sakolsky; Carol Taite; Evan Blair; Cindy Roesel; Noel Frankel; Tom Lopez; JoAnn Lederman; Mike and Martha Gilson; Jim and Rhonda Schoolfield; Elaine Terris; Peggy, Arnie, and Sande Harris; John and Barbara Kushner; Rick and Jennifer Schmidt; Kevin Smith; Dan Starer of Research for Writers, New York; Spencer and Calvin.

And, of course, Nikola Tesla for inventing the future.

I'm lucky to have all of you, but I'm especially lucky to be in love. To my wife, Carolyn, the truly talented half of our couple, thank you for being my heart, my life, my dance of light.